IN
PLAIN
SIGHT

JOSEPH BIRCHALL

POOLBEG
CRIMSON

This book is a work of fiction. References to real people, events, establishments, organisations, or locales are intended only to provide a sense of authenticity, and are used fictitiously. All other characters, and all incidents and dialogue, are drawn from the author's imagination and are not to be construed as real.

Published 2025 by Poolbeg Crimson,

an imprint of Poolbeg Press Ltd.

123 Grange Hill, Baldoyle, Dublin 13, Ireland

Email: poolbeg@poolbeg.com

Joseph Birchall © 2025

© Poolbeg Press Ltd. 2025, copyright for editing, typesetting, layout, design, ebook. and cover image .

The moral right of the author has been asserted.

A catalogue record for this book is available from the British Library.

ISBN 978-1-78199-661-4

All rights reserved. No part of this publication may be reproduced or transmitted in any form or by any means, electronic or mechanical, including photography, recording, or any information storage or retrieval system, without permission in writing from the publisher. The book is sold subject to the condition that it shall not, by way of trade or otherwise, be lent, resold or otherwise circulated without the publisher's prior consent in any form of binding or cover other than that in which it is published and without a similar condition, including this condition, being imposed on the subsequent purchaser.

www.poolbeg.com

About the author

Joseph Birchall spent much of his twenties living abroad before returning to Dublin to establish a successful family business.

A lifelong writer, he penned his first play at just eleven years old. Over the years, he explored screenwriting and novel writing, but family and work took precedence. Eventually, he returned to his first love, carving out time in Dublin's early-morning coffee shops to write.

He lives in Dublin with his wife and three children, and still gets up early to write.

To Mam

'Whoever fights monsters should see to it that in the process he does not become a monster.'
Friedrich Nietzsche

Prologue

From the darkness of my usual hiding place, under the sofa, I look at my mammy's body lying still on the floor. I'm on my tummy, my arms tucked under my head. It's dark, and I try to see if her chest is rising and falling with her breathing. But I can't.

It's not the first time I've seen her fall after she's pushed the big needle into her arm, but this time it's different.

After it happens, there are always other voices in the house, but this time everyone ran away. Before, someone would always have carried Mammy up to her bed, or taken her away in a car, and she would be gone for a few days, and I'd have to stay with Mary Whelan at number thirteen up the road and sleep on her sofa and eat chips and beans every day.

Before, though, Mammy didn't ever have blood coming out of her nose.

I wonder if I'll have to wear my black dress again. I've worn it six times so far. Once for my aunt, then two uncles, a boy cousin and a girl cousin who I can't remember, and a friend of Mammy I didn't even know. Six times, but I didn't cry once. Every time, I tried really hard to be sad in the church, but everyone kept telling me how pretty I was, just like Mammy, they'd say, when she used to have long blonde hair the same as me.

People tell me I have my daddy's blue eyes though, not Mammy's.

I don't see him much, but sometimes he takes me to the pub, and all the other men are really polite to me, and Daddy gives them a dirty look whenever they use the F word in front of me. He always holds my hand when he drops me back to Mammy, and I love the way his whole hand covers mine. It makes me feel like nothing bad can ever happen to me. Then he smiles and winks one of his blue eyes at me, and he's gone till ... till the next time.

But my mammy's eyes are closed now.

If I have to wear my black dress for her, that would be seven times. Once every year since I was born.

Here's the blue lights now, flashing in the window. They're like little blue sparks. And just like sparks that start a fire, they'll get bigger and bigger and then more blue lights will fill the street and the house and the room. Those blue lights are so strong, they'll even shine under this sofa. Then the Guards will find me. But that's only because the Guards will look for me. No one else ever looks for me.

I'll just have one more look at Mammy's face. Sometimes when I'm having a happy day, I do that, and then I'll try to hold the picture in my head and remember it later on in case it turns out to be not such a happy day after all.

Then I turn my face away towards the wall and close my own eyes.

Voices and noises fill the house. Big strong voices. I don't move until a hand reaches under the sofa and gently touches me.

'Hello there,' someone says. A woman's voice. I wasn't expecting that.

I slide out from under the sofa. Mammy's gone from the floor. The woman is wearing a dark-blue Garda uniform like the men do. She isn't pretty like me, but she has nice brown eyes.

'My name's Kate. And what's your name, sweetheart?' she asks me.

'Darcy,' I tell her.

I look at the spot where Mammy used to be.

'Was that your mum?' Kate asks. Sometimes people say mum when they really mean mam.

I nod.

'Don't worry, Darcy,' she says with a big smile, but I don't know what she's smiling at. 'Your mum's going to be OK.'

'Really?' I ask.

'Yes. They've taken her away to make her better.'

'I think she had a cardiac arrest,' I tell her.

Kate laughs at me. 'No. She'll be OK. I promise.'

So, no black dress for Mammy. I'm glad. I start to cry. Tears flow down my cheeks. I feel silly, but I can't stop them. Kate gets down on her knees and gives me a big hug. Her jacket is cold, but it makes me feel warmer inside.

Why am I crying when my mammy is going to live, and I couldn't cry for all the others who died?

'Everything will be OK,' Kate whispers into my ear. 'Everything will be OK.'

She holds me away from her, and we look into each other's eyes.

'Do you know where your daddy is?' Kate asks.

I don't move. Ever since I could talk, they always told me never to answer that question.

'That's OK,' Kate tells me and stands up. She holds out her hand for me to take. 'Do you want to come with me?'

I know what she's asking me. I know that if I go with the garda, I will probably go away for a long time. I've seen other kids being taken away. Grace from the next road. Robbie from two doors away. I know they go to new families. New mammies and new daddies. My mammy would cry like the other mammies when their children had gone away. Then someone would give her a new needle, and she wouldn't cry anymore.

But sometimes the children come back. A few anyway. When they're all big and grown up. And when they do come back, they take their mammies away with them. Even their daddies sometimes. In a big car. Or in a taxi.

I wish I could do that for my mammy. One day come back with loads of money and make her better. Better forever. And I'd never ever have to wear the black dress again.

I look up at Kate. Her bright, yellow jacket shines onto her face. She looks pretty now. If only one day I could be so strong. So big. Then I could protect my mammy forever.

So, I take her hand, and I walk out of my house.

Twenty-five years later

Monday

Chapter 1

Darcy Doyle checked her Garmin watch as she slowed her running pace before reaching her house.

Five kilometres exactly.

She pressed STOP, and it reverted to the time of 05.47, the white numbers beaming brightly in the darkness of the early morning.

She was soaked through from an unexpected downpour that came only ten minutes into her run. After a short time, however, the cold rain had felt warm against her skin and, apart from having to wipe it from her eyes occasionally, she had enjoyed the run. The rain gave her even more of a sense of isolation than her usual early run, a feeling impossible to find anywhere in Dublin's city centre in another hour.

She took the door key from a small, zipped pocket in her shorts and inserted it into the lock of her one-bedroom bungalow house. She had bought the house after just one viewing, and what the auctioneer had described as 'quaintly vintage' had since proved to be a money-pit of repairs and renovations that seemed never-ending. Her work colleagues had lamented her misfortune but, if she were honest, she could still afford the mortgage and had no intention of moving out of the Liberties anyway. The Liberties was an old working-class area within walking distance of the city, and she wanted for nothing in her house, despite its size.

By most people's standards, the house would be called 'sparsely decorated'. But for Darcy, that was intentional. The sofa was old, second-hand and exceedingly comfortable. The original wooden floors, which she had painstakingly sanded and varnished over a long Bank Holiday weekend, felt almost soft under her bare feet. The only two paintings were seascapes of Dublin Bay that made her feel melancholic, although she wasn't quite sure why, and her only concession to modernism was three bright-red cushions from IKEA. There was no TV, and there were no photographs.

Even now, upon opening the front door, it was as if her home were a faithful old dog who raised its head slightly as she entered and wagged its tail in delight at her arrival. It was uncluttered and spotless, an oasis of calm in her world which was too often filled by turbulence and disorder. She might easily be accused of OCD when it came to her home but, for her, it was all about gratitude and appreciation of her own little place.

She headed straight to the bathroom, took off her jacket and hung it over the bath. She watched as the droplets fell and splashed into a small puddle. *Drip. Drip. Drip.* A memory came to her of returning home from school one Friday afternoon. It had been in one of her early foster homes. She had hung her damp coat over an electric heater, and it had leaked into the back cover and sparks had flown out and almost caused a fire. That time they had locked her in her room for two days as punishment, only letting her out to go back to school on Monday.

Darcy picked up a towel and threw it over her head. She rubbed vigorously, as if wiping the memory away. She sometimes felt her long blonde hair was too juvenile but, when she had once cut it short, she was constantly being told that she looked like Daryl Hannah from *Blade Runner*.

Her phone beeped in the bedroom where she had left it before her run.

Are you up? It's that Peggy Farrell again. She won't talk to them. Can you go over? I've sent a unit to her house.

The shower would have to wait. The phone beeped again.

Of course you're up!

She tapped the phone.

On my way.

Thanks. You're a star.

She threw the phone back on the bed and went into the bathroom. She stripped out of her running clothes, grabbed a large white towel and roughly dried her body.

Darcy left her house and drove through the Dublin streets, as dark rainclouds prolonged the night over the city.

This was her third year working in Domestic Violence as a detective, and she already felt stuck there, even forced to stay. Her superintendent, also a woman, didn't have enough female gardaí and, since most victims were women, they needed Darcy more than ever. She knew she made a difference in the lives of the women she helped, and it was true that she derived an enormous sense of satisfaction from her work in DV but, every time she passed that old grey building in Harcourt Street, her eyes still climbed to the fifth floor, to the home of the NBCI, the National Bureau of Crime Investigation.

She had already turned down transfers to various units. She lived close to the city centre, and most of the career criminals knew her by sight already, so undercover was out. The option of an armed unit was tempting, but she didn't want to go back to uniform and she feared it would bore her after a few months.

She wanted the NBCI. From her first day after passing out in Templemore College, it was what she had always wanted. In her heart, she felt that with her record, if she were a man, she would have already been offered a position. They hadn't even had the courtesy to acknowledge her last application.

The rain turned into a deluge as she pulled into the street of terraced houses that were squeezed together in a long row, like discarded second-hand books on a shelf. She saw the marked Garda car outside Peggy Farrell's house. Every city has housing areas like these, and every cop hates driving into them. She noticed the lights on in several of the neighbours' windows and could see figures standing in them.

As she got out, it wasn't so much a sense of *déjà vu* that struck her as the fact she had literally been here and so many places like it a hundred times already. The rain struck the roof of an ancient brown car with one red door that looked more abandoned than parked. To Darcy, the rain sounded like a continuous drumroll.

A uniformed garda was standing outside the front door, sheltering under the porch.

'Hey, Gerry!' Darcy called, running a few steps to him. She could hear the muffled screaming coming from inside the house.

'Morning, Detective,' he replied. 'Lovely day for the race.'

'What race?'

'The Human Race,' he said with a smile.

She gave him a half-smile as he opened the front door, and she stepped into the hall.

'*I swear to Christ I'm going to fucking kill him!*' she heard Peggy screaming from upstairs. '*This time I fucking mean it! You hear me, you little prick! Do you?*'

Darcy climbed the stairs, stepping over a toy drum and a yellow tractor, and saw the illuminated jacket of another garda at the top of the stairs.

'Please, Mrs Farrell, calm down,' the garda was pleading with her. 'We can talk this through.'

'*I'm finished talking – this time I'm really going to kill the shitbag!*'

Peggy Farrell was an impressive figure. Short but heavy. Probably as wide as she was tall. Her unruly hair was dyed light-brown, but with dark roots that made it look like a bunch of seaweed had just fallen on her head.

But it was the black poker in her hand that had Darcy's attention.

Peggy banged her fist on the locked bathroom door again.

'*You hear me, you fucker?*' she yelled at the door. '*I'll go to jail! I don't give a fuck! I'll do time!*'

'Mrs Farrell,' Darcy said. 'Please. What's happened now?'

The other garda took a step back, happy to be finally relieved of control by a more experienced garda.

'*What's happened?*' Peggy screamed. '*What the fuck do you think? I warned him. I warned the little fucker if he went near that bitch's house again, I'd kill him!*'

'Detective Doyle? Is that you? Oh, thank God!' a man's panicked voice came from inside the bathroom. 'She's crazy. Arrest her or something. I've been stuck in here for hours.'

'Put the poker down, Mrs Farrell,' Darcy said.

'Do you know what he did?' Peggy asked her. 'Do you?'

Darcy shook her head.

'We're having sex, right? The first time in six months, I might add. He's going at it hammer and tongs, not that it makes much difference with his tiny prick!'

She banged on the door again with her fist.

Darcy's colleague put his hand to his mouth to suppress a laugh. She threw him a stern look and he turned away.

'He was making the effort, though,' Peggy went on. 'I'll give him that much. But then, right as he's going at full gallop, what does he do? *He says that bitch's name!* Calls her name out as if he's in a field trying to get her attention. The bastard!'

'I haven't spoken to her in months, I swear!' a voice pleaded from inside the bathroom.

'*You're a liar!*' Peggy screamed back at him and slammed the poker into the door, cracking open the wood.

'Mrs Farrell, please.' Darcy took a step forward.

'Jesus Christ!' the voice inside the bathroom pleaded.

'Where are your little boys, Mrs Farrell?' Darcy asked.

'I took them next door,' the garda told her.

'Look,' Darcy said, keeping her tone as composed as possible, 'there's been no real damage done yet, except to the door – so if you calm down, we can all go downstairs and talk things through. I'm sure we can resolve this. Please think of your boys, Mrs Farrell. They're frightened and scared right now.'

'*They're* frightened and scared?' the voice in the bathroom called out. '*How do you think I feel?*'

'*Please, Mr Farrell!*' Darcy called to him, and put her hand on Peggy's shoulder.

Peggy's breathing slowed down. 'OK, but if he says one stupid thing, I'm going to clobber him with this!' She held up the poker.

'*Mr Farrell!*' Darcy called in to her husband. 'We're going downstairs now. We'll talk about things in the sitting room.'

'*Tell that crazy bitch to put the poker down!*'

'*I'll shove it up your arse if I find out you've been cheating on me again!*' Peggy yelled.

'Just stay in the bathroom until we're downstairs,' Darcy told him. 'We'll sort everything out.'

Darcy took a step back to let Peggy pass her and go down the stairs.

There was a click and the bathroom door opened.

'*Please stay inside, Mr Farrell!*' Darcy said.

Peggy turned around to face her husband.

'*You should arrest this nut-job!*' he shouted. '*She's as batty as her mother!*'

Peggy swung at him, the poker aimed at his head and the tip of it cut into her husband's cheek. He screamed and slapped a hand to his face. A trickle of blood poured through his fingers.

Peggy swung again blindly. With both her hands, Darcy grabbed Peggy's arm, and slammed her own body into Peggy's, so that Peggy lost her balance mid-swing and fell backwards onto the landing floor.

'Grab the poker,' Darcy ordered the garda, as she twisted Peggy's left arm, forcing her to turn over.

Darcy planted her knee into Peggy's back as she reached behind her belt and grabbed her handcuffs. The extra pressure and pain forced Peggy into further submission and allowed Darcy to cuff her hands.

Peggy lifted her head off the floor and, turning it, saw her husband's bleeding face.

'Oh, my baby,' she said, her voice muffled. 'I'm so sorry. Mammy didn't mean to hurt you.'

'*Get up,*' Darcy ordered.

She and the garda got Peggy's massive frame off the floor.

Peggy leaned into her husband and he wrapped his arms around her, unable to join his hands behind her as his thin body almost disappeared into her.

The garda pressed his radio and called for an ambulance. Darcy looked at Peggy soothing her husband and bent down to pick up the poker. She resisted the urge to beat the two of them with it.

The Garmin on her wrist showed the time: 06.55.

Chapter 2

The electric alarm had been buzzing in the dark apartment for some minutes before Mick Kelly reached over with his left hand and smacked the OFF button.

He fumbled along the bedside locker until his hand settled on a packet of cigarettes with a disposable lighter resting on top. Opening one eye, he removed a cigarette from the packet and placed it between his lips. He sparked the lighter, moved its flame to the tip of the cigarette and inhaled deeply.

Only when his lungs were filled with the first of the day's smoke did he finally sit up and open both eyes. He took a half-filled ashtray from the locker, using his ample belly as the perfect resting place. Then he reached for his phone and opened it. He squinted at the bright screen.

There were two voicemails. He knew both were from his ex-wife. She had phoned him the previous evening but, having had a few drinks too many, he didn't want to answer. She could always tell when he'd been drinking, even if it had only been one, and he didn't need to hear again how she was 'concerned for his welfare', especially since he was fully aware that she wasn't.

He moved the ashtray back to the locker, balanced the cigarette on its edge and pulled the bedclothes off his legs. With more effort than a fifty-two-year-old man should have to make, he planted his feet onto the floor and stretched his back. He let out a loud groan and then roughly scratched at his overgrown grey-speckled beard, like a dog with fleas.

He stood up and, finding his trousers in a heap on the floor, picked them up and pulled them on. Some coins rattled in their pockets as he tightened the belt. He raised his arm and smelt the armpit of his T-shirt. He winced and took it off.

Opening his wardrobe, it surprised him to see a clean and ironed shirt hanging there. He put it on, in the knowledge that its unexpected discovery would probably be the highlight of his day. When he was fully dressed, he opened the curtains. He stood looking out at the redbrick apartment building opposite him, then raised his head until he could see the drab grey sky above the rooftops.

'Poxy rain,' he said and then turned and left the room.

The dank morning reminded the shuffling commuters that their summer months had ended, and soon the dark wet days would settle over Dublin again. Everyone's head was lowered as they paraded along, clutching their takeaway coffee cups.

After a short walk, Mick stepped out of the rain and into Murray's pub on Pearse Street. He had stopped trying to convince himself several weeks ago that he wouldn't have an early-morning drink on his way to work. It was a part of his routine now, and he accepted it, like a limp in a man's walk.

He sat at the bar and nodded at John. John was the owner's nephew who had promised himself he'd only work in the pub for a few summer months to earn some cash before heading off to Australia. That was over six years ago. But that was nothing unusual. The walls of Murray's pub were plastered with unaccomplished dreams and its carpets soaked in unfulfilled and half-attempted goals.

As John poured a Guinness, Mick placed his cigarettes on the bar and casually swept his eyes around the crowd: three gardaí, who had probably just finished their shift at the Garda Station two minutes' walk away, four lads who looked the worse for wear, squeezing the last drop out of a good night, a young couple who from their body language looked like they had only met eight hours ago but didn't want the thrill of meeting someone new to end, and a few regular old lads with stubbled faces and tired clothes that needed a wash, already sipping on their second drink of the day.

The fresh black pint made a welcoming heavy thud as it was placed down on the worn mahogany surface in front of Mick. He grasped the glass in his right hand like a drowning man gripping the side of a lifeboat.

He kissed the lip of the glass and swallowed a third of its contents before placing it back on its spot in front of him. He felt the cool liquid, like cold lava flowing down, and his entire body relaxed in a sigh. John placed his change on the bar and said nothing. If he had learned anything over the last six years, he knew better than to interrupt a customer's first drink of the day.

This was Mick's morning meditation: a drink half full on the bar and the quietness of a pub as the alcohol swirled around inside his body, calming his nerves and bringing peace to his soul. His spiritual respite from the scourge of the streets. Now he could face the day and try to be the man he knew he could be. Or at least the man he once was.

He knocked back the remains of his pint, then slid down off the stool. He saw one of the gardaí glance in his direction. Mick made eye contact with him and held it until the garda looked away.

He looked over at the door for a moment – a moment that was way too long. He knew well that a second pint was the gateway to the dark side, but then, as if someone's hands were gently turning him around, he slid back up onto the stool and gave John a nod of his head.

The Streaky Rasher, off Townsend Street, was located right in the middle of a few blocks that had somehow managed to avoid all attempts at inner-city gentrification. It was known for serving the best (and cheapest) breakfast in Dublin. It opened at 6 a.m. sharp and closed at 11 a.m. Five euro got you a full Irish breakfast cooked in animal dripping. Six euro and you got a pot of tea with it. There was no coffee. Seven euro and they'd throw in some toast. There was nothing for eight euro.

It was run by a grumpy middle-aged man named Dermot, who had a sunken chest, skinny legs, and a protruding stomach that made it look like he was hiding a football under his greasy white T-shirt. If he liked you, then you got a nod from him and some free toast. That was the rumour anyway, but nobody had ever seen it happen. Dermot liked no one.

Mick queued and ordered the seven-euro option before taking a seat beside an elderly lady whose lavender perfume almost hid the fact that she hadn't changed her clothes for days. She glanced at him before deciding he wasn't any immediate threat. Between them sat a large open handbag stuffed with clothes, with her purse resting on top. Mick attempted a smile, but her focus was already back on her eggs and sausages, which she ate as if it were her first decent meal in a week.

Mick started on his own breakfast. He had gone to Lidl on the way home from work last night and had filled his basket with a ready-made meal, milk, bread and eight cans of cheap beer whose Polish name he couldn't pronounce. He had every intention of sticking the frozen meal into the microwave, but it didn't look as appetising in his apartment as it had under the bright lights of the store.

He ate ravenously. Everyone in here did. The café's food was more than filling – it was medicinal. When the plate was empty, he slurped his tea and sat contently for a few moments, allowing the food to settle in the base of his stomach.

From the corner of his eye he saw a snake sliding at waist height between him and the old lady. He blinked and looked down. The snake was an arm that had a black shamrock tattoo on the forearm which looked self-drawn, and the veins were peppered with small red dots – souvenirs from forgotten needles.

Mick shifted in his seat, turned around and looked straight at the owner of the arm. An emaciated face under a blob of grey hair looked back at him. The man put his finger up to his pursed lips and said '*Ssshhh ...*' He managed a smile that practically cracked his face in two like a split tennis ball.

Mick looked down at the hand again. It had a hold of the purse on top of the woman's bag. In one swift move, Mick grabbed the little finger that was holding the side of the purse and yanked it sideways.

There was a cracking sound, like standing on a dry twig in a forest. The man shot up to his feet and looked down at his little finger pointing out at ninety degrees from his hand. He had a grimace on his face that would make children cry.

When the shock had subsided somewhat and the man could breathe again, he exploded in a roar that stopped everyone. '*Yeh fuckin' bastarrrd!*'

Mick returned to his tea and raised the cup to his mouth.

A woman, almost as skeletal as her partner, appeared at the man's side and looked at his finger.

'*Look what you done to him, yeh prick!*' she screamed at Mick. '*Somebody call the Guards! We're goin' to sue you for assault!*'

From behind the grill, Dermot put down his spatula. He peered over across the café at the commotion. He saw the two junkies, and he saw Mick.

'*You two – out!*' he shouted.

'*Fuck you!*' the woman screamed back at him.

'*Jaysus, me fuckin' finger!*' the man cried again, staring at it in disbelief.

Dermot made his way to the end of the counter, a wooden hurley appearing in his hand by the time he reached the end.

The woman pulled at her partner's arm and led him to the door.

Regaining some of his composure, the man shouted over at Mick, '*I'm goin' to fuckin' remember you! Do ye hear me, yeh prick?*'

Mick stayed seated and kept his back to the couple as they left. By the time they were outside, Dermot was back at his station, and the café had returned to its normal sound of chatting and the clanking of cutlery.

Mick finished his tea.

'Thank you,' the woman beside him said.

He looked at her. 'You should know better.'

She nodded and grimaced.

Mick stood up to leave.

'They might be waiting outside for you,' she warned him. 'You should call the Guards just to be safe.'

Mick pulled his jacket a little bit to the right, and the woman saw the gun and holster under it.

'Jaysus, missus,' he told her, 'I'd be in for some slagging if I had to call a few wooden-tops to come to my rescue over a pair of junkies. They'd love that down in the station.'

The woman nodded again and smiled, revealing teeth that had quite possibly never been viewed by a dentist.

'Take care of yourself,' Mick told her and headed for the door.

Chapter 3

Jennifer Delaney placed three plastic shopping bags into the back of her car on top of beach towels, buckets, spades, a Batman toy, and rocks and sticks that all summer long her little boy, Bo, had picked up and carried back to the car.

He was such a – a boy. And, of course, she loved her little man and wouldn't change a hair on his beautiful little head. But now she wanted a girl. A girl to do girlie things with. A girl she'd buy pretty dresses for, and dolls, and play girlie games with. And decorate her bedroom in pinks and purples and a giant doll's house with tiny furniture, and play make-believe games with her, and brush her long hair or tie it up into a ponytail.

Jennifer's life was full of men. Three brothers, a husband, all his male friends and a son. Men and boys. She wanted an ally in her world of testosterone and fart jokes. A little Mini-Me, she often thought.

She started her car, reversed out of her spot in front of the supermarket, and then headed for home. She turned on the radio and tried to listen to the talk show host, but her mind kept barging in with thoughts of her husband and that dark spot in the corner of her brain that was growing bigger every day. That little niggling thought like a stone in her shoe she could no longer ignore.

Was Paul having an affair?

And if he wasn't, then why didn't he want her anymore? Sure, he kissed her and hugged her, and she believed he still loved her, but she knew in her heart that he no longer fancied her. She was tired of trying to initiate sex in bed when he would just roll over or complain of tiredness.

In a strange way, she hoped he was having an affair. At least then it wasn't her who had grown older and less attractive. But she saw how men still looked at her – even in the supermarket just now, a man had almost crashed his trolley because he was staring at her so much.

If he was having an affair, a part of her wanted him to confess it, and then they could go to couples' therapy together, and she could learn to forgive him for the sake of Bo, and then they could grow from it and have a stronger relationship in the future. Of course, another part of her would want to cut his balls off with rusty garden shears.

But today was the day and, while he'd been away on his business trip, she had planned a little surprise for him.

She went over her plan again. He'd said his flight was landing at 10, so he should be home before noon. She'd have time to shower and change and, by the time he got home, she'd have his favourite snacks prepared, flowers on the table and a bottle of champagne cooling in the fridge. Her friend was collecting Bo from school so she and Paul would have the house to themselves until then.

When he'd arrive, she would be dressed in the white lingerie she had bought only yesterday. He would come in and if he chose the food over her then she would know.

She spotted the parcel outside the front door as she pulled into her driveway. At first, she cursed the courier for leaving another package outside for any passerby to steal, but then she remembered what might be inside. She had ordered it online over three weeks ago and was sure that she hadn't ordered any clothes in the last week. Or had she?

She got out her groceries and opened the front door. She placed the bags on the kitchen island and went back for her parcel.

She brought the box into the kitchen and, grabbing a steak knife, sliced it open. She pulled out the cardboard shredding that had been used to protect it, and then held it up in her hands.

It was a clock. A wall clock. A wall clock with a tiny camera in its centre. She had seen it in on an online UK spy store and her mind had begun to whirl. If she could just have some evidence that Paul was actually cheating on her, then all her suspicions would be justified. That depended on him having the nerve to bring the bitch into their home, of course.

She found two AA batteries in a drawer, clicked them in, and the hands of the clock began to move. She held it at arm's length and stared at it. She leaned her face in closer to check if the camera was visible and heard a gentle *tick-tock, tick-tock, tick-tock*. At the centre of the clock's hands was a glass ball, like a small eye. She felt as if the clock was looking at her instead of her examining it, as if it were studying her face.

The doorbell rang.

She almost dropped the clock and her heart quickened.

It couldn't be Paul. It was too early. Audrey. It was most likely Audrey. Oh, God. Audrey. She really didn't have time for her this morning. She didn't care about the latest neighbourhood gossip or what Sarah's husband in number twenty-four was doing behind her back. She had enough problems with her own, for God's sake.

She turned to the door, then looked back at the clock as if she were about to be caught with something illegal.

She hurried into the hall and, looking around, to the left of the front door spotted the framed photo of her and Paul on their honeymoon in Thailand. Rather than loving memories, the photo always reminded her of an argument they'd had that same evening. She quickly removed the photo and placed it on a shelf between an award Bo had won for reading and a photo of her deceased father. She doubted very much Paul would even notice.

Then she carefully hung the clock on the exposed nail.

The doorbell rang again.

'Morning, Audrey,' she said as she opened the door. 'I'm afraid I'm rushing out at the ...'

A delivery man with a large box stood there. He was wearing a baseball cap with a hoodie pulled up over it.

'Yes?' she said.

The man grunted. The box looked very heavy. More of Paul's gym equipment, no doubt.

'Oh, bring it in, please,' Jennifer told him, barely disguising the impatience in her tone.

The man stepped inside before she had time to make way and she was forced to take a few steps backwards.

'Just put it down there,' she said, and he bent down and placed the box on the floor.

She looked at the top of the box. It was open. Then the man reached into the box and pulled something out that was small and black and looked like a cucumber. He glanced behind him through the open door.

She opened her mouth to question him but, as he stood up, his hand whipped upwards at such speed that she was almost unaware of what had happened until she'd been struck. She flew back against the wall and tumbled to the ground. Pain pulsed through her jaw, but she managed to raise herself up off the floor by pushing against the plant pot there for support. The pot overturned and she collapsed back onto the floor. She watched as the man pulled on a pair of latex gloves, then reached behind him to the front door and closed it gently.

She tried to get up, but she couldn't. When the man turned around, she saw his face, and she was consumed suddenly with a deluge of fear.

'There's money upstairs,' she wheezed. 'Take it.'

He bent, pulled her away from the pot by an arm and a leg and righted the pot. She lay there, frozen in fear, looking up at him.

The man removed the hoodie and baseball cap and, looking down at her, he smiled – a grotesque and ugly smile. He reached into the box and pulled out a gym bag. From it, she watched him take out a black mask, like a small gas mask, and place it over his head, covering his face but leaving his mouth exposed. She watched in fascination, as if she were watching him from a different place.

He unzipped his jacket and folded it neatly. Then he did the same with his trousers and placed them both in the bag. He reached in again and pulled out the largest knife Jennifer had ever seen. The blade shone like a mirror and was almost the length of his forearm. He looked at it closely, twisting it in his hand and admiring his reflection, as if Jennifer weren't even there. He stuck out his tongue and licked it from the shaft to the tip of the blade.

Only then did the scream pour out of her as if reality had suddenly punched her in the face. The man turned and looked at her.

Then he got on one knee, and raised the black object above his head. She watched as it came soaring down through the air at her.

Chapter 4

The only modification Detective Chief Superintendent Glenn O'Riordan made when he took over the National Bureau of Criminal Investigation five years earlier was to change the wooden office door to one made entirely of glass. This, he felt, would be a symbol of the transparency he strove for in his squad. He could see all his detectives as they came and went, and they could see him diligently at work behind his desk.

At least, that's what he told everyone, and it was partially true. Growing up on the banks of Lake Corrib in County Galway, O'Riordan had been a big Sam Spade fan, and a glass door with *Sam Spade – Private Investigator* painted on it had always been a childhood dream. As yet, he had not managed to garner the courage to have his own name embossed on the door, and perhaps at this stage he never would.

He spread out the dozen personnel files on his table as if he were about to perform a magic card trick. He smiled, pleased with himself at the analogy. Perhaps that's what he should do: close his eyes, reach down, and pull out a lucky rabbit.

The Commissioner, at the very least, had allowed him to pick his own new recruits. He should be thankful for that, anyway. The problem wasn't their qualifications, however, it was their gender. He didn't see women as second-class citizens, and he certainly wasn't a misogynist. It was just that … well, the job of arresting and detaining hardened criminals and murderers, which was what the NBCI was all about, was hardly the kind of job he'd like his sister or wife to perform. He'd seen and heard things that had kept him awake at night, and he certainly never shared any such details with his wife.

But he also understood, all too well, that being the head of any department made it necessary to make decisions and perform tasks that the politicians above him, in their ultimate wisdom, thought necessary. And if balancing the gender disparity was what they ordered, then bringing more females up to the fifth floor was what he would do.

It wasn't sheer ambition and brute determination that had landed him the top job in Harcourt Street. It was a combination of his seniority (he had over thirty years' service), and his simple ability to avoid pissing people off. When it came down to his nomination for the position, it wasn't that he didn't have the most friends in senior management, it was rather that he had the fewest enemies.

And now, like a marathon runner with only a few kilometres to the finish line, O'Riordan could finally visualise his retirement. He looked out at his detectives. Some were behind their monitors, others were on their phones. In the years to come, whether it was he who sat in this chair or not, nothing would change. Crime was a hardy perennial, and its prevention, or not, would continue with or without him.

The thought cast a shadow over him, but he shook it off. He allowed his mind to drift and daydream about the not too distant future and of holidays with his wife in Lanzarote during the long winter months and pottering about in his vegetable garden back in Oughterard in Galway in the summer while she watched him from the kitchen window and then tapped on the glass to tell when dinner was ready. They had a happy and childless marriage of over thirty years, which seemed to a contradiction to most people, he knew.

He rested both his hands on the pile of new NBCI applicants on his table. He was going to be late tonight. He should call Eleanor and let her know.

Instead, he stood up and walked to the glass door. He had a team of twenty-six detectives. Twenty men and six women. It wasn't like he hadn't tried in his own way over the years to address the gender imbalance, but it was a hopeless cause. The gap already started at rank-and-file level with four male officers for every one female. By the time they reached the senior investigator's level, it was down to one in ten. He considered six in his own department a damn miracle. That's what he should have told the Commissioner.

He sat back down and spent a few minutes arranging the files alphabetically into a neat pile.

Rather than his own career failings and achievements, his thoughts of late had taken on a more dominant resolution. A simple determination that he would not allow his swan song, whenever that might be, to be a total fuck-up. A resolve that his name would be remembered with respect and honour for years after he'd finally handed in his badge.

And if that meant bringing in more female gardaí for the Commissioner, so be it. After all, it'd be the Commissioner who'd be the one to pick up the pieces after he'd gone.

O'Riordan took up the top file, opened it and began to read.

The elevator doors pinged open, and Mick Kelly stepped onto the fifth floor. A few heads slowly raised and looked over at him, but then quickly lowered before eye contact was made.

'Detective Inspector Kelly!' O'Riordan called to him from his glass door.

Mick looked over at him.

O'Riordan beckoned to him with his head and stepped back inside.

Most of the other officers pretended not to have noticed his summoning as Mick stood still for a few moments before heading over to his boss's office.

Two detectives were standing side by side as Mick passed them: Des Burns and Fergal Kane.

Whenever Mick heard complaints of poor police behaviour, he always thought of Burns and Kane. Sometimes he felt the NBCI bore similar idiosyncrasies to a teenage classroom. Burns was a bully and Kane was his sycophant sidekick.

Mick wished sometimes they really were all back in school. Then he would get away with dragging the pair outside and kicking the living shit out of the two of them while everyone else stood in a circle cheering him on.

'Looks like you're about to get fucked, Kelly,' Burns said as he passed them.

Some other officers looked over, and a couple sniggered.

Mick stopped. 'What a coincidence, Detective Burns,' he said. 'That's exactly what your wife said to me last night.'

The expression on Burns' face changed to a scowl. More officers looked over at them and several laughed.

Burns took a step towards him. Kane stood up straighter.

Mick didn't budge.

'*Fucking loser*,' Burns whispered to him through clenched teeth.

Mick opened his mouth to reply.

'*Kelly!*' O'Riordan called again. '*In here!*'

Mick held Burns' stare for one more second and then turned away.

'*Burns, Kane!*' O'Riordan shouted to the two detectives. 'Have you two not got something better to be doing? Because I have some door-to-door enquiries if you're interested.'

'That's a uniform's job, Chief,' Burns said.

'Exactly,' O'Riordan said, and watched them scuttle away.

Mick went in, closed the door behind him and sat down opposite his boss's chair. He looked around the office as O'Riordan switched the kettle on. The chief fumbled with jar lids and spoons behind him until a large mug of black coffee was placed in front of Mick. He watched O'Riordan walk to the other side of the desk and sit down.

'You look like shit,' O'Riordan told him.

'Good morning to you too, Chief.'

'Drink that.'

Mick looked down at the steam wafting off the surface of the black liquid. His eyes followed it as it rose and then vanished into the air above him.

O'Riordan regarded his detective. 'As you know,' he said, 'I'm not one to waste time on chitchat and other bullshit, so I'll get straight to the point.'

'Understood, Chief.' Mick focused again on him.

'I've been thinking a lot about my retirement, and I have a proposition for you.'

Mick took a slow sip from his coffee cup.

'It's to do with what you'll be doing when I'm gone,' O'Riordan continued. 'In three years, you'll be fifty-five.'

Mick said nothing.

'You'll be fifty-five, and you'll have thirty years' service behind you. That's all you need to pack it all in for a pension.'

'Sorry, Chief – can I say something? Because I think I know where you're going with this, and I might save you a bit of time.'

'Go on,' O'Riordan said and leaned back in his chair.

'Are you going to recommend me to take over from you as the new chief when you're gone?'

O'Riordan's face flushed, and he sat up. 'Of course I'm not going to fucking recommend ...' Then he calmed himself. He let out a deep sigh.

Mick smiled, happy to have got a rise out of his boss. He reached out for the coffee mug, took a noisy slurp, and placed it back down on the table.

O'Riordan leaned back in his chair again. Neither man said anything for a while, and it was only when O'Riordan had fully relaxed that he finally spoke. 'How's Marion?'

Mick didn't reply.

'Haven't seen her in ages. Not since your divorce, anyway.'

'I'll tell her you were asking for her, if you like.'

'Do. Thanks. And Lucy? And Michael? How are they doing these days?'

O'Riordan watched Mick's lips tighten. Mentioning Mick's children was like throwing a cup of cold water into his face, but it was sometimes the only way of reaching him.

'What do you want, Chief?'

O'Riordan sat forward. 'I want you to fucking listen to me. I want you to stop being ... stop being yourself for a minute and think about what I'm saying to you. Is that so hard?'

'I'm not interested in listening to your thoughts on your retirement, thanks very much. And I'm certainly not interested in listening to your thoughts on mine.'

'Then when are you going to stop mulling about this place like it's a fucking social club? Coming and going whenever you feel like it. You think the lads upstairs haven't noticed your detection rate these days?'

'I don't give two shites what the lads upstairs think about me or my detection rate.'

'Well, you should. Because I can't keep covering your arse forever.'

'I never asked you to.'

'I need results, Mick. I need solves.'

'Well, then, stop giving me all the shite cases all the fucking time. Or having me acting like a fucking lackey for some of the lads half my age.'

'You don't give me any choice, Mick. You don't have the record for the big cases.'

'I don't have what? Are you fucking kidding me? When you were a sergeant in Rathfarnham getting cats down from fucking trees, I was running with the big dogs in the inner city!'

'I know that, Mick.'

But Mick ignored him. 'Three murder solves and a missing six-year-old girl returned to her parents in my first four months as a detective. Remember that?'

'I do, Mick.'

'Columbo Kelly, they'd say. He always gets his man. Even the criminals used to say, "If Kelly has his sights on you, you're fucked".'

O'Riordan nodded at the memory. 'I remember every garda back then talking about you in the pubs, or up in Harrington Street Club. Because no matter what position they hold, rank-and-file right up to Detective Inspector, when the officers of the law in this city get together with a few pints on them, they can gossip as good as any rag mag out of Hollywood.'

'Then don't talk to me about my record.' Mick picked up his coffee. 'And don't tell me you don't remember who I was or what I've done.'

O'Riordan leaned forward. 'I do remember, Mick. And it wasn't just the cases. Morale had been low, even lower than it is now, but suddenly there was a change among the men and women in uniform. They walked a little taller. Showed a bit of pride in their jobs. Back then, you brought something back to the force that had been missing. Young kids on the streets started respecting us again. Wanting to be a garda when they grew up.'

Mick nodded in agreement and took another slurp from the mug. 'I knew you'd remember.'

O'Riordan leaned forward in his chair. 'The problem is, Mick. Nobody else does. Nobody else gives a shite.'

They sat in silence for a few moments, allowing the words to settle.

'I want you to retire with me,' O'Riordan tried again. 'Call it quits. I'll get you off the fifth floor for your remaining three years. Get you something handy. No shift work. I'm owed a few favours.'

Mick snorted a chuckle. 'And then what? Golf? Gardening? Holidays in Torremolinos?'

'You can do whatever the hell regular people do. Have you forgotten what that's like? I have, anyway. You can go on golfing holidays and spend all the time on the 19th hole if you like. Or get a job in security. Something in the private sector. Double what you're getting paid here. Plus your pension.'

'And have Eleanor invite me round for a Sunday roast?'

'Something like that, yeah.'

Mick shook his head. 'I hate to burst your bubble, Chief, but you and me don't get to be regular people again. With the shit we've seen and done. It doesn't work like that.'

'I disagree.'

Mick shrugged.

They sat in silence until Mick eventually stood up and stretched his back. He let out a groan and walked to the door, but turned to face his boss before leaving.

'Just get me a proper case, will you?' he said, feeling like he was almost on the verge of begging. 'You won't regret it, Glenn.'

'I'll think about it.'

Mick opened the door.

'And you? What about what I said?' O'Riordan asked. 'About retiring?'

'I'll think about it,' Mick said and walked out.

Chapter 5

'Check it out.' Burns nudged Kane as they left by the main entrance of Harcourt Street. 'It's Double D.'

Darcy was aware of the nickname that some of her male colleagues had pinned on her. Naively, she had thought it was because of her initials: Darcy Doyle. The nickname had started in Templemore College during her basic training as a garda but had somehow followed her around like a bad smell.

Back at Templemore, all those years ago, she had felt an initial euphoria of having made it. A sense that she had risen from where she had once been and had finally been able to breathe in the air above water. That she had been liberated. Free from the carers who saw her only as an income in foster money. Free from drinking too much to numb the reality of her teenage years and then eating too little so she might disappear.

Burns and Kane straightened their posture and sucked in their guts as Darcy passed them. She watched them out of the corner of her eye. They knew who she was, or at least they thought they did. And that was good enough for Darcy because she definitely knew who they were.

She knew most of the detectives who worked in the NBCI. She would sometimes see some of them whenever she was dragged to a local bar. They had an aloof air about them that bordered on the superior. It wasn't just that, though. They dressed better, probably because of their higher clothing allowance. Their squad cars were better as they had first choice in the carpool. Darcy drove a green eight-year-old Opel Astra whose interior had a faint, yet constant, odour of vomit and that could barely push above 100 kilometres an hour in a straight line – not that she ever found the need to go that fast.

'Doyle!' the desk sergeant, Eddie Mills, called over to her. 'Fifth floor is looking for you.'

'Fifth floor?' she asked, but he just stared at her until she knew he wasn't going to repeat himself. She walked away, but then turned back. 'Who do I ask for?'

'O'Riordan. Hope you didn't piss him off too much, whatever you did.'

She took a step back to ask him what he meant, but his phone rang and he picked it up.

She stood for a few moments in the centre of the entrance like a boulder in the middle of a river, civilians and gardaí moving around her. Her mind was racing.

The lift doors opened to her right and, without overthinking it, she hurried and stepped inside. She pressed the button for the fifth floor and the doors closed. She stood alone, looking at herself in the reflection of the metallic door as the lift ascended.

She quickly ran her fingers through her loose hair, and then tied it into a ponytail. She fixed her shirt and straightened her jacket, thankful now she had taken the time to go home and shower and prepare her report on this morning's incident.

What if this was the opportunity she had been waiting for? The 'tap on the shoulder' she had dreamed about?

The door opened onto the fifth floor. She could see O'Riordan's office at the far end and its famous glass door. Several heads turned to watch her as she made her way through the room. She kept her eyes on the office and her back straight.

O'Riordan had his head down, studying a file, when she tapped a knuckle on the half-opened door. He raised his eyes without moving his head. They stared at each other for a few moments before he nodded for her to come in.

'Close the door,' he told her.

She did.

'Take a seat.'

She sat in the chair opposite him. She wondered if he too could hear her heart beating. He kept reading the file, so she allowed her eyes to look around the room, breathing slowly in and out: a few framed photos, mementos from previous cases, a dying potted plant.

'Bunch of nosy bastards,' O'Riordan said.

She shifted her focus back onto him. He was staring at her.

'Sir?'

He raised his finger and pointed behind her.

'The lads outside there,' he said. 'Watching you. Wondering why you're here. Why does the chief want to talk to her, they're asking. Or did you think they were all just looking at your arse?'

He tilted the file in his hand slightly, and she risked a glance at the title on its cover. Her heart skipped a beat when she saw the name on it. It was her personnel file. She raised her eyebrows and her mouth opened slightly but then she tried to hide her reaction to reading it, but it was too late. She saw the slight smile on O'Riordan's face.

'You see, that's half their job,' he said.

'Sir? Whose job?'

'Their job,' he repeated, indicating the detectives outside on the floor. 'One man's nosy bastard is another man's inquisitive detective.

It can be a curse as well, though. To be like that. Always watching. Always listening. Always switched on. Trying to figure out something from nothing. A glance. An intonation of the voice. A certain picture in a certain place. But also knowing something missing can be just as important as something there. All the things that can make or break a case. You know what I mean?'

'I think so, sir.'

'Do you?'

He watched her for a second before returning to the file.

'You've an exemplary record here. There's a lot of women you've saved between these pages. And some men.'

'Thank you, sir.'

'Of course, there are no victims for you to save in the NBCI. You realise that, don't you?'

'What do you mean, sir?'

'I mean that by the time we hear about the victim, it's usually too late for them.'

'I understand.'

'Do you? Is that why you're here, Detective Doyle? Because if you've no one else to save, then maybe you have a chance to save yourself?'

'Sir?'

Chief O'Riordan kept eye contact with her.

'Something doesn't add up,' he told her.

'With what, sir?'

He tapped the side of the file and sniffed loudly.

'It's your background, Doyle. It doesn't add up.'

'I underwent a rigorous background check before my training in Templemore, sir.'

'Rigorous would be a slight exaggeration. They checked you out alright, but you're talking to the big boys now. The NBCI don't do rigorous, we do thorough. Tell me where you're from.'

'It says right there ...'

'I know what it says right there. I'm holding the bloody thing in my hands, aren't I? I asked you to tell me where you're from. And I want specifics.'

Darcy felt her throat go dry and her face redden. This was the moment she had feared all her career. The moment she would be found out and, finally, the charade would be over.

She pushed back into the chair as if trying to escape the question.

'Check your emotions, Detective. Your cheeks are flushed, your chest is going up and down like you've been running, and your right hand has tightened into a fist. If I put you in a room with a seasoned criminal, he'd make mincemeat of you. He'd laugh at you. Now, take a deep breath and start again. Where are you from?'

Darcy calmed herself and forced herself to relax into the chair.

'That's better,' O'Riordan told her.

'I was fostered when I was seven years old.'

'I know that.'

'My biological mother was abusive. An addict. Social Welfare took me away from her. I never saw her again.'

'You're lying. You looked her up on the PULSE system. Seven years ago. As soon as you had the authority to access it. Try again.'

'Honest, sir. I checked, but I never visited her.'

'Your own mother? That's some cold shit right there, Doyle.'

'She was a junkie, sir. She never wanted me. I only wanted to see if she was still alive.'

'And is she?'

'You tell me,' she told him, regaining her composure.

O'Riordan smiled at her.

'And your dad?' he asked.

Darcy just shrugged off the question.

He looked down at her file again.

'Four years criminology in UL?' he asked her.

'Yes, sir.'

'That must have been shite, was it?'

'No, sir. I knew one day that studying sociology, psychology and –'

'No,' he interrupted her. 'I mean, it must have been shite living in Limerick for four years.'

He smiled at her, and she allowed herself to smile back.

'My missus is from Limerick. God, her family drives me nuts.' He laughed. 'Talk about a chip on their shoulder about Dublin! Do you know what I mean?'

'Yes, sir,' Darcy said and laughed. 'They always used to say that …'

'Who paid for it?' O'Riordan said loudly, the smile gone from his face.

Darcy gulped. 'Sir?'

'You heard me.'

Darcy felt as if her legs had been whipped out from under her. She tried to compose herself.

'I paid, sir … I …'

'No, you didn't. Last chance. Who paid?'

O'Riordan closed the file and threw it back on the table.

'I don't know, sir.'

'You don't know?'

'I would get the receipts, but the money was always lodged into the university's account.'

'And you never paid for any of it?'

'No, sir. It was always on time and always the exact amount. I worked part time in the evenings in a restaurant and saved the money in case the cheques ever ended but ...'

'But they didn't?'

'No, sir. They didn't.'

'And you never questioned it?'

Darcy looked him straight in the eyes. 'Of course I did. I asked the university, but they said there was no name attached to the payment. I didn't want to ask too many questions in case they thought it was suspicious and kicked me out.'

O'Riordan picked up her personnel file again and leaned back in his chair.

'But you have your suspicions about who it was.'

'Of course.'

'Who then?'

Darcy shifted in her seat. She had never spoken to anyone about this before.

'My English teacher, Mr Benson.'

'Why? Did he fancy you or did he ...?'

Darcy's eyes widened. 'No, sir.'

'Sure?'

'Yes, sir.'

'OK, Doyle. I believe you. So why?'

'Why did he pay for it?'

O'Riordan nodded.

'I honestly don't know. We had a friendly relationship. He knew my background, and he said he would do everything he could to help me. I had talked to him about the course and how I wanted to do it. One day I got a note in the mail saying everything was going to be paid for and that I only needed to apply.'

O'Riordan nodded slowly.

'Why did you change your name?'

'How did you know …?' Darcy sighed. 'I wanted a fresh start away from …'

'Away from your abusive background and junkie ma?'

Darcy flushed in anger. She began to protest but decided against it. 'Yes.'

'Why the name "Doyle" then? That wasn't one of your foster-family names.'

'It was just a name. No reason.'

O'Riordan raised his eyebrows and said nothing.

Darcy lowered her eyes. 'It was because of the film, *The French Connection*.'

O'Riordan thought about it. 'Popeye Doyle?'

Darcy lowered her head further to hide her blush.

O'Riordan couldn't help but smile.

'OK,' he said. 'I bet you never told anyone that before.'

'I've never told anyone any of these things before, sir.'

O'Riordan flipped over the last couple of pages of the file, then closed it. 'I'm going to take a chance on you. And I don't want to regret it.'

Darcy's heart raced. 'You won't, sir.'

'If I end up regretting it,' he said, making full eye contact with her, 'then you will regret it. Do I make myself clear?'

'Yes, sir.'

'You think domestic violence is boring? Screw this up, Doyle, and you'll be processing parking tickets in County Leitrim till you retire. That's not an idle threat. Do we understand each other?'

'Yes, sir.'

O'Riordan's desk phone rang. He reached to pick it up.

'And you can call me 'Chief', not sir.'

'Yes, Chief.'

'O'Riordan,' he said, answering the phone. He listened, said 'OK,' and hung up. He looked down at his desk. '*Fuck!*' he spat out.

O'Riordan stood up.

Darcy, unsure what to do, stayed seated.

'Seems as if our latest murder victim is Detective Kane's cousin. That's him off the investigation, the inconsiderate little bollocks!'

O'Riordan looked around the open office space outside.

'I could, you know,' Darcy said, 'I could take the case.'

O'Riordan scoffed. 'A murder? On your first outing? As much as it's an open-and-shut case, I think a murder investigation would be a bit of a leap for you.'

'Why do you say open-and-shut?'

'All indications point to the husband but, even so, Doyle, it needs someone a lot more senior than you.'

'So, pair me up with someone, then. If it is such a straightforward investigation, then what have you got to lose?'

O'Riordan looked at her as if it were the first time he was really seeing her. Darcy felt uncomfortable under his stare.

'You know,' he said, as if thinking out loud, 'if you mess this up, you won't get a second chance. And that goes for a lot of other female gardaí who are lined up behind you trying to get in here.'

'I won't mess up, Chief,' she told him. But, if she had to be honest with herself, she was unsure where the bravado was coming from and if she could back it up.

O'Riordan nodded as if he had made up his mind. He opened the door to his office and stepped outside.

'I need someone to assist in the case that Burns and Kane went to,' he called out. 'They're off it, and I want a partner for our newest member on the fifth floor.' He looked behind him. 'Detective Doyle here.'

Darcy scanned the faces in the room. Some looked over at her and then looked away. The room had gone very quiet.

'Anyone?' O'Riordan called out. 'Jones? What are you working on?'

Darcy looked over at Jones, a man in his fifties, with closely cut grey hair, wearing a nice suit, who looked like he worked out several times a week. She tried to catch his attention and smile, but his focus stayed on O'Riordan. His eyes had the stare of someone who was trying not to make eye contact with a beggar while walking past them in the street.

'I'm on the Rathmines case, Chief.'

'Still?'

Jones nodded.

'Anyone else?' O'Riordan called again, but now all eyes were busy on their monitors or suddenly focused on a report in their hands.

Darcy saw a hand go up, but O'Riordan's body was blocking the figure so she leaned to one side to see who the arm belonged to.

'Anyone else?' O'Riordan said again, ignoring the raised arm.

Darcy took a step to the side and saw the figure. He looked like he had just woken up, having spent the entire night asleep at his desk. As much as she wanted this case, she felt some relief that the chief was ignoring him.

'I'll do it,' the man said.

Darcy heard a snigger ripple through the room.

'I don't think so, Kelly,' O'Riordan told him.

The man raised himself up from his chair, with some effort, and walked over to them.

'I'll take her out. Show her the ropes,' he told O'Riordan.

He looked at Darcy, and she forced herself to smile at him.

O'Riordan took one more look around the room before turning back to Darcy. He walked back inside, and Mick followed him.

'This is Detective Darcy Doyle,' O'Riordan said. 'And this is Detective Mick Kelly. You two know each other?'

They shook their heads. Mick stretched out his hand and shook Darcy's.

'Kane and Burns are off the latest case,' O'Riordan told him. 'Family issues. You and Doyle go have a look at it. Woman killed in her own home.'

'Yes, Chief,' Mick said.

They both turned to leave.

'And, Mick,' O'Riordan said, 'I'm praying that the husband will be lying next to the dead body with a bloodied knife in his hand and screaming a confession to the uniforms at the scene. Anything else, I want a day-to-day report on your progress. Understood?'

'Yes, Chief.'

O'Riordan stood and watched the two of them walking side by side across his floor, and suddenly he knew the reason, after almost forty years of exemplary service, why he'd never made it to the rank of Commissioner. Because he was a soft-hearted fucking eejit.

Chapter 6

'Are you taking the piss?' Mick told the carpool sergeant. 'Who do you think we are? Starsky and fucking Hutch?'

Following the car allocation protocol for the NBCI, the carpool sergeant had given Mick and Darcy the best car available: a two-month-old white Ford Mondeo.

'What's wrong with it?' Darcy asked, reaching out and taking the keys off the sergeant's desk.

'Yeah, what's wrong with it?' the sergeant asked.

'What's wrong with it?' Mick said. 'It's about as inconspicuous as an ice-cream van at a kids' birthday party. We're supposed to be detectives, not members of the fucking Garda Band! Only nobs drive the fancy cars.'

The sound of car tyres screeching into the underground car park made the three of them turn. A bright red Hyundai tore down the ramp with its blue lights still flashing and parked close to Darcy.

Mick turned to Darcy and gestured as if his point had been made.

'Well, look what we have here!' Burns called out to Kane as they got out of the car. 'If that isn't what they call "scraping the bottom of the barrel"!'

Darcy moved towards them, but Mick put out his arm to stop her.

'I think we have a feisty one here,' Kane said. 'I like a bit of fight in my women.'

'Leave it,' Mick told Darcy, still holding her arm. 'We've got work to do. Where's your car, Doyle?'

Kane and Burns laughed as Kane placed his keys in front of the carpool sergeant.

The carpool sergeant watched them as they made their way out of the car park.

Darcy saw Mick picking up the keys that Kane had dropped on the desk. He squeezed them silently into his fist and put them at his side.

Mick followed Darcy to her car.

'Jesus,' Mick said, staring down at the car.

Darcy felt embarrassed.

'Let's just fucking hope the killer doesn't make a desperate flight down the M50,' he told her and climbed into the passenger seat. 'And what's that fucking smell?'

Darcy got in and started the car.

As they drove up the ramp, out of the garage, Darcy turned on the siren and watched Mick lower his window and discreetly drop the set of keys onto the road.

Mick stared out ahead as they made their way to the crime scene. Darcy watched him from the corner of her eye. He reached over and pressed some buttons on the dash, the radio switching on and then off again.

'Jesus Christ!' he moaned.

'What are you looking for, boss?' she asked him.

'The siren! How do you turn the fucking thing off? It's giving me a headache.'

Darcy reached down under the dash and flicked a switch. The siren stopped.

'Thank God for that,' Mick said. 'If there's one thing I can't stand, it's any Hawaii Five-O shite. Make sure you turn off the blues as well before we arrive at the scene.'

'I always find the beacon helps move a crowd,' Darcy told him.

'Everyone knows we're cops. You don't need the histrionics.'

Darcy looked at him.

'What?' he asked her.

'Histrionics?'

'What about it?'

'Nothing.'

She faced back to the road and hit the brakes to avoid slamming into the back of a cyclist in the middle of the bus lane. She pushed down hard on the horn.

Without looking around, the cyclist gave her the finger.

'I guess he told you,' Mick smiled.

Darcy reached back under the dash, and the siren blared again.

The cyclist wobbled on his bike for a few moments before mounting the kerb out of their way.

Mick smiled to himself.

'Can you tell me a little about what I'm facing here?' Darcy asked him, the siren now turned back off again.

'What do you mean?'

'Come on, boss. Don't have me walk in here like a complete rookie. You know this is my first murder case.'

'Alright, alright,' Mick said. He sat up straight in his seat. 'First of all, stop calling me "boss". I'm not your boss. I'm your partner. And don't call me partner either.'

'So, what do I call you then?'

'How about my name? My ma thought it was good enough.'

'OK.'

'Second, as you are already well know, 90% of the time it's the husband or the partner. Whether he's actually holding a smoking gun or claims to have been climbing a mountain on an island off the coast of Donegal, it's most likely going to be the husband.'

'OK.'

'Third: 9.5% of the time it's a friend, an acquaintance or a family member. They're a little trickier to solve, but with good, honest, old-fashioned police work and a fair amount of patience, we'll get the bastard.'

'I'm no maths genius, but I think that leaves half a per cent.'

'You don't want it to be that other half per cent.'

'Why? Who's that?'

'Usually anyone who lives within a hundred kilometres of the crime scene. If you're lucky.'

Darcy moved down the gears as she came to a junction.

'Also, this is our case. We're the lead detectives, but at the same time there are others who have first swing at the bat, as the Americans say.'

'Like who?' Darcy asked.

'Forensics, CSI and the State Pathologist. If we're lucky, we'll get someone decent in forensics. But, at the end of the day, we're the ones in charge. Don't be afraid to show some muscle, especially with the uniforms. Better they think you're a right bitch at the start than a big softie. Most of them want your job, anyway. Or at least they think they do.'

'Anything else?'

'Yeah, lots,' he told her. 'But that's enough for now. Just remember, a common problem with murderers is that they tend to overestimate their own abilities and underestimate ours.'

'OK.'

'What was the first thing you learned in Templemore College?' he asked her, leaning deeper back into his seat.

'Do fuck all. But whatever you do, do it well,' she said.

'Remember that.'

The next time she turned to look at him, his eyes were closed and his head was reclined back onto the headrest. It took her a few moments to register that her new partner, and supposed mentor, was gently snoring on the way to her very first murder case.

Chapter 7

Dr Phoebe Pepple, Fifi to her friends, was seven years old when she first fully understood that she was different from everyone else in her class. Her father was from Nigeria, and her mother was from Dublin. Up to that particular day, having a black father and a white mother was as normal to her as a stew of beans and yams on a Saturday and a roast dinner on a Sunday.

Then a boy in her class told her she should 'go back to where she came from'. She assumed he meant the school yard where they had just finished their break but when he told her he meant Africa she simply informed him she had never been to Africa and therefore how could she go back to a place she had never been? It was the first time, however, that her skin colour had been used against her.

It would not be the last.

Fortunately for Phoebe, she also discovered, around the same time, that she differed from her classmates in another way. She was smarter than any of them. In fact, she was much smarter.

Towards her final years in Secondary School, she found a passion for two apparently opposing subjects. Her love of art resulted in dozens of acrylic paintings brightening the walls of her home, but it was in the intricacy and accuracy of her school science classes she would truly lose herself.

Her future path was unclear until a school trip to University College Dublin. They had set stalls up in the main hall for students to view the varied subjects on offer. Phoebe found it hard to find excitement for any one specific department until she overheard a lecturer claiming his field suited someone with an artistic mind and a background in science.

Her love of Forensic Science was born that day.

She studied and worked as hard as she had always done. Her father had once told her she would find it a disadvantage in her life being black, and being a woman didn't help much either. He told her she would always have to work a lot harder than anyone else to achieve the same things as everyone else. But, to excel above them all, she would have to be superhuman.

He also told her never to complain or be bitter, but to love life as much as he loved her.

After four years of college, she finished top of her class. She was immediately offered a position with Forensic Science Ireland (FSI). Further studies in Crime Scene Investigation moved her out of the labs and into the field.

That was ten years ago.

She now lived with her partner, Peter, a thirty-five-year-old actor, her eight-year-old daughter Bessie, her two-year-old boy Art, and a cross-eyed Siamese cat named Watson. They all squeezed happily together into a tiny two-bedroom terrace house in Stoneybatter, a five-minute cycle ride to her work at Garda HQ in the Phoenix Park.

She loved nothing more than spending evenings reading to Bessie or playing with Art, and listening to American jazz singer Bessie Smith, after whom her daughter was named, while Peter could be heard practising his lines. After her children were asleep, she would paint late into the night in her small sitting room, whose walls were adorned with her creations, while listening to jazz and drinking Nigerian Lipton tea.

This morning, it had taken her twenty minutes to arrive at the victim's house in the affluent neighbourhood of Rathgar. The house was one of twelve on the tree-lined Dorchester Avenue.

Her usual practice was to start her investigation from the assailant's point of entry but, on viewing the body in the bedroom, she decided to begin there. She wanted to finish with the victim and allow the investigating gardaí to complete their work as soon as humanly possible. Phoebe knew that the victim's family could not begin to grieve properly until the State Pathologist had instructed that the body be removed to the city morgue in Whitehall.

A framed photograph at the top of the stairs showing the victim with her small blond son had a profound effect on her. The young boy was dressed in a judo suit that was tied with a yellow belt. The boy smiled into the camera lens as his mother squeezed him tightly, beaming with pride. The quality of the picture, a quick snap on a smartphone, wouldn't have normally warranted the expensive-looking gold frame, but it was clear that a unique moment had been captured by the photographer. The unadulterated and unconditional love that exuded from the photo made even the gold frame appear dull.

The police photographers worked silently around her, capturing images of the victim which Phoebe prayed the little blond boy in the photo would never get to see.

Darcy turned into Dorchester Avenue and parked her car behind two marked Garda cars. Mick stretched in his seat and let out a deep groan.

'Is this OK here?' she asked him.

'If anyone needs to get out, they'll know where to find us,' he told her. 'And by the way, stop looking so ... so ...'

'So what?'

'So fucking enthusiastic. Watch me and say nothing unless asked. Now get your game face on.'

There was a gaggle of media and police already at the scene, choking the end of the road. Darcy walked towards them but, realising that Mick wasn't following her, she turned and looked back. He was standing away from the car and quietly viewing the road, the houses, even the sky.

She had once read that a good detective thinks from the viewpoint of the murdered victim, but that a great detective thinks from the perspective of the murderer. As she watched her new partner, she knew what he was doing: viewing the road and houses and asking why here and why her?

When she turned back towards the house, one of the armed Emergency Response Unit officers, Jamie Keane, looked over at her and began walking towards her. She raised her hand and signalled him to stay where he was. He stopped.

'You know Captain America?' Mick asked, appearing beside her.

'Who?' Darcy asked, but then realised he was talking about Jamie. 'No comment.'

'Fair enough, then,' he said and shrugged his shoulders.

Thick white tape with '**GARDA – NO ENTRY**' written in blue on it decorated the perimeter of the house. A few of the older reporters recognised Mick as he approached the house. They couldn't help their jaws from dropping slightly, and Mick couldn't help but notice.

'*Columbo Kelly! Is this your case?*' one of them called out as Mick lifted the Garda tape for Darcy to climb under. He ignored the reporter as they showed their IDs to the uniformed garda.

There was another uniformed garda standing at the entrance to the house. He nodded to the two detectives as they approached.

'Where's the body?' Mick asked him.

'Upstairs, sir.'

Darcy walked in through the doorway, but Mick stopped, one foot inside, one foot out. He looked at the young garda's face. The garda stared into the distance, his lips closed tight, his face pale against the dark-blue of his uniform.

'You OK?' Mick asked him quietly.

The garda didn't look at him, but he nodded.

'First body?'

Again, a nod.

Mick patted him on the shoulder, and the garda nodded his thanks. Then Mick stepped into the house.

He took a slow, deep breath in and out as he stood in the hall. Darcy waited at the bottom of the stairs for him but he ignored her, looking all around, taking everything in.

To Darcy it was as if his facial muscles, and even his posture, became energised and animated like the pricking up of ears of a search-and-rescue dog when he picks up a scent.

He bent down and studied the floor. Then he stood up and peered into the kitchen at the back. From his pocket, he took out some blue latex gloves and slipped on a pair. Only then did he look at Darcy and gestured to her to follow him into the kitchen, handing her a pair of the gloves.

As she pulled on the gloves, Mick walked around the kitchen. She took a notepad from her pocket. She caught Mick glancing at it.

'Tell me what you see,' he said.

At first she wasn't sure he was even talking to her.

'Think out loud. Tell me what you see. The crime scene will tell you a lot if you pay close enough attention to it.'

Darcy looked around the room.

'I see cupboards, tidy and clean. I see groceries on the kitchen island. A recently opened Amazon box. A garden in the back that has –'

'*Stop*,' Mick told her.

'What?'

'I don't mean just list what you see. I mean ...' Mick thought about it. 'Remember your first boyfriend? When you were very young. The first one who liked you and you liked him. He'd say something, or he'd write you a note, and you'd try to interpret what exactly he meant by that? That's what you have to do here. Read between the lines, Doyle. It's not only what you see – you need to find out what it means. Understand?'

Darcy looked around the room again.

'OK,' Mick said. 'Now try again.'

'The groceries are still in their bags. Even the things she should have put away quickly, like the meat and the milk. So she's just returned from shopping. Which means that she was interrupted, and that she'd only been home a few minutes. Maybe by the Amazon delivery?'

'Maybe. But the Amazon man is not our killer. Why?'

'Because she had unpacked the box. The Amazon man was long gone by time she was attacked.'

'Good. Go on.'

'If she'd only been home a few minutes, then he might have been waiting for her inside, and he surprised her.'

'See any signs of a forced entry?' Mick asked her.

'No. Not yet anyway.'

'So, something else?'

'He had a key. So, she knew him?'

'Or?' Mick said.

She paused.

'Or she opened the door to him.'

Mick nodded. 'Or?'

Darcy stood up straighter. 'Or he followed her home.'

'And if he did?'

'Then we can appeal for eyewitnesses.'

'Or something better?'

Darcy stared at him as she thought about it.

'CCTV.'

'Good. From where to where?'

She looked back at the table. There was a receipt on the countertop. She reached out for it.

'Don't touch it,' Mick told her, and Darcy pulled her hand back.

She bent forward to get a proper look at it.

'Quinn's Supermarket,' she said. 'In Terenure village at 9.23 a.m.'

'So, we commandeer all the CCTV footage inside and outside the shop, and everything from there to here. Good work, what else?'

Darcy looked at the bags on the table.

'She was planning a special meal: steaks, expensive wine, flowers.'

'Might tie in with the husband's alibi if he was away and coming back. Or it might indicate an affair if he wasn't around tonight.'

Darcy nodded.

'What kind of woman was she?' Mick asked her.

'Tidy, that's for sure.'

'OK, now come back into the hall.'

Darcy followed Mick back out towards the front door.

'What do you see here?' he asked her.

'Again, a nice clean and tidy hall,' she told him. 'Pictures hanging straight and nothing out of place. Coats hung neatly on a stand. No toys or clothes thrown anywhere. No dirty shoes blocking the door.'

'And what does that tell you?'

'She's well organised. Or house proud, perhaps?'

'OK. So anything else?'

'The photos. A seemingly happy family life.'

'Can be deceptive. Anything else?'

'The pot.'

She knelt to look at it.

'It's been moved,' she said. 'The ring formed in the carpet by the pot is misaligned. And there's soil on the carpet. Which is odd considering her obvious tidiness.'

'And what does that tell you?' Mick asked.

She looked up at him. 'That there was a possible altercation here.'

'And?'

'Which means,' she said slowly, 'that he came in the front door. Rang the bell and she answered. And he walked in. She tried to defend herself and the pot got knocked over.'

'Good. Anything else?'

She shook her head.

'Look closer, Detective.'

As she glanced around the hall at floor level, she spotted something. She examined the carpet. It was beige, but she saw flickers of gold in it.

'Her hair,' she said, looking up at him.

Mick said nothing. She looked closer.

'It's little bits of cut hair – not strands,' she said. 'Did he cut her hair?'

Mick shrugged. 'Let's go find out.'

Darcy stood up. 'You spotted all that straight away. Within a minute of coming in here, didn't you?'

'No, no, not at all,' he told her and winked. 'Much less than a minute. Now let's go upstairs. And if you feel like you're going to vomit – don't.'

'That's weird,' Darcy said as he started up the stairs.

Mick stopped and turned around. 'What is?'

Darcy pointed to the clock by the door. 'Might be nothing. But for such a meticulous lady, that clock has the wrong time. And it's working – it hasn't stopped.'

They both stared at it for several moments until one photographer, dressed in white overalls and a mask, excused himself as he passed them.

They followed him up the stairs where the wall to their right was adorned with framed family photos.

When Darcy was a little girl, her mother was either too hungover or too indifferent on a Sunday morning to take her to church, but sometimes she went on her own, especially in the winter, as the church was warmer than her room. She remembered the closer the congregation got to the altar, the more sombre they became. And so too now, the closer they got to the dead victim, the more sober their actions and words became.

Darcy had been to many crime scenes, but none like this. This was different. In the Domestic Violence unit, emotions were always high, and there was a wildness at every location. Now, there was nobody shouting or yelling. There were no raised voices or threats of escalating violence.

Reaching the top of the stairs was like stepping through the doors of the National Library. Even Mick spoke in a hushed tone as he stopped and looked around him.

'You don't have to say anything in here. Just watch and take in as much as you can,' he told her, his voice almost a whisper.

He took a few steps forward and then stopped.

'Look,' he told her.

Darcy looked into a bedroom. It initially looked like a spare room, but there was an empty glass on the bedside locker and the bed was only half made. She nodded to Mick that she understood, and then they moved on.

Most of the activity was focused through the last doorway on the right. People in white overalls went about their business with competence and care, ignoring the two detectives on the landing. A flash of light pulsed from the room into the corridor: the photographer recording every detail from every angle. Photos that would be later hung on a board in an incident room.

There were three people in the room when Darcy entered. All three were dressed in white coveralls. One man was taking photographs, another was dusting for fingerprints and the third, a black woman, was removing a hair from a pillow with tweezers. These things Darcy saw only in her peripheral vision. Her focus was on the body on the bed.

The forensics woman looked up. She was wearing a face mask, but her eyes squinted into a smile.

'Well, if it isn't Columbo Kelly himself!' she said.

'Nobody calls me that anymore, Fifi,' Mick told her.

An image of the 1970's American detective TV show popped into Darcy's head, but she couldn't see any similarities between Mick and the cigar-smoking Columbo.

'I heard you were dead.'

'Stolen Property Department,' Mick lied.

'Really? Who'd steal you?'

Mick turned to Darcy. 'Detective Darcy Doyle, let me introduce you to Dr Phoebe Pepple.'

'Call me Fifi. You'll forgive me if I don't shake your hand.'

Darcy said nothing, but continued to stare at the naked, lifeless body lying face-up on the bed. This was the same woman in the photos on the stairs who had looked so ... so ... *alive*. It was a stupid thought, she knew, but she couldn't think of a better word.

She gazed at the red line that ran along the circumference of the woman's neck, the laceration open slightly like a small crevice in the snow. The woman's face was paler than her short blonde hair, her blue eyes frozen in a stare as if caught in a photograph. They stared away and behind Darcy like those of a blind person. Darcy followed her gaze.

'Does she talk?' Phoebe asked Mick.

'She'll be alright in a minute,' Mick said.

'You were right,' Darcy said. 'Her hair has been cut off.'

She walked towards the chest of drawers in the room. There were various creams and lotions and a single bottle of perfume. A framed family photograph stood in pride of place. She looked back at the woman's face and then at the photo.

'She was looking at her family,' Darcy whispered.

Mick and Phoebe looked at each other.

'What did you say, Doyle?' Mick said.

The other two forensics officers were looking at Darcy too.

'She was looking at her family,' Darcy said again. 'She knew he was going to kill her, and it was the last thing she wanted to see before she died.'

Everyone looked at the picture in the frame of three smiling faces under a blue sky. All dressed in light colourful clothes. A family holiday abroad, perhaps.

It was a photograph of a different time and in a different world. A parallel universe.

Mick turned back to Phoebe. 'Is there anything you can tell us at this stage?' he asked.

'We haven't been here too long ourselves. Apart from the obvious, you'll have to wait until the reports. I've been told the State Pathologist is on his way. I'm hoping to be finished before he gets here.'

'What can you tell us now, then?' Mick asked her. 'Give us the obvious. Just something to go on. And listen up, Detective.'

Darcy was moving around the room slowly, trying not to get in anyone's way. She stopped and looked at Phoebe.

'The husband discovered her and called 999,' Phoebe said. 'Best guess, given a body temperature drop of three degrees, she died about an hour before that. Although probably best to hear that from the pathologist.'

'OK,' Mick said. 'Go on.'

'Cuts on the wrists and ankles from the ropes were probably caused by her struggle, so she was most likely conscious when he killed her.'

'Was she raped?' Mick asked.

'Yes. We'll do DNA swabs next, but for any semen samples you'll have to wait.'

'Anything else?'

'She received several blows to the head with a blunt object, which may or may not have caused a concussion. Also, it's not ...' Phoebe stopped and looked at the body again.

'Not what?' Mick asked.

'It's just that he ... the perpetrator ... he was extraordinarily lucky.'

'How?'

'He got in at the right time, did what he had to do, and got out. Very neat. Also, there are very few defensive wounds. Normally these would be more extensive with a rape or strangulation as the victim fights back – her hands were tied before he began. Nothing in the house seems touched. I have a feeling we're not going to find any fingerprints either.'

'You'll find the husband's fingerprints all over the place, though,' Mick said.

'He lives here,' Phoebe said.

'So the killer got lucky,' Mick said.

'Or …' Phoebe replied.

'Or what?' Mick asked.

'Or,' Darcy said, finishing Phoebe's thought, 'he's done it before.'

Chapter 8

Mairéad Carter stood up from her kitchen table, refilled the kettle and switched it on to boil. The wall clock made a loud *tick-tock tick-tock* as it beat out the seconds in the small kitchen.

She didn't want any more tea, but she needed something to do. Her eldest son, Liam, stayed seated and watched her. Even with her back to him, she could feel his eyes on her.

It was strange how she still felt intimidated by him. He was always dressed so smartly, and he was so clever with his job in finance in those fancy offices on the quays, although she had no idea exactly what he did.

'Mum, I think it would be in the best interests for everyone if you let me go ahead and book the psychologist,' Liam told her.

Mairéad stayed by the kettle. 'Your father never wanted –'

'Dad's dead, Mum. I know it's only been a month, but we can finally get some help. Perhaps it's too late for Conor now, but we have to try.'

She remained silent.

'Look, I'll pay for everything. And whether it's autism or even something else, I'll make sure he sees the best people. This isn't going to cost you a penny.'

'Money isn't the answer to everything, Liam,' she said, with more aggression than she'd intended.

Liam sighed and looked around the room. Its decor and furniture were over twenty years old. The entire house looked tired and jaded –

much like his mother, he thought. The linoleum floor was frayed at the edges. Cupboards whose original colour couldn't be deciphered. And all the time Liam smelt a slight odour of grease and stagnant water. It was in stark contrast to his own two-room apartment in the Docklands overlooking the River Liffey.

It had been an understandable blow to the entire family when his father, Jack Carter, had died in a car crash just over a month ago. And yet, his going could not be seen as a 'great loss' by any stretch of the imagination. Jack's relationship with his wife had been confined to that of non-communicative housemates. He hadn't spoken to Liam for years.

The only person with whom Jack had a relationship, albeit an unusual one, was with his youngest son, Conor.

'Conor is special,' Jack would say, but what exactly classified Conor as 'special' was unknown. As members of the Palmarian Catholic Church, professional or expert advice had not been sought outside the organisation. Outsiders of any kind were not welcome. As Conor grew up, he was home-schooled and often didn't leave the house for months on end.

Now that Liam was back, he intended to right that wrong. Whether it was for Conor's benefit out of brotherly love, or as an act of revenge against his dead father was yet to be determined.

Liam stood up from the kitchen table. His mother remained standing by the kettle.

'This needs to be addressed, Mum.'

She looked at him.

'I only want to help,' Liam said, a little softer this time.

Mairéad knew he wanted to leave. He looked out of place in her kitchen as if he were from a different place somewhere in the future. Even his tie was brighter than anything she had to wear.

'And I can help you too if you'll let me,' he said.

'What do you mean?' she asked.

'Well, I could help with ...' he looked around him, '... with all of this.'

She followed his gaze around the room and saw the disdain in his eyes.

'This neighbourhood is actually quite fashionable, believe it or not,' he said, almost to himself. 'You could make a nice profit if you sold now. Zero Capital Gains Tax. I know a developer who might –'

'And where would I live? This is my home.'

'There are plenty of new apartments being built in the village. For half the money this place is worth.'

'They're a bit small,' she said.

'They're big enough. How much space do you need?'

'And what about Conor? Where would he go?'

'Well,' he said with a little too much enthusiasm, 'there's an organisation that caters for people with special needs. I've looked into it and –'

At the sound of the front door closing, Liam stopped.

Mairéad stood up and opened the kitchen door into the hall.

'Are you OK, darling?' she called out.

Liam stepped towards the door and faced his brother.

'Hello, Conor,' he said. 'Have you been out and about?'

Conor looked at him and then at his mother.

Mairéad looked at the clock on the wall.

'Oh, sorry, honey,' she told Conor. 'I'll get your lunch now.'

Conor didn't look at his brother again, but instead continued back down the hall. Mairéad listened to him climb the stairs to his bedroom, and then the door open and close.

Thunder rumbled outside. Mairéad turned to the kitchen window as the rain began to fall heavily into her back garden and bounce noisily off the roof of the old wooden shed.

It was also raining late one night, twenty-five years ago, when Mairéad Sheehan met Jack Carter in a Carl's Jr., just off the 101 freeway in Ventura, California. A sudden unexpected downpour had caught them both off guard, and water dripped from their clothes onto the restaurant floor. They both stepped up to the counter at the same time and ordered the same double cheeseburger meal. Then they turned to each other and smiled. Outside, the rain came down onto the dark Californian streets like retribution for all the past countless sunny days.

Over the cheeseburger and fries, Jack admitted to her that he drank too much, and his life was a mess, but that he was trying to get things back in order. Mairéad had grown up in a small town in Wexford, where gossip, denial and stoicism were part of everyday life. She had never met anyone so honest before, and she'd found it genuinely refreshing. She told him about coming over to California on the invitation of her cousin in Los Angeles, but that she'd found LA too hot, too noisy and too weird, so she'd ventured further north and found work as a nanny.

He'd found God and joined a Church, he said, and although Mairéad had never heard of the Palmarian Catholic Church, she was happy to hear, at the very least, that the god they worshipped was a Catholic one.

On their first date, Jack drove up the 33 freeway, past Ojai, and into Los Padres National Forest. They walked until they found an area of rocky hills with pine trees, cactus and scrub. There they spread the blanket Jack had brought and had a picnic.

After, she was shocked when Jack pulled out a gun from the picnic basket. He told her it was a .38 Colt revolver and passed it to her.

It felt heavier than she'd imagined it would. Jack reached into his pocket and pulled out six shiny brass bullets.

'You wanna shoot it?' he asked her.

He took the gun from her and slid the six cartridges into their chambers. He stood up and reached out for her hand. She allowed herself to be pulled up onto her feet and they walked until they stood fifty feet from a lone pine tree. Jack wrapped his arms around her and placed the gun in her hands. Then he stretched out her arms and aimed the gun at the tree.

She pulled the trigger, feeling its tension grow on her forefinger. When it fired, she let out an involuntary scream as a flurry of smoke rose into the air. The bang was louder than she'd expected.

After she'd fired all six rounds, Jack held her by the hand and led her back to the blanket. He put the gun back into the basket and then lay her down and began to kiss her. Mairéad was as excited as she'd ever been in her whole life, and when he reached under her shirt to remove her bra, she didn't try to stop him.

Her own integration into the Church was slow and incremental. Small things began to change like her dresses becoming longer until they were no shorter than the regulation five fingers' below the knee. Not that their teachings were suddenly the answers she had been seeking, as some claimed, it was more of a slow awakening that everything they said began to make sense. She tried to talk about it with the family whom she worked for as a nanny, but her questioning their lifestyle was seen as an attempt to recruit, and she was promptly fired.

With no job to go to, and no money for rent, the Palmarian society offered her a room on their farm, located just north of San Diego, in exchange for some light menial duties.

Six months went by and when she had fully cut off all contact with anyone outside the organisation, she and Jack were called to a private meeting with the High Priest.

He commended them on their work within the walls of the farm and praised their devout lives. A position had become available at their world headquarters in El Palmar de Troya, in Spain. Jack, being an American citizen, would have difficulty obtaining the necessary long-term visas required. However, as a holder of an Irish passport with the right to live and work in any European country, these rights would also become available to Jack upon his marriage to Mairéad. Did they, the High Priest inquired, feel their relationship had reached a stage of commitment that warranted marriage?

Mairéad blushed, and Jack smiled from ear to ear. They were married the following week.

They flew to Seville in Spain and were then driven twenty kilometres south to the Catedral Basilica Nuestra Senora Del Palmar, just outside the town of El Palmar de Troya. Their driver, a fellow member of the Church, never spoke nor smiled as Mairéad watched the parched Spanish terrain go by.

Inside the building, they were escorted to a tiny concrete room that contained a bed that was too big to be called a single but too small to be called a double, a chest of drawers, and a wooden table and chair. The window looked out onto acres and acres of vineyards outside the compound walls.

It was noon on the first Tuesday in August and the temperature had already reached over a hundred degrees. Jack stripped down to his underwear and lay on the bed, jet-lagged and exhausted. He was asleep within a minute.

Mairéad looked down at him, his body spread out across most of the bed. Her own clothes stuck to her skin from the heat and humidity. She licked her dry lips and turned to face the closed door. Jack's deep breathing echoed loudly against the walls, amplified by the interminable silence.

Years later, she would look back at that moment and mark it as the beginning of her life's unhappiness.

Liam's birth the following year brought a new focus to her life, but the church took care of most of the responsibility for his upbringing. There was a creche on the compound where the children stayed during the day to 'allow members to maximise their time through work and prayer'.

The day he was born was the first time she told Jack she wanted to leave Spain. It would take another son, Conor, and five long years before Jack finally relented. By then, she had hardly spoken to anyone who wasn't associated with the Palmarian Church for almost a decade.

A house in the suburbs of Dublin was purchased for them, on the assumption they would spread the word of the Church and recruit new members to the true faith.

Mairéad never contacted her family, partly because it was against the Church's wishes, but mostly from shame and guilt. She was in a café off O'Connell Street on her own one day when an elderly woman approached her and said her name. The woman had been a neighbour from her village in Wexford and had come to Dublin for the day to meet her daughter for lunch and to shop.

The old woman didn't move to sit down, nor was she invited to. The woman said what she wanted to say and then left.

Mairéad cried every day for two weeks. The woman had told her that Mairéad's mother had died of cancer two years previously and that her father had died six months later. 'He always said,' the old woman told her, 'that you'd come home one day.'

Her youngest son Conor's unusual behaviour became more pronounced in their new surroundings. To what extent and what his limitations would be, she had read in a local library, could only be determined through a professional diagnosis. These types of visits were explicitly forbidden by the Church and, more importantly, by Jack.

One afternoon, she was vacuuming their bedroom while Jack was out of the house. The vacuum cleaner lifted the carpet in the corner, and she got down on her knees to shove it back into place. In one of the floorboards, she spotted a small, neat hole drilled into the wood. Without thinking, she placed her finger into the hole and lifted the board.

At first, she couldn't see anything, but then she saw a black metal box further underneath. She stretched her arm inside and pulled it out. She had seen the box before and already knew what was inside. The box had a six-digit combination lock, but she knew that too: Jack's birthday.

She opened it. There was a black, folded-up piece of cloth inside and when she unfolded that, she held the .38 Colt in her hand. She felt its weight and thought back to that sunny day in California. The excitement of firing the gun. Then the excitement of Jack taking her for the first time. She could almost remember being happy.

When Liam was eighteen years old and had finished Secondary School, he said he was going out one Friday evening, and he never came back. Conor, as perpetual and stagnant as the dark wallpaper, remained at home with his mother. She loved him, of course, but she was also aware that he would be the anchor that would keep her forever tied to that house. She allowed him to be as unhappy or as happy as he chose to be.

Life plodded along for them all, each of them in their own separate unhappy worlds, until one day everything changed.

Two uniformed gardaí knocked on her door late one rainy night, and removed their caps before speaking, which was never a good sign. One garda was female. Again, not a good sign.

She invited them inside and out of the rain, and they informed her of her husband's sudden demise on a dangerous section of the N81 past Brittas village.

As their luminous jackets dripped rain onto the sitting room's carpet, Jack's charred remains were resting in St James's Hospital. There would be a full investigation, they assured her, but at present it looked like due to poor visibility and the dangerous bend in the road, Jack's car had slammed into the wall. The fire may have been caused by a spark from the engine but, within a few moments, the car had been engulfed in flames.

Jack was probably unconscious from the crash, they assured her, so he would not have suffered much. Mairéad made an unconscious whimpering sound, and they assumed it was her gratitude that he had not suffered in any way. They were incorrect in their assumption.

It didn't look like he'd been wearing his seat belt, they said, so the crash alone may have caused his death. Either way, they repeated, there would be a full investigation.

She thanked them and led them to the door. She refused the female garda's offer to stay with her. She would call her son, she told them, and he would come to her. She saw the relief in the garda's young face as she turned and walked back out into the rain.

Mairéad watched them get back into their car as the rain bounced angrily off their car's roof, her driveway, and the street. She thought back to that night sitting in a burger restaurant listening to Jack's voice above the noise of the rain outside.

And then, suddenly, the rain stopped. Just like that. And Mairéad stepped back inside and closed the door.

Chapter 9

'You're a what?' Mick asked Darcy.

They were seated at a table in a deli off Rathmines Road. Lunch hour was long gone, and the staff were starting to clean up.

'A vegetarian,' she told him.

'Jaysus. You girls and your diet fads.'

'I'm not a girl, in case you hadn't noticed,' Darcy told him. 'I'm a woman. And it's not a diet fad. I've been a vegetarian since I was twelve years old when I saw a pig on the TV having a bolt fired into its brain and then sliced open just so I could have bacon for my breakfast.'

They both looked up and saw a waitress staring down at them. Her name tag said *Agnieszka*.

'What can I get you?' she asked them.

'I'll just have a black tea, please,' Darcy said.

'I'll have the double bacon burger with extra cheese, please,' Mick said without looking at the menu.

Darcy stared at Mick.

'What?' he said.

'You know, most illnesses later in life can be linked back to a person's lifestyle. Their diet and exercise, for example. Or lack thereof.'

She looked down at Mick's protruding belly.

'Whatever,' he said, sucking in his gut.

'Besides, and I know it's a film cliché – but, seriously, how can you eat after what we've just seen?'

Mick's expression changed. 'Yeah, it's a tough one but, unfortunately, I've seen worse, much worse, kid. In your first few years with the NBCI, it certainly feels like death and violence will never be easy to handle. But then something happens, and you'll be amazed at how quickly it does. One day, you just get used to it. Death, the dead and all the shite we have to deal with just becomes a normal part of your life. And so it'll be the same for you. Rape, stabbings, gangsters shot in the face, children left for dead ...'

Agnieszka had returned and was staring down at them again. She seemed a little paler.

'Would you like ketchup on your burger?' she asked.

'Sure,' Mick told her and gave her a wink. 'Loads. Thanks.'

She walked away.

'So, what's our next move?' Darcy asked him, her voice lowered.

'Get back to the station. Set up an incident room. We'll get some uniforms to help with the groundwork. Questioning the neighbours – the usual standard operating procedure.'

Darcy was writing it down.

'You know,' Mick said. 'You don't have to write everything down.'

She put her notepad away.

'First thing though,' Mick told her, 'is to go see the husband. We need to eliminate him from our investigation ASAP. Or not. See if we can find any holes in his alibi. Trace, interview and eliminate. You know the routine.'

'You think it's him, don't you?'

Mick gave her a smile that Darcy couldn't help defining as patronising.

'What's more curious,' he said, 'is why you think it's not. At the moment, he is one hundred percent a person of interest and our main suspect.'

'I'll tell you why I don't think it's him. Because if she died looking at a photo of her family, and I realise that's a bit of a long shot, then she died looking at a photo of the man who was raping her. That makes no sense.'

'You're right. It is a long shot. Who knows what was going through that poor woman's head when she died?'

The café's door opened and noise from the traffic invaded the room until it closed again. Darcy stared outside at the busy street, as the outside din returned to a muffled sound.

'But it's not just that one thing in particular,' she said. 'It's something Dr Pepple – Fifi – said, something you said and some things I noticed myself. More of a feeling. A sort of ...'

'Women's intuition?' Mick suggested.

She looked back at him and saw a smile appear on his face. Even through all her time in Domestic Violence, she couldn't remember wanting to slap a man across the face so much.

'No matter. I still fancy the husband for it,' Mick told her.

'Maybe you fancy the husband for it so you can wrap it all up quickly and go back to ... whatever it was you were doing.'

Any playfulness fell from Mick's face. Perhaps, she felt, she had overstepped her boundary with him.

Agnieszka returned and placed the burger in front of Mick and the tea in front of her. Mick looked at the burger for a few moments before he picked it up and took a huge bite out of it.

Darcy watched him chewing, his beard speckled now with ketchup, the tension in his face easing as he chewed.

'You don't know what you're missing,' Mick said, in appreciation of his burger.

She felt nauseous and wanted to wait outside, but was afraid it would make her look weak.

'You know that processed meat is carcinogenic,' she told him.

He continued to chew, undaunted. 'Well,' he said, 'it's a very tasty carcinogenic.'

Darcy sipped her tea and looked out onto the road.

'What about fish?' Mick asked. 'Can you eat fish?'

'Of course not, and for what it's worth, I'm more of a vegan than vegetarian.'

'Isn't that something off *Star Trek*?' he asked her while still chewing.

'No,' she assured him.

'Yeah, it was your man with the pointy ears. He was a Vegan. Tell me this. Are you able to read my mind? What am I thinking now?'

Mick squinted his eyes shut and stopped chewing.

She looked up at him. 'You're thinking, is it possible I could say something else to make myself sound even more ignorant and uneducated?'

Mick raised his eyebrows and looked genuinely shocked.

'Jaysus, that was a bit harsh!' He took another large bite out of his burger. 'Now that I think of it, I have been compared to William Shatner myself more than once.'

'I think you misheard them when they said you looked like "Shat",' she said, smiling at him for the first time.

Chapter 10

Darcy drove the short distance to interview Paul Delaney, who had temporarily moved in with his sister and her family. Mick spoke into his phone as he jotted down notes on the back of the receipt from the deli. The sun was trying its best to break through gaps in the black clouds and to brighten a world that Darcy knew would never be the same again for Jennifer Delaney's little boy.

'Looks like I was right after all,' he said when he hung up. 'There's a two-hour discrepancy between Delaney landing and then discovering his wife's body. His earlier statement says he came straight from the airport. The fucker's lying.'

'OK,' Darcy said.

Mick continued to look at her, but said nothing.

'What?' she asked him.

'It was him, Doyle. Don't start getting any fancy ideas into your head again, you hear me? He killed his wife, and we're going to arrest him. End of. OK?'

Darcy didn't say anything.

'OK?' Mick repeated.

Darcy nodded, and they drove in silence until they reached the house.

'Mr Delaney, I'm very sorry for your loss,' Darcy said when Paul Delaney answered the door.

He thanked her and escorted her through to the sitting room of his sister's house. Mick strolled in after them and then closed the wooden double doors.

The three-storey redbrick Georgian house was even grander than Paul Delaney's own house. The richly furnished sitting room was elevated above the street and looked out onto a small square city park of neatly trimmed trees and manicured hedgerows. Darcy estimated that the reception room they were in was larger than her entire house in the Liberties.

'We'll be as brief as we can,' Mick told him when they were all seated. 'It's only a few questions that may help our investigation and point us in the right direction.'

'Of course,' Delaney said. 'Whatever I can do to help.'

Paul Delaney's accent was crisp but with a touch of softness that hinted at a childhood outside of Dublin. He was a fit and lean man in his early forties. His clothes suggested a pride in his appearance and, given his physique, also pointed to daily visits to the gym.

'How's your son doing?' Darcy asked him.

'Yes, he's ... he's ... with my sister. They've gone to the park. We haven't told him yet.'

'Oh, I see.'

'Mr Delany, can you explain to us how you found the body?' Mick asked. 'Your wife, I mean. You'd been abroad, I understand.'

'Yes, Edinburgh. We're opening a new branch there. I've been away for five days.'

He let out a dry cough. He picked up a teacup and sipped from it. 'I'm sorry,' he said. 'Where are my manners? Can I get you some tea?'

They both refused.

Suddenly, he threw his face into his hands and sobbed loudly.

Darcy glanced at Mick. His face was impassive. Even unsympathetic.

'I'm sorry,' Delaney eventually said, rubbing his eyes. 'Every time I close my eyes, I see her there. It was horrible. I'm sorry.'

'There's no need to apologise,' Darcy assured him. 'It's perfectly understandable.'

Delaney took a deep breath and for a moment Darcy had the impression he was about to repeat a poem or a story that he had learned earlier verbatim. Maybe Mick was right, after all. 'When I entered the house –'

'Can I stop you there, please, Mr Delaney?' Mick said.

Delaney looked at him, surprised by the interruption.

'In order to get things rolling, as it were,' Mick said, 'we need to have an understanding here. A certain … how can I put it? A level of trust and honesty.'

'Yes, of course,' Delaney assured him. 'We need to get the bastard who did this.'

'Exactly. So, let's back up a little. What time did you land at Dublin airport this morning?'

Paul Delaney caught his breath and put his head to one side. 'I think it was …'

'Now, pause before you answer, Mr Delaney,' Mick said, holding a hand in the air like a stop sign for traffic. 'I can't stress the importance of the correct and vital information you provide for us here today. Do you understand?'

Delaney finally did understand what the detective in front of him was suggesting. His eyes widened.

'I didn't do it!' he exclaimed. 'I can assure you this has nothing to do with me!'

Mick said nothing. Darcy knew better than to interrupt.

Delaney looked from one to the other. He stood up out of his chair.

'Someone has killed my wife. How can you accuse me of having anything to do with it? I loved my wife. I loved our family. Bo is everything to me. I would never ...'

Darcy could sense that Mick had Delaney against the ropes and was about to strike. She knew that a good interview was a vital cog in the wheel of any good investigation.

'Then how do you explain the two hours from when you landed at the airport to when you arrived home?' Mick asked.

'What? What do you mean?'

Mick reached into his inside jacket pocket and pulled out the piece of paper.

'I have a printout of the time you arrived from Edinburgh this morning. You took the first flight out at 8.05 a.m. You landed at 9.10 a.m. You arrived home after 11.30 a.m.'

Delaney's mouth opened and then closed, as if he'd been about to say something but had decided not to.

'Please sit down, Mr Delaney,' Darcy told him.

He flopped backwards into the chair.

'So, I'll ask you again, Mr Delaney,' said Mick. 'You told the garda at the house that you'd come straight from the airport. You lied. I want to know where you were from 9.10 this morning until you discovered your wife's dead body in your bedroom over two hours later.'

Delaney looked like he was going to pass out. His eyes darted back and forth between Darcy and Mick.

'Traffic – I don't know,' he said. 'The M50 was so slow. There might have been an accident. I can't remember. Everything's a blur.'

'We can check that,' Mick told him. 'Do a reconstruction to find out exactly how long it takes to get from the airport to Rathgar after 9 o'clock in the morning.'

'But someone would have seen my car outside my house. If I were the killer, I mean. Several of our neighbours have CCTV outside their homes. You can check them to find out.'

Mick turned to Darcy. 'Is it just me, Detective, or is Mr Delaney starting to sound like someone who's put a bit of thought into this?'

'*What?*' Delaney shouted.

'You could have parked a couple of streets away,' Mick continued. 'Scaled the garden wall – in the back door. Be there when she got home from the shops. Get the job done and be out in ten minutes.'

'*No!*' Delaney yelled.

'That's an expensive house you own. Lovely area. Easily worth over a million. Probably a massive mortgage. I bet there's an even bigger life insurance policy to go with it once we begin to investigate. Any chance your wife's life insurance has been topped up lately, Mr Delaney?'

'*How dare you?* This is preposterous! How can you just sit there and accuse me of murdering my wife? She was the mother of my only child. I loved Jennifer.'

'I'm sure you did, Mr Delaney.' Mick said. 'And, for the record, I'm accusing you of lying as to your whereabouts this morning. I haven't charged you with murdering your wife. Yet.'

Delaney looked down at his hands. He was unconsciously twirling his wedding band with his right hand. He realised what he was doing and stopped. Darcy and Mick let the silence fill the room until they watched Delaney's shoulders slump.

'We, I mean, Jennifer and I, had been having difficulties – marriage difficulties,' he said, without looking up. 'We'd been trying to work it out for months, but I was kidding myself. Maybe we both were. She wanted another baby. A little girl, she said. It was a mess. I was just going through the motions, for the sake of Bo.'

Darcy began to reach for her notebook but forced herself to stop.

'You were sleeping in the spare bedroom, weren't you?' Mick said.

'Yes. Yes, I was,' Delaney admitted, finally making eye contact with Mick. 'I've been seeing someone else. For quite a while, actually. I was with this person this morning. Before I went home. I know how terrible that makes me.'

'Having an affair is not against the law, Mr Delaney,' Darcy told him. 'But lying and misleading an investigation is.'

Delaney nodded like a reprimanded schoolboy, his head still bowed low.

Mick looked over at Darcy, and she shrugged.

'We need her details,' Darcy said. 'To confirm your alibi.'

'His,' Delaney said, raising his head slowly.

'Excuse me?'

'*His* details,' Delaney said.

'But you said you were ...' Mick said. 'Oh, I see. Well, we'll need his details then. I presume you must have been at his address at that time of the morning?'

'Yes, I was.'

He reached into his inside jacket pocket and pulled out a business card and a heavy silver Cross pen. He scribbled on the back.

'Here,' he said, holding the card out to Mick. 'This is his name, number and address. Stephen Fields. I drove out to Howth, to his house, to see him. I had wanted to tell Jennifer, you know, but ... oh, God. Everything's such a mess!'

Mick stood up and took the card as Delaney flopped back into his chair and wept into his hands. Mick went to the corner and dialled the number. Darcy watched him but he didn't speak into his phone.

He walked back to Delaney and peered down at him.

Darcy stood up.

'There's no answer from that number, Mr Delaney,' Mick said.

Delaney continued to weep.

'*Control yourself, Mr Delaney!*' Darcy said loudly.

He sniffled a couple of times and then looked at them, his face tear-streaked.

The wooden double doors opened, and a little boy and a woman walked in.

The woman stopped abruptly when she saw Delaney had been crying.

'Oh, hello,' she said then. 'Bo, come with me, please. Daddy's busy.'

'Daddy?' the boy said. 'Daddy, what's wrong?'

Delaney put his arms out, and Bo ran into them.

Mick looked at Delaney's sister and indicated for her to take Bobby away.

'Come on, Bo,' she said, holding out her hand. 'Let's go make those brownies I promised.'

Delaney held his son at arm's length. He forced himself to smile at the boy.

'Listen to me, Bo,' he told him. 'I might have to go away for a day or two, but I promise I'll be back as soon as I can.'

'But you just got home!' Bo said.

'I know and I'm sorry, son. But I need you to be a big boy and stay with Aunty Karen till I get back.'

'Why can't I go home to Mummy?'

Darcy could see Delaney fighting back another burst of tears, and she admired his ability to control it.

'Come on, Bo – brownie time!' Karen said, and he went to her. She led Bobby back out, closing the doors behind her.

Once they were alone, Darcy took the business card from Mick and showed it to Delaney. 'Is this your personal mobile number, Mr Delaney?'

He looked at it. 'No, but it's one I have with me at all times.'

'Make sure you do. We'll be in touch.' She slipped the business card into her pocket and took out one of her own. In her peripheral vision she could see Mick staring at her, no doubt astonished or perhaps outraged at her taking the lead.

Delaney looked up at her, confused. 'You mean you're not going to arrest me?'

'You need to get in touch with Mr Fields. He might answer for you. Get him to call us.' She handed him her card.

Delaney held the card, staring at it as if afraid to look away, as Mick stalked out of the room.

Darcy took one more look at the magnificent view from the large bay windows and then followed Mick.

Chapter 11

When Darcy entered the incident room on the second floor of Harcourt Street Station, there were three uniformed gardaí present: two male and one female. She didn't recognise any of them.

They stood when they saw Darcy and Mick enter, and she wondered if they stood out of respect or because they'd disrupted their conversation.

'Jaysus, will you look at this bunch!' Mick said, addressing Darcy as if they were alone. 'I asked for three competent gardaí, and it looks like they sent us three arse-wipes that'd be about as useful as a cigarette lighter on a fucking motorbike.'

With that, Mick burst into laughter at his own joke, and Darcy couldn't help but smile.

'I hope to fuck they're not culchies as well,' he added.

'Don't mind him,' she said, smiling, her hand outstretched. 'He's only trying to get a rise out of you. I'm Detective Sergeant Darcy Doyle. And this is Detective Inspector Mick Kelly.'

They introduced themselves as Sam, Aoife and Eoin. Sam seemed to be the eldest, with Aoife and Eoin taking his lead.

'Please take a seat,' Darcy told them.

They sat. She and Mick stood facing them.

'Well then,' Mick began, folding his arms across his chest, 'since you all look like you just got off the bus from Templemore College, let us enlighten you on where we are with this murder investigation and, more importantly, what will be expected of you. OK?'

They all nodded and pulled out their notepads and pens. Mick raised his eyebrows at Darcy.

He spent the next twenty minutes going over everything from that morning. When he'd finished, Darcy saw a tiredness come over him and how, as if to hide it, he ran his hand across his face.

He looked at each of their eager faces.

'Questions?' he said with a sigh.

The youngest-looking of the three, Eoin, put his hand up in the air.

'Is he taking the piss?' Mick asked, turning to Darcy. 'Does he think he's still at school?'

'Put your hand down, Eoin,' Aoife told him.

Eoin lowered his arm.

'I already know I'm going to regret this,' Mick told him, 'but what's your question?'

'I was just thinking ...'

'Mistake number one, but go ahead anyway.'

'I was just thinking,' Eoin continued, his face red at this stage, 'what if it was the husband, or the husband's lover who hired the murderer and then both of them would have each other as an alibi.'

'OK, fair enough,' Mick admitted. 'That's actually not a bad question. It's happened before that husbands or wives have hired outside help in murdering their spouse, but normally a line of enquiry like that only comes to light during the investigation. So, unless we find a book titled *How to Kill Your Wife and Get Away with It* on his bedside table or twenty grand cash in an envelope marked *For the Killer*, then we'll park that theory for now. Also, a paid assassin wouldn't typically go to such extreme lengths to complete their mission.'

'Or it could have been the lover himself who committed the murder,' Sam suggested.

'And raped her? Hardly,' Mick said. 'But you're doing well, lads. Anything else?'

'If there's no signs of a forced entry and she let him in the front door,' Aoife asked, 'then would that not mean she knew him?'

'Maybe you'd like to rethink that?'

Mick stared at her, eyebrows raised.

'Time of day?' he said.

'Oh, of course!' she said after a small pause, flushing. 'She would have opened the door to anyone at that time of day.'

'Yes, she would. But, for now, we don't know if she knew him or not. There were signs of a struggle in the hall but that doesn't mean she didn't know him. Keeping an open mind and dealing only with the facts is very important at the start of any investigation. Don't let assumptions tempt you into making any judgements at this stage without having any evidence to back it up. Anything you'd like to add, Detective Doyle?'

Darcy looked at their three eager faces and could easily remember when she was in their shoes.

'Just remember that you only get one chance to do it right – the first time. So, if you think of it, do it. Because if you don't, then people higher up the line are going to be asking you why you didn't.'

'Anything else?' Mick asked.

No one spoke.

'OK then. Tomorrow morning. 9 a.m. I want you, Aoife, knocking on doors in the neighbourhood, asking if anyone saw Delaney about at the relevant time or anything else of interest. Sam, is it? You go and retrace the route from Quinn's Supermarket in Terenure to the victim's house. Get a list of all CCTV cameras that cover that route, starting with Quinn's. I'll have a warrant with the desk sergeant by 8 a.m. tomorrow. And while you're knocking on doors, Aoife, ask any of them if they have any security cameras or camera doorbells themselves. A lot of these posh houses do.' Mick turned to face Eoin. 'And you – go see the boyfriend and check on Delaney's alibi. And the boyfriend himself needs to be ruled out – so check on his neighbours or any other possible witnesses. Get a photo. You'll need to do a door-to-door with that around Delaney's neighbourhood too. And don't wear your uniform, it'll make him nervous.'

This, undoubtedly the best job – an actual interview – made Eoin smile from ear to ear. Aoife and Sam shot him envious looks.

'And if any of you fuck up,' Mick told them, 'you'll be back on the bus to Templemore for a refresher course. Understood?'

They murmured 'Yes, sir', as they got out of their chairs and shuffled out.

Darcy made her way down the concrete stairwell and out through the front doors onto Harcourt Street. She listened to Mick's heavy breathing as he followed behind her. The bell of a Luas tram rang once as it went by. It was almost 7 p.m., but she felt like it was closer to midnight.

Mick stifled a yawn and stuck a cigarette into his mouth, then sparked up his cheap disposable lighter. As the bright yellow flame touched the tip of the cigarette, Darcy noticed his hand shaking. He blew the smoke up into the air and for a few moments it just floated above him, as if it were unsure where to go next.

'I'm bushed,' Mick told her. 'I'm going to head home. You take the car. There's an old library called Marsh's just behind Kevin Street Garda Station. Meet me outside at 7 a.m. OK?'

'Sure,' Darcy told him. 'You need a lift home?'

'No, I'll walk,' he told her and then turned to look at her. 'You did well today.'

'Thanks,' she said, genuinely pleased.

'Well, what I mean is, you didn't fuck up anyway. That's good enough in this game. Try to get some proper rest tonight.'

Darcy looked down the street. 'I'm going to the gym,' she said.

Mick raised his eyebrows at her.

'It helps me sleep,' she explained.

'Whatever rocks your boat, kid.'

'What about you, Kelly? You got a family to go home to? Kids?'

He looked at her, and she thought she saw a flash of something in his eyes, maybe pain, but she wasn't quite sure. Then he took a drag on his cigarette, and it was gone.

'Just cause we're partners doesn't mean we're married,' he told her. 'Everything in its own good time. Goodnight, Detective.'

Then he turned and walked up Harcourt Street.

She watched him walk away and thought she'd never seen anyone walk like that before, as if he had a limp, but neither leg could decide which one was supposed to have the limp in it.

When she reached her car, she looked back in Mick's direction and saw that he had stopped on the path and was now facing across the street as he puffed on the remains of his cigarette. Her eyes followed his gaze to a bar called The Odeon. Its lights looked warm and inviting in the darkening evening. The front door opened, and two men came out. The laughter and merriment from inside spilled out onto the street for a few moments and then the door closed, and it was gone.

Without looking left or right, Mick stepped onto the street and, with a determination in his stride, marched across to the other side. The pub door opened quickly and then snapped shut behind him like the jaws of a crocodile.

The chime of a bell from another Luas tram as it glided by woke Darcy from her reverie as she stared at the pub's closed door. Then she got into her car and drove away.

It took her only fifteen minutes to drive the short distance back to the scene of the murder. By then it was dark. Darcy hadn't made a conscious decision to go there. She had simply got in the car and driven.

Dorchester Avenue was emptier now. No one was on the road. All the neighbours were locked in their homes, their children trapped inside under the protection of their parents. Darcy had seen this happen before. After a serious crime or act of violence had been committed on a street, a shadow fell on all the houses and, for the families, a sense of vulnerability was suddenly prevalent that hadn't been there before: as if a security curtain had just been drawn open and left them exposed.

A marked Garda car was parked outside the Delaney house and Darcy pulled in behind it. A single garda was stationed at the front door. He stamped out his cigarette when Darcy got out of her car.

'I'm Detective Sergeant Darcy Doyle. How are things?'

The young garda wrote her name in the Crime Scene Logbook as she ducked under the crime scene tape and walked up the driveway.

'All quiet, ma'am. The press left about an hour ago. A few dark tourists, but none of the neighbours have come near the place.'

'Dark tourists' was a term for members of the public who derived some form of entertainment from visiting serious crime scenes.

'How long ago did they remove the body?'

'About two hours ago.'

'OK. I won't be long,' Darcy told him as she slipped on a pair of blue latex gloves from her jacket pocket and opened the front door. She stepped inside and closed the door behind her.

None of the lights were on in the house as Darcy stood in the hall. She waited, listening. It was as quiet as if she were standing in a field in the countryside. No traffic. No faint music. Not even the muffled sound of a TV through a neighbour's wall or the sound of a barking dog. It was as if the whole house itself were in a deep sleep after the most traumatic day of its life.

Not wanting to disturb the peace of the house with the main lights or attract any attention, she took out her phone and switched on the torch.

She turned and looked at the closed front door as the victim had done less than twelve hours earlier. Jennifer Delaney had been in the kitchen when she heard the bell ring. Or had the killer knocked? There was a spyhole in the door. Did she look through it first? Probably not. Darcy looked through it now, and saw the reflective jacket of the garda outside, smoke rising from another cigarette.

She walked through and into the kitchen. The full plastic grocery bags were still on the counter. She shone her phone onto the bags that were bulging with meat that would soon decay, and milk that was souring, and then onto an empty Amazon box. She hadn't paid too much attention to it before, having focused mostly on the bedroom, but she saw that the box had held a wall clock. Of course. The clock in the hall with the wrong time. Jennifer Delaney must have been interrupted before she could set it to the correct time.

She took out her phone and took a photo of the model number. Then she looked out through the wide glass doors and into the back garden.

Eight tall trees. Poplar she thought they were called, lined the back wall. Between the tree trunks were thick bushes of dark green. Over the wall there was a road leading through to Rathgar village.

Darcy opened the sliding glass door and walked out into the garden. At the trees, she turned and looked back at the house. From there, she could see the landing upstairs and two of the bedrooms were within view. The kitchen downstairs and beyond into the hall were also visible. If the lights were on inside, from this vantage point, someone could see almost half of the entire house. She made a mental note to have forensics search the bushes tomorrow during daylight.

She went back inside and climbed the stairs in the darkness, her torch turned off. The carpet felt soft and expensive, even under her shoes. She stopped on the landing outside the bedroom.

This was the reason she had come.

The lights and the noise were all gone. The house had reclaimed itself from its intruders with their industrial lamps and probing equipment. Darcy looked back down at the stairs and wondered if the killer had dragged Jennifer up here, or had she gone willingly?

She felt even more alone in the house with the memory of them. Alone with the traces of them in the room and on the walls. The only thing she could hear was her own breathing as she stepped into the bedroom.

The curtains were still pulled open, and the room was lit by the half-moon from outside. With the forensics crew gone, it appeared a much larger room than she remembered. Jennifer was a tidy woman and a proud homeowner, Darcy thought to herself. Everything in its place, with very little clutter.

Only one thing stood out that marked the room as different from the millions of other bedrooms in the city. Across the unmade bed, large, blotched stains were splattered across the room. They looked black in the moonlight, but Darcy knew they were red.

She knelt beside the bed and leaned over until her head was almost touching the pillow. Then she looked across the room, to where Jennifer had looked.

What had she heard from outside as he had raped her? The sounds of normality? Cars, a child's cry, a raised voice. Like a prisoner from behind a barred window looking out onto a city, she had listened and waited for her time to come to an end.

Darcy looked at the photo of her family, the one she had said Jennifer had stared at. The last view when she knew it was all over. When she knew the man above her was a killer and not just a rapist. When she knew that it was all going to end. When she knew she would never see her little boy again.

Darcy stood up. She had seen enough. She had felt enough.

She was unsure about many things in her life. Things that she had control over and things that she had none. But she knew with certainty deep in her heart that she would catch this fucker. And all she wanted was to catch him before he did it again.

Tuesday

Chapter 12

Darcy's 5 a.m. run was a tough one. Her legs felt wooden and lazy. She could feel her heart having to work harder to pump the sluggish blood around her body.

Back home, she allowed the coffee grains to sit in her cafetière that bit longer as she showered and then dressed. Her usual bowl of muesli and oat milk had an odd taste and after several attempts to finish it, she scraped the remains into the bin. She took the coffee with her in a ceramic takeaway mug and drove the short distance to the Mater Private Hospital. The city was starting to come alive. She checked her watch, remembering her 7 o'clock meeting with Mick, and then parked her car on a double yellow line near the entrance.

As it was a Tuesday, Niall was on duty as hospital porter. Unlike most of the others, Niall barely ever looked in her direction, even as the automatic glass doors noisily slid open and shut.

Darcy took the lift to the fourth floor, which opened onto a nursing station. The nurse, a Filipina named Jasmine, gave her a warm smile as Darcy waved good morning to her.

'A quiet night,' Jasmine told her. 'Not a peep from him.'

'Great. Are you finishing soon?'

'Not soon enough.'

Darcy gave her a sympathetic look and continued down the dimly lit corridor to Room 9.

The curtains were pulled open to allow Jasmine to keep an eye on Seán without having to disturb his sleep. Darcy took a moment to watch him sleeping. He was still as handsome as the first day she had laid eyes on him from across the canteen floor in Templemore Garda College all those years earlier.

Seán Murphy arrived at Templemore Garda College on the same day as Darcy, but it wasn't until the following morning during breakfast that the two of them first laid eyes on each other. Although strictly against the rules, they quickly found themselves in a clandestine relationship that lasted all through their training and that only ended when one morning Seán didn't turn up for breakfast.

Rumours were rife as to what had happened and where he was. The most agreed-upon explanation was that his brother-in-law was a high-ranking lieutenant in the Grennen drug cartel from the Northside of Dublin inner city. This was neither confirmed nor denied by their superiors, so was therefore taken in Templemore as fact.

Darcy, however, believed that their relationship must have been discovered, and he had taken the fall for both of them. She didn't hear from him again.

Then late one night, three months ago, she was returning from a domestic violence call when she saw him. She had stopped at a bar outside of Skerries to use the bathroom before the long drive home. She knew it was him, even though he was twenty yards away and sitting on a stool with his back to her.

She sat outside in her car for two hours until she saw him leaving with two other men. She followed him back into the city where he was dropped off at a house in Ballymun.

The next day she looked up the house address on PULSE, the Garda computer system, and saw that it was owned by Rory Grennen who had links to the Grennen drug cartel. It was not the first time she had searched the name of Seán Murphy on PULSE and again it had no further information as to his whereabouts, but it didn't take Hercule Poirot to figure out what was going on. Having been proven wrong as to why he had so suddenly left Templemore, Darcy felt angry and betrayed. She began following him, often at night. Sometimes in her car and sometimes on foot.

One night she got home late, turned on the lights in her sitting room and saw him lying on her couch. She leapt at him, catching him off-guard, and had him in a headlock before he could even say a word. They fell onto the floor but, as soon as she reached behind to get her handcuffs, he twisted her arm and spun her around so that she was pinned to the floor under him.

She kicked and wailed at him, but his weight and grip on her were too strong. She wriggled her head from side to side as he moved his face closer to hers. She tried to pull away from him, but his mouth bent closer to her ear.

'Some things never change,' he whispered. 'You're still a badass and sexy as hell.'

Then he moved his mouth so close to her she could feel his lips and his breath touching her ear.

'And I'm still a garda,' he whispered.

She stopped moving, and instantly he released his grip on her and stood up. She lay on the floor, looking up at him.

Over the next two hours, and half a bottle of Jameson whiskey, Seán explained how he had been 'kicked out' of Templemore on the pretence of his connection with the Grennen crime lords but had secretly remained an undercover garda ever since. Only six people knew the truth, and Darcy was now one of those six.

'So why are you coming to me now?' she asked him.

'You know why.'

She looked away from him.

'You need to stop following me,' he said. 'If I spotted you, then they will too. These guys don't fuck around, Darcy.'

'I needed to know.'

'And now you do.'

He picked up his glass and drained its remains, which was mostly whiskey-flavoured ice at this stage. He put the empty glass down and stood up.

'How much longer until it's over?' she asked him.

He shrugged. 'Soon. Maybe. Six months. I hope. I don't know.'

'And then?'

'Something handy, I hope. Traffic control down the country.'

She looked up at him. 'I meant about us.'

Without saying anything, Seán walked to the front door.

'I can't think of that now,' he said. 'I can't risk losing my focus. It's not a game.'

'I know. And I know I'm selfish for asking.'

Darcy stood and went to him.

'You're not selfish,' he said. 'I'm sorry I didn't say goodbye back then. So, I'm saying goodbye now.'

Darcy smiled and reached out to hug him. He accepted her hug.

'Thank you,' she said.

He raised his head from their embrace and looked into her eyes. After a long moment, they kissed. They kissed as if trying to make up for all the lost time between them. Lost days and lost nights, lost arguments and lost reconciliations, lost walks together in the summers and lost winters by the fire. All never to be reclaimed.

They kissed and then fell on the floor without any thought of hope for the future or regrets of the past.

For the next two weeks, Seán would park several streets away from Darcy's house and walk back through alleyways and dark lanes before scaling over her back wall. Sometimes he would be there when she came home, sometimes she would wait up for him and sometimes he would never come at all. It seemed at times to Darcy that their relationship was going to be forever hidden inside the walls of her little house. A prison of love. Often, she would question, especially when alone, where the line was between Seán's covert life and what was real, and she couldn't help herself from wondering on which side of that line she lived.

On one of those nights, she waited until eleven before finally accepting that he wasn't going to make an appearance, so she climbed into her bed and tried to sleep. She lay there, puzzling at how her little house was beginning to feel too big without him there. As much as she loved him filling up the space in her home, her bed, and her life, she hated how she spent her time waiting for him, yearning for him. It made her feel both loved and at the same time so very vulnerable.

She texted him then, asking for his whereabouts and if he'd be dropping by. His reply was curt, at best.

Juno's. No.

The abrupt reply disturbed her. Juno's? The assumption was that he was hanging out in one of the top nightclubs in Dublin because of work. Wasn't he? It wasn't like he was having a good time, as he'd much rather be here in bed with her. Wouldn't he?

Suddenly she felt unsure of everything.

Just after midnight, she threw the duvet off, dressed, and got into her car.

Although not dressed for Juno's, the two experienced bouncers stepped aside as she entered.

A flood of music and lights hit her so hard that she put a hand up to her face as if trying to block out the light from the sun. Two women, who seemed to be ninety percent anatomically made of legs, eyed Darcy up and down as they walked by her.

She scanned the room for Seán and suddenly felt like a little girl playing in a grown-up world.

She made her way around the inner perimeter of the club. Bodies were strewn across the long red-velvet chairs. The girls appeared to be in competition as to how little they could wear and still be allowed out in public. The men's dress code was haphazard at best: expensive suits and groomed hair, mixed with designer €500 tracksuits and scruffy hair. Darcy remembered an expression her history teacher often used to describe any period of debauchery: *'It was like a scene from the last days of Rome.'*

Darcy looked towards the dance floor. It was mostly women in the club, and a small group of six of them made drunken attempts at swaggering about to the music while miraculously never spilling a drop from the glasses in their hands. They screamed out the lyrics of the songs when they knew them and shook their heads from side to side when they didn't.

Three of the girls stepped back in unison, and a gap in the crowd opened. Darcy could see through to one of the back walls. A man wearing a white T-shirt with his back to her was bent over a table. When he lifted his head, she knew it was Seán. He was surrounded by a group of women, one of whom had her red-finger-nailed hand resting on him as she caressed his back up and down. Her hair was black and shiny like in a TV commercial and her silk red dress was open at the back, revealing a long, tanned spine.

The woman, as if sensing Darcy's presence, turned to look straight across the dance floor at her. She had a beautiful face with large black eyes that made Darcy think of some exotic princess. Seán saw the woman turn, and he turned around to see what had caught her attention.

Whether Seán had just snorted cocaine off the table, Darcy couldn't be certain.

Time seemed to slow down for a few moments as he made eye contact with her, but then he looked through her as if she wasn't there. Darcy's eyes widened at the thought of him using drugs in a public space. She saw the woman in the red dress leaning slightly to get a better look at Darcy, but then the crowd fused back together like ocean waves and all visual contact was lost.

Darcy continued walking down an empty hall and out the rear fire exit. She opened it and stepped outside. Then the door closed behind her, and she was in a dark alley filled with bins and rubbish bags and graffiti. Even with the rain falling on her, Darcy's ears still rang from the music.

She stood in the rain, her mind racing with thoughts that bounced around her head. Who was the girl in the red dress? Did she or didn't she see Seán snort cocaine? But this was his job, wasn't it? Fuck! What was she even doing here? Had she just compromised him?

The rain suddenly felt cold as it dripped from her hair onto her face. She moved under an overhanging ledge and looked up into the night sky and wondered where all the rain came from. She watched it as it fell and as it appeared momentarily in front of the glow of an orange streetlamp, and then disappeared before hitting the ground.

The back door opened, lighting up the alley as Seán stepped outside. He took an empty plastic drum of cooking oil and used it to prop the door open slightly.

'*What the fuck, Darcy?*' he hissed at her.

She looked at him, so full of rage at her. How could she be so stupid? She suddenly felt like a little girl again in an adults' world. 'I'm so sorry,' she said. 'I fucked up.'

'*Get the fuck home, Darcy. I'm trying to do my job here.*'

'I know. I'm sorry. I don't know what I was thinking. I expected you to come ... I waited. Your text was so ...'

'Go home. We can talk later.'

She took one step towards him. The rain was dripping from his hair onto his face.

'I sometimes wish we could just be normal ... you know?' she said.

'*Normal?* What exactly does that even mean, Darcy? Working in an office? Nine to five? You making a Sunday roast while I wash the car in the driveway? Is that what you want? Is that what normal is to you?'

She wanted to answer him but didn't know where to start. How could she preach to anyone on what normal looked like? What normal felt like?

She stared at him, her eyes blinking. 'I don't know, Seán. And I wish I did.'

'Go home, Darcy. This isn't the time or the place. This is dangerous – for both of us.'

She nodded. And, without saying another word, she turned and walked down the alley and out onto the street. She could sense Seán watching her as she left.

As soon as she was out of sight, she stopped and leaned her back against the wall. Unsure how to get home. Unsure of herself. Unsure of anything.

Then she heard the crack of the gunshot.

Her eyes popped open as if given an adrenaline injection. She turned back into the alley in time to see a male hand pull the emergency door shut and return the alley to darkness.

Seán was standing looking at her. At first, she didn't understand and then, almost as if an electrical plug had been disconnected from his body, his legs buckled under him, and he collapsed onto his knees.

She ran to him and fell to her knees beside him.

He looked at her and then at his stomach.

She saw the blood spreading out like black ink onto his shirt. She looked at his back and saw the entry wound on his lower spine.

Seán tried to move his arms towards his back, but it seemed as if he had no power over them. They flopped to his side. He blinked several times then his body tumbled forwards.

She fumbled for her phone, dialled 999 and gave some instructions.

'Fuck,' she heard him mutter, but it was a mere whisper into the air.

She looked back up at the rain falling out of nowhere, as it appeared momentarily in front of the orange streetlamp glow and then disappeared before falling on top of them.

'He's in recovery now,' the doctor assured her the next day.

She kept her focus on Seán unconscious in the hospital bed, too shocked to respond.

'Surgery went well, but I'm afraid only time will tell how well. He'd lost a lot of blood when he got in here. He's already beaten the odds by being alive.'

Darcy had a million questions but couldn't focus on anything specific.

To fill the silence, the doctor continued talking. 'The entry wound was in the spinal column T10, the thoracic vertebra. We managed to remove the bullet and have attempted to salvage as much spinal function as possible, but of course the damage is irreparable. We've controlled the bleeding and removed any hematoma for now. He'll remain in ICU for three or four days. He'll most likely remain unconscious for the next day or two. Then he'll hopefully start rehab straight away. To be honest, rehab can have enormous benefits to the level of paraplegia that will occur. I've seen cases where the patient –'

'What did you say?' Darcy asked.

'I said that rehab can have enormous benefits,' the doctor repeated.

'Paraplegia? You mean ...'

'Yes. I'm sorry. I thought you knew. Seán's injury will most likely result in full paraplegia.'

'He'll be paralysed?'

'From the waist down, yes,' the doctor told her. 'But as I say, a lot of good can be done through rehab.'

Darcy stood staring at Seán. The doctor looked at her, then down at his watch. He mumbled something about other patients and left the room.

But Darcy just stared at Seán's face. She stared and all she could think of was the first day she had laid eyes on him from across the canteen floor in Templemore Garda College all those years earlier.

Chapter 13

At 7 o'clock Darcy stood where she had been told to stand, outside the door of Marsh's Library on St Patrick's Close. An early autumn breeze blew down the lane and found a gap under the bottom of her jacket. She shivered and looked at her watch again.

A homeless man was wrapped up in a heavy blanket against the back wall of the library. The top of his head poked out, making him look like a giant turtle huddled on the ground.

From the ages of fourteen to sixteen, Darcy's foster parents had been a wonderful couple. Her memories were of long Sunday hikes in the mountains, with picnics on the summit with jam sandwiches, crisps and hot tea from an old flask. They had encouraged her studies and, for the first time, she had excelled in school and won praise from her teachers. But they were both nurses and wanted to travel the world, and when one of them was offered a chance of a lifetime in Australia, they had no choice but to take it.

From sixteen to eighteen, her new foster parents put her in a room with three other teenage girls, all of whom were also fostered. Darcy soon realised that their fostering plan was to receive all the cash benefits of having foster children with none of the responsibility. As sixteen and seventeen-year-olds, they were left to come and go as they pleased.

In the next school, in a poor area of the city, she stood out from the others as the new girl, and as her grades slipped the teachers lost interest in her and then it was open season. The girls called her a scanger and a slut. Told her she had the pox, and that she was a dyke. They swapped seats to avoid sitting beside her and stuck pens in her back.

Her memories of that year were of studying for her final exams of Secondary School in the front porch of the house where there was a permanent light left on, and of being constantly hungry and cold. The joy of receiving good grades two days before her eighteenth birthday was quickly dampened by being informed that she was to leave the house.

She celebrated her birthday on the streets, staring at an empty McDonald's cup that passers-by threw their change into without making eye contact. For the following three weeks, she slept in the doorways at night and wandered aimlessly during the day. They were the longest, coldest and loneliest weeks of her life. Then a priest, Father Brian, stopped and spoke to her and found her a bed for the night. He helped her get off the streets and back into civilization.

She looked down at the homeless man and could easily envision every moment of his night: hunger in his belly and thirst in his mouth, fear of someone kicking him for laughs, or worse, too tired to get up but too uncomfortable not to, trying to sleep but not really sleeping. He moved as if sensing her gaze on him, and she shifted her stare to down the lane.

Mick was late. So late that she decided to go back to her car and let him come look for her. She imagined him curled up in bed, snoring his head off. Possibly with a hangover. She'd heard the rumours and hearsay about his drinking. She could only hope they were exaggerated.

She had turned back towards her car when a door built into the wall beside her, which she hadn't noticed, opened noisily. Mick appeared in the doorframe carrying two takeaway cups, one in each hand. He had to turn sideways to squeeze through the narrow doorway. A uniformed garda stuck his head out, peered at Darcy for a second and then closed the door.

'Morning,' Mick said cheerily. 'I bet you thought I wasn't coming, didn't you?'

'I knew you'd be here,' she lied.

Mick looked at her, letting her know he didn't believe her.

'I got you a cappuccino,' he said, proffering her one of the cups.

'Sorry, I don't drink milk,' she told him. 'But thanks anyway,'

He looked down at the cups in his hand.

'What's with *The Secret Garden* stuff?' Darcy asked.

Mick looked back at the door. 'It's only a secret if you don't know about it,' he told her.

The door to Marsh's Library opened with a creak and a uniformed security man stepped into the street. He eyed them up and down and then walked back in.

Mick stepped inside the library. Darcy took one more look at the homeless man and then followed Mick. The security man held the door open for her and then closed it once she was inside.

'I'm Pat,' he told her. 'You must be Detective Doyle.'

Pat's height and width blocked out almost the entire frame of the door. He seemed to cast a shadow over her and when he stuck out his hand for her to shake, his hand reminded her of an American baseball mitt. She was happy to have him as an ally rather than an opponent.

'Here you go, Pat,' Mick said while looking at Darcy. 'I got you one of them fancy coffees.'

Pat took it off him and gazed at it. Darcy couldn't imagine him drinking anything but tea from a giant mug. She reckoned she was right when he put the coffee cup down and didn't pick it up again.

Mick walked on ahead down the centre of rows and rows of ancient bookshelves that stood like a stoic guard of honour as he marched between them. The shelves of dark wood strained under the weight of thousands of thick brown leather-bound books, stretching high to the ceiling, their top shelves out of reach.

'This is amazing,' Darcy said, her voice instinctively reducing to a whisper.

'Marsh's Library. Oldest library in Ireland. 1707 to be precise.'

'What are we doing here?'

Pat strode after Mick with Darcy having to take two steps for each one of his.

'It's out of the way, and next door to Kevin Street Station,' he explained. 'This place was used for years to meet anyone working undercover. A chance for the detectives working a case to meet up with the undercovers. Sometimes the street knows more about a case than the Guards do. Murder detectives can be like the bride at a wedding party when the groom is banging the bridesmaid – they're always the last to know. This place was central but out of sight and discreet.'

'And are you discreet?' Darcy asked him, taking her eyes off the books for the first time.

Pat laughed. 'It's not used for that purpose anymore, with the likes of text messages and burner phones, but the tradition has continued. The Department of Justice has an 'arrangement', shall we call it, that the night watchman is always an ex-cop.'

'You were a garda?'

'Forty years' service. Had to retire when I reached sixty. Didn't really want to go, but they're the rules. Terrible business yesterday with that poor woman. Back in my day, a crime like that was a once-in-a-year occurrence. Now it seems as if there's one every other week. Dublin's fair city just isn't so fair anymore.'

They walked until they reached an opening with a large table taking up most of the space. Mick was standing at a bay window with his back to them, looking out onto the shadows creeping over a graveyard as the sun rose over St. Patrick's Cathedral.

'This is where James Joyce used to study,' Pat told Darcy.

'The same table?'

'The very one. You know, if you're the superstitious type, they say if you write out "JJ" with your finger on the table, it'll bring you luck.'

Darcy smiled.

'But you don't look the superstitious type,' he told her, smiling back.

Darcy looked at the table and then up at Mick.

'Why are we here?' she asked him as she sat down.

'See, I told you, Pat,' Mick said. 'There's no messing with this one. Straight to the point.'

Darcy looked up at the two men staring down at her. Throughout her career, she'd always been aware that things happened in the gardaí that she was not privy to, that she was always 'out of the loop'. For the first time, she felt as if she was finally being let into an inner circle of information and expertise that had always been shrouded from her before.

'I was hoping that our good colleague here,' Mick said, 'would have some information on our case.'

Darcy looked up at Pat, surprised.

'Not only a member for forty years,' Mick told her. 'Pat has read every murder file case in Ireland, the UK and the US. He has given me more insights and useful tips on my own cases than all the pen-pushers in Dublin Castle.'

Pat gave Darcy a bashful grin that she found charming. He pulled out a chair from under the table and sat on it. The chair groaned in protest under the weight of him and all his memories.

'I mostly worked the nights,' Pat said, almost apologetically. 'It sort of became a hobby of mine to read murder files.'

'Haven't you ever heard of Dan Brown or James Patterson?' Darcy said.

'No,' Pat answered. 'Did they work in the Castle?'

Darcy didn't know whether to laugh or not. Was it a joke? She looked at Mick but he was straight-faced.

'What do you make of this malarkey, Pat?' he asked.

Pat turned his attention back to Mick. 'To be honest, this has got me stumped. The brutality of it all is shocking. Not your regular drug-cartel stuff anyway. Did you get anything out of the husband's boyfriend?'

Mick shook his head. 'We had one of the lads question him to confirm the husband's alibi but, besides that, he got nothing.'

'Did he talk?'

'Did he talk? He wouldn't shut the fuck up! He had the poor lad worn out with his nonstop babbling. Looks like someone forgot to tell him about his right to remain silent.'

Pat looked out into the garden. The room remained silent for almost a full minute. Then Pat turned his gaze back to Mick.

'*Bollox!*' Mick said.

'What?' Darcy asked, confused.

'I know that look,' Mick said. 'Pat doesn't think it's the husband, the boyfriend or anyone with any connection whatsoever to the woman.'

'It doesn't look good,' Pat agreed.

'*Fuck it anyway!*' Mick said and stood up.

At that moment, his phone rang, and he took it out and looked at the screen.

'I should have stayed in bed,' he said and answered the phone. 'Yes, Chief?'

While Mick listened, he walked down the adjacent corridor of books.

Darcy and Pat watched him saunter away, his head bobbing repeatedly as if listening to music. Then they turned back to face each other. They smiled in awkward silence.

'What about him?' she asked.

'Who, Mick?'

'Yeah, what's his story? I heard forensics – Dr Pepple – calling him Columbo Kelly.'

'I bet that pissed him off,' Pat said. He looked out of the window before turning back to Darcy. 'They shipped him to Mayo from Dublin when he first graduated out of Templemore. A local cop in a seaside village called Murrisk.'

'Never heard of it.'

'Why would you?'

'Somehow, I can't see Mick in the middle of nowhere surrounded by fields and farms,' Darcy said smiling. 'He must have been biting at the bit to get back to Dublin.'

'Actually, it was the opposite. He loved it out there.'

'Really? Then why'd he come back?'

Pat raised himself up from his chair to see if Mick was still out of earshot, then lowered himself back into the chair before continuing. He leaned across Joyce's table and lowered his voice.

'Some bastard raped and killed a kid back then. A girl, twelve years old. Unfortunately for him, he dumped the body in Mick's neck of the woods. When they found the girl's body on the side of Croagh Patrick

Mountain, Mick stayed with the girl all night. Shitty weather came in from the sea, and it meant any support couldn't make it up till morning. He watched over her in the ice-cold rain and wind for ten long hours. Lucky he didn't die of hypothermia himself. But he never left the body – all night in the rain and the dark on the side of that mountain with that dead little girl. When they eventually got up to him the next morning, he went home and showered. He put on a clean uniform and started to work on the case. It took him two days to find the killer. Mick had him cornered in a house, but the guy decided to jump off the roof of the building to escape rather than walk down and face Mick. Broke both his legs, internal injuries. He was a mess by the time medics got to him. He was convicted and got thirty years, but he never walked again.'

An image of Seán lying in his hospital bed appeared in Darcy's head, but she shook it off.

'And then Dublin came calling?' Darcy asked him.

'Pretty much, yeah. They offered him the NBCI straight away. Although, again, it's not what you think. Apparently, he still wanted to stay in Mayo. It was the wife who wanted to move back to the big smoke. She comes from money, old money. She likes her restaurants and shopping centres, and I don't blame her for that. All that fresh air and green grass wouldn't exactly be my cup of tea either. Mick was happy to stay though. But he moved mostly because of his two-year-old son. Have you met his son?'

'No. I didn't even know he was married.'

'He's not. I mean, not anymore. His kid has ... well, he's not a kid anymore. He must be a teenager by now. He has ...'

'Come on, Doyle,' Mick's voice boomed over them. 'Let's get going. We're not going to solve anything sitting here, and I've something I need to do before we head out to Whitehall.'

'The pathologist has started already?' Darcy asked.

'Yeah, started and finished. She got in extra early this morning.' Mick walked back down the first corridor, his voice trailing off. 'I told her we'd be out after breakfast.'

'What is it with food and dead bodies with this guy?' Darcy asked Pat.

Pat smiled, but then put his hand on her arm.

'Listen,' he said, leaning in to her and lowering his voice again, 'Mick isn't what he used to be, you know?'

'Meaning what?'

'Meaning if he's going down, it's nothing to do with you, OK?'

Darcy said nothing.

'You've got a long career ahead of you. Mick doesn't. If he's going down, Detective, make sure you're standing well back, or you'll be going down with him.'

Pat left her there and followed Mick.

Darcy looked down at her hand still resting on the table. Joyce's table.

With her finger, she drew a small "JJ" before following her colleagues out of the building.

Chapter 14

'Hey, what's the rush?'

Darcy jogged a few steps to catch up with Mick.

Mick stopped and turned to face her. His face was a little flushed.

'Listen,' he said, 'there's something I need to do. I mean, somewhere I need to go. Let's meet back in Harcourt Square in about an hour, OK?'

'We're on a murder case, Mick. Where the fuck are you going?'

'I have to ... do something. I'll be back in an hour.'

An image of him sitting at the bar in an early house in a back street five minutes' walk from Harcourt Street popped into her head.

'Hold on a second,' she said. 'Maybe I should come with you.'

'That won't be necessary.'

'I'm not covering for you unless you tell me where you're going.'

'For fuck's sake!' he said. 'I'm not asking you to cover for me. Look, I promised someone I'd do something for them. I won't be long.'

Mick turned and walked away. She watched him, her temper rising. Eventually she ran after him and stood in his path.

'I don't know what sort of partner setup you had before,' she told him, 'but that's never how I worked in Domestic or even when I was walking the beat. I don't have mystery meetings, and I don't fuck off for an hour on some secret rendezvous. Now, if there's something you've got to do, even if it's off the books, we'll do it together and then get back to work. OK?'

He studied her for a few seconds and then looked at his watch.

'I need to get a car from the carpool,' he told her.

'We have a car,' she said.

Mick looked back up the street in the direction he was going and then back at Darcy's car.

'Come on then,' he said.

'It's the second house on the right,' Mick told her, as she inched the car along the narrow road.

Darcy slowed down and pulled up to the closed gates.

Dalkey was not a part of the city she would often come to. Each house was more impressive than the next. On the walls outside the houses were names like '*Montecito*' or '*Sorrento*'. Tall iron gates bordered the street with electric keypads and ornately bricked walls, as if each of the entrances were trying to outdo the others.

'Jesus, Mick. Are you loaded?'

Mick let out a short laugh.

'Not a pot to piss in,' he told her. 'This is her family's side of things.'

'Your ex-wife?' she guessed.

'Yeah.'

'Well, you must have had the shittiest lawyer in Dublin. This place must be worth millions.'

They both looked up at the enormous house, its wide glass windows reflecting the sea of Dublin Bay.

Mick reached over and beeped the horn.

'Let's just say it was made very clear and in no uncertain terms by her three-hundred-euro-an-hour lawyer that I had a choice between contesting the divorce and ever seeing my two kids again.'

The gates opened slowly.

'Keep the engine running,' he said. 'He'll be waiting for us.'

Darcy edged the car slowly into the driveway. The house was even more breathtaking from up-close. The front door was made from thick oak and the steps leading up to it were of polished granite. There were more windows than she had time to count.

The door opened slowly and a boy of about fifteen years of age stepped out. A woman stood behind him inside the hall, but she didn't come outside.

When the boy looked up, she saw that he had Down syndrome. Darcy turned to ask Mick was the boy his son but stopped when she saw his expression. Mick's smile covered his entire face. She felt sad, knowing no one had ever smiled at her like that.

When she turned back to the boy, he was walking towards them, mirroring Mick's smile.

'What's the story, Michael?' Mick asked him, rolling down the window.

'Mum said you might not make it, but I knew you would,' Michael told him.

'Get in, buddy,' Mick told him.

Michael climbed into the back seat and said, 'Who's she, Dad? Is she your girlfriend?'

Darcy laughed.

'No, Michael,' Mick said. 'You know I only like pretty girls.'

'Hey!' Darcy said in mock offence. 'I'm Darcy. Pleased to meet you, Michael.'

'How did you know my name?' he asked her.

'She's a detective like me,' Mick told him. 'That's her job.'

'I'm smart, Michael,' Darcy said. 'Even if I'm not pretty.'

'You're very pretty,' Michael told her. 'I'm smart too. If you're not my dad's girlfriend, then will you be my girlfriend?'

'I'll let you handle that one,' Mick told her. 'Drive back through the village. His school is only five minutes outside it. Michael, sit back and put your seatbelt on.'

Michael obeyed his father, and Darcy put the car into gear and drove out.

Mick chatted and laughed with his son on the way to the school. When they got there, Michael got out, and they both sat and watched as he went inside without turning around to wave goodbye.

Darcy drove out of the school and headed back towards the city.

'Nice kid,' Darcy said.

'Yeah,' Mick replied. 'That he is.'

'You're good with him.'

'Of course.'

'No, I mean, you have a special connection.'

Mick gave Darcy a sideways glance.

'I suppose you try to do your best when you're younger so that your parents are proud of you,' he told her. 'Then later you try to do your best so that your kids are proud of you. If everyone lived by those guidelines, maybe the world wouldn't be so fucked up.'

'Unless, of course, you have shitty parents or assholes for kids,' Darcy said.

Mick laughed. 'And which of them applies to you?'

'Definitely the shitty parents bit.'

'Were they Dubs?'

'Yep. True blue Dubs.'

Darcy moved uncomfortably in her seat, and Mick was shrewd enough not to push the subject.

'You said you've two kids, didn't you?' she asked him.

'Yeah, a daughter. Lucy. She's seventeen. Goes to boarding school.'

'You see her much?'

'No. We, ah ... we don't talk much.'

They drove in silence for a few minutes.

'Look,' Mick said, 'I'm sorry we had to come out here. I didn't think I'd be involved in a murder case today, and I'd promised him I'd drop him to school. I've fucked up on more than one occasion in my life, but I do my best never to let him down.'

'No worries,' Darcy said. 'Forget about it. It was nice to see a softer side of you.'

'Go fuck yourself.'

'And *The Grinch* is back.'

'So, what's your story, then? You want kids one day? A family?'

Darcy glanced at him from the corner of her eye.

'Just cause we're partners now doesn't mean we're married.'

Mick smiled. 'Put the foot down then, will you? Before the chief knows we're missing.'

Darcy reached down and switched on the blue lights and sirens, then accelerated to overtake the line of cars ahead of her.

Chapter 15

Although Darcy and Mick had entered the State Pathologist's mortuary an hour ago, they were still waiting to speak to a doctor or see any details of Mrs Delaney's autopsy.

The hundred-year-old building was in Whitehall on the north side of the city. It had an art deco, redbrick facade that had been converted from an old Garda Station. The admin offices were antiquated but clean and occupied by a staff of eight. The brass bannisters and ornate tile floors in the front of the building contrasted with the sterile and modern postmortem rooms where Darcy and Mick waited impatiently.

They were seated in a gallery looking down at an operating theatre, the floor sloping down slightly to a drain. There was a constant hum of motors, which operated the air conditioning and the extractors. Darcy's nose twitched with the mixture of potent smells. She remembered being told in Templemore that pathologists used formaldehyde, but she didn't know if that was what she was smelling.

The garda who initially found the victim was obliged to be present at the post mortem to identify the body to the pathologist. That unfortunate garda sat in a stiff wooden chair on the far side of the operating theatre and had a complexion as pale as any corpse that had ever been wheeled in there. Darcy wondered if this had been his first autopsy – it had certainly been a rough morning for him. She looked at him in the hope of giving him a look of sympathy, but he kept his stare focused on an opposite wall. Eventually, she gave up and leaned back in her chair.

'I'm fucking freezing,' Mick said for the third time, trying to snuggle deeper into his jacket.

'Yeah, you mentioned that,' Darcy told him. 'The room has to be cold.'

'I know the room has to be fucking cold! This isn't my first rodeo.'

'If you know so much,' Darcy asked him, 'then why are we in this room where there are no bodies, and not that other room where all those horizontal fridges are?'

Mick sighed, and a cloud of breath vapour filled up the space in front of his face. 'This room is used for murder investigations and is for only one body at a time. So, when we get the case into court, the defence can't say anything contaminated the body.'

'Oh, I see. That's clever.'

Mick looked at her and was about to say something when the double doors swung open. A technician pushed a stainless-steel table on wheels into the room. On the table, a white sheet lay over the outline of a body. A woman dressed in a blue coverall, a white hair cover and a face mask followed him inside. The technician applied the brake to the trolley and left.

'Good morning, Detectives. Sorry for keeping you waiting,' she said when she'd removed her face mask.

She was in her early forties, Darcy guessed. Her face had a serene glow, and she had intelligent eyes. Darcy thought she looked like the big sister that everyone should have.

'It's not morning anymore,' Mick told her, and Darcy elbowed him in the ribs.

'Oh, yes, you're right, apologies for the wait. Let's hope that's the only thing I get wrong today.'

She flashed her best smile, and Darcy couldn't help but like her and smiling back.

'My name is Dr Catherine Daly. I'm the Deputy State Pathologist, and –'

'Where's Hamilton?' Mick called down to her. 'He usually looks after homicides. He has years of experience dealing with this sort of thing.'

'Professor Hamilton is away on a family matter at the moment. I'm afraid you'll just have to make do with little old me and my twenty years of training as a doctor and forensic pathologist.'

She put on a sad face, and Darcy laughed.

'I think the chilly air is having an effect on my colleague's manners, Doctor. My name's Detective Sergeant Darcy Doyle and this grumpy lump beside me is Detective Inspector Mick Kelly.'

'It's very nice to meet you both.'

She released the brake and positioned the table so it was centred and then locked the wheels in place. She spotted the garda sitting on the chair.

'There's no need for you to still be here,' she told him.

He looked over at her.

'I'm sorry. Someone should have told you.'

'*Garda!*' Mick called out.

The young garda looked up at him.

'You can head off now,' Mick told him.

Without appearing either elated or unhappy, he stood up and began to leave.

'*By the way!*' Mick called out.

The garda stopped and looked back up at him.

'The smell is in the nose hairs,' Mick said, tapping the side of his nose with a finger.

'Sir?'

'After you shower and you can't get rid of the smell from being in this place, it'll be in the nose hairs.'

He looked at Mick but said nothing. Then they watched him walk slowly to the exit door and disappear behind it.

'Now, before we begin,' Dr Daly said, 'I normally like to find out at this point if we have any first timers in the room.'

Mick nodded at Darcy, smiling.

'Well then, Detective,' Dr Daly said, following Mick's cue, 'if at any point you wish to leave the room, there's a bathroom outside, first door on your left, and if you have the misfortune to faint, please try not to bang your head. Most of all, please remember to breathe.'

Darcy nodded.

Like quickly removing a plaster, Dr Daly pulled the sheet from Mrs Delaney's corpse. It made a loud swishing noise that echoed in the room.

Darcy stared down at the body. It was cut open in a Y-shape from the base of each shoulder to the stomach. The inside was like a cave, its walls painted a coppery red. None of the organs appeared to be in place. She felt lightheaded and realised that she was holding her breath. She inhaled the room's air and tried to relax.

Dr Daly looked at her, raising her eyebrows, and Darcy nodded.

Dr Daly gave her an easy warm smile, and Darcy found herself relaxing.

'OK then. I'll go over the basics for your benefit, Detective Doyle, and, if you've any questions, I'll do my best to answer them. Maybe I could call you Darcy?'

'Of course, Doctor,' Darcy said.

'And please call me Catherine. First of all, we collect any trace evidence from the body and clothes. Everything is meticulously photographed and documented. It's rather like what you see on TV, actually.'

She smiled up at Darcy, and Darcy attempted a smile back.

'Next is an external examination to check for bruising or any other related injuries. It's important not to make any assumptions. Even though the body had an obvious deep laceration on the neck, we still did a thorough examination. Samples are also taken throughout for a full toxicology report: drugs, poisons, etc. Blood and urine samples are also taken. Finally, the organs are dissected, and some tiny fragments are sent for microscopic analysis. There are often very subtle factors that may have contributed to death, such as scarring of the heart.'

'With all due respect, Doctor,' Mick said. 'I think the cause of death in this case was quite obvious.'

'Like I said, Detective, we make no assumptions.' She returned to the body. 'Time of death was approximately 10 a.m. It was warm yesterday, so rigor mortis could have occurred earlier than would be normal.' She looked up at the gallery. 'Rigor mortis slows down in cooler temperatures, Darcy.' She returned to the body. 'There are abrasions on the hands that are no deeper than the epidermis, so these would suggest defensive injuries.'

'Can you confirm the victim was sexually assaulted?' Darcy asked.

'Yes,' Dr Daly told her. 'Swab tests would suggest that at this stage.'

'Any sperm or DNA from the attacker?' Mick asked.

'None, I'm afraid. The vaginal swab test found traces of latex, so he used a condom.'

'What about trace evidence, fibres, clothing?'

'I'm afraid not. The only thing I found was a minute fragment of what appears to be rubber under the fingernail of the second finger of her right hand.'

'Rubber?' Mick asked. 'What sort of rubber?'

'I don't know. I've sent it off for analysis. As soon as I get anything back. I'll share those findings with you.'

'Was the rubber there before or after the murder?' he asked her.

'Hard to say.'

'What would be your guess?' Mick asked.

'I would guess,' she told him, 'that it would be your job to find out, Detective.'

Darcy smiled, and Dr Daly smiled back at her.

'For fuck's sake,' Mick said under his breath.

'I'm sorry?' Dr Daly asked.

'Can you give any indication as to what weapon might have been used?' Mick asked.

Dr Daly looked down at the body again. She laid her hand on the corpse's shoulder.

'Ultimately, she died of exsanguination – blood loss to a degree sufficient to cause death. There was a lot of blood at the crime scene. Half to two-thirds blood loss is about enough to cause death. Both left and right carotids were cut open. These arteries supply both the head and the neck with oxygenated blood. The weapon would have to have been large and heavy. The laceration was deep, so the killer would need to be quite strong. Death probably occurred in less than a minute.'

Thank God for that, thought Darcy.

'And one more thing.' Dr Daly said. 'She was pregnant. About four weeks.'

She said it as if she were telling them that there was no milk left in the fridge. They both stared at her, trying to comprehend this latest fact.

Dr Daly reached for the white sheet and covered up Jennifer Delaney's body.

'Thank you, Catherine,' Darcy said when it was clear that Mick wasn't going to say anything.

'Hopefully, next time we meet, Darcy,' she said, giving Darcy her easy smile again, 'it'll be under more pleasant circumstances.'

'I hope so too,' Darcy said. 'But ... can I ask you ...'

'Yes?'

'How do you ... how do you do what you do, Catherine? Does it not affect you?'

"Well, that's a question I'm asked at every dinner party I attend, and every disappointing date I've ever been on! Once, at the scene of a murder of a pimp in Cork, even a prostitute asked me the same question. Certain cases affect me. Some more than others. It's like your job, Darcy. If some cases aren't going to affect you, then maybe you should choose a different profession.'

Chapter 16

According to the discreet sign above its door on Fitzwilton Place, Club Paradiso had the 'hottest and most entertaining girls in Ireland'. It was run by Mary Byrne, the seventy-five-year-old ex-wife of 'Mad Dog' Freddie Byrne, a celebrity criminal in the 60s, who had died in prison many years before.

Mary Byrne ran her club without any permission or links to the city's modern criminal elite. For some years this proved to be a sticking point until a gangland criminal boss in charge of the West Side of the city proposed that Mary Byrne continue to run the club as she saw fit, on the condition that the club be used as an out-of-bounds zone. A sort of no-man's-land for meetings where the criminal landscape of Dublin could be divided up, and where truces, or declarations of an all-out war, could be instigated in the comfort of a cosy retro-styled strip club.

The man who had proposed the solution was a long-running gangland boss by the name of Frank 'The Face' Kavanagh. His patch of the city that covered the western outskirts was relatively quiet. Quiet enough to avoid the focus of the gardaí, and small enough to be deemed not worth fighting over by the other bosses. He was known to be fair but at the same time ruthless enough to avoid a confrontation with, if at all possible. Whenever someone turned up dead or seriously injured and sources pointed towards Frank, it was usually viewed openly by crime bosses and quietly by the gardaí that the victim 'most likely deserved it'.

Also, Frank played a vital role in the peace and harmony of the criminal world. Generally, Frank, at the grand old age of sixty-one, wanted an easy life and had seen enough blood and violence and money in his time to avoid any serious disputes. He was the one person whom all sides could turn to – to help mediate whenever there was a disagreement, or someone had stepped out of line and poached territory from the wrong side of the River Liffey. 'When Frank goes, all hell's gonna break loose in the Dublin underworld,' was the consensus on both sides of the Thin Blue Line.

He got his nickname 'The Face' from his uncanny likeness to the Irish actor Pierce Brosnan. Indeed, he had toyed with the idea of becoming an actor himself in his late teens and twenties, but his disadvantaged background and a peer group of drug-dealers and thugs saw him veer towards a more lucrative and less arduous career path in drug trafficking and larceny. He spent the late fifties and sixties as a feral child on the streets of Crumlin, learning his craft in a band of thieves and thugs. His father went to England for work when he was four years old and was never seen again. His mother had about as much positive influence on him as his absentee father.

'Good evening, Frank,' the tuxedo-clad six-foot-five bouncer said in his deep flat Dublin accent. He peered down at Frank with small dark eyes that were perched above a boxer's flat nose, his entire frame blocking the doorway. 'Mary's not in.'

'That's alright, Johno,' Frank told him. 'I'm here to see someone else. Mark Dunne. Is he here?'

Johno nodded his head slowly.

Johno's real name was John O'Casey, but Mary Byrne could never remember his second name, so she'd always say, 'John O ...' and then pause.

He stepped aside as Frank turned and looked up at the setting sun over a dark-blue sky. 'It's a hell of a beautiful evening to be stuck inside this place,' Frank said.

Johno looked up at the sky, unsure exactly what Frank meant. Rain, snow, or sunshine, Johno stood at that door and wore a tuxedo with little thought of the weather. He gave Frank a shrug, stepped aside, and pulled back the heavy red curtain.

The doors of the strip club had only been open an hour, so Frank wasn't expecting many punters inside. He walked along the dimly lit corridor until he came to the cloakroom.

'Hi, Frank,' the twenty-year-old Croatian seated there said. She smiled at him, brushed her long dark hair off her face and leaned forward as if presenting her cleavage to him for inspection. Her name was Petra. Mary always put her most beautiful girls working at the door or the cloakroom as it helped bring in the customers.

'Petra,' Frank said and removed his Burberry trench coat to reveal a grey Prince of Wales three-piece tailored suit, a pristine white shirt and a navy and pale-blue paisley silk tie. Twice a year, Frank flew to London for the weekend, spending most of his time (and money) between Saville Row and Harrods. Whenever anyone met Frank, he could see them pause and take in his appearance with a hint of reverence he always enjoyed.

'Are you here for business or pleasure?' Petra asked him.

'Strictly business,' Frank told her, his attention already inside the club, looking for his rendezvous.

'*Aww*,' Petra said, feigning a sad face. 'When are you going to take me for a nice dinner, then, Frank?'

Frank turned to her and smiled, looking her up and down. 'You Croatian girls are just like your cuisine, too spicy and full-bodied for me.

Gives me heartburn. And you always forget to mention your boyfriend being on the way back from the gym. I'm getting too old to be jumping out of windows, Petra, my love.'

'I promise next time that won't happen,' she said.

Frank nodded at her. 'If anyone asks, I wasn't in tonight, OK?'

Petra sat up straight. 'Only if you promise to take me to The Ivy for dinner and then to Krystle nightclub, the VIP section and then …'

But Frank had already walked away, leaving Petra holding his coat. She sniffed its collar and then checked the pockets as she hung it up on the rack.

From the small stage, the redheaded stripper, still dressed in her red bikini, watched Frank as he made his way along the back wall of the club. There were about ten customers dotted around the chairs and sofas. All eyes, however, were directed towards the stage, on the only reason they had paid a €50 entrance fee and had drunk €40 a bottle of warm white wine out of IKEA glasses.

Frank liked to hold meetings here when he wasn't too sure what way the other party would react. The club gave the person a misleading sense of security, thinking it was a 'public place' in the early evening, whereas in truth they might as well be meeting down a dark Dublin alley at 4 a.m.

A song from the nineties by Joan Osborne played over the speakers. Mary let the girls play any music they liked until the club got busy. There was a long red sofa towards the very back, far away from the stage. Frank was not surprised to see the man he had come to meet seated there behind the table.

He was, however, surprised to see the woman sitting next to him.

The guy, Mark Dunne, was in his early twenties. He was checking his phone repeatedly and taking quick swigs from his beer bottle. The woman beside him, Sinéad Fay, was Mark's cousin, but more importantly, she was the wife of one of Frank's top men, Tommy Fay. Frank could feel the tension rising in his shoulders. He was not a man for surprises.

Mark looked up and saw Frank watching him. For two seconds, the men stared into each other's eyes, until Frank's expression turned into a warm grin and Mark matched it. Or at least tried to.

'Frank,' Mark said. 'Great to see you, man.'

'Alright, Mr Dunne?' Frank said, but his eyes were on Sinéad. He remained standing.

'I know what you're going to say, Frank,' Sinéad said.

'Really, Sinéad? Then tell me. What am I going to say?'

'You're going to tell me I should stay out of it. Mind my own business. And that I'm not to give Mark any more money.'

Frank raised his eyebrows and nodded. 'I admire your loyalty, Sinéad, but it's misplaced. And unfortunately wasted. So, here's the thing. You need to leave now, because I don't think Tommy would appreciate you being here either.'

Sinéad stood up and put her hand on Mark's shoulder. Just by being there, she had made her point.

'He's a good skin, Frank. Just give him another chance, will you?'

'You said your piece, Sinéad. Now go on about your business.'

She leaned over and embraced Mark, keeping her eyes on Frank. She picked up her handbag and threw the strap over her shoulder. She looked around the room, a look of utter disdain on her face.

'These places are disgusting anyway. Full of creeps and perverts.'

She spotted one of the men in a long coat, sitting alone at a table, looking at her.

'*Eyes on the stage, not on me, you pervert!*' she shouted at him.

Frank smiled. She was not only a rare beauty, but she was also ballsy. He'd give her that. It's not as if Tommy was faithful to her, but he understood why he had married her. She was as loyal as she was vicious.

All three men watched her leave until she was out of sight.

Then the man at the table turned back to the stage as Frank finally turned his attention to Mark, sitting in beside him, so that both men were facing but not looking at the stripper.

'Listen, I really appreciate you meeting me, Frank,' Mark said, too quickly and too high-pitched. 'We can get this whole mess sorted out and get things back to normal, yeah?'

'That's all I want,' Frank told him and smiled back at him.

'Good, good. I'm very happy to hear that, Frank. Honestly, I am.'

The waitress came over to the table, but neither man looked at her or acknowledged her, so she shrugged and walked away.

'Listen, I want to get straight to the point, Frank. I know you're a man who has a dislike for long-winded meetings and too much fucking bullshit. Am I right, what?'

Mark laughed loudly, but Frank kept his same attentive expression.

'Anyway, look. The thing is, like … I … I mean, I was … Well, here's the thing, Frank, and I know you'll understand this when I say it, I –'

'You know how I know when a junkie's lying, Mark? His lips are moving.'

'No, Frank. It's not like that. I'm clean. You go ask anyone. Honestly, I'm not –'

'Where's the money, Mark?' Frank interrupted him again.

'I know, man. I know. I'm getting to that … You see, I was … I mean …'

'*Where's the fucking money, Mark?*' Frank asked him again, slower this time.

'Ah, come on now, Frank! There's no need to be like that. I have every respect for you. You know that. It's only €5K, man. It's not like you're short of a few bob, yourself. You know?'

'That's not how it works, Mark, I'm afraid. It's only €5K from you today. And what, I ignore it? Word gets out. Then it's €50K from someone else. Should I ignore that too?'

'No, that's not what I'm saying.'

'Then one morning, I wake up and there's a man standing over my bed with a shotgun pointed at my face.'

'Ah, come on now, Frank! Come on! I'll get you the dough. You know I'm good for it.'

'I wouldn't trust a junkie to produce €50 if he said he would, never mind €5K.'

Mark swallowed hard and licked his lips.

Frank rubbed his hand across his face. He took Mark's beer bottle up off the table, took a long drink from it and leaned back into the chair.

'Did you know your mother was a stunner in her day?' Frank said. 'Yeah, of course you did. How could you not? She grew up a few streets from me. Did you know that? She could have had any bloke from the criminal elite in the entire city and who does she choose to marry? Your da. A fucking bricklayer from the flats. I should have told her he'd never be able to support her in the way she deserved. Then your dad lost his job in the eighties, and she ended up working in one of my strip clubs.'

Mark turned to face Frank, eyes wide.

'Oh, you didn't know that, did you? Don't worry, she never stripped. Not that I didn't offer her a ton of cash if she would. Only worked the door. Her brickie hubby got a job after a while, and then she quit. Hadn't seen her in years till she comes to me last year. Jesus, a blast from the past or what? The years haven't been too kind to her, though, but I tell you what, she still has that something. I'd probably still do her, given the opportunity. For old time's sake.'

Frank saw Mark clenching his fists.

'So anyway, there she is in front of me going on about her fucked-up junkie son, as in you, Marky boy, her pride and joy, and how he owes five grand to some lowlife dealer, which if she doesn't produce in the next forty-eight hours, he was planning on taking a claw hammer to your knees. Five grand, Mark. Two and half grand a knee, I suppose. A poxy five grand. I carry more than that around in my wallet. So, she's blubbering and snotting all over the place and going on with herself. I used to fancy her, I know that, but then, well, I suppose I just felt sorry for her. Pity is a very powerful emotion and shouldn't be underestimated. She really let herself go, your ma. Women shouldn't have to struggle in life. It's not becoming for them. But there you go. There's not much a minimum-wage bricklayer can do for a fine piece of ass like your mother. But them's the decisions she made. And I'm sorry to have to tell you this, but you haven't made very astute decisions yourself, Marky boy. Have you? Like mother like son, eh?'

Frank let out a small chuckle and looked around the room. Everyone was still facing the dancer.

'I promise I'll –' Mark began.

'*Shhh!*' Frank told him, pointing a finger at him. '*Shut. The. Fuck. Up.*'

Mark sank back into the chair

Frank continued after a moment. He spoke quietly and looked straight ahead as if addressing the room and not Mark. 'I don't want to know the details. I don't want to know where the money went. If I had wanted you disappeared, then you and me wouldn't be having this conversation now. Even you could have figured that one out. So, listen up and pay very fucking close attention.'

He turned to Mark now.

'Look at me,' he told him.

Mark kept his head down.

'*Fucking look at me, you piece of scum!*'

Mark looked up.

'It's simple. So simple, even a loser junkie like you can understand the instructions on the tin. I should have told your mother the truth that day. I should have told her that she was wasting her five grand. "Use the money to get yourself a facial and spruce yourself up a bit," I should have said to her, "and let your offspring's kneecaps have a tête-à-tête with an eight-pound claw hammer. Probably the best thing that could happen to him". But no, I didn't say that. I told her I'd try to help you out. Give you an odd job here and there. I said there'd be a chance you could get clean. What can I say? Ever the eternal optimist, that's me. Maybe I'm getting sentimental in my old age.' He let out a loud sigh. 'I want you today, now, to leave this table and walk out that door and get on a bus, or a train, or whatever your preferred mode of transport happens to be. And get the fuck out of this fair city I call my home. Never step foot on her cobblestones again, until one day, in hopefully the distant future, you hear of my unfortunate demise, and you come to pay your respects at my graveside. But if I hear of your presence on my streets in the interim, then you'll have twenty-four hours left to breathe in this filthy Dublin air.'

Mark looked away from him. Frank could almost hear his brain churning over this information.

'I'm afraid that's the best I can do for you, and you're only getting that free pass because I feel ever so slightly responsible for your unmitigated fucked-up failure at life. And also, I don't want to have to face Sinéad's wrath anytime soon.'

Frank reached into his pocket, and Mark tensed.

Frank pulled out a mobile phone. 'Now, I'm going to check my messages,' he said, fiddling with his phone. 'And when I'm finished, you'll be gone.'

As Frank looked at his phone he could sense that Mark was still staring at him. Maybe, he thought, there really is no hope for this kid, and he'd have to send in the heavies to teach him a lesson after all. But eventually he felt Mark slither along the long red sofa, and when he looked up from his phone, he was alone with only the beer bottle for company. Even the man in the long coat had left.

On the way out, there was a group of four men handing in their suit jackets to Petra and, as she passed out their tickets to them, Frank slipped inside, took his coat and left.

Johno was still at the door and Frank stood beside him, shoulder to shoulder. He reached inside his jacket and pulled out a packet of Lucky Strike cigarettes and a lighter with a Playboy Bunny on the side. He placed one of the cigarettes between his lips, then flicked on the lighter, took a few deep drags and blew the smoke up into the sky.

He was going to say something to Johno but, when he turned and saw Johno's blank stare and deadpan expression, he decided not to bother.

His phone rang, and he looked at the screen before answering.

'Yes?' he said.

He listened for a few moments.

'I'm on my way,' he said. 'Don't let him leave there.'

Chapter 17

She was running late. She hated being late. She was bewildered by the Trinity College campus layout but quailed at the thought of prying yet another begrudging student away from a phone to ask for directions.

As the sun set, the granite buildings loomed above her and cast a shadow across Parliament Square, impervious to her plight as they had been to the multitudes who had scurried across its cobblestones for hundreds of years before her. She dashed past the Old Library, scanning the far too uncommon signposts while mumbling '*Samuel Beckett, Samuel Beckett,*' over and over. She stopped with a sigh of relief when she finally saw a small blue nameplate screwed to a concrete post that read '*Samuel Beckett Theatre*'.

As she approached the auditorium, she could tell that the lecture had already begun. An A4 page was taped to the exterior of the door. She read it as she quietly opened the door and slipped inside to find a seat.

Dr Austin Horris
Forensic Psychiatry, London
'How to Cure a Serial Killer'

'Today in the United Kingdom alone,' Dr Austin Horris told his audience, 'it is believed that there are two or three active serial killers.

In the United States, that figure is estimated to be between twenty-five and fifty. My hypothesis, although I understand it to be controversial, is that we need to reach out and help these victims through mental-health rehabilitation and psychiatric corrective treatment, which will, I believe, ultimately lead to their societal integration and assimilation.'

Horris observed most of the people in attendance shift uncomfortably in their chairs or mutter their disapproval at his reference to serial killers as 'victims'. Philistines, Horris thought to himself. Less than half of the one hundred and fifty seats were occupied in the auditorium and, much to his annoyance, Horris heard his voice echoing around the room.

Attended mostly by academics, journalists, and psychiatrists, there were also a few curious members of the public. Despite misgivings from his publicist, Tamila Williams, he had placed a lengthy and overpriced ad in *The Irish Times* at his own expense. He had expected to sell hundreds of copies of his latest book *How to Cure a Serial Killer*, but now dreaded the thought of lugging the boxes of books back to England.

She was right about one thing, though. The public's interest in serial killers had been waning in recent years. Hollywood had apparently moved on to its latest fad of international terrorism, and mere crimes against the public were becoming increasingly banal and senseless. If his latest book was not a success, he would have to do the unthinkable and revert back to private practice as a mere psychiatrist. The thought made him shudder.

Before summing up, Dr Horris paused and looked at his audience. His eyes fell on the second row. There was a twenty-something female student with the body of a Greek goddess who had been throwing him salacious looks during his entire one-hour talk. Her eyes were willing and, with a thirty-year age difference and a wife far away, it was not an opportunity to be ignored. Despite his age, he still thought of himself as being somewhat dashing. He wore his greying hair slicked back, and his face was freshly tanned from a salon off Piccadilly Circus.

'I believe,' Horris continued, 'that if I were given the resources, it would be possible to transition a killer, even one as cold and ruthless as a Jeffrey Dahmer, or a Ted Bundy or a David Berkowitz, into a normal, everyday member of the public. Many of the characteristics of a serial killer: indifference, callousness, an inability to form bonds with others, and other seemingly harmless personas, can all be 'cured' for want of a better word, by techniques I have used in my London clinic for years. Their motivation to kill, or their more normal feelings of rejection, or power, or the unending seeking of perfection, are psychoses that have been dealt with successfully through my proven methods of psychiatry. Ladies and gentlemen, I believe the mind of a serial killer is not unlike your mind or mine, and is therefore malleable, and with the proper approach can be coerced and altered to eradicate the malevolent forces within it. One day, I promise you, serial killers will only be the work of fiction and Hollywood, and our streets and homes will be the safe havens they should always be. Thank you.'

There was a splattering of polite applause throughout the auditorium as Dr Horris tidied up his notes. Tamila walked on stage and addressed the audience.

'Ladies and gentlemen, Dr Horris has agreed to answer a few of your questions, but please keep it brief. He will sign copies of his latest book, *How to Cure a Serial Killer*, in the hall after a short break. Thank you.'

Tamila cupped her hands over the mic and leaned towards Horris.

'For the love of God, Austin,' she whispered to him, 'can you please stop eye-fucking that girl in the second row and focus on the job at hand here? It's embarrassing.'

Horris, who was straining his neck around Tamila to see if his second-row admirer was still there, twisted back to her and gave her his best false smile.

'Just because you're not getting any,' he told her, 'doesn't mean the rest of us have to be monks.'

She muttered something inaudible under her breath and walked back off stage to her seat.

'Now, folks,' Horris began, and looked at an elderly gentleman in the front row. 'You, sir. Hello. Your question, please?'

There seemed to be no end to the questions. Horris was soon enjoying himself, showing off his psychological expertise while flexing his intellectual muscle for the female student.

Eventually Tamila stepped onto the small stage as he fielded yet another question. She smiled at the audience through gritted teeth, then turned her head away from them, her hand firmly covering the mic again.

'Unless you'd like to pay €200 for another hour in the room, I suggest you wrap it up.'

Horris spoke into the microphone while smiling. 'Looks like my assistant wants to get me to move things along.'

'I'm not your assistant,' she said under her breath. 'I'm your publicist.'

The audience groaned and lowered their hands.

'OK,' Horris said. 'Let's have just one more question.'

Tamila clenched her jaws tighter.

'Dr Horris,' a middle-aged man at the back called out, 'ultimately, what forces a serial killer to turn their fantasies into reality and commit these heinous acts of violence against innocent members of the public?'

Horris paused for effect, as if he were trying to think of an original and spur-of-the-moment answer. He refrained from pointing out that a major part of his lecture had dealt with answering that question.

'Their motivations vary,' he said, 'but it's usually either a fear of rejection, a seeking of perfection, or pursuing a power of one form or another. They're usually insecure individuals who fear abandonment or humiliation. Often, they have sex with their victims, even with the corpse. No possibility of rejection in that situation.' He chuckled at his little joke, but no one else joined in. 'Power is experienced by them when they feel they can decide when their victim should die or not. Having their victims' lives in their hands is a very powerful feeling, as you can imagine. Other killers seek to improve something, such as murdering prostitutes to make the world a cleaner place. Many feel that the world, and even their victims, should be grateful to them for providing a service. Later on, they become addicted to killing and see no reason whatsoever why they should stop. Psychopaths are amoral. They know the difference between right and wrong, but they just don't care. They usually lack any feelings of guilt or remorse. They are meticulous and incapable of empathy. They often shun society and lack any social integration. They are also very effective predators. I suppose you could say they are perfect killing machines.'

Tamila barged her way between Horris and the mic.

'I'm afraid that's all the time we have for now, folks,' she said. 'Please remember that Dr Horris will also be signing books on Thursday afternoon, that's in two days' time, at Reeds of Nassau Street at 4 p.m. I'm sure if you have any more questions at that time –'

A woman's voice could be heard shouting something. Some people were standing up and shuffling along their aisle, but they all stopped when they heard her. It wasn't so much her question, which no one had been able to make out, it was more the animalistic desperation in her voice.

Even Horris strained his eyes into the audience to see who had asked it.

'I'm sorry,' Tamila said. 'There are no more questions.'

But the question came again. '*So you're saying you can stop a serial killer from killing again, even if they've already killed?*'

Horris stepped towards the mic again. Too close. His voice boomed out in the auditorium.

'*Yes,*' he said. '*Yes, I am*. I can.'

His answer was simple, because he believed it.

Mairéad believed him, too.

Chapter 18

Whenever Darcy drove along Pearse Street, cars would stop and allow other drivers to enter the main artery of traffic. Nowhere, Darcy often thought, was it written in any Rules of the Road manual that this was the way things were meant to be.

It was the same for pubs throughout the capital for city cops. Every Garda Station had its 'local' but in the centre there were 'assigned' pubs depending on your rank. For example, uniformed members of the force would never enter Kennedy's. Everyone knew only detectives drank there. But, at the same time, no detective would ever order a pint in Buswells, because only superintendents or above went there.

Again, Darcy often thought, it wasn't written down where you should or shouldn't go at the end of your shift, and yet everyone seemed to know the rules.

So when Jamie had phoned her earlier that day asking to meet up for a drink after work, it was to Kennedy's pub that they went. If she had to be honest, she didn't want to go. She had planned on this being a night for pure relaxation. It had been a rough couple of days and her thoughts had turned to sinking into the hottest bath her skin could take, filled with essential oils and bubbles and watching the light and shadows from lit candles dance around the room.

Jamie Keane, the Armed Emergency Response Unit officer who had attempted to approach her at the Delaney house, had sent her three texts since she waved him away then. They hadn't yet been on any official date – mostly just after-work drinks – but it was as obvious to her as a punch in the gut what his exact intentions were. Jamie wasn't the subtlest of guys, so he wasn't shy about hiding his interest ever since they'd first met.

She sat in a snug as far away from the door of the pub as possible and watched Jamie order her a vodka and Diet 7up at the bar. She wasn't sure exactly why she had finally given in to him. Perhaps she was looking for a distraction, something or someone to listen to that wasn't going to tax her brain for even just a short period. Plus, there had been a lot of 'firsts' this week, and she needed as many allies as she could scrape together.

He leaned up against the bar, taking up space where two people could have stood. Darcy had never thought too much about it but, watching him now at the bar, she realised that he always seemed to wear T-shirts that were about one size too small for him. His visits to the gym seven days a week ensured that he had a physique that was admired or envied by both sexes. This small-T-shirt-physique combination, which could easily be viewed as unintentional, led to his gun holster poking out from under his T-shirt, and his sidearm causing a bulge on his hip that couldn't be mistaken for anything but what it was – a SIG Sauer P226 semi-automatic pistol.

Was Jamie, Darcy wondered, one of those guys that got off on wearing a gun? The force was riddled with cops who had grown up on Hollywood movies of FBI agents having shootouts with bad guys. Darcy saw their type every day. They were usually the ones chewing gum, their hands shoved into their pockets and a smug look of superiority on their faces. She saw them as a cancer in the force, and the ones that gave other gardaí a bad name before they'd even shown up at a crime scene.

She raised her head again and saw three girls at the bar flashing their pearly whites at Jamie. One girl said something to him, and he smiled at her and said something back. Another girl touched his arm, and he laughed.

Darcy lowered her head as Jamie approached the table.

'Here you go,' he said, putting the drinks down. 'This might help take the edge off.'

Darcy looked at him. 'What's that supposed to mean?'

'What?'

'Are you saying I'm on edge?'

'No, of course not. I'm just saying I'm sure it's been a tough couple of days for you. I know the NBCI can be a bit rough at first.'

'You think I can't handle it?'

'No, I didn't say that.'

Jamie looked away, and Darcy saw the hurt look on his face. She knew she needed to calm down, but what would Jamie know about actual detective work anyway? Investigative detective work. Not just showing up after the criminal is long gone and posing with guns like bodybuilders at a Mr Universe competition. But what was the point in going down that road with him? He had done nothing wrong.

She let out a deep sigh. 'I'm sorry,' she said. 'I guess I have been a little on edge. There have been a lot of firsts this week.'

'Yeah, that's OK. You'll do great.'

She made an effort and smiled at him.

He raised his glass to her. 'Here's to the best detective Harcourt Street has ever had!'

She laughed and clinked her glass off his. She took a large mouthful of the vodka and enjoyed its warmth as it sank inside her.

'Actually,' she said, 'I don't think I am the best they've ever had. I'm beginning to get the impression that Mick Kelly had his moments back in the day. I met an old colleague of his this morning. Made me see a different side to Mick.'

Jamie laughed out loud. '*What? Mick Kelly?*'

'*Shhh*, lower your voice! I'm serious.'

'Come on! Really?'

Darcy didn't reply.

'But isn't he a bit too fond of the gargle?' Jamie said.

'Yeah, but there's something about this guy that doesn't quite match up. Also, why do Kane and Burns hate him so much?'

'Kane and Burns hate everybody.'

'*Nah*, there's more to it than that. It's like they're afraid of him stealing the glory from them.'

'No fucking way, Darcy. They're a couple of pricks, no doubt about it, but they've had a good run of solves this year.'

They both looked into their drinks as if the answer somehow lay there.

'Columbo Kelly,' Darcy said, almost to herself. 'I've heard a couple of people call him that. What does that mean?'

'Wait,' Jamie said, sitting up. 'Did you say Columbo Kelly?'

'Yeah.'

'*The* Columbo Kelly?'

'Yeah, you've heard of him?' Darcy asked, leaning forward.

'You think Mick Kelly could be Columbo Kelly?'

'Yes – you've heard of him?'

'*Nah*,' Jamie said and gave her a big smile.

Darcy couldn't help but smile back.

'Prick!' she said.

Jamie laughed again and then took a big swig from his beer.

'You'll have to ask some senior guys, Darcy. Even after ten years' service, I'm still classed by many of them as a 'newbie'. I'm told "I've had more sick days than you've had days of service".'

Darcy scoffed at the suggestion. 'Nobody would talk to me. You know that.'

She let the silence between them grow.

Jamie eventually let out a sigh. 'Alright then,' he told her. 'I'll ask around.'

'Would you? Thanks. I just feel I need as much info as I can get if I've to continue working with him.'

'So, what do I get as a reward then?' he asked her, raising his eyebrows.

'You'll need to produce the goods first,' she told him, smiling.

'Oh, I'll produce the goods. Don't you worry about that,' he said with a cheeky grin.

She allowed herself a big smile, and she felt more relaxed than she had in days.

'Are you sure you wouldn't rather go back for chats with your three admirers at the bar?' she teased him.

'Nah, the three of them wouldn't even equal one of you, Detective Darcy Doyle.'

She had to admit, Jamie did have his moments.

Her phone rang. She opened it and looked at the screen.

'Mick, go ahead,' she said into the phone. She listened for a few moments and then hung up.

'Looks like you'll have to fancy your chances with the Nolan sisters at the bar after all,' she told him as she stood up. 'There's been another murder. Looks like the same MO.'

Before Jamie could even open his mouth, his phone rang.

Several other phones rang throughout the pub but, by then, Darcy was already gone.

Chapter 19

The grass in Mountjoy Square was blue, lit up by the lights from a dozen squad cars that surrounded the small urban park on the north side of the city. In fact, as Darcy looked around the crime scene, everything was blue: the bricks of the towering Georgian buildings that looked down on them, whose occupants now stood at windows and doors watching them from afar, the leaves and branches on the tall trees that hid the park from the street, the abandoned children's playground.

Darcy stood next to Mick and, like the buildings and the trees, they too looked down on the body of the dead woman. Even the blood that splattered the surrounding grass was blue.

'*Jesus Christ*,' Mick whispered. He shook his head and then repeated to himself. '*Jesus Christ*.'

Darcy let out a deep breath.

Garda forensic officers were constructing a makeshift white tent to preserve the scene and to protect the woman's privacy.

They had received an anonymous 999 call, and the first Garda car had arrived at the scene less than an hour before. Darcy assumed that the vomit at the base of the tree was from the first responders. Because of the overgrown bushes and the density of trees in that corner of the park, the location of the body was hidden from the street.

There appeared to be blood everywhere. As if a sacrificial slaughter had taken place, with the grass mound where she lay used as an altar.

With the tent completed, gardaí entered, dressed in white disposable hazmat suits.

'Hi!'

Darcy turned to see Dr Phoebe Pepple. 'Hi!'

Darcy didn't know why, but she suddenly felt a lot more at ease. As if a good friend had appeared at a time in need, as only good friends can.

'What the fuck, Fifi?' Mick asked her, as if she had all the answers.

'As Dr Daly likes to tell all gardaí,' Phoebe said, 'that's your job. I'm just here to tell you the facts.'

'So, what are the facts? Look at her. Give us something.'

'From what I remember, Mick, it was always you who were the blood-pattern expert.'

Darcy looked at him.

'Depending on the blood spatter,' he told her, 'you can normally make a good guess whether an iron bar or a pool cue has been used to bash someone's head in. And I've seen arched patterns that showed a main artery had been cut and sprayed outwards while the victim's heart had continued to beat.'

'And now?' Darcy asked. 'What do you see?'

But Mick just shook his head.

In the centre of the tent lay the naked woman whose throat had been cut so deeply she had almost been decapitated. Unlike yesterday's victim, this woman had not died looking at a picture of her family. This woman had died choking on her own blood.

Such a gruesome scene was witnessed, even by murder cops, perhaps once or twice in their career. For Darcy, this was day two.

Phoebe turned to Darcy who was pale, but still standing. She touched Darcy's arm. Darcy looked at her, and Phoebe silently mouthed 'OK?'

Darcy swallowed and nodded.

'Well, Fifi?' Mick interrupted.

Phoebe looked at the victim and finally relented. 'Looks like there are some similarities to yesterday's killing. Also, looks like she put up quite the fight.'

'How can you tell?' Darcy asked.

'Her nose is broken,' Phoebe told her. 'Hard to spot with all the blood, but he gave her a good whack in the face before he dragged her over here. But there are also slashes on her hands and arms as if she was flailing or lashing out at him. Some are quite deep.'

'Her hair looks like it's been chopped off like yesterday's victim,' Darcy said. 'When we ID her, we must check if she wore her blonde hair long.'

Mick leaned in closer to the woman's face.

'Oh fuck!' he said.

'You know her?' Phoebe said.

Mick nodded. 'Sinéad Fay.'

'Who is she?' Darcy asked.

'Tommy Fay's wife. He's one of Frank Kavanagh's boys, and that's his wife.'

'Frank Kavanagh?' Darcy repeated.

'He's one of the drug lords, isn't he?' Phoebe asked.

'Yeah,' Mick told her. 'He mainly sticks to the west side. Some of his colonels have settled down a little, but he's still up there when it comes to your average vicious bastard.'

'So, what are you saying?' Phoebe asked him.

Mick sighed. 'I need to be sure that this is the same perpetrator as yesterday. Otherwise, what's to say it's not one of Frank Kavanagh's enemies looking at a revenge killing and using yesterday's murder as a cover-up.'

Phoebe shook her head.

'You don't think so?' Mick asked her.

'I can see where you're coming from. I understand you have to cover all your bases, but ...'

'But?'

'For now, if this wasn't Tommy Fay's wife then I'd say it's not a copycat killing, but you'll need to rule it out first. I'll also need to get the lab results back.'

Mick ran his hand through his hair. He looked at Darcy. She seemed to be staring at the wall behind Phoebe.

'What are you thinking?' Mick asked her.

'Well,' she said, clearing her throat, 'I'm thinking we might be looking at something bigger here.'

'Like?' Phoebe asked.

'Like a possible serial killer.'

Phoebe and Mick looked at one another.

Phoebe spoke first. 'You know, technically, it takes three bodies to make a serial killer.'

'I'll go talk to the chief and get this prioritised,' Mick told them. 'Unless, of course, we'd rather wait to prove Detective Doyle wrong.'

Chapter 20

Frank 'The Face' Kavanagh lived in an exquisitely designed and furnished house called The Guardhouse. The irony of its name was not lost on anyone. It was originally the guardhouse for a 17th century manor home. That manor now served as the clubhouse for an 18-hole luxury golf course, while the guardhouse, where Frank lived, was converted into a spectacular residence. The perimeter of Frank's house had the original ten-foot high and three-foot thick granite walls. The walls, however, were unseen from the house because of the tall and fully mature oak, birch and ash trees that ran alongside them. Also unseen by the casual observer was the €100,000 high-tech security system that allowed Frank to view every inch of his property and alert him if any unwelcome visitor foolishly set foot on it. So far that had never happened.

From the living room, whose glass doors opened onto a finely manicured Japanese-styled garden, Frank poured, for the second time that night, two large glasses of Jameson 18-year-old whiskey. He didn't add any water or ice. He walked across the room and handed one of the heavy crystal glasses to the man who sat with his fists clenched together on the sofa.

'Here, Tommy,' Frank said. 'Have another one.'

Tommy Fay reached up and took the glass, but then held it in his hand as if he were unsure what to do with it.

'Drink it,' Frank instructed him.

Tommy poured it down his throat and then winced as it burned inside.

Frank took the empty glass and then sat opposite in a reading chair. He looked across at Tommy. He had a scar running down the entire right-hand side of his face and his unabridged grief and rage made his scar seem even uglier. Frank sipped on his own whiskey, savouring it.

'They butchered her, boss,' Tommy said, the anger in his tone boiling below the surface of his words. 'Fucking animals! How could they do that to her?'

Frank raised his eyebrows at this. Many times, he had dispatched Tommy to eliminate a rival gang member and, of all his men, Tommy seemed to enjoy this part of his work more than anyone. He had once chased a half-naked man around the man's house before dragging him out from under the bed and shooting him three times at point blank in the face.

Tommy did love his wife though. He had to give him that. He was as much a devoted husband to his wife as he was a devoted killer to his boss.

'Have you any idea who could have done this?' Frank asked him. 'Did you notice anything or anyone out of the ordinary in the last few days?'

'No. We went to the cinema this afternoon but then you called me to do that job, so I left her.'

'You left halfway through the film?'

Tommy nodded. Frank leaned forward in his chair.

'I have to ask you this, Tommy, but ... was Sinéad ... faithful? I mean ... do you think there's any chance there was someone else?'

Tommy raised his head for the first time.

Frank sat back in shock at the pain and anger in his red eyes.

'No,' he said.

'OK, fine. I'm sorry. I had to ask.'

There was a knock on the door, and a tall man who looked impossibly skinny and deathly pale came into the room.

'Well?' Frank asked him. 'What's happening, Lurch?'

'The cops are at the scene now, boss. The place is swarming with them.'

'Who's in charge?' Frank asked.

'Mick Kelly.'

'Columbo Kelly? I thought he was dead.'

Lurch shrugged.

'And someone new. A woman. I don't know her.'

'Does she have a name?'

Lurch looked down at some notes he had written. 'Darcy Doyle.'

There was silence in the room as Frank stared out into the garden. He eventually put down his whiskey glass on a small coffee table and stood up.

'OK,' he said, 'here's what we're going to do. Tommy, you need to go with Lurch and deal with the filth. Go to Sinéad. Show them you have nothing to hide by being there. They'll still want to have a proper sit-down interview with you later, but for now that'll keep them at bay. For a while, anyway. OK?'

Tommy looked up at his boss but knew better, even at this time, to contradict him.

'I know that's the shit side of the stick for you,' Frank told him, 'but we need to play by their rules for now. To begin with, anyway. You did the right thing coming here, but you're a suspect in their eyes until you have an alibi.'

'But I was ...' Tommy began.

'Don't worry about that. Lurch will go over everything with you: where you were and what you were doing, and who was with you this evening. I'll have ten witnesses if they want to check it, which they will. Stick to that and say nothing else and then come back here. And Tommy ...'

Tommy looked up at him.

'I need you to fully understand what I'm saying here. You need to man the fuck up. We'll give Sinéad the send-off she deserves, and I promise you ... *look at me.*'

Tommy looked into Frank's shining blue eyes.

'We'll get the bastard who did this to Sinéad and I promise you, Tommy, you can look him in the eye before you put a gun to his head and blow the fucking thing off.'

Frank saw Tommy's eyes turn from grief to revenge.

'Now go, before they come here looking for you.'

Tommy stood up, and Frank stretched out his arms and hugged him.

Frank watched Tommy and Lurch leave and then turned to look for his glass of whiskey. He sat and began to consider the situation and all its ramifications.

Chapter 21

Mairéad sat in a frayed, yet comfortable, armchair in her living room, listening to a radio drama on Lyric FM. A temporarily abandoned novel rested on her lap. The sparse room comprised a worn patterned armchair where her husband, Jack, used to sit, a sofa, the fireplace where a faded colour photograph of her two boys in matching school uniforms stood and a small lit candle gave off the faint scent of lavender. A bookshelf held a slew of James Patterson novels and a decorative yellow Tiffany lamp that was perhaps the only extravagance in the entire house.

There was no television. She hadn't looked at a television in over twenty years. After they'd left the Palmarian Church, they could have bought one, but Jack never did. Then when Jack died, Liam was already gone and Conor ... well, Conor never expressed any interest in wanting one.

After Jack died in the crash, she'd initially felt a sense of freedom, but it hadn't lasted long. Although his death had freed her from a chain of considerable weight, it had also burdened her with sole responsibility for herself and her family. She quickly realised that she had been hiding behind her husband's Draconian personality like a veil and, when that smokescreen had been taken from her, suddenly the imperfections of her own life had become magnified and very real. Her warped and miserable life was no longer because of her warped and miserable husband. She was no longer a sad, lonely woman because of him. She was merely a sad, lonely woman. Any joy she might have inherited from his death or any bliss from her sudden bereavement crumbled like the ashes of his corpse. When Liam had caught her sitting alone and crying at the kitchen table a week earlier, he'd assumed she was crying for the loss of her husband's life. In truth, she had been crying for the loss of her own.

She thought about her two boys, Liam and Conor, and felt ultimately responsible for how they had 'turned out'. Although Liam had flown the family nest years earlier, there was a coldness about him she found somewhat disturbing. Sometimes when he looked at her, it was as if he were looking through her. As if he blamed her for all the troubles in the world.

As for Conor, her poor Conor, there was nothing she wouldn't have done for him, and yet she had done exactly that: nothing. Trapped between her husband's refusal and her own lack of understanding, she had watched his silent frustration with the world. Where she saw resentment in her eldest son's eyes, in Conor she saw disappointment.

Conor had grown more independent with maturity, even venturing out into the world on his own. She had been jubilant at first when he had begun to take walks. But he would be missing for two, then three and four hours at a time. She had even secretly followed him once. On that occasion, he'd gone to a park and sat on a bench overlooking a large playing field. He had sat there for over three hours barely moving. Although she was sure he had not known she was watching him, as soon as she had returned home he returned five minutes after her.

Living in such a quiet house, her sense of hearing had improved over the years. So even above the voices from the radio, when Conor slid his key into the lock of the front door and turned it once, she heard him. She listened to the door close and heard his footsteps going down the hall and into the kitchen. She stood up and followed him.

'Hello, darling,' she said. 'I've kept your dinner for you. Did you have a nice walk?'

Conor was non-verbal, but Mairéad had got into the habit of always talking to him as if he were replying to her conversations. Whenever Liam was there, he found it disconcerting, but she had continued with it for years.

'I'm listening to a very nice play on the radio if you'd care to join me?'

Conor moved about the kitchen as if looking for something.

She picked up a tea towel and squeezed it in her hand for something to do. 'Can I help you find something, dear?'

He took two slices of bread, pressed them together and then sat at the kitchen table taking bites out of the 'sandwich'.

'Can I get you some cheese for that, dear? Or some ham?'

He didn't look at her, so she sat down opposite him. She liked to look at his face. He had such a handsome face, she thought. The face of a movie star, she'd told him. He could even have been another Cillian Murphy. If only for his condition, she often thought, the girls would have been lining down the road to be with him.

'Did you hurt your hand, dear?' she asked him, noticing the slight blemish. She knew better than to reach out and touch him.

He stopped chewing and looked at her. Then he looked down at the scratches on the back of his hand.

In an instant, he rose out of his chair, its four legs dragging along the wooden floor. He dropped the bread onto the floor and covered his face with his hands before storming out of the room. She listened to his rapid footsteps on the stairs and then his bedroom door opening, closing and being locked from the inside.

She stared at the half-eaten bread on the floor. The faint sound of voices drifted in from the radio in the sitting room. For some inexplicable reason, she became overwhelmed with sadness. And pity.

An image of Conor when they had first moved back to Ireland came to her. He had not settled well into their new home. Much to the annoyance of her husband, Conor had cried himself to sleep every night for almost a year.

She would hold his frail body in her arms and rock him back and forth over and over to help soothe his anxiety while singing an old Irish schoolyard ballad that her own father used to sing to her whenever she couldn't sleep. She would gently caress his forehead and patiently console him until he closed his eyes and fell into a deep sleep.

With the memory vivid in her mind, she stared out into the hall and sang the song again.

'There was an old woman and she lived in the woods
Weela Weela Walya
There was an old woman and she lived in the woods
Down by the River Saile.
She had a baby three months old
Weela Weela Walya
She had a baby three months old
Down by the River Saile.
She had a penknife long and sharp
Weela Weela Walya
She had a penknife long and sharp
Down by the River Saile.'

Wednesday

Chapter 22

Darcy's legs felt a little heavier than normal after her morning run. It had been a long night at the crime scene, and she didn't get to leave till close to midnight, when Sinéad Fay's body had been removed to Whitehall for examination by Dr Catherine Daly.

Tommy Fay had shown up a couple of hours before that. He was at the very top of their list of interviewees, but he had been so distraught and uncontrollable that they had ordered him to be removed from the crime scene.

After a visit with Seán in the Mater Hospital before her drive into Harcourt Street at eight, she was hoping to get time to review any results that may have come in during the night. She was surprised to find Mick already in their assigned incident room, hunched over a folder. The coffee cup beside him was empty.

'How long have you been here?' she asked him.

He looked at her. 'Good morning to you too.'

'Sorry.' She sat down opposite him. 'I didn't get too much sleep.'

'You didn't get too much sleep, or you didn't sleep too well?'

'Both.'

'I'm not in long,' he said. 'Besides, it's not a competition. We're supposed to be a team. Remember?'

She didn't reply, but instead walked over to the kettle and switched it on.

'Anything come in overnight?' she asked him, sitting back down while she waited for the kettle to boil.

'No. It's too early. Most of the lab guys work business hours only, and any of them who were at the scene last night are probably still fast asleep under their *X-Files* bed covers.'

Darcy allowed herself a smile at that image.

'I think we'll have to get more help on this one,' he told her.

'Really? Why? There's more than enough of us working on it already.'

Mick looked at her for a few moments.

'What?' she said.

'Nothing. But you're wrong. I'm going to request another twelve uniforms.'

'Twelve?' she said incredulously.

He ignored her. 'And we'll probably need another one or two from the NBCI to assist. I'd be surprised if the chief himself doesn't request it.'

'Look, Mick. If this is too much for you, I understand, but I don't want to be answering to anyone else. I can handle the extra workload. A few extra uniforms to knock on some doors, fair enough, but another couple of detectives? That's not normal.'

'Normal? What do you know about normal? Normal to what? Remind me again, Detective. How many murders have you worked on now? *Hmm?*'

Darcy didn't reply.

'Exactly,' he said.

'I just thought it'd be my – I mean our chance to show the chief ... well, you know what I mean.'

'I know what you mean. But it has to be done right. And finding the perp is more important than anything else.'

Neither of them moved for a few moments. Mick rubbed his hands across his face.

'Look, Doyle,' Mick said, sighing heavily and pointing at the pages in front of him, 'none of this shit is normal. I didn't say it last night, but I agree with you – this is going to happen again. And it's going to get bigger. So, we have to get bigger before it does. We can't afford to be reactive to these murders. We need to be proactive. Do you understand?'

Darcy nodded.

Mick looked at his watch. 'Now let me tell you what I do know. The chief is going to be here in an hour. And he's going to want answers or a plan of action. We don't have any answers, so we'll have to work on a plan. And if we don't have a plan to make him all happy and warm inside, then by 9 a.m. I'll be back looking for stolen credit cards and you'll be back hugging some woman with a black eye who refuses to leave her husband. Do you understand, Detective?'

'I understand, but I just know it's not drugs-related, and it has nothing to do with Tommy Fay or even Frank Kavanagh. I know that. This is some sick, misogynistic killer, and he will do it again.'

'I agree with you, but I'm not so sure the chief will, so it's up to us to show him otherwise. OK?'

Darcy nodded again.

'Now go make your coffee, and we'll go over this stuff together,' Mick told her and he turned back to his pages.

An hour later, three newspapers slammed down on the desk in front of Darcy and Mick.

'Are you two reading your fucking horoscopes?' Detective Chief Superintendent Glenn O'Riordan said, standing over them. 'Because if it's your future you're thinking about, I'd be more concerned with the headlines if I were you.'

Without looking around, Mick opened the papers.

Killer on the Loose

Sadistic Butcher Strikes Again

Double Deaths in Dublin

'They work fast,' Mick said, scanning through the articles.

'Which is a lot more than I can say about you two,' O'Riordan said. 'Read the part where it says, "*Gardaí stumped by the latest killings*".'

'Look at that,' Mick said, pointing to the bottom of the page. 'There's a sale on in Aldi.'

Darcy could feel the rage boiling from O'Riordan. She turned around to him.

'We're working on a plan, Chief,' she told him.

'Oh, are ye?' Whenever O'Riordan got upset, his Galway accent got more pronounced. 'Ah, well then, I wasn't aware that you had a plan worked out. I can go back home now so, can I?'

Mick couldn't help but smile.

'Now you tell me, Kelly, before I wipe that fucking smile off your face, what is your plan? And you've only got one shot at this, boy! One fucking shot. I want clues. I want suspects. I want leads. I want something to tell that pack of vultures at the press conference in two hours' time! And when the Commissioner calls me later today after his daily round of fucking golf, I want to dazzle him with how we're on top of the situation, sir, and how I have my best people on the job, sir. And right now, I see none of that happening. And if I have to tell him the actual fucking truth, then there's two people in this room who are royally fucked. And neither of them is me.'

They both remained seated, staring up at him.

'I've either been suddenly struck deaf, or I'm not hearing any good news,' O'Riordan said.

'We think it could be a serial killer, Chief,' Darcy told him.

Mick closed his eyes.

O'Riordan turned his attention to her. 'Unless the next words out of your mouth are " *We've arrested the killer, and he's made a full confession*" then you better not say another word, Detective. Am I making myself clear?'

He walked over to a chair and dragged it closer to them. He sat down, leaned back, and folded his arms across his chest.

'We have three uniforms chasing enquiries into Monday's murder,' Mick said. 'Results from the Supermarket CCTV are due in today. We've another uniform verifying the first husband's alibi. The autopsy report made for some gruesome reading. DNA results due in today as well. It's last night's murder that has more complications than we need. As you know, Chief, it was Tommy Fay's wife. Normally we'd put it down as a gangland act of revenge, but with Monday's murder and a similar MO, we believe it was just a coincidence that the victim's husband was a gangbanger.'

O'Riordan sighed deeply. He hated hearing American terminology from his officers. 'Go on.'

Mick looked at Darcy, and she took over.

'Forensics have given us the name of the compound found under Jennifer Delaney's nails. Neoprene. It's a hard rubber used in clothing like gloves, wetsuits and face masks, but also in swimsuits and in mouse mats. More forensics are due back today. We spoke briefly to Tommy

Fay last night at the crime scene but didn't detain him. Whoever was responsible for the murder of Sinéad Fay, it wasn't him. We had a car follow him and he went straight to Frank Kavanagh's house. We'll still need to conduct a full interview with him.'

O'Riordan moved in his seat at the mention of Frank Kavanagh's name, but he said nothing.

'We need more uniforms, Chief,' Mick told him.

'How many?'

'A dozen for now.'

'OK,' O'Riordan agreed. 'I'm also going to bring back Kane and Burns.'

'Fuck's sake!' Mick said.

'You've no choice on this.'

'Chief?' Darcy asked.

O'Riordan nodded at her.

'To investigate or to assist us?'

O'Riordan looked at them. 'To assist ... for now.'

Darcy let out an audible sigh.

'We'll review the situation day by day,' O'Riordan said. 'One misstep on this from either of you and you're both gone. Is that understood?'

He stood up and found a page and a pen. He began to scribble some notes.

'Ah come on, Glenn!' Mick rolled his eyes. 'You're not still doing that, are you?'

'*Shhhh!* Those reporters out there can sniff out a liar. And if there's one thing that's been my downfall and spoiled my chances of becoming Commissioner, it's an innate inability to bullshit straight to someone's face. Get over here, Doyle!'

Darcy got up and stood beside him.

He finished scribbling and then handed her the page. '*Read that,*' he told her.

'*Ah, for fuck's sake, Glenn!*' Mick said.

Darcy glanced at Mick, puzzled at his reaction, then looked at the page and began to read. '*We are following a positive line of enquiry but at this stage can't say too much in order not to compromise our investigation.*'

She stopped and looked up.

'Continue,' O'Riordan told her.

'*We have several definite leads and feel that an arrest is imminent in the very near future. Several concrete clues left at the scene will bring about a speedy resolution to this case. We have several witnesses and persons of interest whom we are interviewing.*' Darcy looked up from the page. 'I don't understand, Chief. None of this is true.'

'Of course it's not true. But now you've said it, so I can say that you said it.'

O'Riordan crunched up the page and threw it into a bin. 'Now get back to your horoscopes or whatever the fuck you were doing.'

Chapter 23

Mairéad had not slept well. On her bedside locker sat her radio, which she had switched on every hour on the hour, listening to the news. 3 a.m. 4 a.m. Falling in and out of sleep. Finally, at 5 a.m. she heard what she had been waiting for. Another murder.

The front door slammed. She opened her eyes and listened. The house was quiet. She jumped out of bed, pulled back the curtains and watched the back of her son, Conor, walking up the street.

Everything was starting again. It was just like Spain. This time, there would be nowhere to run. Like father, like son. Or maybe she was to blame, at least in part, for his ... his perversion.

Everything screamed at her not to go into his room but, if she were to get any help for him, she needed proof. Needed evidence. Otherwise, she was just the batshit crazy old lady that everyone thought she was. Dr Horris would laugh at her unless she had something to show him. Something concrete.

She walked to her son's room. The door was closed. She turned the handle and opened it slowly. The curtains were still drawn, and the room was dark. She took a deep breath and flicked the light switch on. She paused and listened to the house. Then she took a deep breath and stepped into the room.

This had been Conor's room since he was a young boy. Her special little boy whom she had tried to protect from the nasty world outside.

But now it was time to protect the outside world from him. She realised, standing alone in his room, that her love for him was now mixed with fear. When did that happen?

For several moments, she tried not to believe her own son, her own flesh and blood, was capable of such atrocities. So why then, she asked herself, was she standing in his room? And sneaking about without his permission?

First, she opened the drawers, trying carefully not to disturb the clothes and items inside, unsure what she was looking for, but knowing that she would know when she found it. Then she searched his wardrobe, his bookshelf, behind his TV – until she stood in the middle of the room and looked down at his unmade single bed. She got on her knees and then lay flat on the floor.

There was one thing under there. She reached in and pulled out a thick brown envelope. It was unsealed. She opened it slightly and looked inside but couldn't make out what it was. She summoned up all her courage and placed her hand slowly inside, and then pulled the object out. It took her a moment to realise what it was: a ponytail of long blonde hair tied both ends with simple hair bands.

She examined it with curiosity and then saw the droplets of blood on the envelope and dropped it and the hair onto the floor. She was suddenly aware that she was holding her breath and let out a gasp that manifested into a cry of horror.

Mairéad felt her heart cave in. She felt light-headed and for a moment she thought she would faint.

She left the room in a haze. She should have closed the door, but didn't have the energy. Her head was spinning. Her mouth was dry and she found it hard to swallow as if there was something caught in her throat.

At the top of the stairs, she looked down into the hall. She tried to focus on the first step, but it was moving from side to side. She grabbed the bannisters to steady herself, but when she reached out she grabbed only air and she lost her balance. As hard as she tried, she was unable to stop herself from falling forward.

There was a place in her heart that wanted to fall. She wanted to end this nightmare and make it go away. Make everything go away. She gave in to a feeling of tumbling forward, almost with a sense of relief.

She fell, head-first. The side of her head hit the third step down and then she rolled, begging for an unconsciousness or blackness that didn't come.

She lay in the hall, her head resting on the cool wooden floor, staring back up the stairs.

She knew what she had to do.

Chapter 24

'*OK, everybody! Listen up!*'

Mick had to raise his voice to be heard above the chatter of fifteen uniformed gardaí. Some were in full uniform, having already been on duty at a nearby station. Others wore their shirts open at the neck, having come straight from home to avail of the overtime. There was a mix of both men and women. Men mostly, as always.

Aoife, Eoin and Sam sat up front, assuming a senior position on this investigation since they were involved from the start, even though that was all of two days ago. Eoin was still not in uniform, milking his temporary promotion while he had fact-checked the husband's lover's alibi.

The possibility of extra overtime in a budget-strapped department, and the fact they were working on an actual murder investigation, added to a somewhat jovial mood.

Mick and Darcy were standing behind a table at the top of the room, large windows behind them.

Mick's request for silence had failed to register. Darcy stood up straight and took a deep breath.

'*Shut the fuck up!*' she yelled at them.

Like reprimanded schoolchildren, they all stopped talking and faced the two detectives.

'Lads,' Darcy said, 'we haven't got time here for catch-ups and chit-chat. We've brought you here to assist in a double murder investigation, and we need your one hundred percent focus on this. OK?'

She had their attention.

'For those of you who don't know us, my name is Detective Sergeant Doyle. This is my partner, Detective Inspector Kelly. Please give us your undivided attention for the next few minutes.'

Darcy had never addressed Mick as her 'partner' before. It gave her a feeling of permanence, which she felt somewhat uneasy about.

'Thank you, Detective,' Mick said and took a step forward. 'Here are the facts of the case so far. I stress the word 'facts' because you are going to read a lot of hearsay, speculation and sensationalism regarding this case. Pay no attention to the media, be it from a journalist of *The Irish Times* or a blogger on social media. Understood?'

Mick waited until his words had sunk in.

'OK then,' he continued. 'We have two murders. Both cases have very similar MOs, so at this point we're deeming that the same man committed both crimes. As always, we need to be careful about making assumptions, especially this early in the case, but there's no denying the similarities. He attacks the victim, strips her, ties her up and then rapes her. At some point during the rape, he slits her throat.'

Mick never felt a need to be overly dramatic with his description of a murder. He found that everyday banal words have more gravity to them. He watched as some of the uniforms squirmed in their chairs.

'Other similarities,' Darcy joined in, 'are that the victims have long blonde hair, which he cuts off and then removes from the scene. They were both in their thirties, and they were both married.'

She looked at Mick, and he took over.

'The first victim was Jennifer Delaney, wife of Paul Delaney, a financial consultant. The second victim was Sinéad Fay, wife of Tommy Fay. If anyone doesn't know that name, then you might have heard of his boss – Frank 'The Face' Kavanagh.'

More shifting of seats.

'As you can imagine,' Mick continued, 'this makes matters more complicated. We've contacted Tommy Fay to arrange an interview, but he has informed us that unless he's under arrest, he had no intention of coming in to talk to us. The fact that any information he could provide would undoubtedly assist in our investigation to catch the person who did this to his wife doesn't seem to click with him.'

'Can't we make him a suspect and just haul him in?' someone asked from the back of the group.

'We could,' Mick told him, 'and we may have to do that but, for now, we'll give him a little time to cool down. If we go in all guns blazing, it may have a counter effect.'

Mick paused before continuing.

'We've had three uniforms working with us so far. Aoife has been doing the ever-popular door-to-door, but apart from the usual shock and horror of the neighbours, she has nothing to report. Either way, it's a thankless but necessary part of the investigation and we'll need it done near the second victim's crime scene. Today. Aoife, take two others with you and get cracking in the area surrounding Mountjoy Square.'

Aoife made a face of exasperation. Mick ignored it. He looked at three members sitting together on the right and pointed at them.

'You three. Examine the habits of both victims: where they shopped, where they went to the gym, where their kids played sports, who did their Botox injections – everything. I want lists and lists and lists.'

'Yes, sir,' the three of them said in unison.

Sam, who was sitting near them, gave them a look of disdain.

'I'm sorry, I forgot your name. What was it again?' Mick asked Sam.

'Sam,' he muttered.

Eoin and Aoife couldn't help but smirk.

'OK, Sam,' Mick said. 'I believe you've had some luck with the CCTV cameras. Can someone at the back please turn off the main lights?'

Sam stood up and wheeled over a TV. The lights in the room went off.

Sam fiddled with some buttons until an image appeared on the screen. Mick and Darcy had already seen it.

The image showed the half face of a man wearing a loose-fitting hoodie. The camera had been far away from the suspect, so the figure was out of focus. Everyone leaned forward in their chairs as if to get a better look. Unsatisfied, they sat back.

'I know, I know,' Mick said. 'It isn't going to win any Pulitzer Prizes for photography, but we can tell a little from it. His height is slightly above average. Maybe about 5 foot 11 inches. Very bulky on the upper torso and legs.'

'How do you know that's him?' someone asked.

'Who asked that?' Mick said, straining to see in the darkened room.

A hand went up, and Mick looked at the female garda.

'OK, great question. Lads, you need to be always questioning everything. Why? Where? Who? What? That's the only way we'll get this guy. Old-fashioned police work. Walking the beat, knocking on doors, checking everything until we get our break.'

Darcy liked the way Mick motivated them. He had them working together for a single cause and made them feel like they were learning and getting something from it as well. They would leave this room with a purpose.

'To answer your question, we have footage of him outside in a stolen white Ford Transit following Jennifer Delaney's car out of the car park. Flick to the next few clips, please, Sam.'

From black-and-white footage in the carpark, they watched the van almost collide with a car pulling out into its path. The car reversed and let the van out. The same figure wearing a hoodie top could be seen in the driver's seat.

'I want you ...' Mick said, looking towards the back of the room. 'What's your name? The one who asked the question.'

'Cara, sir!' she called out. 'Cara Walsh.'

'OK, Cara. You see the registration number of that car?'

'Yes, sir.'

'Find the owner. I want him interviewed, and I want to know what he saw when he looked at our man. Get him in front of a sketch artist and report back to me. Take someone with you.'

The garda to Cara's left nudged her with his elbow as if to say, 'Well done'. She smiled her thanks at him.

'Sam,' Mick said, 'I want you and four other gardaí to start looking at more CCTV footage. Find out where that van went after it left the victim's house. Look for any CCTV cameras around that area. Contact all Garda Stations with its description. It's been abandoned or set on fire somewhere. Also, check out any footage from cameras around Mountjoy Square where Sinéad Fay's body was discovered. We need all the footage from there as well. Find that van.'

'*Jesus!*' Sam complained. 'I'm already half blind from watching the videos.'

Mick stared at him for a second or two. The room was silent.

'But I'll get working on it right away,' he quickly added.

'Are you sure you're half blind from watching *these* videos, Sam?' Aoife asked him.

Everyone laughed as he returned to his seat.

'Turn on the lights, please!' Mick called out. 'Eoin, come up here for a second.'

Eoin walked to join Mick behind the table.

'Who here knows about ping triangulation?' Mick asked.

A few hands went up.

'OK. It's vital we talk to the person who called 999 for the second victim, Sinéad Fay. But first we need that phone number. If they saw the body, perhaps they saw the killer. We've already got the recording, but I need you, Eoin, to get back on to ECAS, the emergency call answering service, and get that number.'

'I thought those numbers were anonymous,' Eoin said.

'Nothing's anonymous anymore. Get me that number.'

Mick moved some objects around the table.

'Look here,' he said, holding his mobile phone. 'Let's say this is the phone we're looking for.'

He placed it in the centre of four objects: a cup, a red marker, a bottle of water and a stapler.

'This technology is not that new, and we've used it before. It's already been used to help get a guilty conviction.'

Everyone in the room stood to get a better view.

'OK, so we send a ping to the mobile phone. It's like ringing the phone without it actually ringing. The guy holding the phone won't even feel it. That ping from his phone will send a signal to possibly four antennas. If it's in Dublin, then they'll be quite close to each other. Whichever is the weakest of the signals is then eliminated.' He removed the stapler. 'Then we work backwards, and by drawing a circle around the three antennas, the marker, the cup and the water, we're able to find the location of the phone in the centre.'

They all took a moment to imagine the phone silently ringing somewhere in the city.

Mick turned and looked at Eoin. 'Understand?'

'Yes, sir. How close could we get?'

Mick shrugged. He looked at Darcy.

'If it's in Dublin?' she said. 'I'd say within six feet.'

Gasps rose from the room.

'Now, if my maths are right,' Mick continued, 'that gives you all something to do except for one person. Whoever's left, I want them sitting by that phone over there.'

Mick pointed to a desk in the corner with a phone on it.

'That's our tip line,' he told them. 'The number is being published today. Most of it will be shite, but either way I want every call noted and a contact name or phone number written down. That's if they give one.'

The room settled down.

'Lads and ladies,' Mick said, 'what are we really looking for here?'

No one said anything.

'Anyone?' Mick asked.

'Leads?' a voice said hesitantly from the middle of the room.

Mick nodded. 'Leads would be fantastic. But we'll be happy with just one lead. That's all we want. Something solid. And then we're going to pull on that lead like a piece of string and it'll be attached to a bigger lead and on and on until we get our break and suddenly ...'

Mick clapped his hands loudly for effect. Some of them jumped.

'... we have the fucker in our sights. There's no such thing as the perfect crime. If you don't believe me, then go ask the thousands of men and women sitting in prison cells around the country right now. This killer is a monster, I'll give you that, but he's a man. And like all of us, he'll fuck up. He's out there right now. In your city. Breathing in your air.'

All eyes went beyond Mick and out the windows into the daylight.

'We don't know his name,' Mick continued. 'We don't know where he lives. And we don't even know what he looks like. But one thing we do know. One thing we are one-hundred-fucking-percent positive about. We are going to get this prick and make sure he never walks the streets of our city again.'

Mick paused and looked at them all. He turned and looked at the TV set again. The image of the killer in the shopping centre was on the screen. He stared at it for a few moments.

'Right then,' Mick said, facing them again. 'Let's get to work.'

Chapter 25

A car screeched to a stop and blared its horn at Mairéad as she stepped onto the road. She looked up and tried to focus on the car that had stopped inches from her.

'*Get off the fucking road!*' a man screamed out his window at her. He beeped his horn again as he drove off.

Mairéad walked on.

She was so tired, she felt disorientated. She couldn't think of the last time she'd had a proper sleep or eaten anything. How could she eat? How could she sleep?

She clutched the large brown envelope with the ponytail in her arms. She told herself again that she was doing the right thing. She owed it to the families of these victims. They needed to know who had done these things to them. She would want to know if it was her daughter, or her sister.

She hoped that her son would now get the treatment he deserved. They would know how to help him like she never could.

This morning her anger had subsided a little, and her rage at her son had eased just enough for her to see a way to protect him. Protection from himself and from others.

The Garda Station was only a ten minutes' walk from her house. She imagined herself sitting with the detectives and explaining her son's difficulties. Her son's disability. She would show them the ponytail and they would understand his struggles in life. He needed compassion and empathy. Doctors could finally help him. And then the killing would end.

She would be alone forever after this. But she had always been alone. What did it matter anyway at this stage of her life?

The foyer of the Garda Station was quiet and she went straight up to the counter. There was no one at the desk and Mairéad looked around to see if there was a button she was supposed to press. She couldn't see anything, so she knocked timidly at the glass partition.

There were three rows of plastic chairs behind her, with one person seated in each row – all were staring down at their phones. She was about to ask one of them what she should do when a door opened behind the counter, and a female garda came out.

'Yes?' she said.

'I have ... *em* ... I have something here,' Mairéad said, holding up the envelope.

'What is it? Forms?'

'No. Nothing like that. It's ... it's ...' Mairéad searched for the word. 'Evidence.'

'Evidence of what?'

Mairéad looked around at the other people in the waiting area. She didn't want to have this discussion in a public area.

'Can I speak to someone?' she asked.

The female garda didn't hide her impatience. She looked Mairéad up and down.

'Do you want to talk to a detective?' she asked.

Mairéad nodded and attempted a smile of gratitude.

'Take a seat,' the garda said, happy to offload this woman onto someone else, and walked back through the door.

Mairéad did as she'd been instructed. She sat in the front row and placed the envelope on her lap. She kept her head low and didn't make eye contact with anyone.

The entrance doors to her left barged open and two plainclothes officers burst in, with another man sandwiched between them, his arms twisted behind his back. The arrested man had his head down.

Mairéad also looked down to avoid seeing something she wasn't supposed to see.

She saw the black shoes of the detectives go by. In the middle of them was a pair of brown soft leather shoes. Mairéad's eyes widened. They were Conor's shoes. She raised her head and looked at the back of the man who was being dragged towards another locked door.

'Open the door!' one detective called out.

Mairéad put the envelope on the seat beside her and stood up.

Conor?

His hair was like her son's. She walked towards them.

'*Conor?*' she said, out loud this time.

One detective turned back to her.

'Stay where you are, ma'am,' he told her.

The arrested man tried to turn around, but the detective on his left shoved his twisted arm further up his back. The man let out a moan.

'*Don't hurt him!*' Mairéad shouted.

'Ma'am, go back to your chair. This is none of your concern.'

Mairéad reached out.

The prisoner tried to turn around again.

'*Open the door!*' the detective called more loudly.

The prisoner squirmed from side to side, and one detective elbowed him in his ribcage.

He groaned out in pain.

Mairéad was close to them now.

Close enough to hear the detective whisper in his ear, 'If you think that fucking hurt, wait till we get you inside, you prick!'

'*No!*' Mairéad called out. '*Please don't hurt my son!*'

'What the fuck?' the detective said.

The door finally made a loud clang as the magnetic lock opened.

'*My son! Don't hurt him!*'

The detective spun the prisoner around to face Mairéad.

'Is that your mother?' he asked.

Mairéad stared at his face.

'I've no idea who the fuck that old bag is,' the prisoner said, and turned back to the door.

Mairéad stumbled backwards. She could see concern in one detective's face, but he was pulled along with the other two and the door swung shut behind them.

Everyone in the waiting room stared at her. She could feel their eyes on her. She walked back to her chair and looked down at the envelope.

She had made a mistake. These men, these brutes, would never understand her son. These people would only hurt him. Her son needed compassion, not cruelty. Conor had no one in this world but her, and she had been about to take that away from him.

I have failed him. She wanted to cry. I have failed him his entire life.

She picked up the brown envelope and held it to her.

I will never fail him again, she thought. *I will protect him, always.*

The Englishman from the lecture would help her, she reasoned. Horris. Yes, he would cure her son. He would treat him and help him and cure him. He was her only hope now.

Mairéad left the Garda Station and went back to her home. And back to Conor.

Chapter 26

'I think I'll pop across the road for a spot of lunch,' Mick said, as he stood on the last step of Harcourt Street. 'Would you fancy joining me?'

Darcy looked over at the front of the Harcourt Hotel.

'No.'

Darcy felt the awkward silence building momentum between them.

'Enjoy your lunch,' she told him, turning back towards HQ. 'I've something I want to do myself. How about we meet back here after four?'

'OK.'

Darcy forced herself to slow down as she walked back into the building. She couldn't hear Mick's footsteps walking away, but she didn't turn around to see if he was looking at her.

Walking back into the foyer, a woman carrying a brown envelope bumped into her and, without apologising, rushed out the front doors. Darcy watched her before heading for the stairs.

The skipping of her footsteps echoed throughout the stairwell until she pushed open the door into the carpark. She greeted the carpool sergeant, who had barely enough time to look up from his newspaper as she went by.

Her car started on the third try but only after she had banged the steering wheel several times. She pushed it into gear and followed the exit signs, the sergeant looking up from his paper again as her tyres squealed on the concrete floor.

She slowed slightly before reaching the top of the off-ramp. Slipping her hand into her jacket pocket, she took out her phone and glanced at the time on the locked screen.

When she looked up, Mick Kelly was standing six feet from her moving car. She slammed on the brakes, her body jolting forward.

Initial anger at having almost knocked him down turned to anger at his very presence. She watched him slowly walking towards the passenger door. He opened it and bent over so he could peer inside.

'*What the fuck, Mick?*' she yelled at him.

He said nothing for a moment.

Nothing phased this man, she thought. She had to at least give him that.

'And where, may I ask you,' he said, 'are you going in such a hurry?'

'I'm working the case, Mick. That's what I'm doing.'

'Without me?'

'You can't be in two places at the same time, can you? If you want to go and have your ...' she paused, 'lunch, that's fine.'

He stared at her, and she had to force herself not to break eye contact with him.

'Fine then,' he eventually said, tapping his stomach. 'I'll come with you, so. I was thinking of giving that intermittent fasting a go anyway.'

Darcy swallowed down her infuriation as Mick climbed into the passenger seat, but she managed to offer him a smile through clenched jaws.

'What was your plan, then?' he asked her.

'I was going to try to see if I could get Tommy Fay to talk to me. To us.'

Mick raised his eyebrows. 'You mean in Frank Kavanagh's house?'

'Yeah, why not?'

She realised Mick could probably come up with a dozen reasons why not.

'OK,' he said and leaned over to put on his seat belt.

'OK?' she said.

He nodded.

'OK, then,' she repeated and manoeuvred the car out into the Harcourt Street traffic.

Darcy drew up at the front of Frank Kavanagh's house. She looked through the black iron gates towards the house, hidden mostly behind tall leafy trees.

'And they say crime doesn't pay,' Mick said, unsuccessfully trying to hide the bitterness in his tone.

There was an intercom on the wall, and Darcy rolled down her window. She reached out and pushed the button. A bell rang, but nothing happened. She looked at Mick, and he shrugged. She pressed it again.

'*Yes*,' a voice crackled out.

'Gardaí here to see Tommy Fay,' Darcy said.

There was silence for a few moments, then voices in the background.

'Do you have a warrant?' a crackled voice came again.

'No.'

'Then fuck off.'

The connection went dead.

Darcy looked at Mick and he gave her a shrug, as if to say – well, what did you think was going to happen?

'You've met Kavanagh before, right?' Darcy asked Mick.

'A few times.'

'Doesn't he owe you any favours?'

'Frank?' Mick chuckled. 'Frank owes nobody nothin'.'

'Can I try anyway?'

She stretched her arm out again and pressed the buzzer.

'*What?*' a voice said.

'Tell Frank it's Detective Mick Kelly and Detective Darcy Doyle.'

Silence again.

There was a sudden loud buzz, and the tall gates began to open slowly.

'Looks like you're more famous than you think,' she said.

She put the car into gear and drove in. The gravel driveway crunched under her tyres. She spotted several cameras in the trees as they silently moved in their direction, watching them as she drove by. She parked her beat-up unmarked Opel between a black Land Rover with tinted windows and a large dark-grey Mercedes.

They both got out and looked at their battered Opel Astra sandwiched between the other two expensive cars. The thick oak door opened as they stepped onto the porch. A man wearing a tracksuit, who had a black tattoo crawling up from under his T-shirt onto his neck, stepped outside.

'Please raise both your arms so I can search you,' he growled.

'Fuck off!' Mick told him.

Instinctively, the man did what he had done to everyone who'd ever made the mistake of saying those two words to him, including his own father: he grabbed Mick by the collar and lifted him into the air.

As Mick's feet rose off the ground, Darcy removed the retractable metal baton from her jacket and flicked it open to its full length of thirty inches. With one swipe, she smashed it into the man's knee.

'*Oh, you fucking cow!*' he yelled, loosening his grip on Mick.

Mick's feet found the ground as the man fell back holding his knee and crashed up against the open door. Mick watched Darcy step forward, the baton raised again to hit if necessary.

From behind her, Darcy felt a grip on her arm.

She looked around at the tallest and palest man she'd ever seen. His grip seemed metallic, like a robotic hand had clasped her and with one twist could easily snap her arm in two.

She lowered her baton and the man eased his grip, but not before a gun was shoved in his face.

'*Get your fucking hands off her*,' Mick snarled.

Lurch took a step back. His expression remained unchanged. Everybody froze.

'*Whao, whao, whao!*'

Frank Kavanagh walked into the hall, dressed impeccably in a three-piece suit. He had his arms raised in defence. Tommy Fay stood behind him.

'Tell your dogs to back the fuck off,' Mick said, his gaze never leaving Lurch's face.

'Everybody just relax,' Frank said.

Lurch and the gorilla at the door walked back behind Frank.

Darcy stood up. Mick holstered his gun.

'Well, well, well,' Frank said. 'Columbo Kelly. I thought you were retired. Or dead.'

'Frank Kavanagh,' Mick said. 'I hoped you were retired. Or dead.'

Frank smiled at him. His mouth smiled, at least, but his eyes remained impassive.

'And you, Miss Doyle,' Frank said. 'You're very welcome to my humble abode. The cops sure didn't look anything like you in my day. Am I right, Tony?'

Tony was bent over, rubbing his knee, his face contorted in anger at someone having got the better of him physically.

'No, boss.'

'Detectives, Tommy is here to help you in any way he can with catching the perverted scum you're looking for. Shall we make ourselves more comfortable in the sitting room?'

Frank turned and walked back through a door leading from the hall. Tommy, Lurch and Tony the gorilla followed him.

After a few moments, Darcy and Mick followed them.

The room was huge with a view out onto a landscaped garden. Darcy couldn't hide her admiration.

Frank was standing behind a wet bar built into the corner, pouring whiskey into a glass of ice.

'Can I get either of you something to drink?' he offered.

'To be perfectly honest with you, Frank,' Mick told him, 'I'd rather just do what we're here to do and get the fuck out of this house.'

Frank made an exaggerated sad face. 'What? You don't like my house?'

'The house is very nice,' Mick told him, 'considering it was built on the suffering of so many.'

'You're wrong, Mick. This house was bought and paid for by my many business interests: construction, security, a couple of restaurants. I'm what you'd call a successful entrepreneur.'

'Is that what they call it now?' Mick said, almost to himself, and walked over to a set of twenty screens with views of every corner of the property.

Frank watched him.

'Do you like that set-up? Security is very important to me, Mick. It's all high-tech stuff these days. I have a few security firms, you know. I can get you a discount if you like. Oh, I'm sorry. I forgot. She kicked you out of that nice, big house in Dalkey, didn't she? Where are you living now? Some poxy bedsit in the inner city, no doubt.'

Mick didn't react to Frank, but instead viewed the screens. He pointed at the two at the top that showed the front gate. The point of view was from across the road.

'I notice a couple of your cameras are mounted on public road signs,' Mick said before turning to face him. 'I'm sure you've received permission to have them positioned there, because if you don't then they'll all have to come down. It'd be a pity to have to do that, wouldn't it?'

Mick saw Frank's mouth tighten.

'Tommy,' Frank said without losing eye contact with Mick, 'why don't you tell the nice detectives everything you can, so they can go back to doing what they do best … wasting taxpayers' money.'

'A legitimate businessman and you're a taxpayer now as well, Frank?' Mick said as he sat down opposite Tommy. 'I must give the Criminal Assets Bureau a buzz and let them know.'

Darcy joined Mick on the sofa and faced Tommy seated opposite them. He didn't have a face she'd like to meet down a dark alley. His scar seemed swollen as his face was contorted into pure anger. He made no attempt to hide his contempt for them both.

'We're very sorry for your loss,' Darcy told him in as calm and soothing a tone as she could command.

That was as far as any pleasantries were going to go. Darcy had read the file on Tommy Fay. He'd been in and out of Dublin District Children Courts since he was twelve years old, serving multiple sentences in Oberstown Detention Centre. As an adult, he moved on to Mountjoy Prison, always serving longer sentences than he'd initially been given, due to violent offences against other inmates or prison officers. Darcy reckoned that, at thirty-one years old, he'd spent over half his life in prison. Most likely, though, if he hadn't been in prison, he'd already be dead.

'We have several questions we'd like to ask you,' Darcy continued, 'that may help in discovering the killer or killers of your late wife Sinéad.'

Tommy's grimace relaxed slightly at the mention of his wife's name.

'On the day of her ... death, could you please tell us how she spent the hours leading up to that?'

Tommy's eyes glanced over in Frank's direction, as if looking for approval to talk.

'We went to the cinema,' Tommy said, his voice hoarse as if it hadn't been used in days.

'Very good,' Darcy said. 'What cinema was it?'

'Why?' Tommy asked.

'Because it's possible, Mr Fay, that the killer could have stalked you, I mean your wife, in the lead-up to his attack on her.'

Tommy thought about this.

'Liffey Valley,' he told her.

'The time?'

'After twelve.'

'What film did you see?' Darcy asked him.

'I don't know. A comedy or something.'

'You don't remember?'

'No, I left.'

'You left the cinema during the film? On your own or together?'

'On my own.'

'Why?'

'I got a call from ...'

A chair shifted in the background as Frank stood up.

Darcy, Mick and Tommy looked over at him.

'Have you something to add, Mr Kavanagh?' Darcy asked him.

Frank didn't reply.

'I got a call from a mate who needed a lift,' Tommy said.

'And you left your wife at the cinema?'

'Yeah.'

'Alone?'

'Yeah.'

Darcy let that information sink in before responding.

'That's some mate. And are you sure you didn't see anyone following you or your wife at the time?'

'No,' Tommy said impatiently. 'I didn't.'

Darcy looked at Mick. She was sure he was thinking the same thing. Tommy's wife was killed a few hours after that. Could there be a CCTV tape at the cinema with an image of the killer on it? Phoebe had already told them it had been a more impulsive kill than the first one, so that could mean he was careless.

Darcy took a few deep breaths.

'Can you think of any reason,' Darcy asked him, 'why your wife was targeted by the killer?'

Mick couldn't help but raise his eyebrows at this question. There were perhaps a hundred reasons Sinéad Fay could have been killed because of the actions of her husband. This wasn't a road Mick wanted to go down. For now, anyway. It would mean hours and hours of work that would probably lead nowhere.

'No,' Tommy lied.

Darcy nodded.

'Do you have a current photo of Sinéad?' Darcy asked him.

Tommy thought about that. 'On my phone,' he said.

'May we see it?'

Tommy took his phone out of his pocket and unlocked it. He scrolled through a few photos before handing it over.

Darcy took it and looked at the image. Mick leaned over to see it. Sinéad Fay was a strikingly beautiful blonde lady and the similarities to Jennifer Delaney were not lost on either of them.

'Mind if I take a photo of her?' Darcy asked, taking her own phone out.

Tommy shrugged.

After Darcy took a photo, Mick took Tommy's phone and looked more closely at the image. He slid his thumb up onto the screen and flicked it to the left a few times. There were photos of a dark-haired woman naked in the photos. Then a topless, skinny blonde.

Tommy realised what he was doing. '*Give me that fucking thing!*' he snarled and snapped the phone out of his hand.

Mick gave him a smile.

Tommy shoved the phone deep into his pocket. 'Is that it?' he asked.

'Yes, for now,' Darcy told him. She reached into her pocket, pulled out her card and handed it to him. It was several moments before she realised that Tommy had no intention of taking it.

'Very well,' she said, and left it on the table.

'Well, then, if that's everything, folks,' Frank said out, 'allow me to show you off my property.'

Darcy and Mick stood up. Tommy stayed seated, and Darcy looked at him. Now that the focus was off him, the mask of aggression had fallen away, and a look of sadness showed on his face. A real-life Beauty and the Beast story, she thought.

'Detective Doyle,' Frank called out. 'Or may I call you Darcy?'

'No,' she told him.

Frank smiled at this. 'Are you what they call Kelly's protégé? Imagine that, lads. Columbo Kelly, the mentor!'

Tony let out a bellow of a laugh. Lurch remained as stoic as ever.

'Will I tell you about the first time I ever heard of Columbo Kelly, Detective Doyle?' Frank said.

Darcy saw Mick's face harden. It was obviously a story he'd heard before.

'You're OK,' Darcy told him. 'We've a lot to get on with, Mr Kavanagh.'

Frank ignored her. 'Now, this isn't something that happened to me personally or that I was involved with in any way whatsoever, you understand.' He offered her a large smile. 'But I heard about this snitch, Charlie Cleary. He was passing on info to the Guards while he was serving five years in the Joy for possession. He only had six months left, so we … I mean, so they waited for him to get out. He knew he was a marked man and should have fucked off out of the country, but the fucking eejit wanted to stay with his wife. He promised her he'd go straight and all that shite. Anyways, he starts wearing a bulletproof vest under his shirt …'

A woman wearing only her underwear walked into the room. Frank stopped talking and looked at her. Everyone looked at her. She was a tall, attractive brunette and seemed impervious to anyone else in the room.

She walked over to the wet bar, opened a bottle, and poured herself a large measure of gin. She added ice and some tonic water. Then all eyes watched her as she casually left the room, sipping on her drink.

'So anyway, he gets a little braver with the bulletproof vest on, you see,' Frank continued. 'Even occasionally pops down to his local for a few jars. But one night there's a couple of boys waiting for him, shooters at the ready. Superman in his bulletproof vest even stands up to them, thinks he's fucking Clark Kent. The two boys know about the vest, so what do they do? *BANG! BANG!* Two in the head.'

Frank looked for a reaction, but only Tony was laughing.

Maybe he was one of the assassins, Darcy thought to herself.

'They throw him into the back of the car and head up the mountains. They have a spot already picked out and they pull over. Now here's the kick in the bollocks. As they're offloading him, one has him by the legs and one has him by the shoulders when, un-fucking-believable, an unmarked squad car comes up the road. The two boys freeze, not believing their bad luck. And the two dicks freeze, not believing their good luck. And guess who was one of them? None other than Columbo Kelly himself. Some say he was tipped off but, personally, I think he was just lucky. That's what makes Columbo a force to be reckoned with. He's a lucky fucker, and you're always at a disadvantage against those born with luck on their side. Fortunately, I'm one of them myself. Anyway, all hell breaks loose. They drop the body onto the ground and jump back into the car. The coppers jump out after them, but the boys are too quick. They're away and down the road like a hot snot. One of the dicks stays with the body and the other one tears after them. A hot pursuit ensues through the Dublin Mountains. Now, this is not the lads' first rodeo, so they know what they're doing, and flashing blue lights and sirens wailing aren't going to rattle their nerves, as they would many. Plus, the BMW they're driving is a touch faster than a five-year-old Toyota Corolla. Sure, if truth be known, the cops didn't really have much of a chance, and the two boys sailed away into the sunset. They were never caught, but I heard they had a good laugh about it in the pub the next night.'

By now, Tony was chuckling loudly. Darcy couldn't help thinking he was laughing at the memory of it, rather than the story itself. She looked at Mick to see how he reacted to the story. His face gave nothing away.

'I remember that alright,' Mick finally said after the laughter had died down. 'Although I remember Charlie's wife more than I remember him.'

'His wife was a junkie hooker,' Frank told him.

'Maybe,' Mick said. 'Maybe that's what she was when she died, but she wasn't like that when Charlie got out of the Joy.'

'She was a fucking junkie!' Frank told him again, his voice slightly raised.

'No, she wasn't, Frank,' Mick said, pointing a finger at him, the rage palpable in his voice. He took a breath before continuing. 'You know how I know?'

Frank didn't reply.

'Because I was the one that Charlie was spilling the beans to while he was in the Joy.'

'You fucking liar!' Frank said.

Mick just smiled and shook his head. 'I was driving up the mountains that night because I was looking for him. An eyewitness in the pub car park had called it in, and I knew where to go looking for his body.'

Again, Frank said nothing.

'And you know why Charlie was ratting you out? It wasn't in the hope of earning a Get Out of Jail Free card. It was so his missus would be looked after. By us. He never really cared for his own safety. He knew he was fucked either way. *That's* why he didn't run.'

Mick looked over at Tommy on the sofa.

'It seems,' he said, 'that even lowlife dealers still make the mistake of falling in love just like the rest of us.'

Mick walked up to the bar and then went behind it. He took down a bottle of Bushmills whiskey and poured himself a generous glass. He held it up to the light and then put it down on the counter.

'To be honest, Detective Doyle,' he said, looking at Darcy, 'I probably wouldn't have told you the rest of Mr Kavanagh's story but, since we're all here, chit-chatting about the old days …'

Tony stood up, but Frank raised his hand for him to sit back down.

Mick ignored them both.

'I had just finished my shift. It was about a month after Charlie had been killed. A call came into the station. There was a bad smell coming from an abandoned apartment that I knew Charlie and his wife had hung out in a few times. I had done the rounds all week looking for her, the usual places, but no one had seen her. She was using again, that I knew. She'd been clean for five years while Charlie was away, but she fell apart after his funeral, the poor cow. She went from depression to heroin in a matter of hours. It's an easy enough path to follow once you've been down it a few times already. So, I head over with a couple of uniforms, and we break the door down. Junkie, bad smell, person not being seen, even a rookie uniform can put that one together. We found her in the bedroom. She'd put a plastic shopping bag around her head and duct-taped it tight on her neck. She was weak, so the forensics said she probably died in less than two minutes. Now, here's the real kick in the bollox. A maggot or an egg must have been inside the bag. A normal head weighs about ten or eleven pounds. The brain itself weighs about three on its own. Even being a junkie, that's a lot of meat for one little maggot. Leave that alone for a week, and you get a bag stuffed with millions of the little fuckers. Eggs, maggots, flies. All duct-taped around her neck. It sounded like a little motorbike was going off in the bag. Like a giant, black balloon on her shoulders, resting on top of her emaciated body. I'm not ashamed to admit it, but it was the only time I puked my ring up at a crime scene. In fairness though, all three of us did. People think it's the shock of seeing a mutilated body that makes you vomit. But it's never that. It's the smell.'

Mick looked down at the glass of whiskey in front of him. He lifted it to his nose and inhaled the fumes. Then he placed it on the bar and touched its rim as if touching an old photograph of a distant friend.

Darcy stood up.

Mick looked up from the glass and followed her out of the room.

Chapter 27

Tony pressed the remote fob for the wide iron gates to open and watched Darcy and Mick drive out. He dawdled out onto the road after them and then watched them turn the corner in the distance.

Tony was Frank's longest serving and most trusted personal bodyguard. He had spent most of his youth bullied by older boys for being both the fattest and the poorest kid in the school. It was only in his final year that he realised he had become taller and stronger than anyone else, including the teachers.

One lunchtime, outside a food truck that sold junk food to the kids on their break, three big lads started pushing him. They weren't looking for money or food or cigarettes. They were just looking for some fun. Something to pass the time.

Tony couldn't tell why that day was different from any other. He didn't even get angry. All he knew was that he felt tired. Tired of the accumulated abuse. Tired of the belittling and the humiliation. It was as if over all those years a giant jar of hatred had filled and filled, and today there was simply no more room and it had just spilled over.

Tony broke the first guy's jaw in two places with the same effort it took him to swat a fly. As the second boy looked on in horror at his friend reeling with pain, Tony punched him square in the face and broke his nose. The sight of the blood sent the third boy running backwards, but he was unfortunate enough to trip and fall. Although the guy had the sense to put his hands up to protect his face, Tony kicked him hard in the balls. He screamed the loudest of all three.

Tony was suspended for two weeks but when he came back, he systematically began to terrorise anyone who crossed his path. It could even be said that he forgave those other bullies, as he now genuinely saw the attraction to being a bully himself. He would have been expelled if it weren't for the fact that the principal himself feared some form of retribution. Those final six months were perhaps the happiest days of his life.

A few years later, a couple of bouncers tried to throw him out of a bar, and he knocked them unconscious. The bar belonged to Frank Kavanagh, and Tony was summoned to explain himself. As fearless as Tony was, he knew better than to refuse a summons from Frank Kavanagh.

But instead of punishing him, Frank saw Tony's 'talent' for callous violence and offered him a job. Over the next ten years, Tony became his closest minder, and Tony's presence in any part of the city was as feared as if Frank himself were present.

It was an unusually warm late afternoon as Tony watched Darcy's car drive out of sight.

At first Tony thought that the figure who climbed out from the bushes on the other side of the road was a golfer from the golf course that surrounded most of Frank's house, and that perhaps he'd strayed too far in search of a lost ball. Tony's second thought, as he watched him cross the road towards him, was that he wasn't a golfer at all. To be fair, though, Tony wasn't that familiar with the nuances and traits of a skilfully crafted game of golf, but he could spot a worthless junkie from a mile away.

A name popped into his head that matched the emaciated face as it came closer to where he stood.

'Mark fucking Dunne!' Tony said and smiled like a bulldog that had just spotted a wounded cat.

'Tony, I need to see Frank,' Mark said, stumbling across the road.

Tony knew enough of Frank's business to know that Mark Dunne should not be walking around Dublin, let alone on the road in front of Frank's house.

'I know what you're thinking, Tony, and I know I'm not supposed to be here, but I have to see Frank and let him know what's happened. And what I saw. I've tried to call him a few times, but he didn't answer.'

'Why didn't you just knock on the front door, then?' Tony asked.

'Because I saw the coppers. I had to wait for them to leave. Just tell him I know about Sinéad. He has to listen to me. Jesus Christ, man. It was awful!'

The smile fell from Tony's face. 'Now, what would a smackhead like you know about Sinéad Fay that'd be of any use to the likes of Frank?'

'I saw it happen, man. I swear. I couldn't do anything, though. You have to tell him that. You have to believe me. I puked my guts up. I saw who done it.'

'You're a fucking liar.'

'I'm not lying to you. I swear on my ma's life. Sinéad said she'd meet me and give me few quid to get out of Dublin for a while. I was waiting for her. I don't want Tommy thinking it was my fault though.'

'You're a liar like every poxy junkie in this city.'

'Honest to God, Tony. I saw it happen, and I saw who done it. I heard her scream. I saw the man following her into the park. I thought he was one of Frank's men, so I waited outside. If I'd have known what was going to happen – Jesus! What he was going to do to her. I swear to God, Tony. I even called the cops to help her, but it was too late.'

Tony said nothing.

'I followed him,' Mark said, calming himself a little. 'I followed the man afterwards. I saw him come out of the park. He had on a long coat. I know where he lives.'

Tony looked up and down the road.

'OK,' he said, taking his own phone out. 'Here, take this. You tell him yourself. He'll answer this phone.'

Mark stared at the phone in Tony's hand. He too looked up and down the road but saw no one.

'Go on,' Tony encouraged him. 'Talk to him and arrange something with him. I'm sure he can meet you somewhere.'

With his mind made up, Mark pocketed his own phone and took two steps forward, reaching out for Tony's left hand. Tony stepped to the side and with his free right hand punched Mark hard behind the ear – a classic unexpected punch that he had learned in his earlier years. The smack reverberated through the skull and jolted the cerebellum of Mark's brain enough to make his eyes roll into the back of his head. He began to swoon, but Tony caught him in time and hoisted him over his shoulder.

Mark's phone fell out onto the road. Tony looked at it and thought about leaving it there, but then squatted down, picked it up and slipped it back into Mark's jacket pocket.

He glanced up and down the road as he turned and marched back towards the house, the weight of Mark Dunne on his shoulder barely noticeable to him. He pressed the remote fob, and the wide iron gates, like the leaves of a Venus fly trap, closed behind him.

Chapter 28

Reeds Bookstore on Nassau Street was not Horris's first choice for his book signing. He had asked for the larger Eason store on Dublin's main thoroughfare, O'Connell Street, but had been told by his publishers that the smaller Reeds would be more 'fitting'.

They had been right.

Despite several radio and press interviews over two days, it had been a poorly attended event that had only further helped exasperate his working relationship with his publicist Tamila.

'And to whom should I dedicate this book?' Horris asked, seated behind a large table with copies of his book arranged neatly in piles. Of course, he recognised the girl immediately from his lecture two nights before – the Greek goddess in the second row.

She had waited to be one of the last in the hope of having some private time with him. And she was almost the last, except for that dodgy-looking woman who seemed intent on being last to speak to him.

'Samantha,' she told him.

'Well, Samantha, I hope you enjoyed the talk the other day.'

'I certainly did, Dr Horris. It was simply fascinating. But I have so many more questions.'

Horris looked up at her. His eyes shamelessly studied her body for several moments, then he wrote a note in her book: *The Chesterfield Hotel. Room 310. 10pm x*

'I'm always available to help develop any enthusiastic young mind,' he told her as he handed back the book.

Tamila turned her head away in both embarrassment and annoyance.

Samantha opened the book and read Horris's note. Her smile broadened. She held the book against her ample chest, then turned and skipped away.

Horris watched her leave, like a ravenous tiger eyeing a wounded deer.

As she left, he caught sight again of the woman at the back of the room. Now that he was alone with Tamila, the woman walked towards him. He was sure that she was the woman who had asked the final question in his lecture.

He could think of no reason for it, but he felt his heart beat faster as she approached the table.

'Good evening,' he said to her.

Tamila was watching.

'Hello,' Mairéad said.

Horris stirred in his seat.

'Did you want me to sign a book for you?' he asked.

Mairéad looked down at her empty hands as if searching for something that wasn't there. Seeing the stack of hardback books on the table, she reached down and picked one up, then stared at it as if unsure what it was.

'It's OK,' Tamila told her and stepped forward. 'You don't need to buy a book.'

Horris grunted. 'I see little point in me being here if no one buys any books.'

'*Shhh*,' Tamila told him, putting her hand on Mairéad's arm. 'It's OK,' she said to Mairéad. 'Was there something specific you wanted to ask?'

Mairéad nodded at Tamila.

Horris let out a loud sigh.

'Yes, there was. I mean, there is.'

'Go ahead,' Tamila told her. 'You can ask your question.'

Mairéad swallowed. 'It's my son,' she said.

'Your son?' Tamila said.

'Yes.'

'Do you think Dr Horris could help him?'

Mairéad nodded again.

'I'm afraid that I don't do private –' Horris began, but Tamila quieted him again by raising her hand.

'What sort of help do you think your son needs?' she asked.

Mairéad looked behind her. It was just the three of them now. The cashier was busy on her phone and the security man was in the distance, peering out onto Nassau Street.

Mairéad leaned forward. Tamila leaned towards her. Even Horris leaned across the table to hear her.

'I think my son is a serial killer.'

'I'm not sure,' Horris said. 'Meeting a possible serial killer outside of a safe clinical environment is beyond abnormal. Maybe we should postpone any meeting until such a time that a suitable –'

Tamila grabbed him by the arm. 'Are you out of your fucking mind?' she said. 'This opportunity could be a career-defining moment for you.'

They had both sat with Mairéad for thirty minutes while she explained everything about Conor, his comings and goings, her suspicions, and their family history and, of course, the discovery of the blonde ponytail.

Despite Horris's misgivings, Tamila arranged for them both to meet Mairéad and her second son, Liam, in the National Gallery of Ireland across from their hotel.

'There's a Jackson Pollock exhibition tonight,' Tamila had told her. 'I was there last night. It was quiet. I'm sure there'll only be a few people there. And they say it's going to rain for the rest of the evening. We could meet there at, say, 8 o'clock? There's a café in the gallery. It opens late. We could meet you both there. OK?'

Mairéad had smiled for the first time and walked out of the room as if all her prayers had been answered.

'I actually have an appointment at ten,' Horris told Tamila.

'What? With that little girl you were gawking at all evening? Give me a break. You can keep your erection in your trousers for a couple of hours till this is all over.'

'If we make it out with our lives, you idiot! Think about it for a second,' Horris said, his face growing redder. 'We're going to meet the mother of a potential murderer. This may be some personal vendetta against me. He could have forced her to do this. You could see how nervous she was. She could barely talk for chrissakes.'

'That's why I arranged to meet her in a public place along with her hopefully sane other son.'

Horris threw up his arms in exasperation.

'Look,' she said. 'Don't you see? This could be the big one. *Your* big one.'

'What are you talking about?'

'I'm talking about the big bucks. The talk shows. A number one bestseller. I'm talking about a movie deal. Netflix. Who knows?'

'What?'

'Listen to me,' she said.

'No. You're as bat-shit crazy as she is!'

'Fucking listen to me for a minute!'

Horris folded his arms across his chest, but he was listening.

Tamila took a breath and spoke slowly. 'Think about this. Serial killer expert meets serial killer. Befriends him. Makes him see the error of his ways. Reforms his behaviour. Think of the possibilities, Austin. You'd be revered by not only your peers, but you'll be hailed as a hero to the public.'

Horris sat staring at her.

'And what's in it for you?' he asked.

'Thirty percent. And I'll even come with you.'

Horris looked out onto the same damp grey street that the security man at the door stared at. He wondered what the man was thinking about.

'Look, I'll be honest with you,' Tamila said, taking her coat. 'I shouldn't tell you this, but if this book isn't a big hit, and right now the numbers aren't great, then they're going to drop you.'

'*What?*'

Tamila just shrugged.

'Simon said that?' Horris asked.

'It's not up to Simon anymore.' Tamila had her coat on now. 'It's your choice,' she told him as she made her way to the exit.

He watched her squeeze by the security man, open her umbrella and walk up the street. She didn't even glance at him as she walked by.

It was then that he realised that Mairéad had left with a copy of his book without even having paid for it. Horris slammed his fist down onto the table.

Chapter 29

Darcy punched the bag hard with her right fist. Twenty minutes into her workout, she was already feeling tired, but that only forced her to work harder. She gave a right-side kick to the bag, then switched to her left foot. Over and over, she kicked the bag. *SMACK. SMACK. SMACK.* Some men stopped to watch her for a few moments before returning to their own workouts.

'You're late,' a voice said beside her, as she stopped to take a breath.

Amos Levy, her personal trainer, stood at her side.

'Work,' was her succinct reply.

Originally from Israel, Amos had come to Ireland during his one-year-around-Europe trip. Upon completion of his mandatory three-year army conscription, he had worked almost every day in a chicken farm on a kibbutz for eighteen months to save enough money for his trip.

The longest he had stayed in any one country was Germany – four weeks. The least amount of time was Switzerland – four hours. His last port of call was on the edge of Europe – Ireland. After hostelling along the West Coast, getting soaked in the rain, and then drying in front of a warm turf fire in a pub with a pint of cold Guinness in his hand, he felt as if he'd found the real land of milk and honey.

Then he met a redheaded Irish girl in a bar in Galway. She was being thrown out by a bouncer for being drunk. He was the bouncer. He calmed her down outside and offered her a cigarette. They spoke for over an hour and then met the following night.

A three-month sex-driven meteoric relationship, which culminated in a Registry Office marriage, crashed six months later in a tiny Dublin apartment situated across the road from a noisy pub and a busy gym. On the positive side, he ended up with a resident's visa that allowed him to stay and work in Ireland. What she benefited from the stormy, albeit passionate, marriage was anyone's guess.

She went back to Galway, and he walked across the road to the pub. Every night, after work, he sat at the bar downing pints of the black stuff until he spoke English with a slight inner-city Dublin accent. One evening when getting dressed to go to the pub, he couldn't close the upper button of his jeans. He removed his shirt and then the rest of his clothes and looked at himself naked for the first time in a long time.

It wasn't a pretty sight. He sat back on the bed and rubbed his protruding belly with his hand. He wasn't sure how long he sat there, but when he got up he rooted out an old tracksuit bottom and a T-shirt. Instead of walking into the pub, he went next door and joined the gym.

A year later, he was unrecognisable to older friends. Since he spent so much time in the gym anyway, they suggested that he become a personal trainer. That was four years ago, and two years since he started his own gym.

Amos Levy had a crush on Darcy from the first day he met her. It had never gone away, but she had used the terms 'my boyfriend said that …' or 'my boyfriend and I …' enough times for him to take the hint. He also never asked her out for fear of things becoming awkward between them, and her then moving to another gym.

'Come on,' he told her. 'The ring is free. Let's go a few rounds.'

He noticed her hesitation before she fell in behind him. He climbed up into the ring and lifted the ropes for her.

The boxing gym was in the basement of a multi-level car park five minutes from her home. Amos had acquired a ten-year lease when it sat under an abandoned warehouse. The new owners demolished the warehouse to build the car park, assuming Amos would leave. They assumed wrong. The room still had many of the old brass features when it was a clothing factory sixty-years ago, with some memories from its staff engraved on the walls.

There was some newer equipment, kettlebells and kick bags, but just as popular were the tractor tyres and the empty kegs of beer. It was ice cold in the winter and oven-hot in the summer. Anyone who joined whenever the gym was written about as a trendy hardcore gym quickly left after a few weeks, but it had enough regular members for Amos to pay the bills.

Darcy kicked Amos's punch pads, following through with several roundhouse punches. She grew tired quickly and held up her hands.

'I'm sorry,' she told him, bent over, her hands on her knees. 'Early start and a long day.'

'No problem,' he told her. 'Let's pick it back up tomorrow. Everyone needs a break now and then. Even you, Darcy Doyle.'

She fist-bumped him with her glove, ducked under the ropes and headed for the changing room, all the time aware of Amos's eyes on her as she left.

Darcy had just pulled away from the gym when her phone rang. She smiled at the predictability and persistence of Jamie as she took out her phone but was surprised to see a number she didn't recognise.

'Hello?' she said.

'Hi. Detective Doyle?' a woman's voice said. 'Darcy?'

'Yes. Who's this?'

'It's Fifi. Did I catch you at a bad time?'

'No, not at all, Fifi. Is everything OK?'

'Yes, yes, everything's OK.'

'So, what can I do for you, Fifi?'

'Are you driving?'

'Yes.'

'How about dropping in to see me? I'm at home, but I'm not too far out of the city.'

Darcy paused, not sure she had time or even wanted a social visit. Then, again, perhaps it had something to do with the case.

'Unless you've other plans?' Phoebe said.

'No. I was only heading home.'

'OK, great. Here's my address.'

Darcy memorised the address and then hung up the phone. She looked at the blank screen, still surprised that Jamie hadn't called or even texted at his usual time and was even more surprised to realise that she had been looking forward to it. Then she turned the car around and headed for Phoebe's home in Stoneybatter.

Chapter 30

A cluster of several hundred cramped houses, Stoneybatter was wedged in, like an elbow joint, between the Phoenix Park, the River Liffey and the North Circular Road. It was built at the start of the last century for a cavalry regiment of the British Army, but now mostly housed small families in small rooms with smaller gardens.

Darcy parked the car a block away from Phoebe's address. She found the house, Number 221, and rang the doorbell. It was opened immediately by a skinny girl of about eight years of age with light-brown skin and big dark eyes, her head awash with thousands of bubbly brown curls that cascaded across her face.

'Oh, hello,' Darcy said.

The brightness from the hall lights and loud music, something by Christy Moore, she guessed, poured out onto the empty street.

'I'm Bessie,' the girl said.

'I'm not sure if I'm in the right house,' Darcy said, trying to peer behind the girl and down the hall.

Then Phoebe appeared, holding a pot in one hand and a large wooden spoon in the other.

'Darcy! Come in, come in.'

Darcy looked down at Bessie, as if waiting on her approval to enter. Bessie stepped to the side and Darcy walked in.

The music was even louder when the front door closed. It was a fast, traditional song. The sitting room was to her right, and she looked in. There was an unlit stove fire, a worn but cosy-looking sofa and a bookshelf. Paintings of various sizes and all obviously originals decorated every inch of every wall.

She peered down at Bessie who was staring up at her, not breaking eye contact. Darcy felt self-conscious under her gaze. She smiled, but the girl did not reciprocate.

'*Turn off that music!*' Phoebe yelled.

Bessie jumped with fright and ran into the sitting room. The music stopped as Phoebe appeared again.

'Come on through,' she beckoned, still holding the spoon.

The end of the hall opened into a kitchen with a wooden dining table at its centre and a short but wide living room. A glass patio door looked out into a small, neat garden that was lit by several wall lamps and that gave a more spacious feeling than Darcy would have imagined there.

As she entered further into the room, a man stood up. He had been lying on the living-room floor among a heap of cushions. He was tall and thin, like his daughter, Bessie, and had a messy flop of hair and a grey speckled beard. Darcy thought she recognised him, but then that was true for most handsome men – they emit a sort of inviting familiarity.

She was about to say hello when she saw the little boy at his side. He hid behind his father's leg as Darcy approached, smiling at him.

'Hi,' the man said, an easy smile appearing on his face. 'I'm Peter.' He looked down at the boy. 'And this little fella is Art.'

'Hello, Art,' Darcy said, looking down at him. 'Nice to meet you.'

Peter took a step forward and extended his hand, which Darcy shook. He had green eyes and again Darcy thought she recognised him.

'Mummy,' Bessie said, appearing from nowhere at Darcy's side, 'is this the pretty new detective you were talking about?'

'Bessie!' Phoebe said. 'What have I told you about repeating home conversations? Sorry about that, Darcy.'

'Not at all. I'm sure you could have said something a lot worse!'

'I'm sorry too,' Bessie said. 'I'm an extrovert like Daddy, but Art is an introvert like Mummy, so it's not completely my fault.'

Darcy laughed.

'We're about to eat,' Phoebe said. 'Why don't you join us for dinner?'

'Oh God, no!' Darcy blurted out too quickly. 'But thank you. I'm still in my gear from the gym and, besides, I've eaten mostly plant-based for years, so I don't eat a lot of typical dinners, I'm afraid.'

'That's no problem at all. Bessie here, much to our consternation, went vegetarian last year. We try our best to accommodate her. Although she has been known to cave in for some fish and chips at the seaside. This evening is her favourite though: Quorn mince and spaghetti.'

Darcy glanced at the door and wondered how she had suddenly gone from a sweaty gym to finding herself invited to a family dinner. She felt a small hand take hers and looked down to see Bessie looking up at her. Her touch eased Darcy, and she allowed herself to relax.

'OK,' she said. 'Thank you.'

'Great,' Phoebe said as Bessie led her to the table. 'Sorry for throwing you in at the deep end, Darcy. I'm sure you imagined me as a spinster living alone in some perfect little house, all pristine and clean surfaces, and no TV.'

'Actually,' Darcy said, 'I think that describes my house exactly.'

Phoebe stopped, unsure whether she'd offended her guest, and threw her husband a look.

Bessie, happy not to have been the only one to make a *faux pas*, blurted out, 'Awkward!' and they all laughed.

After dinner, and at the end of a conversation between Bessie and her mother as to why Bessie couldn't get a tattoo of a dolphin on her shoulder just like her favourite YouTuber, Peter stood up and told the children it was way past their bedtime. Bessie and Art duly kissed their mother goodnight and then were heard scampering up the wooden stairs as Peter shook Darcy's hand again and told her he was pleased to meet her. She thought again that she had met him somewhere before and hoped it wasn't someone she had arrested back in her uniformed days.

'You're a lucky woman,' Darcy said as she and Phoebe listened to the babble of her children's bedtime routine upstairs.

'I know,' she said, smiling.

'Is it hard, you know, dealing with the victims and then coming home to a house so full of life and so full of ... innocence, I suppose?'

'I think it makes me enjoy my children more,' Phoebe said. 'But the victims themselves become something like a friend to you, in a way.'

'Really?'

'Sort of. They're the ones who have all the answers to your questions. During a case, you need to pay more attention to them than to anyone else. You need to find out everything about their life. It's a strange intimate relationship, and yet they'll only ever be a dead body lying in a room, but they may also be the only witness to whatever horrific thing happened to them. In many ways, I feel as though I work for them. That they're my boss. Does that sound silly?'

'Not at all. I know how you feel.'

They heard Bessie shout, 'I *am* brushing them properly,' and they both smiled.

'And what about you?' Phoebe asked.

'You mean a husband?'

'Or a family?'

'No, it's just me. I was fostered by different families. But the good ones were too short, and the bad ones went on for way too long.'

Phoebe said nothing.

'When you're a child, though,' Darcy continued, 'you don't realise how bad it is.'

'So how bad was it?'

'I knew that I wasn't like most of the kids I went to school with. I knew that their parents didn't want me playing with their own little darling bullies, and I certainly knew I was struggling.'

'I'm sorry,' Phoebe said.

'Apologies are only when there's someone to blame or take responsibility,' Darcy fought against the bitterness in her tone, 'and I'm not so sure there is anyone. Not anymore, anyway.'

Darcy looked at all the leftover food on the table, untouched and unwanted.

'All I wanted for a long time was for someone to say that what actually happened did happen. That it was all real, and that I actually experienced it all.'

'Are you OK?' Phoebe asked her.

Darcy had been asked that question many times in her life. *Are you OK? Are you OK?* It was a bullshit question.

'Yes, I'm fine. I'm just very tired.'

'And what about now?' Phoebe asked her. 'I should tell you that I know about you and Seán Murphy.'

'Oh!' Darcy was startled. 'Well, a lot of people think they know about me and Seán, but they don't really. They hear rumours. And cops love rumours like kids love lollipops.'

'I'm sorry if I've offended you,' Phoebe said.

'No, you haven't. It's just seeing you with your kids and your husband and how normal you all are – I suppose it makes me realise how *not* normal my life is.'

'We're not that normal,' Phoebe laughed. 'I'm black, he's white. I'm a scientist, he's an actor. Our kids are insane.'

Darcy smiled and felt the tension leave her. 'Well, you're more normal than I'm used to, that's for sure.'

Phoebe let that hang in the air.

Darcy looked out into their little garden.

'You know, I visit him every day. Seán, I mean. I do try to make an effort with him, and I do still love him. But every day it gets harder, and every day I dread the thought of going back into that hospital just a little more. It's just that …'

Darcy stopped talking and took a deep breath.

'I'm sorry,' Phoebe said. 'I can't imagine how hard it is for you to see him like that.'

'It is, but that's not what upsets me. I haven't been able to even start to deal with that yet.'

'What is it then?'

Darcy looked straight at Phoebe. 'He doesn't want me.'

'What do you mean?'

'I mean, when I visit him, he never looks at me. When I try to talk to him, he just turns away.'

'I thought he still couldn't speak.'

'It doesn't take words to see that he doesn't want me. He reacts well to his parents, God help them. He responds to the nurses, but he shuts down whenever I arrive. He's angry at me, and he has every right to be. I don't know if you know ... and I don't want to go into it ... but it was my fault he was shot.'

Phoebe thought about that. She looked up at the ceiling.

Darcy looked out into the garden. The clamouring of the children had ended, and they could hear the murmur of Peter singing them a lullaby, and they listened to him for a while.

'You know,' Phoebe said, 'if I were in Seán's position and it was just Peter and me, and not the kids, I'd want him to forget about me. I wouldn't want him to have that life. Not with me, anyway. I think I'd shut down on him, too. It would be the only way I could set him free.'

Darcy looked at her. 'I'm sorry,' she said. 'I'm not usually this open. You have a nice way about you, Doctor.'

'*Nah*,' Phoebe said. 'It's probably just the Quorn.'

They both laughed.

'I need to get going,' Darcy told her, looking at her Garmin watch.

Phoebe straightened up in her seat and stretched.

Darcy's phone beeped in her pocket. She took it out and looked at the screen and then let out a sigh.

'Bad news?' Phoebe asked.

'No. Sorry. It's just someone.'

Phoebe smiled and raised her eyebrows. 'Just someone?'

'Someone very persistent,' Darcy said. 'A colleague.'

'Anyone I know?'

'I doubt it.'

'Try me. I've worked with a lot of detectives.'

'He's not a detective.'

'A uniform?'

'God, no. He's ERU.'

'I've heard that they even have names sometimes.'

Darcy smiled. 'Jamie.'

Phoebe thought about this. 'Jamie. Jamie. Not Jamie Keane, is it?'

'Yeah, you know him?'

Phoebe let out a deep breath. 'Who on the force hasn't heard of Jamie Keane from the ERU? Most of them wouldn't mind getting a late-night text from him. At least the female members, anyway. And probably a few male members. If you pardon the pun.'

She burst out laughing at her own joke, and Darcy couldn't help joining in.

'*Wow!*' Phoebe said. 'Jamie Keane, *eh*?'

'Oh, he's very keen alright,' Darcy said, and they both had a fit of laughter again. 'Mick calls him Captain America.'

Ten minutes later, at the front door, Darcy turned to say goodbye, and Phoebe gave her a hug. Although it surprised her, it felt natural.

'Where are you parked?' Phoebe asked, yawning loudly.

'On the next street.'

'OK, goodnight then. Thanks for dropping by.'

Darcy walked away but then turned back.

'Everything OK?' Phoebe asked.

'It's just ... you know, I thought you'd called me over to discuss the case, and I ended up talking about myself the whole time. I'm sorry. We should have just talked on the phone. It would have been a lot less time-consuming for you.'

'It's never time-consuming to spend it with friends, Detective Darcy Doyle. It's what time was invented for.'

Darcy didn't know what to say to that, so she just walked back to her car, her footsteps echoing in the chilly night between the rows of houses.

Chapter 31

After a shower, Darcy walked around her house in her pyjamas, turning off all the lights. It was eleven and already past her normal bedtime.

The rain was coming down with a vengeance, as if trying to make up for its two days of abstinence. The soaked square outside her window looked like the setting of a film noir from the Hollywood fifties. Like always, whenever it rained heavily at night, she thought of the homeless on the streets of Dublin. She had walked that beat in a uniform many a night and knew that it added only further misery to their already miserable lives.

Then she thought of Seán, and she wondered if he was awake and lying in his hospital bed, and if he were thinking of her as she thought of him.

She picked up a novel called *The Lost Children*, a recent nominee for the Booker Prize. She had been taking it to bed for the last month, falling asleep after a page or two. At 609 pages, it was going to be a long read. Sometimes she wished she'd just bought the latest easy-read thriller she'd seen in the bookshop, but she felt like she'd be letting someone down if she'd done that. Who exactly that someone was, however, was unclear.

As she walked into her bedroom, the doorbell rang. She stopped and looked at the door. It rang again, followed by knocking.

The urgency of the knocks put her on edge, and she stepped quickly into her bedroom and pulled out the small gun safe from under the bed.

She removed her gun, checked it was loaded and the safety was on, and then approached the door.

She looked out her window, but the figure was pressed into the door so she couldn't identify who it was. She looked through the spyhole but the person's upper body was blocking her view. A tall man, then.

'*Who is it?*' she called out.

'It's me! Open up.'

'Jamie?'

'Open the door, Darcy. I'm soaked.'

She pulled at the locks and opened the door. He wasn't lying. Jamie was soaked from head to toe. He rushed past her and into the bathroom.

'OK if I grab a towel?' he called out.

She went into the bedroom to put her gun away. When she came out Jamie's head was covered by a large white towel. He continued to dry his face and hair as Darcy stood looking at him.

When he was finished, he handed the crumpled and damp towel to her, smiling. Her expression was obviously not the one he had expected. The smile fell quickly from his face.

'What are you doing here?' she asked him.

'I'm sorry. I just finished work and thought it'd be OK to call over. I did text you but there was no answer. I know, I should have phoned.'

Darcy didn't say anything.

'I can go if you'd prefer?'

The look on his face reminded her of a scolded, damp dog who'd been caught chewing a garden hose, and she was forced to smile at the image.

'No, no,' she told him. 'Don't be silly. But I'm tired, and I was just about to go to bed.'

'Even better,' he told her, his voice a lot more cheerful.

'To sleep.'

'Fine, I can tell you tomorrow.'

'Tell me what tomorrow?'

'Oh, but I thought you were tired and about to go to bed,' he teased.

Bastard, Darcy thought, but didn't say it.

'OK, tell me and then go,' she said.

'No probs. Mind if I make a quick coffee?'

'Help yourself. You must be the only person in the world who drinks coffee before bed.'

He walked into the small kitchenette and opened the cupboard to find the coffee.

'So, what news have you got?' Darcy shouted to him.

'Just something about Mick, that's all,' he said, coming out of the kitchenette.

'What did you find out? Don't tell me. He used to be a woman in a previous life.' She laughed nervously.

The kettle popped, and Jamie went back to making his coffee.

Darcy let out a sigh. In her eagerness to do a background check on Mick, she was beginning to regret getting Jamie involved. The thought of the shoe being on the other foot and Mick asking someone to do a background check on her made her shudder. She listened to the spoon clanging off the side of his cup and hoped he wasn't making a mess. He came back into the living area, plopped down on the sofa and put his cup down on a side table.

Darcy got out of her chair and put a coaster under his coffee cup.

'So,' she said. 'What have you got?'

He sipped his coffee, taking his time as he looked around the room. He was obviously enjoying letting her wait. Darcy knew it was unusual for him to have the upper hand with her, and she sensed he was savouring it.

She bit on a nail. 'Why are the only paintings in your house of Dublin Bay?'

'Just get on with it, Jamie. Please. I'm tired.'

'OK. I asked around this morning about your Columbo Kelly,' he said, taking another mouthful of coffee. He looked at the cup. 'What coffee brand is this?'

'Jesus fucking Christ, Jamie! Just tell me what you heard.'

'OK, OK,' he said and placed the cup back down, on the coaster this time. 'Seems like your boy was a sort of Rambo in his day,' Jamie began.

'The poet or the soldier?'

'Poet?'

'Sorry, nothing. Go on.'

'OK. So, it looks like he had detection rates through the roof. And not just a few lucky breaks either, but for over a decade. Even had a couple of attempts on his life. From what I'm told, he was quite the crusader when he was in his thirties and forties.'

Darcy had suspected something like that. She tried to imagine him in his thirties, lean and fit and working a case, but the image just wouldn't come to her.

'So, what happened?' she asked him.

'He was one of those cops that just couldn't let go of a case. You know the way they say that every detective has one case that haunts them forever, even in their retirement? One case that gets too personal and under their skin. Well, that's how Columbo Kelly worked on *every* case. So anyway, one day, the SCMU (Sexual Crime Management Unit) asks Mick and his partner, a guy named Flynn, for their help on a persistent child-abuse case. The case had a litany of child victims who had suffered serious sexual abuse by seemingly the same perpetrator. Apparently, every time the investigators got close to him, he'd disappear. This had been going on for about a year. Mick had always been fond of the gargle, but it was about that time that he really started to drink. I don't know how those guys in child-abuse crime do it. Anyway, Mick starts working the case and makes good progress but, again, twice when he thought he had the paedo, the guy was gone. Then, after about two months, Mick arranges to meet his partner Flynn in a disused warehouse. Tells him he's got a tip as to the identity of the sex offender. When Flynn turns up, Mick takes out a hurley from his car and pretty much beats him to within an inch of his life.'

Darcy sat up in her chair, an astonished look on her face.

Jamie was happy with that reaction from her. He took a moment to sip his coffee.

'He was the offender?' Darcy asked.

'No.'

Darcy thought about it. 'He was tipping off the offender,' she said.

Jamie couldn't hide the disappointment on his face.

'But why?' she asked.

Jamie put his cup back down before answering, but Darcy beat him to the punch line.

'He was a watcher,' she said, more to herself than to Jamie. 'He liked to watch. So, he tipped off the sex offender in exchange for his own voyeuristic gratification.'

Jamie let out a sigh like a deflated balloon.

'So, what happened?' Darcy asked. 'If Mick is still in the force, then they must have cut a deal with him.'

'Yeah,' Jamie confirmed. 'They told Flynn that if he didn't press charges against Mick, they'd let him away with a dishonourable discharge.'

'And Mick agreed to that?'

'No. But it wasn't about Mick at that stage. The government was involved. The Department of Justice didn't want the case all over the media. Said it would do irreparable damage to the public's trust in the gardaí and all that shite. Mick had no choice. He had to suck it up.'

Darcy said nothing. She thought about that for a while.

When Jamie saw her nodding to herself, he continued. 'They gave Mick a month off. Sent him to the psychologist, but by then it was too late and he was over the edge. He spent the whole month drinking. A few months later, his marriage fell apart.'

'How long ago was this?' Darcy asked.

'I think about five years ago.'

'So why don't they just get rid of him?'

'Well, for one, they don't want him spilling the beans about Flynn. They have to keep Kelly sweet somehow. And two, Chief O'Riordan and him go way back, and he's supposed to be keeping him out of harm's way.'

'I think O'Riordan was sure this would be an open-and-shut case. That's why he gave it to Mick. And me.'

'I'd be careful, Darcy. If Mick looks like he's going down, then you need to step away. If he falls, or when he falls, you could easily be pulled down with him.'

'You're the second person who's told me that.'

Jamie let out a giant yawn and stretched out his arms. 'I'm going to head off,' he told her.

He finished the remains of his coffee and stood up.

'I forgot to tell you,' he said. 'I called my FBI guy today.'

Darcy smiled but decided not to comment on it. As part of Jamie's ERU training, he spent a week at Quantico in Virginia for specialised training, but with the frequency that Jamie managed to get "FBI" into his conversations, you'd think he'd spent several years in the place.

'And what did your FBI guy say?'

'Nothing yet, but I gave him your killer's full MO, and he said he'll run it through their system. You never know what'll come up.'

'Thanks,' she said and stood up to walk him to the door.

Jamie stretched again. She thought back to what Phoebe had said, and couldn't deny that he was, in every way, a fine specimen of a man. Her eyes lingered a moment too long on him, and she saw him notice. She was sure he knew that look that a woman might give a man, their glance resting on them for a moment or two longer than was normal.

Darcy saw the smile in his eyes, and she cursed herself.

'I'm on earlies tomorrow,' he said, 'but if I hear anything from Quantico, I'll let you know.'

Darcy followed him to the door. He seemed to take up half the space in her sitting room and she understood why certain women might find that attractive. He had an aura about him that seemed to guarantee a certain amount of protection and security. As if by being in his presence, you could feel safer in the world.

He turned at the door, and she was suddenly too close to him. Her head was in line with his chest, and she smelt the rain and a faint musky aftershave that still lingered despite the lateness of the day. Her eyes raised up to his, and he was looking down at her, all serious now. He had dark eyes that were warm and inviting.

Is this what she really wanted? Maybe it was what everyone wanted.

He took a step closer to her and placed a hand on the side of her face. It felt rough and strong. She closed her eyes, and Jamie took it as a signal and lowered his face to hers.

Darcy's heart thumped in her chest as he gently raised her face to his until his lips touched hers. She steadied herself with her hand against his arm as he drew her closer.

They both ignored her phone when it first began to ring in her pocket, but the ringing became like an alarm bell that pulled Darcy from a dream back into reality.

She pushed Jamie away and took out her phone.

'Mick,' she said. 'Everything OK?'

'Did I wake you?'

'No.'

'Too bad, because you're probably not going to get any sleep tonight.'

'What's happened?'

'That little grafter, Eoin, has come up trumps. Fair fucks to him. We've got the caller's location for the second victim. The phone's location, anyway.'

'Where is it?'

'You'll never guess,' Mick said. 'Meet me in Harcourt Street in half an hour.'

Thursday

Chapter 32

A large brown van slowed and parked on the street opposite Frank Kavanagh's house. The digital clock on the dash read 5:04 a.m. The driver cut the engine. He wore a T-shirt, jeans and a baseball cap. He leaned his head back on the headrest and closed his eyes.

In the back of the van, on two benches facing each other, sat one woman and six men. All were dressed in dark-grey uniforms, black combat boots and black ballistic vests. On the side of each of their legs was strapped a SIG Sauer P226, and in their hands they each held a Heckler and Koch HK416 assault rifle. They wore tight black helmets and clear plastic goggles over black balaclavas. Each sat perfectly still, taking slow, deliberate breaths.

The Emergency Response Unit's HQ, based in Dublin's Kevin Street Station, had a tactical support team ready twenty-four-hours a day to assist in any execution of high-risk situations, including counterterrorism and hostage-taking.

The ERU van was the only vehicle allowed to park within sight of the house. All other vehicles had to park further away, and the gardaí had to walk back. Two streets from the van, Darcy switched off her lights and rolled to a stop. Besides Mick and Darcy's, two other unmarked detective cars were already parked at opposing points a block away, Kane and Burns in one of them.

'You ever been to one of these before?' Mick asked.

Darcy shook her head and then stretched.

'Late night at Fifi's?'

'Not so late.'

There was some chatter over the radio as everyone finalised their positions.

'She has a nice home,' Darcy said. 'Nice family. Although I couldn't help thinking I knew her husband. I'm hoping I didn't arrest him at some point back in my rookie days. I got the impression he was expecting me to know him.'

Mick chuckled to himself.

'Don't you own a TV?' he asked.

'No.'

'He's an actor from that soap opera, *Northsiders*. He's quite famous, I think. I bet he was pissed off you didn't recognise him.'

'Thank God it was only that. I was genuinely worried.'

'Vehicle One in position,' Jamie's voice came over the handheld radio.

There were four other Garda vehicles at a distance from the house, and Mick called out to each of them to confirm they were ready. In each of the cars were at least three uniformed gardaí. They had two roles. Primarily to block the access roads to the house, preventing any members of the public driving into the area. And, secondly, in the event of there being any runners over the walls at the back of the house once the ERU had gained entry at the front.

'Section One, are you ready?' Mick called to the ERU members sitting in the van.

'Affirmative,' Jamie whispered into his headset from the back of the van.

'Chief,' Mick said, 'are you there?'

'Proceed,' came the unmistakable voice of Chief Superintendent Glenn O'Riordan.

'Yes, Chief.'

Mick looked at Darcy. 'OK?' he asked her.

Darcy nodded. Mick handed her the radio. 'So, give the command,' he told her.

She looked at the radio before taking it.

'Section One. On my command,' she said into the radio.

Jamie heard her voice over his headset and corrected himself when he realised he was smiling.

Darcy pressed the button on the radio again. 'Proceed when ready.'

Dylan Keyes was a low-level, low-life criminal who carried triple the weight intended for his forty-year-old frame. He was a cruel sadist who loved only one thing more than threatening and torturing people: food.

He sat in front of Frank's multiple screens, watching every angle of the house. It was the perfect job for him. He was as lazy as he was loyal, and he spent most of every night playing violent games on his Xbox and eating whatever he could find in Frank's fridge. He kept several small vials in his jeans pocket that had enough cocaine in them to help him through the night.

He had noticed the van pull up outside but, when no one got out and he saw the driver lying back in his seat, his attention went back to shooting terrorists in some unnamed Middle Eastern country. He made a mental note to check back on the van after he got through to the next level of his game, but his mind wandered and he forgot.

So, when Jamie opened the back door of the van from the inside and stepped outside, Dylan Keyes' attention was elsewhere. Jamie looked up and down the empty street, his assault rifle raised at forty-five degrees.

The street was empty. He signalled to the other members of his team to follow him. One by one, and without making a sound, they stepped onto the road and, in tight formation, crossed over towards the main entrance of the property.

Suddenly, Jamie raised his hand for the team to halt. They stopped, waited and listened. They could hear a rhythmic squeak and, as it grew louder, a postman on a bicycle turned the corner. He did not notice the seven armed ERU officers until he had almost ridden into them. His bike came to a gentle stop, and he stared at them.

Jamie made eye contact with him and nodded for him to move on. He didn't need to be told twice. His feet slipped off the pedals as he struggled to ride his bike out of the way as quickly as possible. The squeaks increased in speed as he pedalled out of sight.

Jamie signalled to his team to continue. They reached the main gates of the property. The last member of the team walked to the front, and from his pocket took out four bundles of 50 grams PETN explosives. He placed one on each of the four hinges of the gates.

When he was finished, he gave a thumbs-up to Jamie and then joined the rest of the team, out of sight behind the wall. Jamie scurried up to the gate intercom and pushed the button.

Inside, Dylan Keyes almost fell out of his chair when he heard the buzzer. He glanced at the front gate camera and saw an armed garda at the intercom. For several moments, he was unsure whether he was watching reality or his video game.

'*Armed Gardaí!*' a voice shouted over the speaker. '*Open the gate!*'

About the same time as Dylan realised what was really happening, the four explosives detonated simultaneously, blowing the gate into the air. This time, despite his heavy bulk, Dylan fell out of his chair and onto his arse in front of all the security monitors.

From where Darcy and Mick were waiting, the explosions sounded like one big bang. Darcy started the car, drove it slowly to the entrance and stopped.

They unholstered their weapons and got out of the car.

The explosions woke Frank Kavanagh up. His bedroom door was locked, and he sat up and looked at it. The girl beside him sat up.

'What the fuck was that?' she said.

'It's a raid. Stay calm.'

'*A raid?*' she screamed at him. '*Stay calm? Fuck you!*'

She ran, naked, to the door, unlocked it and raced into the corridor.

Frank sighed, got up, closed the door and locked it again. He turned and kicked a bright red Persian mat on the floor to one side, then knelt on one knee.

At the corner of one of the floorboards was a small finger-sized hole. Frank inserted his finger into it until he heard a click. He pushed on one of the boards and a door about three feet by one foot popped open.

He moved the wads of cash in various currencies to one side. There was also a British passport and a driver's licence with his photo ID but under the name of Charles Redding. He pulled out a gym bag that was squeezed into the bottom of the space and unzipped it.

Taking out an Israeli-made Uzi submachine gun, he loaded the magazine into its handle. On the side of the weapon, he switched it from S for Safety to R for Repetition. There was no need to go fully automatic at this stage. Then, with the Uzi pointing squarely at his bedroom door, he leaned against his bed and waited.

Lurch watched the screen as the ERU came through the gates. He hurried to Frank's room and knocked.

'Cops,' he said and left.

Frank gave a short sigh of relief. He quickly removed the magazine from the Uzi, switched back on the safety and put it in its bag. He shoved everything back into the floorboard space, clicked the wooden trapdoor into place and spread the rug neatly on top.

Then he unlocked his door (no point in them ruining it, he figured) and went into his walk-in wardrobe to get dressed.

Dylan Keyes had regained his composure. He was in the bathroom emptying his cocaine into the toilet. Lurch sat patiently on the sofa with his hands placed on his knees. The girl was still running around screaming, trying to find a hiding place.

Tommy Fay lay in his bed. He hadn't been asleep when the gates were blown off, and since then he had remained in his bed. Lurch had opened the door but when he saw the expression in Tommy's eyes, he said nothing and closed the door again.

Mark Dunne was pacing his small room. He had tried several times to open his door even though he knew it was locked. He eventually sat on the bed and waited, biting his nails, his eyes focused on the door handle.

Once they were through the gates, Jamie's team had spread out around the house. He and three other officers went to the front door. One of them was carrying a battering ram, and he stepped up to the door. He turned to Jamie for the command to go. Jamie and the other two officers raised their weapon at the door as Jamie nodded to proceed.

A car pulled up alongside Darcy's car.

Kane stretched as he got out. 'Morning,' he said. 'Did someone here order two experienced and professional detectives?'

'Yep,' Mick told him. 'Keep an eye out and let me know when they get here, will you?'

Kane was about to reply, but then they all turned as the front door was smashed open, and Jamie and his team entered the house.

Screams of '*Armed Gardai!*' and '*Drop your weapons!*' sounded throughout the house.

Kane turned to Darcy. 'Ladies first,' he said, and gestured with his arm for her to go ahead.

Darcy didn't say anything and stepped over the demolished gates. She approached the front door alongside Mick with their guns pointing at the ground.

The door was badly damaged and left wide open.

All four detectives waited at the entrance for the ERU to give the all-clear.

'You know, Kelly,' Kane said to Mick, 'you shouldn't look at the fact that us being back on this case is a bad thing.'

'To be honest with you, Kane, I can't imagine your presence anywhere being a good thing.'

Kane gave a forced laugh. 'It's not that the chief doesn't trust you or think you're going to fuck it up, as usual – it's just, well, he just wants someone reliable. Someone who – I don't know – how can I put this subtly?' He turned to Burns as if looking for inspiration.

'I think I know what you're trying to say,' Burns said. 'Basically, Mick, he's looking for someone who isn't going to make a complete and utter balls of it. Again.'

Kane laughed. 'Well, in fairness, I wouldn't have put it so bluntly, but I think you've hit the nail on the head. But do you know what I'm more worried about?'

'What's that?' Burns asked.

'I'm more worried about the rookie here,' Kane said, nodding towards Darcy. 'This poor kid has barely got a taste of the NBCI and already she's going to fuck up her career by associating herself with Columbo Kelly.'

Burns gave a short chuckle.

'You know,' Kane said, lowering his voice and taking a step closer to Darcy, 'if you asked nicely, I wouldn't mind taking you under my wing and showing you the ropes. In fact, I'd love to show you my rope anytime.'

Darcy looked him straight in the eyes and then lowered her stare to between them. Kane had stepped right into her firing line. Her weapon was pointing at forty-five degrees towards the ground, and now Kane's genitals almost touched the nozzle of her gun. Kane followed her gaze.

'Be careful you don't lose your head,' Darcy told him, smiling.

Kane took two steps back. 'Watch yourself there, Doyle,' he said, growing red with anger. 'You think just because –'

Jamie walked out the door. He looked at the four detectives.

'Everything OK here?' he asked.

'Everything's fine,' Mick told him.

'It's all clear,' he said. 'Kavanagh's in his bedroom. You can follow me.'

Kane and Burns walked in quickly after Jamie. Mick and Darcy followed behind them. In the hall, an ERU officer was holding a half-dressed girl in the air. She was screaming and swearing, and everyone was ignoring her. Tony was face-down on the floor with another ERU officer standing over him. As Darcy walked around the prone figure, she saw Kane lift his foot and, instead of stepping over Tony, plant it onto his head. Tony screamed out in pain.

'*Oops!*' Kane said. 'Sorry about that.'

Frank was sitting on a chair in his bedroom.

'Good morning,' he said cheerfully. 'And to what do I owe this pleasure?'

He was fully dressed and looked like he was about to go into a business meeting.

'Shut your fucking trap!' Kane told him.

'*Wow*,' Frank said. 'Aren't you a real charmer?'

Kane took a step towards him, but Mick grabbed his arm.

'We'll handle this,' Mick said.

Kane hesitated and then backed off.

'Good morning, Frank,' Mick said. 'I was kind of hoping I wouldn't have to come to this house again for a long time.'

'And why are you here, then? You missed my company?'

'There's a charge sheet being prepared for you at the station. It'll be read to you there.'

'Are we going on a trip?'

'I'm afraid so. Cuff him, Detective.'

Darcy stepped forward.

'Is that necessary?' Frank asked.

'Yes,' Mick said. 'We're doing this one by the book. Frank Kavanagh, you are not obliged to say anything unless you wish to do so, but whatever you say will be taken down in writing and may be given in evidence.'

Frank never said a word as Darcy escorted him downstairs and out of the house.

Mick found Mark Dunne and cuffed him. Then he called the number of the missing phone and heard it ringing downstairs.

Outside, Darcy put Frank into the back seat of Kane's car and slammed the door.

Jamie walked over to her.

'You OK?' he asked her, touching her on the arm.

She turned to face him but, as she did, she saw Frank looking out at her from the back seat of the car. He smiled up at her. She raised her arm and shook off Jamie's hand.

Mick exited the front door with Mark Dunne, and headed towards one of the Garda cars.

'You get the phone?' she asked him as he passed her.

Mick grinned and tapped his jacket pocket in confirmation.

Kane and Burns got into their car.

Jamie looked into the back seat and saw Frank gazing up at him. Frank winked and blew him a kiss as the car drove off. It swung onto the road, the blaring sirens waking up the neighbourhood as the sun peeked above the horizon.

Chapter 33

Darcy held Mark Dunne in front of her as she marched him towards an interview room. He felt like a frail child in her hands. He looked like he needed food and a drink, but she knew that all he really wanted was a hit, and all that was going on in his head right now was when and how he was going to get it.

'I'll take care of this guy,' Mick said, grabbing Mark by the arm. 'I'll make sure he gets some strong coffee and settles in before we start our enquiries. Let's take care of Frank first, OK?'

'Sure. Will I wait for you?'

'No. You can have the pleasure of telling Kane and Burns to get the fuck out of our interview room.'

'I don't have a problem with that,' Darcy said, smiling.

'But, listen,' Mick said, lowering his voice and pushing Mark away at arm's length, 'when you're alone with Kavanagh, don't let him rile you up into any "banging on tables" techniques. That shit is for amateurs. Your job as an investigative detective is to open up a line of communication. He has information, and we want it. We need to tease it out of him, not force it out. Going balls to the wall against any interviewee will only shut them down.'

Darcy nodded. 'OK.'

'I won't be long,' he told her and led Mark Dunne towards the stairs.

Darcy found out which interview room Frank was in. As expected, Kane and Burns were already in there. There was a monitor outside the room, and it gave a live feed from inside. She spent a few moments looking at it.

Frank Kavanagh sat, leaning back in his chair, while Burns and Kane took it in turns to yell at him. This wasn't even a good cop, bad cop routine. It was just bad cop, bad cop. Kane picked up a pack of cigarettes from the table and shoved them in Frank's face, then threw them into the corner of the room.

'*Fuck you and fuck your cigarettes!*' Kane was shouting in Frank's face, when Darcy stepped into the room.

All three of them turned towards her. She took her time and looked from one to the other. She stepped further in.

'Detectives Burns and Kane,' she said, 'thank you for your assistance. I'll take it from here.'

Both Burns and Kane sneered at her.

'You're alright, Detective,' Burns said. 'I think we're managing just fine without you.'

'Yeah,' Kane agreed, 'why don't you go ... I don't know ... go do some paperwork or something and come back later.'

Darcy stood and watched them. Then she turned and walked back to the door. She opened it.

'Now, where were we, Frankie?' Kane said, leaning across the interview table.

'*Kane and Burns. Outside, please.*'

They both looked at her and looked genuinely surprised that she was still even there.

Kane shook his head. 'For fuck's sake!' He turned to Frank and winked at him. 'Don't go anywhere. I'll be back in a minute.'

Burns laughed. 'Don't go anywhere. That's a good one!'

They stepped outside and Darcy closed the interview room.

She turned to the two detectives and pointed her finger at Kane.

'*If you ever fucking talk to me like that again, I'll take your fucking head off. Is that clear?*'

The smile fell off Kane's face, and it took him a moment to compose himself.

'Listen ...' he said.

'No,' Darcy said, and took a step closer to him. '*You* fucking listen. Both of you. This is *our* investigation. This is *our* interview room. This is *our* interviewee. You are here to assist *us*. Now, if that's not clear enough for you, how's this? *Fuck off, the pair of you!*'

'Watch your fucking step,' Kane told her, his face hardening. 'You're only here to fill in a statistic for the chief. A bit of skirt to make him look good. You'll never be one of us. You'll never be the real NBCI.'

Darcy laughed at that. 'One of *you*? I'd rather do crowd control in Marlay Park for the next forty years than be one of *you*.'

They both glared at her.

Darcy took a step back and put her hand on the handle of the door again. She took a deep breath and, without saying another word, she walked back into the room.

Frank didn't turn around when she walked in. She pulled out the chair and sat down opposite him. On the table, the voice recorder was still whirling, recording the interview. She reached over and shut it off.

Frank stood up. She didn't look at him. He walked to the corner of the room behind Darcy, bent down and picked up his packet of Lucky Strike cigarettes.

The room was silent, and Darcy could feel Frank standing behind her, watching her. She didn't turn around.

He walked back to his chair and sat down. He picked up his Playboy Bunny lighter and pulled out a cigarette. He flicked the lighter, lit his cigarette, inhaled deeply and blew the smoke up towards the ceiling.

'And how are you, Darcy?' he asked her.

She looked at him for the first time. She shook her head from side to side.

'You're some fucking piece of work,' she said.

'Ah, come on. There's no need to be like that. I'm only asking how you're keeping.'

'What the fuck do you care?'

'Of course I care,' he told her, blowing smoke away from her. 'Isn't that what all dutiful fathers are supposed to do?'

Darcy's blue eyes burned into his, an almost mirror image of her own.

Chapter 34

'How long have you known?' Darcy asked him.

'Known what?' said Frank. 'That there's no such thing as Santa?'

'Don't fucking play games with me, Frank. How long have you known I was a garda?'

'Ah, here! Can you not at least call me dad?'

Almost as if it were somebody else's body, Darcy felt her hands form into fists on the table. Frank noticed them.

'Control yourself now, Detective. It wouldn't be the first time I've experienced police brutality, but I'd expect a little more restraint from my own flesh and blood.'

Darcy forced herself to breathe deeply. She relaxed her hands and put them on her lap.

'And don't be fretting yourself, Detective!' Frank held a hand up. 'You think I want it known that my own daughter is the filth? Get the fuck! If that's all you're worried about, you can put your mind to rest. Have no fear – I'd have a lot more to lose than you would.'

'I somehow doubt that.'

'Really?' He laughed. 'Then you know nothing of my life. Nothing about how our worlds work. You'd lose your job. End up in some shitty security company on the night shift. Me? I'd lose my fucking life. *Guaranteed*.'

He leaned back again and stubbed out his cigarette.

'So, don't worry,' he told her. 'I won't be moaning to anyone if I don't get any Father's Day gifts from you next year. Although I can't see you up for any Kid of the Year Award either.'

'From you? Are you joking me?'

'Not from me, you sap! I'm talking about from your mother.'

Darcy didn't want to have this conversation with him. In particular, she didn't want to have it in an interview room in a Garda Station.

'You must have looked her up on the PULSE system as soon as they gave you access, didn't you?'

Darcy didn't look at him.

'You broke the poor woman's heart when you ran away on her,' he told her.

'I didn't run away, you prick! They took me away.'

'Maybe, but there wasn't any sign of you running back, was there?'

'And there wasn't any sign of anyone running looking for me either. You want to know how I felt at the time? I felt like I'd been rescued.'

'Rescued? Rescued from what?'

'Rescued from the life I had. From the future I was going to have. Rescued from the bad health and bad food, the burnt-out cars and the barricaded houses, the ice-cream vans selling drugs. That's what my life would have been if I'd have stayed. I escaped, Frank.'

'And how did it fare for you with all your foster families? Three tasty and nutritious meals a day, was it? Pony camps at the weekend? Living the dream, were you?'

Darcy said nothing.

'You really think you've escaped?' he said. 'You think it's all about economics? Just because now you've enough cash in your pocket to pay your bills? And a roof over your head? Is that it? You can never escape your background, or who you really are. It's your identity and you can't shake it off. You don't fit in with these other goons. It's a part of you and everyone can see it. They can smell it off you, like a wet dog.'

Darcy didn't say anything to that.

'Not proud of where you're from, is that it?' he asked.

'Proud? I don't know. I'm not ashamed anyway.'

Frank let out a short laugh. 'Either way,' he said. 'You've done well for yourself. Big garda now with her gun and her badge. Think you're the big *I am*, do you? You must be very proud of yourself.'

'No thanks to you.' She dropped her gaze.

Frank kept his focus on her but said nothing.

Eventually she looked up.

'I suppose I can take a bit of credit for the way you turned out,' he told her.

Darcy laughed. 'You?'

'Why not? Look at you. You're the toughest bitch on the block, Darcy Doyle. You don't get like that by going to a private school and doing piano lessons on a Saturday morning and ballet classes in the afternoon.'

'You want to take credit for every shitty foster home I went to? And ran away from. Thanks a lot! I had a blast.'

'Was that your boyfriend back there? I must invite him around for some tea and biscuits.'

'Fuck off!'

'You make an attractive couple. It's funny. That's what they used to say about me and your mother.'

Darcy shook her head. 'You've done as much for her as you've done for me. Nothing.'

'Bollocks to that! How would you know anyway? I've always looked after her. Thrown her a few quid whenever I'm in the area. You probably know her address anyway, don't you? Who do you think got her that house in the first place?'

'It's a council house,' Darcy said. 'You didn't buy her shit.'

'Council houses get given out by councilmen. That's my patch of Dublin, in case you didn't know, and I have more than one councilman on my payroll.'

Darcy didn't say anything. She was unsure whether he was lying. She figured he probably wasn't.

'It's more than you've ever given her anyway,' he said.

Again, she said nothing.

'You know, she cried for weeks, months even, after you'd gone. Her little blonde beauty, taken away. She was inconsolable, the poor woman.'

'Go fuck yourself! *You* left her, not me. I was trying to look out for myself. If I'd stayed, I wouldn't have stood a chance.'

'And was I not entitled to look out for myself too? I hope you at least go and apologise to her someday.'

'Apologise to her?' Darcy felt she was going to explode. 'Where's *my* apology? Where's *my* sorry for all the years of neglect? Jesus Christ! I'm really trying here not to swing at you. You've no idea how close you are.'

Frank smiled at her. 'It's funny,' he said. 'In many ways, we're very similar. I can see a lot of myself in you.'

She stood up out of her chair.

'*I am nothing like you!*' she shouted at him. '*You hear me? Nothing!*'

Darcy banged her fist down on the table just as the door opened. She turned and saw Mick. He paused and looked from her to Frank, then slowly entered the room.

Darcy lowered herself back into her seat and Mick took a seat next to her.

He leaned across the table and switched back on the voice recorder.

'Interview of Frank Kavanagh by Detectives Darcy Doyle and Mick Kelly.'

Mick leaned back in his chair.

Everyone remained silent for several moments. Mick didn't take his eyes off Frank.

'Do you still have to pass the torch test before becoming a garda these days?' Frank asked.

Mick said nothing.

'Maybe it was before your time,' Frank said, turning to Darcy. 'They used to get a torch and switch it on. Then they'd hold it up to the recruit's ear. If any light came out the other side, he'd be hired. And if it was a full beam, they'd make him a detective.'

Neither Mick nor Darcy said anything. For a moment, though, Darcy could see what all those women found attractive about Frank Kavanagh. It wasn't just his looks. He was like the kid with the stick who liked to poke the big sleeping dog in the neighbourhood. Everyone knew it was a bad idea, but everyone was also dying to see what was going to happen next.

'What did Mark Dunne tell you about the murder of Sinéad Fay?' Mick asked.

'Who?'

'OK,' Mick said. 'If you want to go through the motions. Mark Dunne made a 999 call after witnessing the murder of Tommy Fay's wife, Sinéad. Mark Dunne was found on your premises. What information did he give you about that incident?'

'Did you ask him?'

'We will. But we're asking you too.'

Frank shrugged.

Darcy began to imagine what Mick must have been like in the old days, shooting from the hip, as Jamie would say. She would like to have seen him back then instead of the man that he was today.

'Whatever you know, you need to tell us. If you decide not to cooperate, I can't do anything for you later. Maybe there's some evidence on your property we could easily get a warrant for? Plus, who knows what else we might find when we have a good root around in your gaff?'

'Was there a hidden threat in there somewhere, Columbo?' Frank asked.

'I'm sorry. It wasn't supposed to be hidden.'

Frank looked at Darcy, but Darcy kept as stoic an expression as she could muster.

'Can I see my charge sheet now, please?' Frank asked.

Mick said nothing.

Frank recited from memory. *'When you are brought to the Garda Station, details of the offence must be set out in a charge sheet. A copy of the details must be given to you. The garda will formally charge you by reading each charge over to you and you will be cautioned after each charge is read out. The garda must keep a note of any reply you make. If you –'*

Mick stood up. 'Darcy,' he said, and flicked off the voice recorder. 'Fuck this.'

'You do what you have to do, Kelly,' Frank said and leaned across the table to pick up his cigarettes. 'And I'll do whatever I have to do.'

Mick turned back to him. He looked angrier than Darcy had ever seen him before. For a second, she thought he was going to smack Frank. Evidently Frank thought the same as she saw his head move backwards ever so slightly.

'There's a psycho out there, and he'll kill again, unless we get him,' Mick said through gritted teeth.

'I agree one hundred percent with you, Mick,' Frank said, relaxing and then lit his cigarette. 'But don't worry, we *will* get him.'

'There's no *you* in *we*, Frank,' Mick told him, his words slow and precise. '*Understand?*'

'I understand completely,' Frank said, with an expression on his face as if he were trying not to smile.

Outside the room, Mick caught Darcy's arm and stopped her from walking away. He stood close to her.

'I don't know what was going on in that room between you two ...'

'It was just ...'

'*Ah, ah, ah!*' Mick said, holding his finger up to her. 'And, although I want to know, I don't want to know now. You will tell me, Detective, but we've got too much shit on our plate now for your shit too.'

Darcy nodded her consent.

'For now, we've got Mark Dunne to interview,' Mick said. 'Before that, though, go down and tell the desk sergeant, Eddie Mills, not to let that fucker out until I say so. No doubt his vulture lawyer is on his way already. They waste no time, those fuckers.'

She felt her phone vibrating in her pocket.

As soon as Mick had turned away, Darcy took it out.

Jamie's name flashed up on her screen.

'Guess who've I've just been on the phone to?' Jamie's voice said with the excitement of a little boy.

'Who?'

'Go on. Guess!'

'Jamie, what the fuck? I haven't got time for –'

'Have a guess.'

'I don't give a –'

'The FBI!'

'What?'

'The FBI.'

'The FBI? What are you talking about?'

'I told you! I called my guy in the FBI. He got back to me.'

'Oh! OK? And?'

'He got a match. Same MO. Same victim profile. Everything.'

Darcy watched Mick disappear around the corner at the end of the corridor.

'Hold on!' she told Jamie and ran after Mick.

Chapter 35

Mairéad had never been to this part of the city. But, in fact, Mairéad had never been to most parts of the city.

She walked into a coffee shop overlooking the Docklands in the Irish Financial Services Centre. She looked around in awe at the colossal walls and the tall ceilings, which were all antique redbrick and modern steel, fused with bright lights and speckless shiny glass. The past and the present. Just like her being in this place, she thought, the stylish and the dowdy.

At the counter, one barista tried to take her order, but Mairéad stared up at the enormous chalkboard and failed to see anything she recognised. For several moments, she thought it was written in a foreign language. Italian, she guessed. Eventually, after too much tutting and looking at watches from other customers behind her, she said she'd take a seat and wait until her son arrived.

Liam had chosen this place. She'd rather he'd have come to her home, but he had told her he'd been out sick the previous two days and didn't want to take any more time off work.

She watched the young people coming and going and ordering and walking out with their coffees. Even when they had their food and drinks, they still tapped away at their computers or on their phones. They all seemed so busy and confident and important. Everyone had a role to play, and they all played it so well. They appeared to not even have a few minutes to sit and drink and watch the world go by. Somebody somewhere always needed their attention.

She, on the other hand, had all the time in the world but nowhere to go.

She had only Conor. Conor needed her. Conor would always need her. She could feel the well of sadness bubbling up inside her again. She tried to push it back down. Bury it along with her regrets, her failings, her Jack, her distant memories of hope.

She had spent years silently blaming Jack for her unhappiness but now that he was gone the unhappiness remained. The rotten sod couldn't even have done that for her. Only now, the misery was accompanied with a perpetual and profound loneliness.

She saw Liam appear at the entrance of the café. He looked so handsome in his grey suit as he scanned the café for her. He spotted her and waved and then queued to order his coffee.

Everything had been so easy for her eldest. Just as everything had been so difficult for Conor. Liam had so many friends when in school, none of whom he had brought home but who had nonetheless invited him to their homes or to their birthday parties. Conor had never once received an invitation to a party.

She had at first forced and then later bribed Liam to take his little brother, but eventually Conor didn't want to go with him either. When Liam once told her that some of his friends were mean to Conor and called him names, she stopped forcing him to go.

It was inevitable, she knew, but sometimes even inevitability comes with its own pain, and even surprise. Like when Liam left home one day and never came back. She cried for weeks after he was gone. He was the only one who had brought any normalcy into the house. She had used his normality as a mask for fifteen years pretending she was just a typical mother, like all the other mothers in school or in the shops. Until he was gone, and the veil was lifted.

The sorrow of his absence eventually turned to envy of his escape, and then finally resentment for his increasing happiness. She hid that resentment from him for years. Even today, looking at him now, and at the carefree way in which he blended in with this crowd, which was so foreign to her, she felt a bitterness that made it necessary to force herself to smile as he approached the table.

'Hiya, Mum,' he said as he sat down.

'Hello, Liam,' she said.

She hated being called 'Mum'. He had always called her the more Irish 'Mam' until after he'd run away. She'd never got used to it.

He noticed the table in front of her was empty. 'Did you not get yourself some tea, Mum?'

'No, no, I'm fine.'

'I can get some for you if you like?' he asked, raising himself halfway off the chair.

'No, no,' she insisted, 'I don't want to cause a fuss.'

'It's no fuss, Mum. I can get you some?' he repeated, but he didn't raise himself any higher off the chair.

'No, thank you, Liam,' she said, and he settled himself back down.

She noticed he had asked for his coffee in a takeaway cup. He obviously wasn't planning on this being a long talk. There were a few moments of silence as he sipped his coffee. Her perception of the relationship she had with her son was often different from her actual relationship with him. It took several minutes before they each found their place and felt comfortable again in each other's company.

'How is work?' she asked him when he'd put his coffee down.

'Oh, the usual. I wouldn't mind a change, to be honest.'

'Really?'

'Yeah.'

'To do what?'

'No, not to change my job,' he told her, as if the very thought were preposterous. 'To change my location.'

'You're moving again?'

'Again? I've never moved away. I've always ... Oh, you mean out of your house.' He cleared his throat and sat up straight. 'No, it's just a thought that's been running around in my head. The company has an office in London, you see, and I was thinking ...'

He paused and took another sip from his takeaway cup.

She didn't know quite what to make of this.

'Anyway, Mum,' Liam said, putting his coffee down with some sort of finality, or was it impatience, 'what was it you wanted to see me about?'

For a moment Mairéad had completely forgotten herself and stared at him blankly.

'Mum?'

'Oh yes,' she finally said, then coughed, leaned forward and lowered her voice. 'It's about Conor.'

"*It's about Conor*" was a phrase that Liam had grown up listening to. He said nothing, but his silence and the folding of his arms easily gave him away. Mairéad ignored it.

'He hasn't been well since your father's ... passing.'

'When was he ever well?' Liam shot back too quickly and then looked regretful.

Mairéad leaned back in her chair.

'I'm sorry,' he told her.

She sniffed. 'It's not his fault he's the way he is.'

'I know, Mum. I know. I'm sorry. Go on, please. What is it?'

Mairéad took a moment to gather herself.

'He's been acting a little ... strange lately,' she said.

Liam raised his eyebrows at her. She allowed him that.

'OK then,' she said. 'He's been acting a little stranger than normal.'

'Such as?'

'Well, he's gone for most of the day.'

'Gone? Gone where?'

'Just gone. He goes on long walks. Like your father used to do. He gets up, has his breakfast and then he goes out.'

Liam sat forward in his chair. 'And when does he come back?'

'Evening. Night-time. It depends.'

Liam thought about this for a minute.

'Anything else? I mean, anything else unusual or out of the ordinary?'

'He's more distant,' she told him.

Liam sipped his coffee absentmindedly.

'What?' she said.

Liam looked up at her.

'Tell me,' he said, 'does he ever have any ... I don't know ... marks on him?' She didn't say anything, so he continued, his voice almost a whisper. 'You know, like bruises? Or perhaps blood?'

She tried to swallow, but her throat was too dry. She looked around at the other tables, then leaned forward.

'Yes,' she whispered.

Liam leaned in too.

'I found something,' she said.

'Tell me.'

She looked from side to side again. 'Evidence.'

'What evidence?'

Mairéad shook her head. 'Not here.'

'I fucking knew it!' Liam said.

'Watch your language,' she scolded him.

'Mum, you should go to the police if you have anything.'

But Mairéad was shaking her head. 'I can't. They wouldn't understand. They'd lock him away. They'd treat him like an animal. I know they would. Beat him and break him. I couldn't do that to him. No matter what he's done, he's my son. My Conor.'

She lowered her head and began to weep. Liam reached out to touch her arm but then drew it back in. People at the next table were staring at them.

'What do you want me to do?'

She looked up at him and wiped her face with her sleeve. He pushed a paper napkin across the table at her. She picked it up and gripped it in her hand but didn't use it on her face.

'I'm going to talk to an expert, you know, someone who really knows about these things.'

'I don't know, Mum. I think the police …'

Mairéad slapped her closed fist with the napkin in it onto the table.

'Mum, please,' Liam said, and looked and smiled at the group beside them who had stopped talking and were still looking over at them.

'Not the police,' she told him.

'OK, OK. Who then?'

'A professor, I think he is. No, a doctor. He can help. I've arranged a meeting with him. Will you come with me? Tonight? Will you do that for me, Liam?'

'Who is he?'

'Someone who can help your brother. Will you come with me? Please?'

Liam let out a long sigh and leaned back in his chair.

'OK, Mum. I'll meet up with this expert if you like.'

'Thank you.'

'But if he tells us to go to the police, then that's what we'll do. Is that agreed?'

Mairéad thought about it. She had little choice, so she nodded.

A tall blonde woman walked by their table. 'Hi, Liam,' she said in a strong Australian accent. 'You heading back to the office soon?'

'Hey, Jeannie,' he said. 'Yeah, I'll be along in a minute.'

'Cool. See you up there.'

Mairéad watched her son watch the back of the woman as she walked away, swaying from side to side.

Liam turned back to his mother.

'You know,' she told him. 'I was young once, too. And I had many admirers.'

She looked at him and couldn't help but see the pity in his eyes.

'I wasn't always like this,' she said, as she picked the paper napkin apart in her fingers. 'Your father …'

There were so many ways she could have continued that sentence but she just couldn't pick any specific one.

'Why didn't you leave him, Mum? You could have left with me when I was thrown out of the house.'

Mairéad's eyes widened. 'Thrown out? You were never thrown out. Is that what you tell these people? You ran away, Liam. *You* left me.'

'You could have come with me if you had wanted to,' Liam snapped back.

'And what about Conor? Leave him there? Who would have minded him? Your father? Don't make me laugh.' She took a deep breath. 'I stayed because I had to. I stayed when you were a little boy because I had to. I could have disappeared at any time, but your father would never have allowed me to take his sons from him. I stayed. I stayed for you. You ran away from us. From me!'

Liam reached out to her again, but she pulled her hands back and withdrew her whole body back into the chair.

'I don't want to argue with you, Mum.'

She nodded.

'When are you meeting this doctor?'

'Tonight at eight. In the National Gallery of Ireland.'

'I'll come over and collect you at seven. OK?'

'OK,' she said, taking a breath.

Liam stood up, but Mairéad stayed seated. She was unsure whether she could stand or not.

'I hope you're feeling better today,' she said.

Liam paused. 'What do you mean?'

She looked up at him. 'You were off work the last couple of days. You were sick, you said.'

'Oh yes, that. I forgot. Yes, I'm feeling much better. Just a ... thing ... a head cold.'

He stood while she sat, for the same moments of silence as when he had first arrived. He eventually nodded and offered her a half smile before walking back out of the café.

Mairéad continued to look at the empty chair as if he were still sitting there. Several minutes went by as she allowed her mind to wander and wonder how things might have been, if only. If only what? If only so many things.

A voice woke her from her daydream. She looked up, and a waitress was standing over her.

'Sorry?' Mairéad asked her.

'I said, are you waiting on anyone?' the waitress asked again.

Mairéad suddenly felt very thirsty. Thirsty for the tea she had never drunk, or the life she had never led.

'No,' she told her. 'No one's waiting on me.'

Chapter 36

'Before I begin,' said the slow American-accented voice from the conference phone on Superintendent O'Riordan's office table, 'Officer Jamie, can you please inform me who's in the room with you?'

'Sure, Agent Miller,' Jamie said. He was as excited as a kid, thinking he was on the phone to the real Santa Claus. 'That's no trouble at all, sir.'

Darcy thought his accent had also taken on something of an American drawl.

'Sorry, I don't mean to be a pain in the ass. This is sensitive intel, and I gotta follow protocol – you understand, buddy.'

'Absolutely,' Jamie said. 'No probs at all. Buddy. I understand you need to follow the rules Stateside.'

Mick looked over at Darcy, but she forced herself to look away from him, knowing he would trigger her to laugh.

'Detective Chief Superintendent Glenn O'Riordan is here, along with the two detectives working the case, Detective Inspector Mick Kelly and Detective Sergeant Darcy Doyle.'

'We appreciate your time, Agent Miller,' O'Riordan said. 'I've spoken with your Director of Intelligence, and she's told us you may have some useful information regarding our case here.'

'Anything I can do to help you guys is my pleasure,' Agent Miller said.

Mick made a face at Jamie and moved his hand in a circular motion for Jamie to speed things up.

'You know my wife's family is originally from Ireland,' Agent Miller told them. 'We've been meaning to get over there sometime for our summer vacation.'

Mick's head flopped back in his chair, and he stared up at the ceiling. Darcy imagined Miller wearing a cowboy hat and snakeskin boots that were crossed on the table in front of him.

'Well, we'd love to have you over some time, Agent Miller,' O'Riordan said. 'Now, if you could just give us any information you have, we'd appreciate it immensely.'

'Sure, sure,' Agent Miller said, and they could hear him riffling through pages. 'This guy was one badass motherfucker, if you pardon my French. His name is Jack Carter, but he's used various aliases such as Carson and Baker. He was born in 1967 so he's in his late fifties now. And before you guys ask, no, we do not know his whereabouts at this time.'

They listened to more pages being turned.

'Most of this stuff is based on interviews with neighbours, witnesses, our own profilers and the interview tapes after his arrest. You understand that, right?'

Everyone sat up at the same time. It was Mick who spoke first. 'Wait a second. You have him?'

'We did,' Miller said. 'They arrested him after a spate of killings in northern California and a couple up in Oregon. They weren't dissimilar to your own over there. Unfortunately, during his first court appearance, one of the prison officers let him use a toilet in a public area, and the son-of-a-bitch jumped out of a second-floor window.'

'What happened to him?' Mick asked.

'Well, he was new in the job, but either way he was fired soon after.'

'No,' Mick said. 'I meant what happened to Jack Carter?'

There was silence for a few moments.

'Well, obviously he was never seen again,' Agent Miller told them, the embarrassment in his voice barely concealed.

Everyone in the room looked at one another. No one dared to speak.

'I can also organise to have you sent his mug shots?'

'That would be appreciated, thanks,' Darcy said.

'No problem. Do you still want the rest of this info?'

'Yes, please, Agent Miller,' O'Riordan said.

'OK, then. Our guy was originally from Oxnard. That's in Southern California, in case you guys didn't know. No father to speak of. By all accounts, his mom was an attractive lady and had more than her fair share of male visitors while Jack was growing up. Neighbours said she was an out-and-out racist, to boot. Many of her lovers had links with White Supremacist groups and such like. Local cops were called out on more than one occasion when she'd be in the street screaming derogatory names at her Mexican and black neighbours. Anyhoo, young Jack spent most of his time in his room watching TV. His mom continued bringing men into the house and apparently when Jack got older, him and his mom had fights about it. Again, that's in reports from the local Sheriff's office. It says here one of our profilers thought his anger had more to do with him resenting losing his mother's attention than anything else. He wanted his mom all for himself. Classic Oedipus Complex, it says here, if you're into any of that horseshit.'

Mick smiled at that. He was starting to like Miller.

'Sorry to interrupt,' Darcy said. 'What colour was his mother's hair?'

'Pardon me, ma'am?'

'Her hair,' Darcy repeated. 'Does it mention the mother's hair colour?'

The sound of more papers being turned back and forth.

'*Em* ... here it is. She was a natural blonde. Probably the only one in California.'

They could hear Miller chuckling at his own joke.

Darcy nodded at Mick. 'OK, thank you,' she said. 'Sorry to interrupt. Please continue.'

'No problem, ma'am. Anyways, he'd spend every other night listening to his mom and some new guy having sex in the next room. This next part is from the transcript of his interviews. He claimed as he got older he pleasured himself as he listened to his mom and the different fellas she was with. Then he spied on them. Voyeuristic kind of thing. Now, here's where it gets weird, folks.'

'Oh, *here's* where it gets weird,' Mick said.

'*Shh*,' Darcy told him.

'He said his mom caught him spying on her, and that she stayed looking at him while the other fella was on top of her screwing away. He said it became a regular thing for them to do. Then one night, one of these men decides to play it rough and slaps her around and chokes her. Jack gets into a rage, grabs a hammer, and while the poor guy is humping on top of her, Jack smashes the guy's head in with the hammer. His mom starts screaming and going crazy, so Jack holds her down and rapes her. Seems like each of them was as big a psycho as the other. She starts bringing men home and Jack would finish them off as they were ... how do you say? Mid-coitus. Sometimes she'd go to their houses, and she'd let Jack in through a window or a back door. He'd kill the guy, then they'd have sex in the same bed and then rob the place for any cash or jewellery. They moved out of Oxnard as the body count started adding up and travelled north along the 101 toward Frisco. The FBI was involved at this stage, and we found bodies in Ventura, San Luis Obispo and all the way up to Monterey. We're not sure what happened then, and Carter wouldn't tell us. Either way, one night after killing a guy she'd picked up in a bar just outside San Jose, Jack cut her throat from ear to ear. CSI said he did it while they were having sex. Sick part was, and I'll never forget it, but they told me the sperm deposits were both antemortem and postmortem. They even got a word for it. Necrophilia. Means he continued having sex with her after she was dead. Climaxed then too. The sick fuck.'

'Are you sure about that, Miller?' Mick asked.

'As sure as shit,' came the response. 'I don't need to look up that detail. Unfortunately, it doesn't end there. His little double act turned solo, and he moved further north. He was top of our Most Wanted for a while back then. We threw a lot of resources at it. There were four more killings after that. Then, like I said, we got him. One of his victims managed to escape, flagged down a passing black-and-white, and he was arrested. But then he just disappeared. Years later, a Wells Fargo bank account in his name was emptied of the few thousand dollars that was in it. It set off alarm bells here in Quantico, and we flew down to investigate. The money was taken out at a branch in San Diego. The bank clerk said she recognised the guy and that he was a member of the Palmarian Church. They had property not too far from the bank. We raided the place. There was a bit of a standoff. For a while, I thought we were going to have another Waco on our hands. Eventually they conceded, thank God, but when we went in he was gone. Of course, everyone there claimed they didn't know shit. Goddam religious freaks.'

'Can you repeat the name of that Church again, please?' Darcy asked.

'Sure. The Palmarian Church. They're a Spanish sect of some sort, if I remember correctly. Even got their own pope. We did follow-up visits with the Church for a while, but we might as well have been knocking our heads against the wall for all the good it did us.'

Darcy looked at Mick, but he shrugged. There was silence in the room for a few moments. A phone rang in the background.

'Just one more question,' Darcy said then. 'What colour hair had his victims?'

'Oh, shit,' Miller said. 'Yeah, I should have mentioned that. They were all attractive blondes.'

'And I assume Jamie told you about the cropped hair from the victims?'

'He sure did. That's what set our alarm bells ringing. It's quite typical that a serial killer often collects a memento from his victims as a sort of reminder or a souvenir. It's believed they use it to help them reminisce and then relive the act itself. It's a very well documented matter.'

Darcy looked over at Mick. 'It's him. It has to be,' she said, and turned back to the phone. 'And forensics were never able to get anything from the crime scenes?'

'No, not a goddamn thing,' Miller said. 'We doubled and even triple-swept the crime scenes for prints, DNA, fibres, blood. You name it. That's why the media gave him that nickname.'

'Nickname?' Darcy asked.

'Yeah, all serial killers have a nickname. Wasn't a bad one now that I think about it.'

'And what did they call him?'

'They called him *The Ghost*.'

Chapter 37

Darcy and Mick left O'Riordan's office. They walked side by side, each deep in their own thoughts. It was only afterwards that Darcy realised she had not thanked Jamie or even said goodbye.

'What the fuck is the Palmarian Church?' Mick asked, more to himself than Darcy.

'I'll get a couple of the uniforms to look into it,' Darcy told him.

She stopped walking.

'You really think this Ghost character could be our man?' she asked.

'I don't know, but it's as good a lead as we have right now. I'll get in touch with –'

Darcy's phone rang.

'Yes, Garda Browne, this is Detective Doyle.'

Darcy listened as she watched Mick take out his cigarettes and light one. He looked up and down Harcourt Street until his eyes stopped on the pub across the road. Darcy watched him. She thought he had the eyes of unrequited love as he gazed across the street.

'*Mick!*' she called to distract him. 'And where's the camera situated?' she asked into the phone. 'OK, great work, Garda. I appreciate the call. Thanks.'

Darcy put her phone away.

'What is it?' Mick asked.

'There was an Amazon box, an opened cardboard box on the table in the Delaneys' house. It had a barcode on the side. I gave it to one of our uniforms to investigate it.'

'And?'

Darcy was smiling now. 'It's that clock. That fecking clock.'

'What clock?'

'The clock I said had the wrong time. In her hall. Remember?'

'So?'

'It has a camera in it. She must have been using it to either watch her kid, or more likely catch her cheating husband maybe coming home with someone. How do you think that'd look in a divorce court?'

'The deceiving little –'

'Oh, so the husband is cheating on her and *she's* the deceiving one?'

Mick thought about this. 'Fair enough. You think the camera was rolling when she was attacked by the killer?'

'Don't see any point in having a surveillance camera without any actual surveillance going on. Do you? We need to get over there.'

'Hold on,' he told her as he dialled a number on his phone. 'Fifi?' he said when it was answered. I need you to meet me with one of your techie lads at the Delaney house. The clock in the hall – it has a camera in it.'

He listened to her reply and then looked at his watch.

'See you in thirty minutes.'

He hung up before she replied.

'What about Mark Dunne?' Darcy asked.

'He'll have to wait,' he told her. 'I swear to God, Darcy. You could be a hundred years in this job and still something will happen that you never saw coming. Come on. You're driving.'

Chapter 38

Phoebe introduced Darcy and Mick to her tech support member, Big Tom, who weighed over 300 pounds and took up most of the space in the Delaneys' hallway.

Mick couldn't resist asking, 'So why do they call you Big Tom?'

Mick felt Darcy's punch in his back.

'Because I'm into country music,' Big Tom told him, without a hint of irony in his voice.

Darcy and Mick stared at him.

'You know, like the singer?' Big Tom tried to explain.

Darcy laughed as Mick couldn't make out if the joke was on him or not.

'Forget about it,' he told Big Tom. 'How much longer until we can see something?'

Phoebe and Big Tom had got to the house before Darcy and Mick. Big Tom had removed the clock from its nail and had already found the tiny hard drive and connected it to his laptop.

'It's downloading the drivers now,' Big Tom told him. 'Just a few more seconds.'

Darcy looked around the hall and into the kitchen. She shivered. It seemed like weeks had passed since she'd first been in this house. She also had the sense that all the life and happiness that had once made this house a home had been sucked out of it. It was nothing now but four walls and a roof. If she had her way, she'd have the whole building knocked down and rebuilt.

'*Got it!*' Big Tom called out.

They all pressed forward and huddled around the laptop.

The kitchen appeared on the monitor. It wasn't top quality, but they could make out the view into the back garden. Jennifer Delaney's face appeared at close range. They all drew back slightly as if seeing a ghost.

The video jumped and then she appeared again as she walked from the kitchen and through to the hall.

'Looks like the camera is motion activated,' Big Tom said. 'That means ...'

'We know what it means,' Mick said, cutting him off.

Big Tom's focus went back to the screen, his face turning a crimson red.

They watched Jennifer Delaney as she positioned the clock on the wall. Darcy thought she was even more beautiful than the photos on the surrounding walls.

Jennifer turned to the right. She was looking towards the front door.

She vanished from the screen for several moments and then reappeared. She was talking to someone.

Darcy and Mick huddled closer together and leaned forward. A man wearing a hoodie appeared, with his back to the camera. Under his hoodie, the peak of a baseball cap poked out. He was carrying a box, and Jennifer had to back into the hall for him to enter.

They all watched him place the box on the floor. Jennifer was looking down at the box when he stood up quickly and smacked her hard across the head with a small leather blackjack in his hand. She dropped to the floor.

'*Turn around, you fucker!*' Mick said. '*Let's get a look at you!*'

But instead of turning around, the man reached back and closed the door shut. He bent down and pulled her away from a potted plant which had been knocked over, then righted the pot. With his back still to the camera, he pulled the hoodie from his head and removed the black baseball cap. He was wearing what appeared to be a tight black hood that covered his entire head and neck. He bent down to his bag and pulled out a small mask.

Before standing back up again, he slid the straps of the mask over the back of his head. He unzipped the front of his hoodie. Then, with Jennifer staring up at him, frozen to the spot, he slowly removed his trousers and his shoes.

Under his clothes, he was wearing a skin-tight black suit.

He bent down and took a large blade from the bag. His head turned sideways and licked along its surface. Jennifer's mouth opened as she screamed. Then he got on one knee and hit her again with the blackjack. This time, her body went limp.

With all his belongings now in the bag, he pushed the mask over the full length of his face and stood up. He stretched out his arms in the hall in what appeared to be a ceremonial manner and then turned in a complete circle, slowly revealing himself at last to the camera.

'*Holy Mother of God*,' Darcy whispered.

'*Fuck. Me*,' Mick said. Then repeated, '*Fuck. Me.*'

Phoebe put her hand up to her face.

The man was wearing a full black wetsuit. It covered every part of him, except for his eyes. The mask covering his face had two little vents on either side. Darcy thought it looked like a mini gasmask.

The rotation completed, he squatted down and lifted Jennifer into his arms. Then he turned and walked up the stairs.

'*Pause it*,' Mick told Big Tom.

He did.

The four of them didn't move for a full minute.

Eventually, it was Phoebe who broke the silence.

'No wonder there's no DNA evidence at the scene,' she said.

Mick's gaze hadn't left the laptop screen.

'Let it play,' he told Big Tom. 'And let's see if we can see this fucker coming back down.'

Chapter 39

Tamila had been right, Mairéad thought. Only a handful of people had come to the Jackson Pollock exhibition at the National Gallery of Ireland. She was grateful to have Liam with her.

'Are you sure she said eight?' Liam asked her for the third time, looking at the time on his phone. It read: 8:10 p.m.

'Maybe he got delayed,' Mairéad said. 'He's a very busy man.'

'I'm also a very busy man,' he told her.

'We took ten minutes to find this café, so he's probably lost.'

They sat in silence for another two minutes. Liam stood up quickly.

'I'm going to look for him,' he told her.

'But she said to meet here in the café.'

'He's obviously walking around looking for it. This place is a maze. You're right, we were lucky to find the café after only ten minutes.'

'And what if he arrives and you're not here?' she asked her son.

'I'll come back soon and check on you.'

'*Oh, wait!*' she called to him.

He stopped.

'How do you know what he looks like?'

Liam saw the book *How to Cure a Serial Killer* on the table. He walked back, lifted it up, and turned it around. 'His photo's on the back. By the way, are you sure Conor was home when you left?'

'Yes, I told you.'

'And you definitely said nothing to him about this.'

Mairéad didn't answer. Liam had already asked her that question several times.

'OK, then,' he said. 'I'll be back in a few minutes.'

Horris was convinced he had passed by that same Jackson Pollock painting twice already. The fucking things all looked the same to him. He had never been a proponent of the inkblot Rorschach test and found most Swiss psychoanalysts to be egocentric narcissists. Rorschach died in his thirties if he remembered correctly. Bet he didn't see that coming in his squiggles. As far as he was concerned, one could just as easily ask a patient to stare at a bloody brick wall and get an interpretation of their mental state.

Earlier, when he and Tamila had come in the entrance of the gallery, a lady had offered him a map, but he had foolishly refused it. Tamila had told him where the café was, but that she needed to use the bathroom first. He had set off through the labyrinth of corridors and rooms. That was fifteen minutes ago. He'd go back, but now he had no idea where the entrance was.

If this turned out to be the disaster he predicted, as soon as he got back to London he would make sure that bitch never worked in the publishing world again. She should thank her lucky stars she even got to work for someone like him. Thirty fucking percent! On all royalties. How had he agreed to that? He'd find a way to wriggle out of it.

Horris heard steps behind him, but when he turned around no one was there. There was no one anywhere. Shouldn't there at least be a security man minding all the paintings? Sure, they were all blobs of paint as far as he was concerned, but they must have something of a monetary value. He much preferred paintings of things: a house or the sea or something tangible.

His mind drifted to the student he was meeting later. He couldn't wait to get his hands on her. He'd impress her and order champagne to the room. Nothing too expensive, just something to get her tipsy. Maybe he could persuade her to take a shower with him? He could tell her he'd just come from a meeting with the prime minister or someone like that and needed to freshen up. Would she care to join him?

Horris looked behind him again, sure that someone had walked into the hall, but no one was there. He looked at his watch. 8:15 p.m. He cursed Tamila again.

Fucking Horris, Tamila thought. Why did everything have to be so difficult with him? Oh, yeah, because he's a whiney, over-educated, condescending arsehole, she reminded herself. How was he unable to see the opportunity in a case study like this? Research into a subject of this magnitude was a once-in-a-lifetime shot at the big time. How could he not see that?

She thought about what he had said about it being a set-up, but she pushed it from her mind. She'd admit that the old woman was as mad as a March hare, but she seemed genuine. Besides, this is what ambitious people did – they took risks. They rolled the dice of life and came up trumps. This was pioneering in a new field, and the world would know that soon.

She turned into a large room. It had only one enormous painting in it that took up an entire wall. The colours and size were impressive. She had stood here yesterday for a full ten minutes. Why were there not more people here to appreciate this genius? Wasted on the bloody Irish!

She felt drawn again to the splashes and intricacies of the work of art. She took a few steps closer to it and bent over to see how the different paints played off one another, crisscrossing and entwining like colourful shooting stars with such apparent purpose and yet without logic. It gave her a moment of calm in an otherwise agitated evening and even brought a small smile to her face.

It was only when Tamila stood up that she knew someone was behind her. Before she had time to turn around, she caught sight of a shadow in her peripheral vision. Something caught the light. Metal.

At first, she felt a sharp pain in her throat. Her head turned slightly to the right in the direction of the shadow as it moved away from her. The sudden realisation of what was happening sent her body into shock.

Tamila tried to scream, but her windpipe had been severed and only a choking sound emitted from her mouth. Instinctively, she grabbed her throat with both hands. She felt the warm liquid running through her fingers. Her head flopped forward towards the floor, and she saw her shoes had turned red and a pool of sticky blood was already forming around them.

She could hear a loud pounding in her ears and knew it was her heart desperately trying to compensate for the blood loss. Her head grew light and her vision blurred. She fell forward, and her right hand shot out in front to prevent herself from falling. But she was too weak, and her hand slid down until her knees buckled, and she crashed to the floor into her blood.

Her last sight was of the Pollock painting, the multitudinous stripes of colourful paint woven together, and now defaced by a red handprint staining the artwork.

'I'm wasting my time here,' Liam told his mother as he sat back down at the table. 'He's obviously not here.'

'Can we just give him five more minutes?' Mairéad pleaded.

Liam looked at his phone again. 'I don't know, Mum. I'm beginning to suspect your Dr Horris was only humouring you. Besides, he –'

A scream shrieked through the corridors of the gallery. Everyone in the café turned and looked in its direction. No one moved. Then it came again. Louder this time.

The manager rushed out from behind the counter and ran in its direction.

Again, the scream. And again.

Everyone who was seated stood up. Some followed the manager.

Liam grabbed his mother by the arm.

'Come on,' he told her. 'Let's get out of here.'

'What was that?' she asked.

'I have no idea. But I don't want to be here when they find out.'

Liam gripped his mother's arm more tightly, so she had no option but to comply.

Mairéad looked back towards the screams as she was quickly led away.

Chapter 40

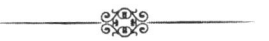

Darcy watched Mick struggling with the coffees in each of his hands as he climbed into her car.

'I got you a cappuccino,' he told her, handing her one of the takeaway cups. 'It's going to be a long night.'

Darcy wondered if the smell of the coffee was there to hide the smell of alcohol and to help sober him up.

'Thanks,' she said and placed it in the cup holder.

'What?' he asked. 'Too late for you for coffee?'

'No,' she said. 'It's just that ... well, it's the milk. I appreciate the coffee, but I don't drink milk. Remember?'

'Jesus Christ,' he said. 'It's milk. It's from cows. They don't kill the cows. What could be more natural?'

Darcy didn't want an argument or even a discussion, so she said nothing. Mick sipped his coffee in silence until they reached the National Art Gallery.

The rain had stopped, so they parked near Merrion Square and walked back towards the entrance of the gallery. White tape that read **CRIME SCENE – NO ENTRY** was blocking every street and road within two blocks. Blue lights pulsed from several Garda cars, reflecting off the windows of the buildings, turning everything and everyone blue.

They showed one of the uniforms their IDs, and he lifted the tape for them to duck under.

'Did you put this Crime Scene tape up all by yourself?' Mick asked him.

'Yes, sir,' the garda said, standing taller.

'Remind me to get you some for Christmas. Looks like you used a whole fucking year's supply.'

The garda lowered the tape and bowed his head.

'I'm just guessing,' Darcy told him as they entered the building. 'You're not much of a night person, are you?'

'No, I'm not, and I might as well warn you now – I'm not much of a morning person either.'

'Lucky me,' she said.

'I should have given him your coffee though. Wouldn't have gone to waste then.'

A uniformed garda was walking past them, and Mick grabbed him by the shoulder.

'What the fuck?' the garda said.

'Show us where the body is,' Mick ordered him.

'But I'm just finishing up,' the young garda told him. 'Get somebody else.'

Mick squared up to him and was about to say something, but Darcy stepped in between them.

'We'd appreciate it if you'd point us in the right direction, Garda,' Darcy said.

He looked between Mick's threatening face and Darcy's far more appealing one and backed down.

'This way,' he sighed and walked back into the building.

'*It's ruined!*' a high-pitched female voice could be heard as they approached the room. '*Absolutely destroyed! This collection was on loan from the MoMA in New York.*'

Darcy looked around the room. A woman's murdered body was face down in front of a large, colourful painting. Her handprint was smeared along the lower part of the painting and then continued down the wall. She lay in her own blood, which looked more like black oil. Her face was turned to one side and her dead eyes stared out, as if focused on something in the far distance.

A forensic photographer dressed all in white stepped around the body, taking photographs from every angle. There were two other forensics, also in white, with their backs to her.

A well-dressed middle-aged woman was yelling at one of the uniforms who was trying to take her statement. She heard the garda ask, 'How do you spell that, ma'am?'

'Spell what?' the woman asked.

'Jackson Bollock, is it?'

The woman looked like her head was about to explode.

When one of the forensics stood up, Darcy recognised Phoebe. Mick was walking over to her. She joined him.

'How are you here before us?' Darcy heard Mick ask Phoebe.

'Because I'm more important than you,' she told him.

'I'm not going to argue with that,' he told her.

'Congratulations, Darcy,' Phoebe said.

'For what?' Darcy asked.

'We had a bet in forensics you wouldn't last more than two days with this grumpy SOB.'

Darcy smiled.

The well-dressed woman raised her voice again. 'No, you don't seem to understand. I need to start work on its restoration immediately. Time is crucial.'

'Who's that?' Darcy asked Phoebe.

'The gallery's Art Director, Mrs Siobhán Campbell.'

'Excuse me, excuse me,' Campbell said to the photographer. 'Would you mind not using the flash on the painting, please? Thank you.'

Mick stood up. '*Hey, you!*' he called over to Campbell. '*Put a sock in it, or I'll have you removed!*'

Campbell stood with her mouth open for several moments before pulling herself together.

'This is my gallery, sir, and I get to decide –'

'No, you don't get to decide nothing.' Mick took two steps towards her. 'It's my crime scene now and if you want to stay you'll pipe down. There's a dead woman on the floor. Have a bit of fucking respect.'

Darcy walked over to her. 'Mrs Campbell, is it?' she asked.

She didn't reply.

'Mrs Campbell. We'll need all the CCTV footage of the gallery from last night. Do you have access to that?'

She looked at Darcy for the first time.

'Of course,' she said.

'Good.'

'Garda,' Darcy addressed the garda who had been taking her statement. 'Please go with Mrs Campbell and get all the video from last night and bring it to Harcourt Square.'

The garda nodded and gestured to Campbell to move. 'You lead the way, please, Mrs Campbell.'

'You know, Columbo,' Darcy heard Phoebe whispering to Mick behind her back, 'maybe if you had her as your partner all those years ago, you wouldn't be –'

'Wouldn't be what? Wouldn't be a washed-out, drunken detective on his way out?'

'I'm sorry,' Phoebe said. 'I didn't mean that.'

Darcy's phone went off in her pocket.

'Yes,' she said into it.

'Good evening, Detective. It's Sam here.'

'You're working late, aren't you?'

Darcy walked back to Mick and signalled for him to listen in to the call. He leaned his head close to the phone.

'Yes, ma'am. I've been working on this FBI tip. I managed to find an ex-member of the Palmarian Church. He's local. I thought you might get some information from him about your man Jack from California. It's a small organisation. He's bound to have heard something.'

'OK, sounds good. Text me the address.'

'Have you found that van yet?' Mick demanded.

'No, sir. So far nothing. After it left the Delaneys' house it headed towards the Dublin Mountains, and we lost sight of it. We're still searching all cameras around Mountjoy Square, but it's not a very affluent area, so it's not like everyone has video doorbells.'

'Well, keep looking!'

'Yes, sir.'

'Thanks , Sam. Goodnight,' Darcy said.

'One more thing, ma'am,' Sam said.

'Yeah?'

'I was wondering if I could sit in on the interview?'

'Why?'

'It'd be a good experience for me.'

Darcy looked up at Mick. He blew out a breath of air and then shrugged.

'OK then,' she told Sam.

'Great, thanks,' Sam's enthusiastic voice could be heard down the line.

'Tell him to make sure he doesn't fucking say anything,' Mick said.

'Detective Kelly says –'

'Yeah, I heard him, ma'am.'

'We'll meet you there at …' Darcy looked at Mick.

'7 a.m.,' Mick said into the phone, and Darcy hung up.

'Isn't it a little early to be knocking on someone's door?' Darcy asked him.

'We're gardaí, Doyle. We're not delivering pizza. We can knock on someone's door whenever the fuck we want. It's sort of a perk of the job. God knows there aren't that many.'

'Excuse me, excuse me!' Horris called out, marching his way across the gallery floor.

A rather large female uniformed garda was chasing after him.

'Excuse me,' he addressed Mick, ignoring Darcy. 'Are you the SIO here?'

'I'm sorry,' the garda said. 'He ran off on me. We were in the café awaiting instructions.'

'That's alright, Garda,' Darcy told her, and smiled at her to ease her obvious nervousness.

'Am I the what?' Mick asked Horris.

'The Senior Investigating Officer.'

'No. She is.'

Horris turned to Darcy, unimpressed. 'Well, how very modern of the Irish police force,' he said. 'Either way, I can't stay around here all night. I am missing a very important appointment.'

'And you are?' Darcy asked.

'I am Dr Austin Horris,' he said, as if declaring he were royalty.

Phoebe stepped up to him, removing her face mask. 'I know who you are,' she told him. 'I went to your lecture in Trinity a couple of nights ago.' She turned to Darcy and Mick. 'He's a serial killer expert. A psychiatrist.'

'Well, it's fortunate that someone knows my credentials.'

'I thought I recognised the victim. She was your publicist, wasn't she?'

'More like an assistant actually,' Horris told her.

'My God,' Phoebe told him. 'That's awful. I'm so sorry for your loss.'

'Well, thank you and I appreciate that, but perhaps you could tell this lady here that I have a very important appointment and need to get out of here as soon as possible.'

'Why were you here so late, sir?' Darcy asked him.

'I was supposed to meet some crazy lady who needed my professional opinion about her son. I was totally against the idea, I'll have you know, but it really has nothing to do with this …' He quickly glanced over at Tamila's body. 'An unfortunate coincidence.'

'We'll need you to stick around, sir, I'm afraid,' Darcy told him. 'If you go back to the café with this garda, please, we'll meet you there as soon as we finish up here.'

'I'm afraid that's impossible. You see, I was supposed to meet someone at ten and I'm already frightfully late.'

'It would very much help our case, sir, if you don't mind.'

'Well, actually I do mind. I don't believe you have any jurisdiction over me and, unless I'm under arrest, then I'm quite free to go at my pleasure.'

Darcy stared at him. 'You're right, Mr Horris,' she said, and he let out an audible sigh of relief. Darcy beckoned to the garda who had been chasing after him.

She stepped forward. 'Yes, ma'am.'

'Arrest this man on suspicion of murder and take him to Harcourt Street Station and put him in a cell overnight. We'll get to him sometime tomorrow. Or the next day. As you're so familiar with Irish law, Dr Horris, I'm sure you're aware that with extensions, I can have you detained for up to seven days. OK?'

'Now, hold on a minute!' Horris yelped, but Darcy had turned her back on him. 'I never said that I wouldn't cooperate with this investigation. I know Tamila was merely my assistant, but I cared for her in my own way. This is as much a shock to me as anyone.'

'So, you don't mind waiting for us in the café, then?'

'Of course I don't mind. I merely meant that I didn't want to waste your time, as I see no connection between my rendezvous and this murder.'

The uniformed garda looked from Mick to Darcy to Horris.

'Come on, come on, then, young lady,' Horris said to the uniform. 'Let's go and have some more tea and wait until we're called.' He walked away.

Darcy winked at the garda who smiled and followed him.

Mick looked around the room, then turned to Phoebe.

'We'll be back later, OK?' he told her. 'Once you lot finish fucking around, we'll come and do a proper job.'

Phoebe was already back down on her knees, examining a part of Tamila's sleeve.

'Whatever,' she said without looking up.

'Let's go have a look at that CCTV,' Mick said to Darcy as he walked away. 'Bet you're wishing now you had that coffee, aren't you? Even with the milk.'

Friday

Chapter 41

Mairéad stood up from her kitchen table. The dawn light had finally arrived and was lurking behind her blinds. The pins and needles feeling in her legs almost caused her to collapse onto the floor. She had barely moved a muscle for hours.

She clutched the side of the table, the wooden legs groaning under her weight. She leaned forward, waiting for the pain and discomfort to pass. It was as if she could feel the entire weight of the house on her back. She was just so tired.

For the entire night she had sat on the verge of tears that never came. She wanted to lie on the floor, or in the corner of a room, or to crawl into a ball and wait for everything to go away. Not face the reality that was crushing in on her from all sides.

She took two deep breaths and straightened herself. The pains in her legs passed. She opened the blinds and turned her face away from the light. She flicked on the kettle, more out of habit than anything else, and sat back down.

Last night, after Liam had driven her home, he'd returned to his own apartment. He had begged her to come with him, but she wanted to stay in her own home. Whatever was true about Conor, she knew her son would never harm her.

Liam had waited downstairs until she checked to see if Conor was in his room. He was. She had slowly opened the bedroom door and seen him sitting in darkness on the side of his bed. He was fully dressed and didn't look in her direction.

She closed the door and went back down to Liam.

'He's asleep,' she lied.

'Please, Mum,' Liam pleaded. 'Come home with me.'

She shook her head.

'I'll go to work as normal,' he told her. 'And remember, I stayed with you all evening at home. Just you and me, OK?'

She nodded and then went into the kitchen. When she was seated at the kitchen table, she heard Liam leaving. That was hours ago, and here she still sat.

She felt as if she had used all her energy to open the kitchen blinds. She was now unable to move. Unable to think. Could only just wait. But wait for what?

She closed her eyes, lay her head back down on the table and felt a flood of tears pressing behind them.

The front door slammed shut and woke Mairéad. She jumped up from her chair and fell back onto the floor. Her heart raced as she looked all around the kitchen. She was alone. How long had she been asleep? She got up, walked into the hall and looked up the stairs to see Conor's bedroom door open. He was gone.

With one hand on the door to steady herself, she dropped slowly back onto the floor in the hall. She pulled her legs tight into herself, her back pressed against the wall.

With utter exhaustion and heartache, Mairéad rocked back and forth, unable to stop her uncontrollable wailing even if she had wanted to.

Chapter 42

As Mick and Darcy turned the corner in their car, they saw Sam sitting alone in his patrol car a few doors down from the Palmarian Church ex-member's house.

'At least he had the sense not to park right outside the house and tip the guy off,' Mick said. 'There might be some hope for this kid after all.'

Darcy did park directly outside and cut the engine. They both turned and looked at the house. It was a normal semi-detached three-bedroom suburban house. Apart from an unkempt garden, old-fashioned curtains on the windows and a facade that could do with a lick of paint, it was as unexceptional as the other houses in the estate.

A car door slammed, and they watched Sam making his way over to them.

They both got out.

'Good morning,' Sam said.

Neither Darcy nor Mick replied. They were both staring up at the closed curtains on the second floor of the house.

'How do you want to play this?' Sam asked Mick.

'I say we kick the door in, drag him out of bed and then get him back to the station for an interrogation.'

'*Jesus*,' Sam said. 'Really?'

'Yeah,' Mick said, walking towards the house. 'Fuck him and his so-called rights. Let's kick some ass, as they say.'

Sam looked at Darcy, who was smiling.

'Come on,' she told him. 'Just remember to keep your mouth shut.'

Mick stepped onto the sheltered porch and gave the wooden door a few loud knocks. The sound echoed on the street.

'Well done on getting this address,' Mick told Sam.

'Yeah, no probs, sir. You see, what I did was, I found a source of all members of the Church on the Net and I –'

Mick banged on the door again, louder this time.

'*Wakey, wakey,*' he said under his breath.

'Maybe he's not in,' Sam said.

'Maybe. But then, how do you explain a wet umbrella in the corner of a sheltered area? It rained last night. Someone put it there when they came home rather than take it inside and get the house wet.'

Sam looked at the umbrella propped up against the wall.

'I didn't notice that,' he said.

'I know,' Mick said. 'That's why they pay us the big bucks.'

Sam smiled. 'I guess that's why they call you Co–'

Mick looked straight at him.

Sam subsided.

The front door opened. They could see a male figure through the partially opened door.

'Hello,' he said. 'Can I help you?'

'Good morning, Mr Hogan,' Darcy said as Mick was still glowering at Sam. 'Gardaí. Can we have a few words?'

'Is there something wrong?'

'There's nothing to worry about, I assure you,' she told him. 'We'd just like to take up a few moments of your time if that's OK?'

'Do you have a warrant? Do I need a lawyer?'

Darcy forced herself to chuckle. 'No, we don't have a warrant. And no, you don't need a lawyer. You're not in any trouble. We were hoping you might help us with some information. Just a few questions, I promise, and we'll be out of your hair.'

The man stood for a few moments, surveying them through the gap in the door. Eventually, he sighed and opened the door fully.

'Come in, then,' he told them and walked back into his house, leaving the front door open.

Mick nodded his approval at Darcy, scowled at Sam and then stepped into the hall. Darcy and Sam followed.

The exterior drab theme continued inside. Darcy imagined that the sitting room where Hogan brought them had not been redecorated in over thirty years. It reminded her of a house rented to students by a landlord who didn't give a shit as long as it was on the legal side of squalor.

There was a stack of old newspapers with four skinny, wooden legs poking out from it, the coffee table hidden underneath. An open fire smouldered, ash and pieces of wood scattered around the hearth. The heavy patterned cream curtains, perhaps a reminder of someone who had once tried to brighten up the place, remained closed.

Declan Hogan sat in a single armchair close to the unlit fire. His tracksuit bottoms and hoodie had obviously been thrown on to answer the door. Darcy figured he was younger than his grey complexion and balding head suggested. She guessed somewhere in his late forties.

Darcy and Mick sat uncomfortably close to one another on his two-seater couch. She could smell Mick's last cigarette and the rain on his jacket. There were no more chairs, so Sam stood, leaning against a wall.

'Can I get you coffee or tea?' Hogan asked.

'No, thank you,' Mick said, answering for them all.

'Should I ask for your ID cards?'

'If you like,' Darcy said, reaching into her jacket.

'You know, on second thoughts,' Hogan said. 'Forget about it. I wouldn't know a real one from a fake, anyway.' He gave a nervous laugh.

'Like I said, Mr Hogan,' Darcy began.

'Declan. Please, call me Declan. It's been a long time since anyone called me Mr Hogan. It sounds strange. Makes me feel like my dad.'

'OK, Declan,' Darcy continued. 'My name is Detective Darcy Doyle, and this is Detective Mick Kelly.'

She didn't introduce Sam.

'We're here to ask you some questions about an organisation you were involved in.'

'Ah, come on, I left the IRA years ago,' Declan said with a laugh.

Darcy and Mick looked at one another. Mick leaned forward on the couch.

'You were in the IRA, Mr Hogan?' he asked.

Hogan stopped laughing and shook his head. 'No. No, I wasn't. I was just trying to make a joke. I guess it was funnier in my head.'

Mick leaned back. A silence filled the air, and Darcy let it sit there for a moment.

'What we're looking for, Declan,' she tried again, 'is some information from your time in the Palmarian Church.'

Hogan sat back in his chair as if he'd just received bad news, and then gazed into the fireplace as if it were a blazing fire.

'I'm not proud of that period of my life,' he told them without looking up. 'But I never did anything illegal.'

'Oh, we know,' Darcy tried to assure him. 'That's not why we're here.'

Hogan turned to face them again.

Darcy sat forward. 'We're looking for information about someone you may have known or perhaps met while you were involved in that organisation.'

'I didn't know too many people, to be honest,' Hogan said. 'Most of my time was spent in Spain.'

Darcy looked at Mick.

'Spain?' Darcy asked.

'Yeah. That's where the main headquarters are.'

'Would you mind telling us how you first got involved with them?' Mick asked.

Hogan looked back into the ashes of a fire where any heat was a long-distant memory. 'I suppose it was about twenty-five years ago or so. I was going out with a girl, Tanya, for a couple of years. We drank and partied every night. We were young. Had no responsibilities. But then one morning we woke up and had vodka for our breakfast. My best mate, Danny, said he'd help us, and we started going to AA meetings.'

'Good for you,' Darcy said. 'Did it work?'

'Yeah, it did actually. It worked too well. They told us, I mean our AA sponsor, that we needed to fill the void left by alcohol. Religion filled my void. So much so I joined the Palmarian Church. And Danny, my so-called best mate, filled Tanya's void.'

Sam let out a loud chuckle. They all looked at him.

'Sorry about that,' Sam said.

Darcy and Mick looked back at Hogan.

'I guess if you don't laugh about some things in your life,' Hogan said, 'you'll either kill yourself or, worse, kill someone else.'

Mick cleared his throat. 'Was it then that you moved out to Spain?'

'Yeah,' Hogan said. 'I didn't have anything here. I broke off contact with my family. The Church persuaded me to do that. Didn't take much persuading, to be honest. Tanya moved out, so there was nothing here for me anymore.'

Hogan lowered his head in defeat.

Darcy wanted to slap him in the face and tell him to stop being such a pitiable excuse of a man. Instead, she asked him, 'When you were in Spain, did you ever come across a man named Jack?'

'Yeah, I sure did. If it's the same Jack I'm thinking of.'

Hogan's mind seemed to wander back to that time.

Darcy took out her notebook and pen.

'I knew it,' he said to himself.

'Knew what, Declan?' Darcy asked him, but his mind seemed to be somewhere else. 'Declan?'

'Sorry. I just knew one day that guy would do something crazy.'

'Do you remember his last name?' Mick asked, unable to stand the tension.

'No,' Declan said. 'I mean, we didn't do last names. Most of us didn't know each other's surname. They said it only tied us to our pasts. But I seem to remember Connor or O'Connor.'

'Jack O'Connor?' Darcy asked.

'Maybe. I don't know.'

'Did he have a wife?'

'Yeah, and two kids. Two boys.'

'What was the wife's name?' she asked.

'*Emm* ... Marie, or Maria. No, Mairéad. Jack and Mairéad. That was them. She was Irish. He was American.'

'And their boys' names?' Darcy asked.

Hogan thought about it for a while, but then shook his head. 'No, sorry. I can't remember their names. I never was very good at names,' he said. 'Two little shits if you ask me, though. One of them, the youngest, he never spoke. Something wrong with him. The other one never shut the hell up.'

'What about their parents?' Darcy asked.

'Mairéad was nice enough. Quiet, you know. Barely ever heard her say anything. I suppose she never got a chance with that son of hers.'

'And what about her husband?' Mick asked. 'Jack?'

Hogan let out a breath. 'Jack was … Jack was the strangest one of all. And that's saying a lot when you're that closely involved in the church.'

'Crazy how?' Mick asked.

'Just weird, you know. Wait a second,' Hogan said, sitting up straighter. 'Are you here about those bodies?'

'What bodies would they be?' Mick asked.

'Those women. Out in Spain.'

'Spain? What women?'

'OK,' Hogan said, settling his voice. 'I was there for about a year, and a woman from the nearby village was killed. It was a gruesome murder as far as I remember. Then six months later, the same thing happened.'

Darcy wrote in her notepad. 'Do you remember the year?'

'Probably late nineties,' Hogan said. 'I was getting disillusioned at that time, and I left soon afterwards. Went to England for a while. I was in London for the Millennium, so it must have been mid-1999.'

'What's this got to do with Jack?' Mick asked.

'He disappeared after the first murder and then came back. Then the second woman was killed, and he disappeared again. One day we woke up and the whole family was gone.'

'Where?' Darcy asked.

'Here,' he told them. 'Ireland. No idea where exactly.'

'Do you know why? Why he left?'

Hogan looked from side to side as if afraid someone was listening. 'They kicked him out. I heard he'd been responsible for the murders of those women. Some said he was the one who cut their throats. But the top dogs in the Church were tipped off by someone in the *Guardia Civil* that they were about to do a raid.'

'So rather than face the embarrassment of a murder conviction for one of their members,' Darcy said, 'they thought it best to throw him out of the Church?'

'No,' Hogan said.

'No? What then?' Darcy asked.

'They made a deal with Jack alright. But what I heard was that the Church said they'd cover his tracks and help him disappear if he'd go back to Ireland and recruit more members.'

'And you've never met or even seen him or any members of his family since then?'

'Never. I told you. I don't want to have anything to do with any of their sort.'

'So they knew he had murdered those women,' Darcy said, 'and they let him go so he'd recruit more people?'

Hogan nodded. 'Yep. Never underestimate the power of a few crazy religious nuts in a room, Detective.'

Chapter 43

After a cursory briefing with the chief, Darcy and Mick continued to the incident room in Harcourt Street. Mick told Darcy it was always a good idea to give the uniforms a little pep talk after a few days on a case. Otherwise, they felt irrelevant, and their minds wandered.

Darcy spotted Eoin and Aoife huddled around Sam and his monitors. She caught a snippet of their conversation and overheard Sam saying 'while we interviewed him'. The other two failed to disguise their envious expressions.

Mick stood at the top of the room.

'*OK, everybody!*' he called out. '*If I could have your attention, please!*'

All the uniforms settled down.

'I want to take a couple of moments with you to go over where we are now. Often in a big case like this, there's so much going on from so many different angles that we lose sight of what's important. Too much noise can cause a lot of confusion. OK?'

They all nodded.

'We believe our primary suspect's name is Jack, and he's married to a Mairéad, and they have two sons. Revenue has been informed and we're trying to crossmatch the names with them now. Garda Cara Walsh has managed to track down the only person who got a good look at him. Our man, Jack, almost collided into him with his van. Unfortunately, the artist's sketch is not going to be the great crime solver that we were hoping for. Jack likes to wear a hoodie and keep a baseball cap low on his face, but it's better than nothing. We're waiting on approval from higher up before passing it on to the media. Either way, we're close to this guy. I know it and I can feel it. What's more important is that he knows it too. We're putting pressure on him, and he will fuck up. This case, like most cases, is going to be solved by old-fashioned police work, following up on all leads, checking CCTV, forensics, dotting the i's and crossing the t's. As much as we like the credit, most cases are not solved by the leading detectives bursting open a door or apprehending the suspect in a car chase. It's often solved by someone like you answering a phone call and asking the right question or spotting something unusual in a photo. Stay focused, keep being persistent and we'll all get this guy and put him right where the fucker belongs. Now, let's get back to work.'

Mick went over to Sam and looked over his shoulder at the three monitors in front of him. Mick signalled for Darcy to come over. She walked over to him and recognised various rooms in the museum on each of the screens.

'Have a look at that, Darcy,' Mick said.

The black-and-white image showed the café. The camera's point of view showed most of the seated area with the counter and till at the top of the screen.

'Go ahead. Play it again, Sam, as the man said,' Mick ordered.

Sam pressed a button on his computer, and the image's next frame jumped a little.

'It's taking a photo every five seconds,' Sam said. 'It's not the best of technology, but it's good enough for what we're after.'

The image jumped ahead through a few more scenes.

'See this couple here?' Mick said to Darcy, pointing to a couple sitting together at a table.

Darcy watched everyone in the café look towards the hall. Some of them stood up. The manager came out from behind the counter, and they watched him running out of the café and into the hall.

Other people slowly followed him. The man and the woman stood up then, and the man could be seen hurriedly escorting the woman out.

'Everyone's running one way,' Mick said. 'But this couple go in the opposite direction. Why?'

'Because they already knew what everyone else would find in that room,' Darcy suggested.

They watched the paused screen of the man and the woman as they left the café.

'Go back,' Darcy said.

'Back to where?' Sam asked.

'Back to when they first sat down.'

Sam rewound the tape until he came to the image of the woman at the table and the man joining her.

'Where was he?' Darcy asked.

'What do you mean?' Sam said.

'Where was this man while she was already sitting down?'

'I don't know,' he said. 'Taking a leak?'

'Go back further,' Mick told him.

Sam rewound it again until both the man and woman were seated together. He paused the image of them.

'How long was he missing?' Darcy asked.

Mick looked at Darcy as Sam calculated the missing time.

'He was gone for just over ten minutes,' he said.

'Get me some stills of these images,' Mick told Sam.

'They'll be quite pixelated.'

'Just get them and pass them around.'

Sam nodded.

Mick spotted a uniform coming into the room and looking around him. He spotted Mick and made his way over. He was holding a piece of paper in his hand.

'What is it?' Mick asked him.

'A message was left at the front desk for you.'

'Go on.'

'A Mr Declan Hogan.'

'Our church guy from this morning,' Darcy said.

The garda read from the piece of paper in his hand.

'He says, "*It wasn't O'Connor. The younger, quiet kid's name was Conor. His shitbag older brother was called Liam*".'

All three of them stood in silence looking at the paper as if it held all the answers in the world. Darcy clicked her fingers and Mick and the garda looked at her.

'The Department of Education,' she said.

'What about it?'

'She, the mother, Mairéad, would have had to register her children with the D.O.E. before getting them a place in school. We need to open their database and find any kids who were registered at that time, maybe at the end of 1999? Isn't that what Hogan said?'

The uniformed garda perked up. 'You know, there can't be too many kids registered at that time. I mean, after the school year started.'

Darcy and Mick stared at him. Then Mick nodded for him to run along back to the front desk.

Darcy was already on the computer, logging in by the time Mick joined her.

One hour later, it popped up onto the screen.

Father: Jack Carter. Nationality (Dual) USA and Irish

Mother: Mairéad Carter (née Sheehan) Nationality: Irish
Liam Carter. Nationality: Irish (Born in Spain)
Conor Carter. Nationality: Irish (Born in Spain)
14 Loftus Avenue,
Dublin 14
Marital Status: Married
NPC: No Prior Convictions.

Darcy looked at the screen calmly. She took long deep breaths, but inside she felt as if she were looking at the winning lottery ticket numbers.

Chapter 44

Conor was sitting at the kitchen table, his mother opposite him, a large brown envelope on the table between them. Mairéad couldn't find the courage to remove the severed ponytail of blonde hair from it but felt that the droplets of blood on the envelope were enough to stir her son's admission of guilt.

She tried to speak, but her throat felt clamped and tight. Only one word came out.

'Why?' she asked him.

Conor looked at her.

'Why?' she asked him again.

Conor just looked at her.

Her feelings of anger, sadness and hopelessness were finally overtaken by sheer exhaustion. The tears burst out of her like a sudden downpour. She put one hand to her face and covered her eyes as if trying to stop them.

Then she felt something she couldn't remember happening before. Her son put his hand on her other hand. She looked at his hand on hers on the table, touching her skin, then she looked up at him.

Was this an admission of guilt or a final show of empathy for his mother?

When he eventually removed his hand, she stood up and went to the kitchen counter and pulled off a paper towel. She wiped her eyes and sniffled. She took a few deep breaths in and out and then walked back to the table.

The door into the hall was open and above Conor's head Mairéad saw the smallest of blue lights flicker in the glass panel. She stopped and looked at where it had been. She walked into the sitting room and looked out onto the road. There was a Garda car with two gardaí sitting inside it. As she was behind the white lace curtains, they couldn't see her, but she could see them, and they were looking straight at her house. A chill ran down her spine. They have come for him, she thought. They have finally come.

She hurried back into the kitchen. Panic was setting in and her breaths became short and quick. She looked at Conor and around the kitchen, her eyes finally resting on the wooden shed in the back garden.

Chapter 45

Darcy ran down the four flights of stairs in the Harcourt Street building and into the underground carpark. By the time she was out in front, Mick was coming down the exterior steps.

Her phone rang as he got into the car. She answered it and put it on her lap.

'Darcy?' Jamie said.

'What is it?'

'Chief O'Riordan has informed me of the development and requested the services of the ERU.'

'Good.'

'You are not to enter that house until it's secured by ERU. Is that clear?'

She didn't answer as her car joined the traffic on Harcourt Street.

'Do I need to get the chief to call you and give you an order?' Jamie asked.

'OK. Just hurry the fuck up!'

'We're on our way.'

Darcy looked down at her lap and ended the call. When she looked back up, she was racing towards the back of a car stopped in traffic. She slammed down on the brakes and came to a stop inches from the other car.

Mick's hands smacked hard onto the dash. *'Jesus Christ!'*

She stuck the car back into first gear, pulled out into the oncoming traffic and drove hard again.

Less than three minutes after Darcy had left, two Audi Q7 jeeps and a black Range Rover roared out onto Kevin Street and into the traffic. The ERU vehicles' sirens blared and echoed off the 18th century Georgian buildings.

They weaved in and out of the cars as if attached by links to each other. Each vehicle held four uniformed and armed personnel. Jamie sat in the front passenger seat in the leading jeep. Unlike the covert operation on Frank Kavanagh's house, this raid would be sparse of any subtlety.

Darcy and Mick arrived first. They parked a block away and ran the remaining distance but kept back from the house as instructed. They spotted the uniforms sitting outside the target house and Mick was tempted to risk his cover just so he could drag them out of the car.

'If those two have blown the surprise by parking there, I'll fucking ...'

As Darcy expected, the ERU vehicles turned into the street moments later. They blocked the entrance and exit to the road. The doors of the vehicles were already opening before they'd come to a complete stop.

A team of four went to the front entrance. One of them, the breacher, carried a battering ram – more commonly known as the Enforcer – and held it to the front door, awaiting his order. Two more officers stood at the side gate, ready to gain entry to the back of the house. The garda with the Enforcer kept his eyes on Jamie, who stood at the back, his Heckler and Koch assault rifle pointed to the ground.

Jamie nodded, and the garda swung the Enforcer back and burst open the door. The officer shouted, '*Door breached!*', and the team went in.

Darcy didn't wait. She heard the shouts of '*Armed gardaí!*' through the house as she stepped into the hall. She saw Mairéad sitting at the kitchen table, with her back to her, looking out into the garden at the back of the house.

'The search of the house has not been completed, ma'am,' one of the ERU officers informed her, but she ignored him and walked into the kitchen.

She turned to face Mairéad. She looked dreadful, like she hadn't slept or eaten in days.

Mick stood in the doorframe watching, but he said nothing.

'Mairéad Carter?' Darcy said.

Mairéad looked up at her.

'*Where is he?*'

Darcy looked away. Then her hand formed into a fist, and she slammed it down onto the kitchen table.

Mairéad jumped.

'*Where the fuck is he?*' Darcy screamed into her face.

Tears fell down Mairéad's face and her whole body shivered.

Jamie brushed by Mick into the kitchen.

'Darcy, Mick,' he said. 'There's no one here.'

Darcy turned away towards the garden. Two ERU officers were there. Another was inside the wooden shed.

Darcy rested her hands on the kitchen counter. Her eyes looked around the shelves and rested on the sink.

There was a single mug in the sink. She picked it up, then turned back to face Mairéad, the mug still in her hand. She looked down at the table. There was another mug in front of Mairéad.

Mick understood. He walked to her and took the mug.

'What is it?' Jamie asked.

'She knew we were coming,' Mick answered for her.

'How?'

'I don't know. Maybe those two fuckers outside in the squad car tipped her off. They got the call the same time as us and decided to park outside her bloody house instead of keeping their distance until we arrived.'

'The cup is still warm,' Darcy said. 'Someone was here a few minutes ago.'

Mick looked at Mairéad. Mairéad's head was lowered.

He leaned over her. 'You know what he did to those women, don't you?'

Mairéad lowered her head even further.

'*Don't you?*' Mick screamed at her. '*Where is he?*'

'Mick,' Jamie said, 'he must have gone over the back. We'll get an Alpha Sierra chopper up in the air. We'll find him.'

'Arrest her anyway,' Mick told him.

'On what charge?'

'I don't give a fuck. Obstructing justice, I don't care.'

Mick glanced over at Mairéad. Her head was raised now, and she was trying to look into the back garden. When she saw Mick looking at her, her head shot back down.

Mick turned and followed her gaze into the garden. He looked back at her and then back to the garden. The shed. She was looking at the shed.

Mick walked out the back door into the garden, and Darcy followed him.

'What is it?' she asked him, but he continued outside.

The three ERU officers were standing together, chatting. Mick looked at the shed and walked over to the opened door.

'We've already searched in there, sir,' one of the ERU said.

Mick ignored him and stepped inside. Darcy followed him.

It was full of the usual bric-à-brac that every family shed holds, half-full tins of paint, a kid's rusted bike, a lawnmower, shelves that held various rusted tools.

Darcy's eyes searched everything until they saw emergency supplies in the corner. Unlike the rest of the items, these were newer. Large plastic containers of water, a first aid kit, rain gear, a torch, tins of beans and powdered milk. Darcy bent down and picked up the torch to see if it was working.

'Lads,' Jamie said, standing in the door.

Darcy turned to look at him.

'We have the other son, Liam. He's being brought back to Harcourt Street now. Do you want to interview him?'

Darcy looked back at the torch, unsure why she was holding it. She clicked the button. The light came on and off.

'Before Kane and Burns get their hands on him,' Jamie said, lowering his voice.

Darcy stood up and put the torch back on the shelf. They walked back through the house, ignoring Mairéad, who still sat in the chair.

'Why don't I stick around here for a while?' Darcy asked Mick when they were out of earshot. 'Perhaps I can get some info out of the mother.'

'Woman to woman, you mean?'

'Something like that. Would help also if there weren't so many guns and uniforms around. Put her a little bit at ease.'

'OK but take her into the sitting room. I want to have this place pulled apart.'

'OK,' she said and walked back into the kitchen.

The two uniformed gardaí who had been outside in the squad car were standing at the front door.

'You two,' Mick said to them. 'You're to stay outside this house. Make sure no one leaves or comes in without us knowing about it.'

'OK, sir,' one of them replied. 'But we're actually just finishing our shift, so we'll call in someone to replace us.'

Mick glared at the pair of them.

The colour drained from their faces.

'*What did you fucking say?*'

They both stared back at him.

'Did I tell you to call in for someone else?'

They shook their heads.

'Get back in that fucking car and don't move until I tell you to move. Call your girlfriends or boyfriends and tell them to cancel whatever the fuck you had planned for your little Friday night together. And I hope whatever the fuck it was, it involved expensive tickets. Is that clear?'

'Yes, sir,' they both answered together and hurried back to their car.

Chapter 46

Liam knew his arrest was inevitable. When the uniformed gardaí and the two detectives had been shown into his office, it had been almost with a sense of *déjà vu*. Under the gaze of his colleagues, he was silently escorted out of the building and into the awaiting squad car outside reception.

The interview room at the Garda Station was also what he had imagined. He breathed in the stench of cigarette smoke and sweat, which wasn't so much in the air – it seeped from the furniture and the concrete walls. Only the room being reduced to rubble would ever stop that smell. The table was metallic, and the chair was riveted to the floor. The colour of the paint on the walls could only be described as institutional. He felt rancid just by being in the room.

He sat alone for thirty minutes. This, he believed, was part of their plan to unsettle and unnerve him. The silence and anticipation could drive anyone crazy, so that when the door was finally opened, anything would be confessed to end one's anxiety. He derived comfort from the plan he'd gone over in his head a hundred times: say as little as possible and call his lawyer.

Mick marched down the corridor like a pissed-off Rottweiler on a long leash. He stopped outside the interview room. There was a garda stationed outside.

'Were you one of the arresting officers?' Mick asked him.

'Yes, sir.'

'How did he seem?'

'To be honest, it was like he was waiting for us.'

Mick let out a long sigh. 'Why do I always get the impression that everyone else is one step ahead of us?'

He put his hand on the handle and opened the door. Stepping into the room, he closed the door behind him. He sat on the chair opposite Liam, placed the large brown folder to his right on the table and pressed the red button on the recorder. Only then did he look across the table.

The folder was mostly packed with blank pages, but Mick had found that the larger folders always gave the impression he had more information than he actually had. He saw Liam's eyes glance in its direction and knew it had achieved its desired effect.

Mick leaned back in his chair and folded his arms across his chest. His eyes surveyed every visible part of the man sitting opposite him.

Liam knew this game of 'first one to break the silence loses'. He had won many good business deals by using it himself. He didn't mind losing today however, as he had nothing to lose.

'I want my phone call, and I want my lawyer,' he said.

Mick didn't respond for a while. 'You young fellas watch too much fucking Netflix these days,' he said then. 'That's not exactly how it works.'

He fell silent again.

'Where is he?' he finally asked.

'Who? My lawyer?'

'You know who I'm talking about. Where is he?'

'Weren't you at my mum's house? If *you* can't find him, then how can I?' Liam said, and then immediately berated himself for having engaged in a conversation.

'I have you on video tape leaving the scene of a crime. A murder crime scene. With a good lawyer, a very good lawyer, you're still looking at an open-and-shut case, a plea bargain, and five years max. How does that grab you?'

Mick watched Liam's lips tighten and a vein in his neck pulse. He wasn't expecting him to be so composed, but at least he had his attention now.

'Where is he?' Mick asked again, unfolding his arms.

Liam shook his head.

'Do you know what you're up against here? Do you? Have you any fucking idea?' Mick asked him. 'Just in case you're not in the loop, as they say, three women have been butchered in the last week by your miserable excuse of a father.'

Liam sat up in his chair. 'What did you say?'

Mick was disconcerted by the interruption.

'Did you say my *father*?'

'Don't start playing games with me.'

'Jack? You're looking for Jack Carter?'

A smile spread across Liam's face. Mick felt like slapping him.

'OK then,' Liam said. 'I can tell you exactly where Jack Carter is. I can even pinpoint his precise location. Mount Jerome Cemetery.'

Mick was stunned.

'Jesus,' Liam said, 'you really need to update your data sources.'

'What the fuck are you talking about?'

'Jack Carter, the miserable piece of shit that he was, died in a car accident a month ago. And good riddance to him.'

Mick tried to make sense of this new information.

'And here I was thinking you were looking for …' Liam stopped talking, biting down on his lip.

'Looking for who?' Mick asked him. 'You thought we were looking for who?'

Liam remained tight-lipped. Mick picked up the folder and leafed through the pages. When he came across what he was looking for, he glanced back up at Liam.

'Conor? You thought we were looking for your brother, didn't you?'

Mick's mind was racing. He tried to decipher all this information. Was Conor their man? Had he been at his mother's house?

Mick's phone buzzed in his pocket. Distracted, he took out the phone and looked at the screen.

Darcy's number. Without saying another word, he stood up and went to the door.

'How long am I going to be here?' Liam called out, but Mick ignored him and stepped into the corridor again.

'It isn't the father,' Darcy told him.

'I know. It's the other son we're after. What else is the mother telling you?'

'Not much, to be honest. She mentioned a few parks he liked to frequent, that's about it. Looks a bit of a "like father, like son" sort of scenario. We found a severed ponytail in an envelope in a drawer in the kitchen.'

'*Jesus!* Do we have any good images of him to circulate?'

'Not really. I get the impression he wasn't a happy, snappy sort of guy, if you know what I mean. You want me to bring her in now?'

'No. There's still a chance he'll come home. Like most people, killers are also creatures of habit. Lower the Garda presence but keep a few ERU officers there. On site, but out of sight.'

'OK, Mick. You know, I'd almost feel sorry for this Conor fella if I hadn't seen the evidence myself.'

'That's a jury's job, not yours. I'll come back and pick you up, and we'll assist in the search. Check out some of those parks.'

'OK.'

'I'm still in Harcourt Street, so I'll get on to the chief now and get him to throw every garda on this. We'll find him.'

'What about the brother there?'

Mick looked back at the closed interview room.

'Let him stew for a while. I get the impression some fancy lawyer is already on his way right now. They always are.'

Chapter 47

'You look tired,' Darcy told Mick as they stopped outside her house, Mick at the wheel.

'That's because I am tired. You don't look too fresh yourself.'

'Thanks. You're a real charmer.'

'You're not the first person to tell me that.'

Darcy got out of the car. They had spent the remainder of the day driving around the parks that Mairéad had mentioned, and then throughout the city, as had every other available unit in the Dublin area. But without an up-to-date photograph of Conor Carter, the task had so far been futile. A search of his home had produced a single photo of Conor as a schoolboy. If one more person had complained to her that it was like 'looking for a needle in a haystack' she'd most likely have punched them.

She walked around to the driver's door, and Mick lowered the window.

'Make sure you get some sleep,' he told her.

'No problem there. See you in the morning,' she said and walked back towards her house.

She heard the car drive away, but she didn't watch it go. Her phone beeped.

Want me to call over?

Darcy let out a deep sigh.

I'm exhausted, Jamie. Going straight to bed.
No probs. Night.

Darcy opened her front door. The running gear she had put on and then taken off that morning was thrown across her sofa. Even as she had driven up to her house with Mick and felt the tiredness in her limbs, she knew she would have to exercise before going to bed. It was the only way she would ever get to sleep. She changed, set her Garmin watch for a fast five-kilometre jog, and then left the house again.

A misty rain fell when she was halfway through her run, and she welcomed it. The images of the dead women she had tried to push from her mind fell away, if only temporarily. Her mind and body, despite the fast run, relaxed, and the adrenaline that had ebbed and flowed through her all day seeped away.

She thought of the man in the hall of Jennifer Delaney's house. She imagined his eyes that lurked behind his mask. She imagined his hands on those women. His hand on the knife.

She raised the volume on her iPhone, and the music blared in her ears. It propelled her forward, and she ran faster. She ran so fast that it was as if the rain fell heavier to keep up with her. She wiped the rain from her face as she turned onto her street.

One more big push to finish, she thought, as she powered along towards her house.

Later, she would blame the loud music in her ears, the rain on her face and even the high speed at which she ran as the reasons why she didn't notice the thin steel wire that was stretched across her path.

Her neck struck it at full force. Her legs and body shot forward as it choked her throat, and it slammed her down onto the wet ground. The back of her head hit the concrete, and she heard a crack.

Although the wire was not touching her, she felt as if it were still choking her. She heard a vehicle's door open and close, and then footsteps getting louder. Someone not in a rush. Someone with all the time in the world.

She tried to look around, but all she could see was the rain falling on her from the night sky.

Then a man stood over her. A man wearing a hoodie, but the rain blurred her vision, and it shrouded his face in the darkness of the night. She was trying so hard to focus on his face that it was several seconds before she even noticed the gun pointing at her body.

She tried to call out, but no sound came from her windpipe. She tried to raise her hands to protect herself, but only managed to lift them a few inches.

He fired the gun, but even as the pain shot through her, she knew it was a taser. The darts stuck into her abdomen and 50,000 volts hammered through her. Her body spasmed and her muscles cramped up in pain.

Then the blackness came as she felt the cloth of a hood being shoved over her head. She was dragged through a puddle and although she felt the cold water on her back, she was unable to react to it. She felt herself being lifted into the back of a van. Every muscle in her body ached with pain.

When inside the van, the man pushed and pulled at her arms and legs. Darcy heard the zipping sound as he fastened cable ties around her hands and feet. She felt him rummaging with the Velcro of her iPhone holder on her arm and take out her phone.

Again, she tried to call out, but the sound caught in her throat. She raised her head slightly, but that's all she could do. She listened to her heavy breathing, but it was as if she were trapped inside a useless body, a paralysed body. And then she thought of Seán, and she wanted to cry.

She desperately fought against the urge to black out, but she was fighting against her own body that wanted to shut down, to shut itself down from the pain that was there and perhaps from the pain that was certain to come.

The door slammed shut, and she lowered her head back onto the floor of the van, and the blackness crept in from behind her eyes, and she stopped fighting it.

Saturday

Chapter 48

Darcy Doyle consciously relaxed her breathing. The darkness closed in on her like a suffocating blanket. She could feel it touching her skin and moving around her. Her eyes darted from side to side, desperately searching for some crack of light where she could focus.

There wasn't any part of her body that didn't hurt. Some parts, like her head and her stomach, hurt more than others, but everywhere pulsed with pain.

How long had she been unconscious? Minutes? Hours? Longer?

The cloth hood was gone, and she tried to adjust her eyes to the dark, but there was only blackness. There was barely any difference whether she opened or closed her eyelids. Even so, she looked in the direction of where her hands and legs were. She could feel the cable ties cutting into her skin. If she tried to move her feet or her hands even slightly, a sharp pain ran up her arms and legs.

She was seated on a cold surface. Metal, she thought. She could feel it on her back too. Her clothes were still wet from the rain. That was probably what was causing her to shiver. At least, that's what she told herself – that it wasn't pure terror.

She breathed in and out steadily through her nose. Her mouth was closed shut with what she imagined was duct tape. The man hadn't just sealed her mouth with a strip of the stuff, he had wrapped it around her head several times.

There was an unmitigated stench in the room that was making her want to vomit. She feared what exactly might explain the putrid odour that was tangible in the air all around her.

She remembered him picking up her limp body from the floor of the van, and she had kicked out at him with everything she had. But then he punched her with the worst type of punch there is: an unexpected one. She had learned in Templemore about the different types of punches someone might receive. To knock someone unconscious was quite difficult, the instructor had told her. The skull had evolved its shape to be near perfect for diminishing blunt force trauma. Location and surprise, he had told them, were more important than force. Her brain had felt like it had rattled around inside her head and a white light had flashed behind her eyes before her body had gone limp in his grip.

She now squinted in a desperate attempt to gauge the room. For some inexplicable reason, her not knowing where she was scared her the most. Not being able to see the floor or the walls frightened her almost to the point of panic.

A loud *clang* rattled through the room. She moved her head from left to right, unsure which direction it was coming from. Then another loud metal-grating-metal noise that seemed to echo inside her head.

Not light, but a lesser darkness, appeared before her as a door opened. It was so far away that she momentarily felt as if she were falling backwards into a hole. Even at that distance, however, she felt the cool air of the night rushing in.

She thought about what she was seeing and hearing. Then she knew where she was, or at least what she was sitting inside: a metal shipping container.

A figure appeared in the door. She knew it was the man. What had he come to do to her? She tried to stay alert and present, and not to allow her mind to conjure up images from the darkest part of her imagination.

His footsteps echoed through the container. She tried harder to focus her vision. She shook her head. He stopped a few feet from her and stood perfectly still.

She shook her head again, trying to clear her thoughts, her vision. She couldn't stand the silence any longer, and she let out a loud scream at him. All that came out was a pathetic, muffled sound. She moved her feet and hands in pure frustration, but the pain caused her to wail again.

Tears poured down her face. She didn't want to cry. She didn't want this fucker to see her cry.

She watched the shadow of his arm rise up in front of her. He had something in his hand. Another taser?

A knife.

It soaked up the light in the room like a twelve-inch narrow mirror. Darcy felt her insides cave in, and a panic and fear took hold of her that rendered any movement impossible.

He reached out and grabbed the hair on her head and pulled her head closer to him. She tried to kick and wail, but his grip was vice-like.

He pulled her head back sharply and the wound on her neck caused by the steel wire opened, and the pain shot through her body. But the pain finally shook her into life, and she thrashed and wailed and kicked with everything she had.

She saw the glimmer of the knife as it descended, the man holding onto her with his other arm, steadying her for the cut. She heard the slice, and then he threw her back onto the floor.

Her hands tried to reach up for her neck, and her breath was caught in her throat. It took her several moments to realise that she could still breathe and that her neck had not been cut.

But what had he sliced?

Her eyes looked up and around for him. He stood back from her, motionless. In his hand he held her blonde ponytail. She stared at it as if he had sliced off her arm.

He stuck the knife into a sheath attached to his belt and took out a phone. It looked like her own phone.

He pointed it at her, and it flashed.

The flash of light was like pins being stuck in her eyes. She jerked away from the bright flash and smacked her head off the wall of the container. She had heard the click. He had taken her picture.

He turned around and walked away. The phone flashed again and again. This time, the camera was pointing at the floor. He kept flashing the camera on the phone as he left. All she could see of him was the silhouette of his back as the sound of his footsteps echoed off the metal walls and roof.

He vanished into the night. The door slammed shut and a heavy metallic bar was placed across the outside.

Then complete darkness again.

Complete silence.

Complete helplessness.

Chapter 49

As Mick pulled up outside Darcy's house, he tried one last time to phone her. It went straight to voicemail again.

He glanced down at the two cappuccinos on the passenger seat in the cardboard holder, hers with soy milk (it had embarrassed him asking for it) and left them there. He got out and banged on her front door. Just like her phone, there was no answer.

He cupped his hands and put his face against the window. He peered inside and then knocked on the window and listened. A dog barked in one of the back gardens of a neighbour's house.

He took out his phone and flipped through the contacts.

'Good morning, Detective Kelly,' Jamie said. 'To what do I owe the pleasure of this early call?'

'Have you heard from Darcy?' Mick asked.

'No. I mean, I texted her last night, and she replied. Why? Is there something wrong?'

'Probably not. She's not answering her phone and there doesn't seem to be anyone at home.'

Mick could hear the cogs in Jamie's brain whirling.

'She might have gone for a jog.'

'Without her phone?'

'Maybe she forgot to charge it.'

Mick looked around the small square of houses. He thought he saw curtains twitching in one of the houses opposite.

'Try looking in the window,' Jamie suggested.

'Jesus, that's a great idea. I wish I'd thought of that.'

'And?' Jamie asked, either ignoring or unaware of the sarcasm in Mick's voice.

'I can see the clothes she wore last night thrown on the sofa.'

'Well, there you go.'

'There I go, what?'

'She obviously got up and went for a run, and she forgot to charge her phone. I'm sure she'll come running around the corner soon.'

Mick looked over at the entrance to the square, expecting her to suddenly appear.

'Maybe I should be the detective, Detective?' Jamie asked.

'Maybe. Just something's not right.'

'I'll call over straight away. I'm leaving for work now anyway. If she's back by then, I'll call you. OK?'

Mick looked into Darcy's sitting room again.

'OK?' Jamie asked.

'OK. I have an idea where she could be too. I'll check there.'

He disconnected the phone.

He wished he could shake off that feeling of uneasiness. Previously, he would have acted on instinct and kicked the door in, but he was older now. Maybe his instinct wasn't what it used to be. Maybe he was being melodramatic and could put his feelings down to simply being tired. Maybe he was losing it.

He banged on the door one more time, in frustration more than anything, and stepped away from the house.

He heard a closing door echo through the square and looked over to see an elderly lady walking out onto the main road.

'Morning, ma'am!' he called out.

She scowled at him. '*Dirty feckers!*' she snarled.

Mick raised his eyebrows. 'Fair enough,' he said and got into the car. He looked down at the two coffees side by side and then drove off.

Chapter 50

Mick took the lift to Seán's room in the Mater Hospital, but when he opened the door Darcy wasn't there.

Seán was looking out at the early morning but turned his head towards the door.

'Good morning,' Mick said.

Seán nodded a greeting, his eyes fixed on Mick, as Mick surveyed the room.

'You know who I am?' Mick eventually asked him.

Seán nodded his head slightly.

'I'm sorry to barge in, but I'm looking for Detective Darcy Doyle. Has she been in this morning?'

Seán raised his eyebrows in concern.

'Don't worry. It's probably nothing. I don't think so, anyway. I was over at her place this morning and –'

Mick's phone rang. He looked at the screen and put it on speakerphone.

'Jamie. Any news?'

'No. I'm at her house now. There's no sign of her.'

Mick looked out of the hospital window.

'Something's very wrong here,' Jamie said.

Mick was silent. Seán watched him.

Jamie's voice came over the speaker again. 'Mick, she could be gone since last night. What time did you drop her off?'

'Wait a second,' Mick told him. 'Let's look at all the obvious possibilities first. You call all the hospitals. I'll get onto the stations and see if any accidents were reported in the area. I'll head over to Harcourt Street now.'

Mick's phone beeped. He looked at the sender's name and let out a big sigh.

'Thank fuck,' Mick said.

'What is it?' Jamie asked.

'It's Darcy. I just got a text from her.'

'Thank God for that!'

He opened the message from Darcy's phone. It was a picture text.

Mick felt the room spin around and his heart stop beating in his chest. He stared down at the image.

Seán looked at him and strained to talk or move.

'Where is she?' Jamie's voice came out of the phone.

Mick was unable to talk.

'Mick,' Jamie tried again, louder. 'What is it?'

Mick took a deep breath and let it out slowly. He had trained himself over the years, even in the most time pressing of situations, to breathe in and out and count to ten before acting. He did this now and then spoke into the phone.

'He has her. The bastard has her. Get back to Harcourt Street now.'

'Where is she?'

Mick could hear the panic in his voice.

'I've no idea where she is. I'll have the IT guys try to locate her phone. Now do as I say and get the ERU ready if we get a location.'

Mick ended the call. He looked down again at the image of Darcy's slumped body on the floor. Was she dead? Was it already too late?

Mick looked at Seán, and Seán let out a groan that filled the room.

'I'm sorry, Seán. I have to go.'

But when Mick tried to leave his bedside, Seán groaned louder.

'Seán,' he said more loudly. 'I need to go.'

Mick could see the strain on Seán's face.

'Seán?'

'*Gg ... gggg ...*'

'What?'

'*Ggg ... ga ... ga ...*'

'Seán, I'm sorry. I don't understand.'

Seán became more agitated, and spit formed on his mouth as he tried to speak.

'*Nurse!*' Mick rushed to the door and yelled down the corridor. '*Nurse!*'

'*Gaaarm ... Gaaarm ...*' Seán groaned.

A nurse was hurrying down the corridor. Mick went back to Seán.

Seán closed his eyes tight as if summoning up every grain of strength in his body.

'*Gaaarmin ... Garrrmin ... Garmin ...*'

The nurse came in and rushed to Seán's sider. 'What is it?' she asked Mick. 'What happened?'

'*Gaarminn!*' Seán screamed.

Mick looked at Seán. '*Garmin?*' he asked.

He thought he saw a slight nod of Seán's head.

'What does *Garmin* mean?' Mick asked.

'It's a watch,' the nurse said. 'I have one. It's a runner's watch. Used to track kilometres and time and stuff like that.'

'What else does it do?'

'It can track your heart rate, tells you the route you took, *em* ...'

'Your route? How does it do that?'

'GPS, I assume.'

Mick suddenly felt as if the muddy waters in his head had cleared. He fumbled with his phone and ran out of room, the phone pressed to his ear.

Chapter 51

'Jamie,' Mick said into his phone.

He had run out the front door of the Mater hospital before realising he had no idea where he was going.

'Go ahead, Mick.'

'Where are you now?'

'On the way back. Should be at HQ in about five minutes.'

'What do you know about a Garmin watch for Darcy?'

'I know she wears one on her runs.'

'Any idea when she got it?'

'She said someone had bought it for her recently.'

'How recently?'

'No idea.'

Mick said nothing.

'Mick? What is it?'

'I need the box it came in.'

'I think she still keeps it in the box when she's at home. I've seen it in her kitchen.'

'Go back and get it. Kick the door in if you have to. I need the serial number off it.'

'GPS,' Jamie guessed. 'You think they can locate her from it, right?'

'We'll make a detective of you yet. Call me as soon as you have it.

Jamie hung up the phone, reached over to the centre console and switched on the blue lights and sirens of the Audi Q7 Armed Support Unit.

'Head for the Liberties,' he told the driver.

Every vehicle on the road stopped as the driver swung the Audi in the opposite direction and roared up the street.

Mick was in Chief O'Riordan's office by the time Jamie phoned him back. Garda Con Maher from Information and Communications Technologies (ICT) was on the speakerphone, listening.

'Go ahead,' Mick said.

'I have the box and the number,' Jamie said. 'You ready?'

He called out the long number.

There was silence from Maher's side.

'You get that?' Mick asked.

'I got it. Hang on.'

They listened to the sound of a computer keyboard being tapped.

'Anything?' Mick asked again.

Mick got up off his chair and paced back and forth in the room.

'Talk to me, Mick,' Jamie's voice came over his mobile.

'We're waiting,' Mick told him.

'Waiting on what?'

'Waiting on –'

'I got it!' Maher's voice called out.

'Thank fuck,' Mick said. 'Where?'

'At the moment, it's just a rough location. But I can try to pinpoint it with a little more time.'

'Where?' Mick said.

'Brittas. County Wicklow.'

'You hear that, Jamie,' O'Riordan said.

'On our way,' Jamie said.

'*Wait!*' O'Riordan shouted. '*Get back here and pick up Mick!*'

There was a moment's silence, as if Jamie were about to disobey him. They listened to the sirens wailing in the background over the phone.

'Be outside in two minutes, Mick,' Jamie told him. 'I'm not waiting for you.'

The phone went dead, but Mick was already running for the door.

Mick sat in the back of the Audi jeep as it roared along the N81. He held his phone to his ear, waiting for more precise directions from Maher as soon as she had them. Two other jeeps and the BMW followed behind them. They had dispatched an ambulance and fire engine from Tallaght, but they were both struggling to keep up.

'We're coming into Brittas village now,' Jamie told Mick, turning around in his seat up front.

'Brittas village,' Mick told Maher. 'Where to now?'

'Hold on,' he said.

'*For fuck's sake!*' Mick barked.

Maher ignored him.

The convoy slowed as they drove through the village. People turned to stare at the convoy slowly creeping along the small village's main street.

'At the end of the village,' Maher said, 'there's a turn to the left. Take that.'

'You hear that?' Mick asked the driver.

The driver nodded and slowed down. He swung the jeep into the left turn.

'Over the bridge,' Maher told him.

Mick brought the phone closer to the driver's ear.

'Left at the T-Junction when you're across the lake.'

The road narrowed, and the driver was forced to drive more slowly. He turned left and followed the country road.

After another minute, Maher could be heard saying, 'OK, stop.'

The driver stopped.

They all looked out of the windows. There were trees and fields and even cows, but what else they were supposed to be seeing they had no idea.

'There's nothing here,' Jamie said. 'There's nothing fucking here.'

'That's what the Garmin satellite is telling me,' Maher said.

'Well, it's wrong,' Jamie said.

'*Hold it!*' Mick said. '*There!*'

He pointed out of the front window at a small sign. Even the driver had to lean forward to see what it said.

CONTAINER STORAGE

The driver didn't need to be told what to do. He drove the Audi forward and saw the opening between the trees. There were the remains of an old open gate when tractors had used the road.

The trees on the road were overgrown, and their low branches scraped off the roof of the jeep. After about a hundred yards, the road widened and opened to a field. They drove into its centre.

On the field's border, in the shape of a square, were about a hundred forty-foot containers – the type used to ship goods from China or abroad. Each side of the field had about twenty to twenty-five containers, their doors facing the centre.

'Bolt cutters,' Mick said.

Jamie ran to the back of the jeep and took out a large metal cutter. He ran to the first container and broke open the lock. The others, including the fire personnel, did the same.

The door creaked as Jamie and his colleague prised it open. They poked their heads around the door and shone their two Maglite torches inside.

'*Empty!*' Jamie called back to Mick.

Mick walked along the front of the containers, looking them up and down. He heard another lock snap open and the doors screeching with rust. After passing about thirty containers, he stopped at one. He studied it for a few moments.

'*Jamie!*' he called.

Jamie ran over with the cutters.

'The lock is newer,' Mick said, 'and the door has scraped along the ground recently.'

Jamie pressed on the handles of the bolt cutter until the lock snapped open. They both pulled at the long metal door. It didn't creak like the others. They got it open enough for Jamie to shine the torch inside. At first, he thought it was empty like the others. Then the light caught movement at the back of the container.

Something squirmed as the light hit it.

She was alive.

Jamie ran inside.

'*Over here!*' Mick yelled. '*Paramedics!*'

He walked back to the jeep. He felt as if he was going to have a heart attack. He banged his chest with his fist.

He reached inside his jacket pocket and pulled out a crushed packet of cigarettes. He pulled one out from the pack and straightened it with his fingers. He lit it and breathed in the smoke as if it were the first time he was able to breathe since that morning.

He called the Chief and told them they'd found Darcy.

Jamie came out of the darkness of the container, carrying Darcy in his arms, her head hidden under a blanket from the brightness of the day.

Chapter 52

The man stood in front of Darcy, looking at her as she lay in the hospital bed. He was dressed all in black, almost like a shadow. How did he get there without her hearing him come in? From behind his back, he pulled out a large knife. It shone in the fluorescent light from the ceiling. Where was the nurse? Where was everybody? She tried to call, but no sound came out. He stepped closer to her. She tried to see his face, but it was a blur. He raised his hand with the knife. She lifted her arms to protect herself, but they were strapped to the bed with cable ties. She was powerless. She couldn't move. She felt her heart pounding in her chest with fear and panic. The knife glistened as it came down on her, as if winking at her before …

Darcy shot up in the bed. She breathed heavily in and out. The heart monitor was beeping loudly beside her. She looked down at the IV going into a cannula in the back of her hand and tried to calm her breathing.

A nurse opened the door to her room and went straight to the heart monitor. She pressed a button, and an alarm switched off that Darcy had not been aware was ringing.

'It's OK,' the nurse said. 'It was just a nightmare.'

Darcy nodded her thanks as her breathing returned to normal. She rubbed her wrists. They were still red and sore from the cable ties. Jamie had been on the chair when she fell asleep, but he was gone now.

'Where's my friend who was sitting on that chair?' Darcy asked.

'I sent him home about an hour ago,' the nurse told her. 'I told him to get some sleep and to come back in the morning.'

'I need to go home too,' Darcy said.

'I don't think that's a very good idea.'

'I want my own bed. I want to have a bath.'

Darcy swung her legs out of the bed.

'Can you take this off me, please?' she said, indicating the IV.

'You really just need to rest and be monitored for the next day or two,' the nurse told her.

'Are all my vitals OK?'

The nurse nodded.

'Then, please?' Darcy said and held out her hand with the cannula in it.

'I'll have to inform the doctor.'

'OK.'

The nurse stood still for another moment, but then began to remove the IV.

'Make sure you get plenty of rest and drink lots of fluids,' she told Darcy.

'Thank you, Nurse. I will,' Darcy said. 'Do you know if I have any clothes here?'

'The man that was in the chair brought a bag of clothes for you. It's in the wardrobe.'

Jamie, she thought. Always the hero.

Darcy watched her removing the needle.

'There you go. That's all finished now. I'll give you some privacy to change.'

'Thank you, Nurse.'

She put on some comfortable leggings, a T-shirt, and a hoodie.

The corridor was empty. She didn't know what time it was and wished she had asked the nurse. She held herself up as best she could and walked along the rooms until she came to Room 9. She gave the faintest of knocks on the door and opened it.

The main lights were off, but it was bright, given the number of monitors in the room. The window blinds failed to block out the orange glow from the streetlamps.

Seán turned his head as she walked in and closed the door behind her. He smiled at her and she returned the smile.

'How are you?' she asked.

He nodded.

'I'm going home,' she said. 'I just wanted to drop by before I went. I'll come visit you properly tomorrow. I promise.'

She walked closer to the bed and reached out for his hand. She took it and squeezed it.

'I also wanted to say thank you. Mick told me it was you who ... you know, the watch and stuff.' She could feel a lump rising in her throat. 'I ... I thought that was it for me, you know?' The tears came to her eyes. 'I was ... I was so helpless. Vulnerable. Weak. I've never felt like that before. And, believe me, there have been plenty of rough times in my life. But he could have done anything to me, Seán. Anything.'

She raised her hand and wiped away the tears.

'How am I supposed to save anyone if I couldn't even save myself? Maybe I'm not cut out for the NBCI after all.'

Darcy took a deep breath in and exhaled slowly.

'I'm not saying that I understand completely what it's like for you here, but I think I understand a little bit more, you know?'

She cleared her throat.

'I'm sorry,' she said. 'I'm sorry for everything.'

Seán shook his head.

She took a step closer to him and leaned in to kiss him on the cheek. He turned his head towards her, and she paused. She looked into his eyes and cupped his face with her hands. Then they kissed. A long overdue kiss.

Chapter 53

The kitchen was so quiet. Mairéad could hear her heartbeat. To her, it was as if a tidal wave of upheaval had washed over her house in one fell swoop, and now the waves gently lapped the shore once again.

She tried to think back to when she had last had a good night's sleep, one that had not been interrupted by bouts of worry.

She opened the curtains a little and peeked out into the garden at her shed. She could see the luminous jackets of the gardaí patrolling the fields behind her house.

She walked into the sitting room and looked out at the two gardaí sitting in their car. She looked up and down the street and then went back into the kitchen.

'Would you like something to eat?' she asked Conor, who was seated at the table.

Mairéad pulled out pots and pans.

'I'm going to make your favourite,' she told him. 'Would you like that?'

Conor turned to look at her, a sign of his approval. Now that she knew what she was going to do, she felt a weight had been lifted from her.

'Don't you worry about anything, son,' she told him. 'They will never take my boy from me.'

She burst into tears but then controlled herself. She sniffed and wiped the tears away before opening the fridge and removing the food.

'Those men will never lock you away,' she told him. 'I'll make sure of that. Not my Conor. Not my little boy. Never.'

'I was told to sign out before I leave,' Darcy told the nurses at the nurses' station.

'Sure thing. What's the name, please?'

'Doyle. Darcy Doyle.'

'She's not going anywhere.'

Darcy turned around to see Mick.

'I'm not going to argue with you,' she told him.

'Good, then go back to bed like a good girl.'

'Don't patronise me, Mick.'

'She doesn't have permission to leave this hospital,' Mick told the nurse.

Darcy reached over and took the clipboard from the nurse's hand.

'Pen, please,' she asked her.

The nurse looked from Mick to Darcy and then back to Mick.

Mick let out a sigh and took a pen out of his jacket. He handed it to her.

She took it, signed the form, handed it back, then gave Mick back his pen.

'Thanks,' she said. 'You prick!'

Mick smiled and then followed her down the hall.

Darcy stood at the lift. 'I think I spend more time in this hospital,' she said, mostly to herself, 'than I do at the station.'

'Maybe they'll hire you as a doctor or a nurse. Even if it's just for your lovely bedside manner.'

'Maybe,' she said and smiled.

They stood in silence for a few moments. The corridor was quiet. They could hear the rain lashing off the windows outside.

'I blame myself,' Mick said without looking at her. 'I should have broken down your house door or at least reacted quicker than I did.'

'It's normal to think that. Everyone always thinks like that.'

'I know. Everyone always thinks it's their fault.'

'No. I mean, everyone thinks it was *your* fault.'

Mick looked at her and smiled.

'What's next?' she asked.

'We have everyone available looking for him. All the exit routes, the train and bus stations.'

'What about the airport?'

'Jasus, we never thought of that. I'll run and say it to them now. No, best not. He's probably not that clever, to think of leaving an island by plane.'

'Why are you always an asshole?'

Mick shrugged. 'Everyone needs a hobby.'

The doors to the lift opened with a ping.

'Excuse me,' a nurse said, pushing a trolley out of the lift and into the corridor.

They both stood out of her way. On the trolley were painkillers, sterile eyewash, antibiotic ointment, antihistamines, and an assortment of medical supplies.

'You must be expecting the end of the world with all those supplies,' Mick joked with her.

She returned a half-hearted smile as she pushed the trolley past them.

'Can't say the medical staff here have much of a sense of humour,' Mick said.

Darcy looked at Mick.

'What?' he said.

'What did you just say there?' Darcy asked him.

'I said the medical staff don't have much of a sense of...'

'Before that!' she snapped.

'I don't know. Her trolley had a lot of emergency supplies. End of the world stuff, you know?'

'*Fuck!* The shed.'

'What shed?'

'It was right in front of us, and we didn't see it.'

'Didn't see what?'

'Everything in that shed was old and rusted, except for what? The medical supplies, the painkillers, the ointment, the tins of food, the torch. I even turned the bloody thing on. How the hell does a torch work in a shed full of old crap? Not a drop of dust on any of it. That's what she was looking out at.'

Darcy pressed the ground-floor button of the lift.

'We need to get back to that house.'

'We checked the shed.'

'He took out all those supplies to make room, and then he got in there himself. A false wall or a false floor. I'm telling you he was there, Mick. He was in the fucking shed.'

Solace came to Mairéad with this thing she was about to do. For a woman of her age, she had very few physical ailments or complaints. However, inside her, everything was broken, bashed and bruised.

The darkness of the night had come quickly, and she was glad of it. With it had come the rain. Where did all the rain come from, she wondered? Did it come from the same place as all her pain? This interminable pain and torment.

She stood up, opened the door, and stepped out into the back garden. There was no sign of the gardaí. The rain pounded down on her, as if it fell only for her. It saturated her from her head to her toes. She stretched out her arms and raised her head to the falling cold rain. It soaked through her and into her, absolving her of the past, baptising her for what lay ahead, and cleansing her for the deed to be done.

She went into the shed and opened the false floor where Conor had hidden. From the corner, she pulled out the small safe. She twirled the metal wheels until the code snapped open its lid. She took out the handgun and checked the bullets were still inside, its feel and smell bringing her back to a hot Californian afternoon with Jack. Her life had started that day with him and had led her to this very moment when a new life would start once again for her.

Back in the house, the rainwater dripped from her clothes onto the kitchen floor. She left a trail of wet footsteps behind her as she walked into the hall. She looked up the stairs and into the darkness of the landing. She climbed, her wet feet sinking into the carpet at each step.

Outside Conor's room, she paused and placed her palm against his bedroom door. *My boy*, she thought. *My beautiful boy*. He had been the most beautiful baby in the hospital, and she had been so proud that day. It would always remain the happiest day of her life.

They will never harm you or cause you suffering as long as I have an inch of willpower in my body.

Her hand curled into a fist, and she knocked on the door. Then she reached for the handle and opened it. There was a small night light in the wall socket, so she could make out the outline of his body as he sat up in bed.

Her hand went to the gun, and she raised it slowly. There was no need for any more words or thoughts. With this act would come an end. An end to everything. And, please God, some peace. Yes. Please God, some peace and solace.

The two gardaí sitting outside Mairéad's house jumped as the gun fired. They looked towards the house and saw a flash in the top bedroom window, and then heard another crack.

At that moment, Mick turned Darcy's car into the street.

The two uniformed gardaí were out of their car by the time Mick pulled in behind them. He got out as they were about to run up the driveway.

'*What is it?*' Mick shouted to them.

'I think it was a gunshot,' one of them said. 'The bedroom.'

They all ran to the door. It was locked. Both uniforms stepped to the side as Mick kicked it. It burst open.

'Behind me,' Mick told the gardaí, taking out his gun but, as they stood aside, Darcy darted in.

'*Darcy, wait!*'

Darcy went straight up the stairs with Mick behind her. There wasn't enough room for him to pass her.

The bedroom door was open.

Darcy held up her hand. She slowly moved into the doorway.

She listened and thought she could hear someone singing. She took another two steps and saw the gun at the entrance on the floor. She pointed to it.

She stepped in further and then saw them. Mairéad was sitting on the bed behind Conor. The front of his T-shirt was bloody, and his eyes were lifeless. Mairéad had her arms wrapped around her son and was rocking him back and forth, caressing his forehead.

Mick lowered his weapon, and with his foot slid the gun on the floor further away from her.

Darcy stood looking at Mairéad as she rocked her son back and forth in her arms, while gently kissing him on his head and singing softly into his ear.

'She had a penknife long and sharp,
Weela Weela Walya
She had a penknife long and sharp,
Down by the river Saile.
She stuck the penknife in the baby's heart,
Weela Weela Walya
She stuck the penknife in the baby's heart,
Down by the river Saile.
Well, that was the end of the woman in the woods,
Weela Weela Walya
And that was the end of the baby, too,
Down by the river Saile.'

Sunday

Chapter 54

After knocking on the front door of Darcy's house for the third time, Mick was about to walk back to his car when a small light came on. He stood back from the door. It opened slowly. Darcy stuck her head outside.

'Coffee?' he said.

She looked at the two Starbucks disposable cups in his hands.

'It's made with that plant milk shite that isn't really milk, if you know what I mean.'

She smiled and walked back in, leaving the door open.

Mick followed her into her sitting room and made himself comfortable on the sofa. Darcy sat opposite, wrapped in a white bathrobe.

'What time is it?' she asked him.

'Eight o'clock.'

'It's Sunday, right?'

'All day, yeah.'

She took the coffee from where he'd left it on the table and sipped it. She winced as the warm liquid went down her throat.

'Not good?' he asked.

'It's good. Very good. Thanks.'

'Maybe next week I could even tempt you to try the best breakfast café in Dublin – *The Streaky Rasher.*'

'I doubt it.'

She gripped the warm cup in both her hands as if she were warming herself. She sat back in her armchair.

'You working today?' she asked him.

'Sure am. Lots of paperwork and details to sort through. Why get paid on Monday when you can get double the pay for doing it on a Sunday?'

She smiled and took another sip of her coffee, then stared at him.

'What?'

'This isn't over, Mick.'

'Our Chief Superintendent begs to differ.'

Darcy looked away from him.

'Fifi has all the evidence now,' Mick told her. 'Knowing her, she's probably already at work and going through it all.'

'It's ... it's just that it's all a little too neat. You know what I mean?'

'No, what?'

'How did he get out of the house to attack me?'

'Who knows? Maybe he had a tunnel into a neighbour's garden. Maybe one of the uniforms went for a piss and he escaped. It wouldn't be the first time.'

'It was too easy,' Darcy said to herself.

Mick leaned forward on the sofa.

'You think this case was too easy? Are you fucking kidding me?'

'I don't mean the case. I don't know. I'm not sure. My thinking isn't a hundred percent yet.'

Mick looked at her for a few moments. He stood up but couldn't think of anything else to say except, 'We'll see. Anyway, duty calls.'

'Can you give me ten minutes to get ready?'

'What? No fucking way. The chief's already going ballistic that you were on the scene last night.'

'This is still as much my case as it is yours, Mick. I want to finish it.'

'No one's denying that. But you've done more than your share on this one.'

Darcy ignored him and stood up.

'Darcy,' he said. 'There's no need to come in.'

'I know,' she said, and walked back towards her bedroom. 'But why should you get all the overtime?'

Mick walked over to the window and looked out. When he turned around, Darcy was standing in front of him still in her bathrobe.

'What?' he asked.

'I don't do mushy stuff very well, but I need to say thank you for … you know, for finding me.'

'It was everyone. Not just me.'

'I know. But Jamie told me you did everything you could. And I wanted to say thanks.'

Darcy could feel the emotion rising in her again. She stepped closer to him, stretched out her arms and hugged him. Then she let go and turned back to her room.

'Well, then, can I say thanks to you too?' Mick said.

She turned back to him.

'To me? For what?'

He paused, searching for the words.

'This is the longest period I've been sober in about three years.'

She looked at him. It was the first time she saw a vulnerability in him.

'For what it's worth, it was never me taking a chance on you this week,' he said. 'You were the one taking a chance on me.'

She nodded at him, accepting what he was saying to her.

'And it's even longer since I was awake at 8 a.m. on a fucking Sunday morning,' he told her.

'Do me a favour then,' she said. 'Next Sunday morning, go knock on your son's door and not mine.'

'I will,' he said as she went back to her bedroom to get dressed.

Chapter 55

A white business card slid across the counter at Harcourt Street Garda Station. Garda Sergeant Eddie Mills looked at it without taking his full attention away from *The Sunday Mirror* that was opened on the sports pages.

Fintan Dawson – Solicitor

Mills glanced up at the solicitor.

'I'm here to see my client Mairéad Carter,' he told Garda Mills.

Mills made an exaggerated effort of looking at his watch.

'That psycho bat? Bit early in the morning, isn't it?'

'Detective Mick Kelly said to come whenever I could.'

Not wanting to fall on the wrong side of Mick Kelly, Mills closed his paper. He pressed a buzzer under the counter, and the side door clicked open.

'Come through, then,' he said as he stood up with great exertion.

He grabbed a bunch of keys and walked around into the corridor that held the cells. The lawyer followed him without saying anything.

When they came to Mairéad's cell, Mills opened the eye hatch and looked inside.

'Looks like she's asleep,' Mills told him. 'Only the guilty ones ever sleep. Want me to wake her up for you?'

He shook his head.

'Right you are, so,' Mills said and stuck one of the keys in the lock. It opened with a loud clunk, and he pulled the heavy door open.

The lawyer stepped inside and Mills closed the door shut, locking it again.

'I'll leave the hatch open,' he said. 'Just give me a shout when you want to leave.'

The lawyer nodded his thanks, but Mills was already on his way back to his Sunday newspaper.

Mairéad had heard the door open but was too tired to turn around. She thought it might be breakfast. She wasn't hungry.

'Hello, Mairéad,' he said.

Mairéad's eyes shot open. She must be mistaken. That voice. Was she still asleep? The grey wall of the prison cell was only inches from her face, but this was not her reality. It was a dream. A nightmare. Her mind playing tricks on her.

'Well, aren't you going to turn around and say hello?' he asked her.

With the greatest of effort, Mairéad rolled her body around and sat up in the bed. She stared at the ghost standing opposite her. She barely recognised him, but those were his eyes, and that was his voice.

'Well, say something,' he told her.

She tried to swallow, but it was as if something were stuck in her throat.

'Jack?' she whispered.

'In the flesh,' he said and smiled at her.

'What is this? Are you a ... a ghost?'

Jack laughed. 'In a way, yes. I guess I am. That's what they used to call me, anyway.'

He sat down on the only chair in the cell and placed his briefcase on the small metal table.

'I don't understand.'

'Of course you don't understand, Mairéad. Unfortunately, you were never that smart. It was one of the things I found most endearing about you, despite our mundane and pointless marriage.'

'*It can't be real,*' she whispered.

'What can't be real? Me? Why is it so hard to believe?'

'They buried you. I saw your burnt body.'

'The eyes see what they want to see.'

'This is a dream,' she said, putting her hand to her head. 'I haven't been sleeping. It's exhaustion. The doctor gave me some medication last night. You're an illusion.'

'I'm afraid I'm not, honey. I am the real deal. Would you like me to pinch you? Or punch you in the face? That'd wake you up.'

Mairéad had so many emotions and questions running around her head, but only one word escaped her.

'How?'

'It really wasn't as difficult as you'd imagine. The hardest part was getting a body. But even that wasn't too tough. It needed a bit of planning, of course. I had to have most of my teeth removed.'

Jack opened his mouth.

'I had them replaced with new ones.'

He gave her a big smile, showing off his teeth.

'It's a wonderful thing "confirmation bias". A few teeth from me, a charred body roughly the same size as mine and soon two plus two suddenly equals five. Not even my own sweet wife questioned it.'

'But I buried you. I mourned your death.'

'You buried a man who had been out walking his dog too late at night and whose wife still hopes he'll return one day. As for mourning me, I'd say that's a bit of a stretch, wouldn't you? You no more mourned my death than did those two boys of mine.'

'You've been in my house? Haven't you? I thought I was going mad.'

'I still have my key. I'd often pop home occasionally when the need arose. Two days after the funeral, when I came by to get my daddy's handgun and discovered it wasn't in its usual hiding place, well, I have to tell you, it took every inch of my willpower not to wait for you to come home and beat you until I had it back in my hand.'

Mairéad rested her head in her hands. She felt faint.

'How else do you think that ponytail ended up under Conor's bed? Although you could call it divine intervention.'

A groan escaped from Mairéad. 'Oh, God, Conor. My poor Conor!'

'Yes, poor Conor. He relied on you for everything, and you killed him. I know it's a lot to take in, but I'm afraid that's the easy part over. Time is pressing, and I can't stick around just for shits and giggles. Are you listening to me?'

Mairéad raised her head. Her look surprised Jack. She had such hate in her eyes.

'I'm here to help you,' he told her and took out two small pills from his jacket pocket. He placed them on the table. 'Think about what you've done, Mairéad. You've taken the life of our son. Your own sweet boy. An innocent boy with a disability. I believe he knew the truth, and you chose to ignore him. Instead, you accused him. You laid the guilt of all those crimes at his feet like the Jews accusing Christ. And who murdered that innocent Christ? His own mother. I suppose I am Barabbas who was released by Pontius Pilate. And, like Barabbas, I am free to kill again. Free to live the life I choose for myself. Little did I know how well it was all going to turn out in the end. It was easy for me to enter the house and add a few bits and pieces to help you and those fucking cops to join the dots.

And now think of the life you have in front of you. When the killings continue, and I assure you they most definitely will, as I'm having far too much fun to stop now, and when the horror doesn't end, then those cops will be back for you. Questioning you. Humiliating you. For now, they believe you've killed a monster. That is your only saving grace, but when they discover the truth, whatever empathy they have for you now will quickly evaporate, and they'll be out for blood. *Your blood.*'

Jack slid the pills across the table.

'I'm giving you a way out. Don't worry, it won't hurt. It will be like falling asleep. Think of them as my parting gift to you. We did share some happy moments through the years after all, didn't we?'

Mairéad shook her head from side to side.

'I won't take them,' she said. 'I want them to know the truth.'

'What truth? That you killed your own mute son for no reason. Is that what you want them to know?'

'No. I want them to know my whole life has been a lie. I want them to know Conor was innocent.'

The smile fell from Jack's face. He took the two pills off the table and curled them up in his hand.

'Fine,' he said and stood up. 'I'll tell your other son that you refused to do the honourable thing as I cut his fucking head off.'

Mairéad stood up.

'*What?*'

'Someone has to die, dearest. If not you, then why not Liam? The little prick had it coming for years.'

'*No!*'

'Calm yourself, woman. You know how I hate a scene.'

Mairéad fell back onto the bed and burst into tears.

Jack let out a heavy sigh and looked at his watch.

'I'm afraid I need to go. It's not the way I had hoped we'd part, but we can't always get what we want, can we?'

Jack picked up his briefcase from the floor. He put his mouth to the open hatch in the door and called out, '*Guard!*' Then, without turning back to her, he said: 'Goodbye, Mairéad. I'll give Liam your regards.'

'*No, wait!*' Mairéad sobbed.

A smile slid across Jack's face. He turned around to face her.

She sat up on the bed, her face a mess of tears and anguish.

She slowly reached out her hand and opened it.

Jack placed the two pills in her palm. She closed her hand around them.

'You promise not to harm Liam?'

'On my word. Crush them with your teeth before swallowing.'

Garda Mills' footsteps could be heard in the corridor. The key was inserted into the lock, and it clicked open.

'All done?' Mills asked.

'Yes, thank you,' Jack said.

He turned one last time to his wife.

'*Vaya con Dios,*' he told her and followed Garda Mills into the corridor.

Chapter 56

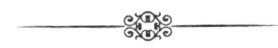

'I blame you,' Chief O'Riordan told Mick in his glass-door office.

'For what?' Mick asked.

'For her. She should be back in the hospital. Why didn't you tell her that?'

'You think I didn't? I told her I'd drive her back. Didn't I, Darcy?'

'He did, Chief,' Darcy said.

'And now this shit-storm with the mother,' O'Riordan continued. 'Fortunately, the Commissioner is too busy with his golf buddies to work on Sundays, but tomorrow he's going to be in here looking for facts and information, so you know what I want from you today, don't you?'

'Facts and information, sir?' Darcy said.

'Correct.'

O'Riordan looked from one to the other.

'I honestly think it would have been easier if you two hadn't succeeded this week,' he told them both. 'Now I don't know what to do with the pair of you.'

'Sir?' Darcy said. 'I'm not so sure we did.'

'Did what?'

'Succeed.'

'What the fuck are you talking about? Haven't you the mother locked up downstairs, the body of the killer in the morgue, ropes of hair found under his bed? What more do you want? A signed confession?'

Darcy looked at Mick, unsure how to proceed. Mick's phone rang. He saw Phoebe's name on the screen.

'You must be costing the State a fortune, Doctor,' Mick told her.

'Where are you?' she asked him.

'I'm in the chief's office with Darcy,' he told her.

'Put me on speaker,' Phoebe told him.

Mick put his phone on speaker.

'Good morning, Chief. I'm sorry you had to go through that, Darcy. If there's anything I can do?'

'Thanks, Fifi. Maybe a girls' night out sometime?'

'Sounds great.'

'What is it, Fifi?' Mick asked.

'The ponytail in the envelope you brought in last night,' she said.

'Yes?'

'We can't find any prints of Conor Carter on them.'

'So he wore gloves.'

'But we did find other prints. Mairéad Carter's.'

'And?'

'We also matched her prints to the gun. But we also found a thumb print on the corner of the envelope that held the ponytail. And another matching one on the gun.'

'Whose prints?' O'Riordan asked, leaning into the phone.

Darcy answered for her. 'Jack Carter.'

'Jack Carter?' O'Riordan asked. 'The husband?'

Mick stood up and paced the room.

'What are you thinking?' O'Riordan asked him.

Mick leaned over O'Riordan's desk phone. 'Fifi, I'll call you back.'

He cut her off before she had a chance to reply and then he dialled two numbers. It rang three times before being answered.

'Yep?' a voice asked.

'Where's Mairéad Carter now?' Mick asked.

'Who is this?' Garda Mills asked.

'*Fucking answer the question!*' Mick shouted at him.

'She's in her cell,' Mills said. 'She was asleep, but I just woke her.'

'Why did you wake her?' O'Riordan asked him.

'When I let her lawyer in.'

'*Her lawyer?*' Mick asked. 'At this hour on a Sunday morning?'

'I thought it was strange myself, to be honest. But he said you told him he could come!'

'Did he show you ID?'

'Yeah, of course. Well, his business card anyway.'

'*A business card?*' Mick shouted at him.

'He's just leaving now,' Mills told him. 'I can see him getting into his van.'

'*He's driving a fucking van?*' Mick screamed. '*We're coming down. Call ERU now.*'

Mick ran out of O'Riordan's office and headed for the stairs. Darcy struggled to keep up with him.

———

Garda Mills picked up the phone to call ERU but then looked out at the lawyer. He was rolling down the window of the van.

Beside Mills's desk was a large truncheon. Mills knew he had already fucked up, whoever the lawyer was.

If I don't stop this guy, Mills thought, the chief will have me writing parking tickets for the next ten years.

He grabbed the truncheon and came out from behind the counter. He walked as quickly as he could out of the building, the truncheon hidden behind his back.

When he was outside, he called out, 'Hey, hold on there!'

Jack looked in his side mirror and saw the garda hurrying quickly towards him. His first thought was to put his foot down heavily on the accelerator, but he stopped himself. Instead, he gripped the handle of his knife that was wedged in the door.

What had the cop called Mairéad earlier? Jack remembered. *A psycho bat.*

'I need a word,' Mills said as he approached the van.

Mick burst open the doors into the reception area and saw there was no one at the desk. He ran to the front door and looked out into the small parking lot.

The revving of an engine caught his attention, and he saw a van leaving through the main entrance. He was about to rush back inside when he saw Mills collapsed in a heap on the ground.

Mick raced over to Mills. He got down beside him and lifted his head. It was covered in blood. His throat was completely torn open.

'*Mick!*' Darcy called from the door.

Mick screamed out. '*Fuck! Fuck!*'

Darcy appeared beside him. She leaned over and saw Mills' neck.

'*Ah Jesus,*' she said and turned away.

Mick lowered Mills's head down gently and stood up.

'Mairéad,' Darcy said.

They sprinted back into the building. Mick ran behind the desk and grabbed the keys to the cells.

They hurried down the corridor of cells, looking from one hatch door to the next.

'*No!*' Darcy yelled into the open hatch of a cell door.

Mick pushed her to the side.

Mairéad was lying on her back, facing the ceiling, her body convulsed, and foam and spit formed on her lips.

Mick opened the cell door and Darcy ran in. She held Mairéad's upper body in her arms, but she could see the life in her eyes slowly slipping away.

She looked back for Mick, but he was gone. She could hear him on the phone yelling for an ambulance.

Darcy held Mairéad tightly to herself until the convulsions eased and her gasping and choking came to a sudden end. Then Darcy rocked Mairéad gently in her arms as the final flickers of life drained slowly away from her.

Chapter 57

Jack felt a rush of euphoria as he drove away from Harcourt Street Station. He wondered if Mairéad would take the pills, but ultimately it didn't really matter now. Her death would give him more a sense of 'tidying up loose ends' rather than it being a crucial part of his overall plan. She would die a decrepit, lonely old lady, either in a cell or in her house. In many ways, he was doing her a favour. He was too sentimental and kind for his own good.

He thought about the future as he drove. He would move to England. England held so many possibilities it was hard to imagine. He couldn't wait to get there, but first he was going to have a little fun. He was going to pay a visit to that jumped-up little shit of a son of his, Liam. It was long overdue, and he was going to take his time with him. Once he was out of the way, then he could make a proper fresh start.

Suddenly a high-roofed white van pulled in front of him and stopped. He braked hard and jerked to a stop very close to it. It had a large amber light on its roof, which began to flash. A construction worker wearing a yellow hard hat and a hi-viz jacket got out of the side door and walked to the back of the van. He opened a door and took out some traffic cones.

Jack's anger flared when the worker had the audacity to wave his apologies. He looked in his rear-view mirror to reverse. There was already a car queuing behind him. He couldn't move.

Another worker jumped out and assisted the first one, also lifting out some cones.

As he turned, Jack saw the side of his face under his hard hat. He thought he recognised him but wasn't sure from where. His hand went instinctively to his knife in the door.

'Sorry about this,' the worker told Jack, stepping up to the car. 'We'll only be a minute.'

His right hand was tucked into his luminous construction jacket.

Jack's eyes widened as he recognised him. There was a jagged scar running up the side of his face. It was the man from the cinema. The husband. He had watched him leave halfway through the film.

Tommy Fay pulled his right hand out from his jacket at the same time as Jack's hunting knife slashed at him. Tommy instinctively pulled back, but not far enough. The tip of the knife sliced open a gash from his ear across his cheek.

Tommy's right hand continued to straighten. Jack saw the gun in his hand.

Tommy's first bullet missed its target and lodged into the headrest of the seat next to Jack's head. The air cracked with the noise of the blast. Jack rammed the gearstick into reverse and pressed down on the accelerator as the second bullet hit his shoulder. Jack cried out but kept his foot down. He slammed into the car behind him. Tommy panned in his direction and fired again. The third bullet hit Jack's neck. Blood spurted out like a geyser from his throat. Jack's hand went up to stop the blood.

The next bullet hit the right side of his chest. Jack's foot fell off the accelerator and the engine's high revs died down. Tommy took a step towards Jack and fired again. This time, Jack spun in his seat as the bullet went through his cheek and out the other side.

'Let's go!' the driver called, already back in the van.

Tommy looked one last time at Jack and then jumped into the back of the van. The door closed behind him and the van drove off.

Epilogue

Darcy parked her car outside a terraced house that had all its windows fully boarded up. The house to its left had four cars in the driveway in various states of disrepair. Weeds grew up and through the wheel arches of two of the cars. To its right, another house had a beautiful display of flowers and hanging potted plants in an apparent attempt to compensate for the entire housing estate. On a grassy area in front of the row of houses were the remains of a burnt-out car.

She opened her car door and got out.

Only some of the houses had numbers displayed, but she didn't need them to find the one she was looking for. When she reached the house, she spent a moment looking at it. It was surprisingly well kept, she thought. The small front garden had potted plants dotted around, and the grass was neatly trimmed. She opened the gate and walked up the pathway leading to the front door.

For a moment, she felt like turning back around, but she rang the doorbell before she could change her mind. She ran through the numerous opening lines she'd already rehearsed in her head a hundred times. She heard the latch click from the inside, and the door opened.

A woman, older-looking and shorter than she'd anticipated, stood in front of her. Even in a line-up of a thousand similar women, Darcy could easily have picked this woman out for who she was. Her mother.

The woman stepped outside and looked up and down the street as if she were expecting someone else to be there. Without saying a word, she walked back inside, leaving the door open. Darcy stood there before following her in and closing the front door behind her.

The house was dark even in daylight, but it was clean and tidy. Darcy smelt a mixed aroma of jasmine from a burning candle and cigarette smoke. The door to the sitting room was open, and she walked in. Her mother was sitting in an armchair that was the centrepiece of the room. There were some newspapers and several piles of books by mostly female Irish writers stacked beside her. A small table to her left held a mug, a pack of cigarettes, a half-full ash tray and an opened paperback novel.

Darcy sat on a worn sofa. It was a different sofa but was positioned in the same place where she had hidden on many occasions as a little girl – and on that night she was taken from the house. No, not taken. She had left. It had been her decision.

'*Hello there,*' the young garda had said. '*My name's Kate.*'

For Darcy now, it was a lifetime ago. And yet she remembered it as if it were yesterday. Her spine tingled as if someone had walked over her grave.

She looked up at the only two paintings in the room: they were seascapes of Dublin Bay that were uncannily similar to the ones in her own house.

Her mother picked up the cigarettes, took one out and lit it.

'I've just made tea,' she said. 'If you want any, you can go and make some yourself.'

Darcy looked behind her and into the kitchen. It, too, was clean and orderly.

'No, thank you,' she said.

Her mother blew out a line of smoke. 'Nice to see you still have your manners,' she said.

Darcy studied her. She had been young when she had Darcy, so was only now in her early fifties. She looked older, though. It wouldn't take a doctor to recognise she had some medical issues. Her skin was pale and grey, and she sat awkwardly in the chair.

'What do you want, Darcy?' she said, her voice hoarse.

'A few answers.'

'Why? Am I a suspect or something?'

Her mother chuckled at her own little joke and then laughed, which eventually turned into a coughing fit. Darcy stood, but her mother waved her to sit. She took a gulp of her tea and the coughing stopped.

'Frank told you I'm a garda?'

'Even if he didn't, I could smell it off you.'

Of all the possible scenarios in Darcy's head, this wasn't going the way she'd planned. Her mother pointed at the chest of drawers in the corner.

'Open the top drawer,' she told her.

Darcy looked over and then stood up. She went to the drawers and opened the top one. In it was a plastic bag stuffed with photos. She brought it back to her chair and spread some of them out on the small table between them. There were still several hundred photos inside the bag, some black and white and some in colour, but each photo had one thing in common: Darcy was in every one.

As far as she could see, they started when she was about two years old and ended in the last year or two. She was with friends in some, and alone in others. They captured her when she was both sad and happy. There were even photos of her graduating from Templemore.

'What is this?' she asked.

'Frank. He has you followed every now and again to keep tabs on you. I guess he thought I'd be interested to see how you turned out.'

'This is a gross invasion of my privacy,' she said.

Her mother remained calm and took another drag from her cigarette.

'To be honest with you, I thought you'd be flattered to know I was keeping an eye on you over all these years. I had asked Frank to look out for you.'

'And what right has he to do this?'

'I suppose he also felt since he paid for you, it entitled him to a few snaps as a memento. Make sure he was getting his money's worth.'

'Paid for me? Paid for what? I got nothing from him. Nothing. He's not entitled to anything from me.'

'So where did you think all that money came from for your fancy university and your fancy courses? More than he ever gave me, anyway.'

'They came from an old teacher of mine. They came from someone who believed in me. Unlike you or Frank.'

Her mother laughed. 'Fair enough, dear. You tell yourself whatever you have to in order to get yourself through the day. God knows that's what I do.'

Darcy's mind was going over all her years of study. The mystery funds that would suddenly appear when they were needed. Could they really have come from Frank? Everything?

'He told me he saw you one day when you were about eighteen years old,' her mother said. 'You were living off the streets, and you'd got into a fight with two scumbags who were trying to rob you, and that you ended up beating the crap out of them. Is that true?'

Darcy nodded her head.

'He said he spoke to some local priest who promised to look out for you.'

'Father Brian?' Darcy said, remembering. 'He found me a place to stay. Then helped me go back to school. That was all Frank?'

'The right word in the right ear by the right person. It goes a long way. He's not a bad old skin, your dad.'

Darcy's head shot up. 'He's a criminal gang lord who should be locked up for life.'

Her mother shrugged. 'We all have our faults, dear. No one's perfect.'

'Some are less perfect than others.'

Darcy saw the hurt feeling cross her mother's face.

'I suppose the only thing not perfect about your life is me. Is that what you're saying?'

'That's not what I meant.'

'It's OK. I know what I am. I've made my fair share of mistakes.'

Darcy could feel her heart aching, and she didn't like the feeling.

'Why didn't you come look for me?' Darcy asked, her voice almost a whisper.

'You left me, Darcy. It was your choice to leave. Why should I look for you?'

'Because you were my mother.'

'Yeah, but I don't admit to being a very good one. You were an accident. I was practically a child myself when I had you. What did I know about anything?'

Darcy looked at the stack of photographs on the table and in the bag.

She still had so many things to say, so many questions to ask, but she also felt like she couldn't breathe. She looked around the room.

Her mother watched her.

'Remembering, are you?'

Darcy didn't look at her. 'I don't remember much,' she said. 'I remember a three-bar electric fire and making toast in front of it. There was smelly brown carpet when I lay on the floor. You drying me after a bath and singing "Crazy" by Patsy Cline as you rocked me back and forth.'

Darcy looked at her mother.

'I also remember being neglected. But I knew there'd be no point in asking anyone where you were. I remember being left on my own, left to roam the streets and knowing that no one would ever come looking for me.'

Darcy watched her mother's face screw up in a rage. Her hands stretched out onto the table as she searched through the photographs. She picked one up and shoved it at Darcy.

'You weren't happy, were you not? What's this then?'

It was a photograph of a little blonde girl about six years of age, smiling in a field.

'You had it well enough. Better than I ever did!' She threw the photo at Darcy. It fell onto the floor. 'It wasn't me. It was Frank who didn't want you in the first place when you were inside me. He's the one that booked me on a boat to England. "Get rid of it," he told me, but I didn't. I never got a penny from him for years because he was so pissed off at me for having you. That's why we didn't have a pot to piss in at the start. You can thank Frank for that. No matter how bad things were at the very beginning, if it wasn't for me, you wouldn't even be alive. It was only when you started to walk and talk that he took any interest in you. Only then did he sort me out with a few quid.'

Darcy bent down and picked up the photograph. She studied the pretty little girl in the photo, her summer dress, her blonde hair, her shy smile.

'It wasn't my fault,' her mother told her, calmer now.

Darcy stared at the smiling girl in the photo. She desperately wanted to cry. But not for herself. To cry for that little girl.

'Maybe it wasn't,' Darcy admitted. 'But it wasn't my fault either, Mam.'

She looked up from the photo at her mother's face that was too old for her age, a woman who had struggled all her life, a woman who had grown up herself in abject poverty into a dysfunctional society and who had fought to survive where winning and losing, and life and death happened every day, and where the only real escape from her own trauma was through drugs.

'If you want to blame anyone –'

Darcy cut her off. 'No. I'm not so sure I want to blame anyone anymore,' she said. 'Suddenly I don't see the point.' She stood up. 'I have to go.'

Her mother nodded.

Darcy turned, but then stopped. She took a deep breath in and out.

'I'm sorry,' she said. 'I'm sorry, Mam. For running off on you.'

Her mother said nothing, but Darcy didn't want or need her to say anything. She looked around the room again.

'Maybe I'll come back again? Some other time.'

Her mother picked up her novel and flicked through it to find the page she was on.

'It's a free country. And I'm not going anywhere.'

Darcy kept her back to her mother, not wanting her to see her smile as she left. She waited until she was in the hall before she slipped the photograph of the little girl into her jacket pocket, and her mother waited until she heard the front door close before she too allowed herself to smile.

Acknowledgements

Writing a book is a solitary business, but publishing a book is a collaboration. Each needs the other to survive. Unfortunately, though, there's only room for one name on the cover!

This book would never have made it onto the shelves without the support and belief of Paula Campbell at Poolbeg Press, to whom I am eternally grateful. Editor Gaye Shortland helped smooth the edges and polish its surface and made me look like I know what I'm doing. Many thanks to David Prendergast for the cover design work.

Thanks to John Coffey of Edge Photography for his time and talent.

Helen Falkoner was there from the start to help untangle the plot and bring the characters to life.

Author Jean Grainger has had my back from day one of our writing careers, and I am very grateful for her advice and friendship.

Early readers (and typo-spotters) included Claire, Kay, Mary, Pat and Hazel.

Special thanks to Fabian Dunne for his technical advice.

Thanks to you too, the reader. Without readers, we wouldn't have books in the world. And without books, we wouldn't have you in our world.

A special mention to all the women and men on the front line in An Garda Síochána, who go about their jobs without the fanfare they richly deserve.

The last word goes to my family. None of this would have been possible without the unending support and encouragement of my wife and best friend Eileen, to whom I will be forever grateful.

Thanks to you three too: Kai, Christopher and Jamie.